FORG

ALSO BY ANN BAUER

The Forever Marriage

FORGIVENESS 4 YOU

A NOVEL

Ann Bauer

The Overlook Press
New York, NY

This edition first published in hardcover in the United States in 2015
by The Overlook Press, Peter Mayer Publishers, Inc.

141 Wooster Street
New York, NY 10012
www.overlookpress.com

For bulk and special sales, please contact sales@overlookny.com,
or write us at the address above.

Cataloging-in-Publication Data is available from the Library of Congress

Book design and type formatting by Bernard Schleifer
Manufactured in the United States of America
ISBN: 978-1-4683-1023-8

FIRST EDITION
1 3 5 7 9 10 8 6 4 2

*For everyone who lies awake at night aching with regret,
I dedicate this to you and send a little absolution your way.*

*"It is the confession, not the priest,
that gives us absolution."*

—OSCAR WILDE

FORGIVENESS 4 YOU

I

I T BEGAN LIKE THIS:

I was in the bookstore, sitting behind the counter reading Dostoyevsky, when a small woman walked in: short red coat, long dark hair, black boots with buckles down the sides. She stopped inside the doorway, unwinding the scarf from around her neck.

Her face was interesting—strange and sad. Not beautiful according to the surgically-nipped-news-anchor style of our time. Yet striking and very beautiful in a way that evoked something ancient: deserts, roiling storms, hieroglyphics on the side of a cave. Her forehead was clear and broad, her nose a little hawkish, her mouth full and nearly as red as her coat. She stood looking me up and down, her large, dark eyes moving over my body like hands.

This happened to me often. Over the years, I'd grown accustomed to being leered at when I was wearing my robes. What surprised me was that this didn't stop when I switched them out for the uniform of the underemployed forty-two-year-old: khakis, sweater vest, cracked leather shoes. Some women, not all but a large minority, seemed to smell something of my old life—candle wax, incense, the ether of old unanswered prayers—because they pressed up against me on the L, breathing deeply, their excitable nipples making little dents under my upraised arm.

That's how this one looked at first glance: as if she were following my scent, preparing to leap the counter and take me in her teeth. So I cleared my throat and said, "May I help you find something?"

At which point she swallowed and cleared her throat a couple of times. Her large dark eyes were damp.

"Can you help me?" she echoed—incorrectly, I first thought. Then I realized she'd actually meant it as a question. *Was it possible I could help her?* She assessed me shrewdly, narrowed eyes gleaming even through her tears. Then she glanced around the room, and I followed along, seeing the neat, shabby shelves as if they were from a grade school library, as I imagined she might. Books spilled from everywhere—half-full boxes and glass cupboards and stacks on the floor. We had run out of space; it was part of the charm of the shop.

"Do you have anything on regret and what to do about it?" the woman asked briskly. "Or maybe how to make it go away? Because I'm not sure I can . . ." Here, she broke off and stared down at her pointed boots. "I apologize," she said after a moment, speaking again in her firm, certain voice. "That was terribly inappropriate—and completely unlike me. I don't know why this is happening. I should probably leave."

This wasn't unusual, I wanted to tell her: the sudden outpouring of sadness followed by apology and confusion. It was the way these things had to be unraveled; for two decades I'd specialized in exactly this, parsing the blame and responsibility and absolving the guilt for everyone but myself.

I was marked. It had happened even before I took my oath, the day I went to God with what I'd done and He appeared to me in the form of a tattoo artist named Sol. Since the moment I confessed and his needle pricked my chest, I'd been unable to slip through life like a normal man. People regularly dissolved in my presence—even those who didn't realize they were harboring shame. Old, young, every race and color, even dedicated atheists and thieves. Nine times out of ten it scared them, so they would abruptly say goodbye and leave.

But this woman was—however reluctantly—standing her ground. Slowly she raised her head, and I watched as she recognized the Sol in me. I put my book down and came out from behind the counter, walking with my head straight forward, hands folded, in the slow, reverent way I was taught.

It was just the two of us, which was not unusual for Brooks Books at 3:30 p.m. on a cold Tuesday in February. I put my hand on the woman's shoulder and pressed down through her wool coat to the bones below. She was a 110-pound warrior dressed in thick winter clothes.

"Would you like to sit?" I asked, pointing to the beat-up leather chairs that Oren, our owner, keeps near the gas fireplace—a set-up that encourages people to settle in and read, but not buy.

"I'm so sorry!" she said again, pulling a pair of rhinestone-studded sunglasses from her purse and slipping them on, as if the sun—which had been in hiding for weeks—were suddenly breaking out in our shop. "Something is going on. I never do things like this! I actually just came in for a . . ." She gestured oddly with the toe of one boot, a masked Midwestern Audrey Hepburn in glittering frames.

"Book?" I prompted.

"No," she said. "A manicure." She pulled off one leather glove and presented me with a small, chapped hand. "There used to be a place. They had a paraffin wrap I loved. I could have *sworn* it was here."

"Next door," I said, tipping my head to the east. "It closed in January."

"Well, I should go then," she said uncertainly. But still she stayed, and I moved forward another inch or two.

I didn't want this one to leave. The image of an empty afternoon yawned in front of me. And it had been a long time since I'd met anyone who stirred my desire to minister. The last person who found me was a loud, bald man clearly in search of a quick fix. He'd been buying a guidebook to Prague, talking rapidly about his mother's Alzheimer's. She didn't remember him anyway, so what did it matter if he saw her? That was the refrain. I'd kept my mouth shut and handed him his receipt without a word.

But this sprite of a woman, hiding behind her dark glasses and fighting the urge to confess, was definitely different. I tested the air, leaning forward and then back. There was definitely something compelling me toward her. My spiritual radar was rusty, yet her appearance felt like a sign.

"My name is Gabe," I said, shaking the hand she'd offered as evidence. My own swallowed hers whole. "Why don't you stay and warm up? I can't help you with your nails, but I'll make you a cup of tea."

Just then there was a brief flash of light through the door's half-window. "Thundersnow," she said and shivered. We slid slowly toward the chairs in unison, as if on a conveyor belt.

I flipped the switch on the fireplace, producing an immediate wisp of heat and a chemical orange glow. "I remember that manicure place," I told her, chatting to put her at ease, "because when I started working here—it was a couple weeks before Christmas—I'd go home every night with the smell of chemicals on my clothes."

"Acetone," she said, tucking into her wingback and nodding.

I nodded, too, though this was the first time I'd heard the term. I didn't tell her about those nights when I would walk through the lighted streets yearning for my old life the way children want their mothers, remembering until it was painful the candlelit silence and safety of a chapel at dusk. I didn't tell her about climbing the stairs to my shoddy one-room apartment where the acetone—if that's what it was—would rise in a vapor as I shucked off my coat. Or about how I would stand there, paralyzed, still aching to go back twenty-two years and save myself.

At least, not yet. Some of this would come later at the nightclub down the street, over martinis she charged to her business account. Some of it would come much later, when I once again had everything to lose.

"Listen," she said, removing the sunglasses, her eyes an endless brown-black and once again unwavering. "I don't know what that was back there. I'm not the sort of person who cries in front of strangers. I guess I've been under a lot of stress."

"That happens," I murmured as I plugged in the hot pot.

"It's work," she said, slipping off her little pointed boots and tucking her feet under her. "Which has been crazy. I mean, you don't know crazy until you've run an ad agency single-handed." She seemed to be warning me, in case I was considering doing such a thing.

"That sounds very challenging," I murmured, my back to her as I rummaged in the cupboard. When I get into the groove, I'm like a backup singer; all most people really need is to hear the familiar echoes and refrains. This woman was different though. She kept going off script.

"It is. But, oh! I apologize. That sounded really pompous, didn't it?" She shook her head. "This is exactly what my ex-husband used to accuse me of: 'You're constantly telling people how successful you are, Madeline.'" Her soprano had gone several notes deeper to become a parody of a man. "But he's right, I shouldn't do that," she said in her own voice.

The water was boiling, and luckily there were two packets of Earl Grey left. I made the tea and handed a cup to the woman. Madeline. "Sugar?" I asked. She shook her head no, hair rustling over her shoulders with a brisk and pleasant sound.

"He was my second husband. My second *ex*-husband now, I suppose." She set her tea down and removed her coat. Underneath she wore a tight, buttoned suit. "Damn. What an error in judgment that was. Second marriages! They never seem to work."

She glanced at me, and I was tempted to agree. *Imagine*, I might say to her, *trying for a second marriage when your first spouse was God*. Sometimes, inside my head, I'm kind of an ass.

"But there was Cassidy." She paused and looked into her lap, and I watched guilt draw its white blind down over her face. "This is ridiculous. I'm making a fool of myself, talking about all this. It's just the surprise, I think. Finding you here. The thunder. Hormones, probably." She spoke matter-of-factly, like the commercials for women's remedies on TV. "Thanks for the tea. I should go."

It was the second time she'd announced her departure, and there was no earthly reason for me to delay her. I had books to unpack and an H. P. Lovecraft display to build. Yet there was something compelling me to keep her. Goodwill, loneliness, attraction, it didn't matter. I acted on whatever it was.

"You haven't even tried your tea," I said with more authority than I'd assumed in a year. "Sit. Tell me what happened. Maybe I can help."

She shook her head. But she didn't get up. "You can't help. No one can. I did a terrible thing to that girl, and there's no way for me to ever make it up."

"Go on," I said, settling back. There was a feeling of security: I knew exactly how this part should go. "It's all right. What did you do?"

She sighed and warmed her hands around her cup. "When I started seeing Kevin," she began, "Cassidy was four. She was so sweet, and I really, truly thought I loved her father. So I took her out, to the zoo and Six Flags and the Christmas show at Marshall Fields. All the things I never got to do as a child."

"You grew up poor?" I asked, feeling a kinship.

But Madeline shook her head again. "Not exactly. I mean yes, my parents survived mostly on welfare and food stamps. There was family money somewhere, a lot of it, from what I understand, but my grandparents kept cutting us off. And when my parents took us places it wasn't to zoos or amusement parks, it was to union rallies and protests." She looked at me squarely. "By the time I was in third grade, I knew how to chain myself to a fence."

I laughed, the image in my head of Madeline now in her nice suit with shackles around her arms. "So you wanted something different for Cassidy?"

"God, yes. I wanted everything for her. Kevin and I were married when she was five, and Cass was the maid of honor. She had this gorgeous little blue dress. White flowers in her hair. She looked like an angel, you know?"

"Yes." This time I spoke with actual knowledge. I knew how it was to look down an aisle and see little girls floating toward you like seraphim.

"Then, I don't know what happened. It was like the minute we got married, Cassidy started to go . . . bad. She did disgusting things, like eating with her mouth wide open or picking her nose when we had company. And I mean *aggressive* nose picking, shoving a finger up there and twisting it and pulling out these long . . ."

Madeline grimaced and shook herself. "Then there was her room. I tried promising her rewards, an allowance, more TV time, but she kept gathering trash. More and more of it, until the whole house smelled." Again, she sighed. "Ooh, so awful. It was the kind of smell that made you just not want to come home. I spent every weekend cleaning her room, throwing out moldy applesauce containers and half-full cups of juice."

She stopped and took a sip of tea, looking around as if to reassure herself that she was no longer surrounded by filth.

"Cass must have gained ten pounds that first year. And we're talking about a six-year-old! Her hair was always snarled, and she wouldn't let me brush it. She screamed like I was killing her whenever I tried. Then when she was in first grade, the real tantrums started. I told Kevin he had to deal with her. It was his responsibility. She wasn't my . . ." She broke off as if startled.

"Child," I finished for her.

"Right," she said. "Only the thing is I'd promised at our wedding that she would be. There was a little part of the ceremony where I 'married' her. *I, Madeline, take you Cassidy as the daughter of my heart, to love forever.* I wrote it myself. It was . . ." Madeline sniffled, then her face grew stiff and disapproving. "A really good script, that's what it was. Crowd pleasing."

"I see."

"Her mother was long gone; she took off when Cass was six

months old. Never sent so much a birthday card. It was like she just zeroed out her own daughter. Moved on. But then I . . ."

We sat staring into the licking tongues of our cozy fake fire.

"You . . .?" I tried to resist, but the man I used to be squatted inside me, patient, offering up his psalms and birds of hope. "You did the very same thing?"

That's when Madeline wept. Not as she had before, the held-back tears of a woman standing at a counter in an unfamiliar shop. This was serious and personal. She turned slightly so I would not witness her shame.

"Yes. By the time Kevin and I finally divorced, she was nine. And impossible. We'd have split up even without her problems, but Cass was a constant issue—she was all we ever talked about. She snuck food, stole it if she had to. She outweighed me by twenty pounds and she was only four and a half feet tall. She had no friends. There was an incident at school where she hurt a younger boy." Madeline was staring at her hands, clenching them in her lap.

"Cass was acting out constantly at school; at least twice a week we'd get called in to talk to the principal. We were considering sending her away to a special place for children with . . . issues." She sighed and drew herself tighter in the chair.

"That sounds like a hard decision." As always when I heard a story like this, calamity building inevitably, I felt the pain of my penitent. But I also felt—corny as it sounds—like an instrument of God. Or at least like something finer than myself.

"But we couldn't. Kevin lost his job, and there wasn't enough money. We started fighting all the time. The bills for Cass's therapy were piling up. It seemed like there was no way out, except . . ." She held her hands up, palms open to the heavens. "I moved out, told him I was just done. I quit, as Kevin's wife and as Cassidy's mom. It was so freeing." She shivered. "The relief was incredible. I don't think anything in my life has ever felt that *good*."

"This is the problem with being human," I told her. "We're given incentive to do all the wrong things."

"Exactly!" I could feel the wind of her vigorous approval and watched the calm settle in the valleys of her face. In the confessional at St. John's I'd been unable to see, contained in the privacy of my own little upright coffin box. This was better, talking to people up close. But also confusing in that the rules seemed to disappear.

"I was elated for about a year, as if I'd awakened from a bad dream. You know how you think, *Oh, I'm so glad that wasn't real?* That's how it was. I kept telling myself I couldn't have stayed even if I wanted to; I never belonged in that family. Then Christmas came, and it was like this door opened."

Madeline looked at me. Her gaze was naked and afraid. "Do you know what I mean?"

I could not answer but simply sat, silent, remembering. Every Christmas I could recall, that door had opened widely: for me, for my parish, for the entire city it sometimes seemed. Sadness poured from some endless spring, infecting the people of my congregation, leading them to kneel before me and go limp. I was for the entire month of December patching together souls and sending them back to their lives still bleeding. I could see sadness leaking from them like drops of icy, gray rain.

And between ministering to those other souls, during this season I confronted my own yawning door. There was something about the silence of snowfall; it sent me right back to the streets of my youth. I would see the same skinny boy, hunched in his jacket, walking alone in the dark. Over and over I would dream of him alone in his bedroom, back against the chipped blue wall, heart beating so fast he was struggling to breathe.

I don't know how I would have responded, but just then, the bell over the shop's door chimed and a woman entered, roughly Madeline's age but dressed in jeans and clogs, her long graying hair pulled back in a clip. She clopped into general fiction, and I rose—one hand extended, palm flat. The beginning of a benediction.

"Please stay," I said. "I'll be right back."

My customer was standing in J–M, scanning the shelf, her body alert and tense. I'd been at the bookstore only two months, but I knew what this meant. It was a situation that had to be handled delicately, depending upon the disposition of the woman herself. Some were furtive, whispering their request. Others opened the book to read right there, crowing and hooting, backing helplessly into cartons and stacks.

"May I help you?" I asked, and she turned suddenly, as if I were a cannibal on her stairs. Definitely a type-one woman; she'd need to be nudged.

"We have some of our more *popular* books on display in front," I said, nodding toward the table of ladies' sex thrillers that Oren told me accounted for 60 percent of his sales and had probably saved him from bankruptcy for two years running. The woman blushed and muttered something that could have been "thank you," rushed to the table to pick up a book with silver handcuffs on the cover, coughed noisily as I processed her credit card, grabbed her plain paper bag, and left.

When I returned, Madeline was grinning through her tear-stained face. "Poor baby," she said, chuckling. "Probably hasn't been laid in years."

For one panicked moment, I thought she was talking about me. But I recovered quickly, clearing my throat and finding my pulpit voice. "People come here seeking solace for all manner of things."

"I suppose." Madeline looked at me, wary but also amused. The shamed, apologetic woman of only a few minutes before had vanished. "What is it that makes you such an expert? Why am I sitting here telling you my life?"

I leaned back in my chair. Doubt. This second phase of penance had come quickly to Madeline, but I could tell already she was smarter than most of the strangers who poured out their lives.

"I don't know," I said. "I just seem to understand these things." Then I shrugged, a gesture I've adopted only since coming to the outside.

There was a stretch of silence, and I thought Madeline might have moved on in her mind, deciding this was ridiculous, talking to a stranger about her past. But when she stirred, she did not gather her things and leave. Rather, she went on, "It was temporary, that first feeling I had about Cassidy. It went away right after Christmas. Then the next year, it came back. I ignored it, and it went away again. But now *this* year . . ." She paused and looked at me for assistance.

"It's not going away?" I supplied.

She shook her head. "Nope. And it's late February. Every day I wake up and expect it to be gone, only I feel worse. Less like the person I intended to be. It's, um, sticky. Sometimes . . ." She paused for a moment and when she spoke again I had to lean in to hear. "I think I'm going crazy. We're all alone: just me and this ominous thing in my head."

"Did you try contacting Cassidy?" I asked.

"About two weeks ago," she said, nodding. "She has a new mom. Kevin's on to wife number three, would you believe?" Madeline snorted, and I saw, as clearly as if the devil were waving a flag, where her guilt was all stopped up.

"Cass said . . ." she swallowed. "She said they're a real family now. Mary—that's the wife's name—helps her. Mary understands her. Mary would never . . ." Madeline swallowed hard. "Mary would never disappear the way I did. I asked Cass if we could meet sometime for lunch, and she said no, that she had no reason to see me. I'd been a terrible mother, and she was glad I'd left. But it wasn't nasty, the way she said it. It was just . . ." A look of pure terror crossed Madeline's face. "True," she said.

"You know the answer," I said softly. "Cassidy is happy now. She has a new family. You can't disrupt that."

"Oh, I know. Only . . ." In the background the hot pot burbled, reminding me that I'd forgotten to switch if off. A cello suite played on the stereo. And Madeline crumpled into her chair, a pile of de-signer clothes crowned with hair. "It means I never get out of this. Cassidy won't forgive me. I'm here forever. I'm stuck."

I thought about how often in my life this had happened: I would listen to the story someone told about selfishness and wrongdoing, and mostly I would be thinking, *You do not deserve absolution.* Some-times, in my own dark heart, I would lobby for those people to suffer more. It would be tempting to banish them from my church.

Once, when a parishioner confessed to having gotten drunk in col-lege and beating up a homeless man for no reason other than boredom, I'd sat clenched with the desire to rip open the door of my little compart-ment, then his, and strangle him in the aisle with my knee to his neck.

"What bothers you most?" I asked now, looking—as I'd learned to do—for the way toward God.

Madeline raised her head, and oddly she looked as if her face had been washed clean. If she'd cried off her makeup, I wondered, where had it gone? And how did her bare skin make her appear both older and younger than before?

"I think about her, Cassidy, going to bed on those nights after I left. Lying there, waiting for me to come back, maybe crying. Realiz-ing that another mom had left her." No self-pity, little drama. I soft-ened. Madeline, despite her confession, was good.

"But Cassie's doing well now," I said. "In fact, she's better off than before. It sounds like she has a wonderful stepmother, and your leaving—as badly as you may have done it—had to happen in order for Mary to come into her life. For Cassidy to have a stable, happy family, which you and Kevin couldn't provide." Madeline blinked as if she were awakening. Damn, I was good.

"You can't change the past, but even if you could I might argue in this case that you should leave well enough alone. You will never know what caused your ex-husband to seek this woman out. It may even have been related to something you did or said."

"Is this an it-was-meant-to-be lecture?" Madeline asked, her tone wary, and I struggled not to laugh.

"Hardly. That's a philosophy for radio ministers and embroidered pillows. What I'm saying is, if you wouldn't change things for Cassidy now, you need to move forward. Take this lesson, learn from it. Be better. And move in the only direction that's available to you."

Madeline was rapt. And why was she listening to this from a bookstore clerk? Because she so desperately wanted what I was offering. That's the only answer I have.

"That makes sense," she breathed, alive now and re-inhabiting her clothes. "But how do I get Cassidy to see it?"

"You don't. You leave Cassidy alone, because going forward you're going to do what's right for her."

"But . . ." I watched her struggle, looking at her hands. "I want to be forgiven."

"Done," I said. "I forgive you. And God already forgave you, long ago."

Finally she looked skeptical. Angry, even. Her eyes narrowed. "It's not that easy," she said, reaching for her handbag and beginning to rise. "You can't just forgive me. It doesn't work that way. You don't speak for God."

I leaned back in my chair and stared at her calmly until she stopped and sat back down. "You'd be surprised," I said.

To: isaac36@comcast.net
From: mmmurray@gmail.com

Dear Isaac—

How's Austin? I imagine it's all warm and dusty with gorgeous men in cowboy hats dancing to country music in the streets. I've never been to Texas in my life but if we get one more blizzard, I swear I'm going to fly down and plant myself in your guest room—maybe find one of those country-western guys. Though I probably won't be able to get on a plane because every time you turn around this year O'Hare is closed.

Speaking of men, I met an interesting one today. I cried in front of him within ten minutes (and by cried, I mean bawled) in the middle of a bookstore. Do you see what's happened to me since you left??? I have no one to talk to or go to movies with. I have to play dragon lady all the time. It's lonely! Damn you and your baby-seal-killing oilman boyfriend. How is Foss, by the way? If I come down, will he explain fracking to me? Never mind, I don't really want to know.

Work is a horror show. (Are you sure you don't want to come back?) We were runner-up on the Prudential pitch, spent about $150K that I personally signed off on. Then they went with Razorfish, which I kind of knew all along they would. The venture capital guys are really pissed! Saatchi was all set to buy us if we got Prudential and a piece of Toyota, but now they're backing off and I'm going to have to fire maybe 12%. Your old pal, Scott? First to go. Don't tell him, or I will have you killed. ☺

'Cause, sweetheart, I have this crazy idea for how I might be able to get us back on track. And it could be a cash cow if it works. But I've had a few drinks, and it's possible I'll wake up tomorrow and realize this was the dumbest drunken scheme ever. I'll write and let you know. Right now, I need to get in bed with my Rabbit.

I still hate you for leaving.

Love,
MMM

II

I WOKE AT 10:22, THE MORNING AFTER MADELINE'S VISIT, TO THE sensation of my brain pulsing like some dark star and threatening to detach itself from my head. I rolled to the side of my bed and lowered myself, moving as carefully as a bomb squad, to kneel on the floor. It was a familiar position, one that gave me comfort. So I paused there, hands clasped on my sheets, eyes closed, head bowed.

When I was able, 10:31 by the clock, I staggered to my feet and into the bathroom, where I took three aspirins and drank seven glasses of water straight from the tap. Hangovers are half dehydration; this I knew from long-ago experience. But the rehydration took time, and if you rushed it, you risked getting sick and having to start all over. I swayed, holding my cup of water, peering into the mirror as I sipped.

This morning I wore the vestments of the down-and-out: boxer shorts and a dingy white T-shirt. A pair of black socks would have finished the look, but my feet were bare, stiff as frozen fish on the icy tile floor. Craving punishment, I removed all my clothes and stood shivering in front of my naked reflection, examining what I saw.

My hair was going gray at the temples, across my tattooed chest, and between my legs. I found this both strange and amusing. I was beginning to look like a man of experience when I was, in fact, just newly born to this world.

The day before I'd talked to Madeline about her stepdaughter. And I'd done what I always do, dispensing wisdom as I understand it, closing my eyes and reaching for the right thing to say, telling her what I believed would bring her closer to God. We'd still been there, she and I in front of the fire, when evening had fallen and closing time had come. I'd risen from my chair to lock the door and put out the sign.

"Do you have time for a drink?" she'd asked in a throaty voice. "I'd like to repay you for everything you've done."

I'd turned to look and had met her endless eyes. Had I been hoping she'd meant something else? In truth, I had. There was something about this woman—her dark hair and strange face—that bewitched me. And do not think that a man who's been mostly celibate loses his ability to judge; rather, I'd become more selective during those dry years, more aware of the women who possessed some denser light than others. This one had a holy spark—flinty, yes, but real.

"I'd like that very much," I'd said, turning my back to her as I'd hurried through my paperwork, using a pencil to mark the total (a pathetic $54) and securing the receipts with a rubber band.

We'd moved down the street to a bar where Madeline had insisted on buying Bombay martinis with her American Express. It was lucky, I'd thought foolishly at the time, that the sacraments had kept me drinking alcohol despite my twelve-step cohorts constantly demanding that I come completely clean. *What is a priest without his chalice of wine?* I had said. *A lonely ex-cleric without the comfort of his very cheap Scotch?* I might ask my fellow addicts now.

"You were a priest?" Madeline had repeated at least four times when I'd told her. "A real *priest*? That's . . . extraordinary." Her eyes had looked, impossibly, even wider than before.

I'd described to Madeline how I'd left the church—omitting the part about my breakdown on the altar one Easter morning—and settled into a life of authentic poverty. No more housekeeping service, no more daily delivery of flowers, no more regular supply of clothing courtesy of the Cardinal's secretary.

"I haven't dressed myself since the early nineties," I'd joked. (This was one of my standard lines.) "Which I'm sure explains quite a bit."

She'd laughed and rested one small unmanicured hand on my thigh, while raising the other to order another round. The gin had done its work and I'd warmed, becoming more the smooth-talking kid of my distant past, relating my entire history as if it were one of those droll, English comedies—all mix-ups and low stakes. My descent, which I'd downplayed out of manly pride, had in fact been dramatic. A squalid apartment and a minimum-wage job. Canned soup and ramen noodles that weren't exactly good for my blood pressure. No health insurance, no pension, no work history—nothing I could list on a form, anyway.

"So you're working a minimum wage job while you dispense advice and grant forgiveness to people like me on your own time?" Madeline had been gazing across the empty bar as Barry Manilow crooned over the sound system. "But there's no compensation for any of it. You live without any of the things you used to enjoy when you can perform this great service. Why?"

Because people like you come to me and lay their guilt at my feet as if it were a rag-wrapped orphan, I'd thought. *Because I have a bizarre gift for forgiveness—or perhaps a deficit where blame is concerned.*

This was what I'd wanted to say, what I probably should have said. Unfortunately, I'd been at this point too drunk.

So I'd bobbed and shaken my head, more to sharpen the blurry, levitating Madeline before me in the booth than to attempt an answer. It hadn't worked; she'd kept rising. But she'd taken my helpless gesture as a sign.

"Nothing! You receive nothing in return for your help, for your work and experience and . . . and . . . compassion. That's wrong. Wasn't that church of yours passing around a basket, asking people to kick in every time you gave out a what-do-you-call-it? A benediction?"

"Well, sort of." It hadn't seemed the right time to critique her liturgical knowledge. Madeline was ordering yet another round of drinks.

"Listen, Gabe. No one else is doing this on a volunteer basis. Think of the Catholic Church. Do you think the Vatican bought all that art by hearing people's confessions for free? Isn't it the wealthiest state in the world, or did I just make that up?"

I'd assumed it was the booze, plus Madeline's relief, that had made her talk that way—drunkenly framing my spiritual work in transactional terms. Tomorrow our conversation would be forgotten, evaporated along with her guilt. I'd been keeping track, and she'd had enough to drink that I could not in good faith have touched her even if she'd ripped open her clothes, laid herself on the table, and begged. So after draining my fourth Bombaytini I'd stood with difficulty, lied that I had an early morning, and tottered out the door and up the block to my lonely cell where I'd dived headfirst into bed.

But when I dragged myself through the door of Brooks Books that afternoon to begin my shift, I was told that Madeline had been calling the store repeatedly and with growing intensity since before nine o'clock.

She, apparently, was more practiced in the ways of gin than I. After Oren left to run his errands, I listened to the first of the voice-mail messages. *I'm looking for Gabe McKenna.* Madeline's voice was crisp and bright. *As per our conversation last night, I'd like to get some time on the calendar. Please call me with your availability*, she'd chirped with no audible hint of headache. She left her number and signed off with a cheery, *Later! I hope.*

It was an unusually busy day, and I actually had a burst of customers (a burst being five) that consumed quite a bit of my time. One older gentleman wanted avidly to discuss the meaning of *The Plague*, though I assured him existentialism was not my area of expertise. Yet he insisted, droning on about the "universal condition" in professorial tones.

My head was beginning to throb again, and finally, in a supremely unprofessional gesture, I unbuttoned my shirt and pulled down the neck hole of my white T-shirt to show him the large black cross with its thorns and three scarlet drops of blood tattooed just above my heart. "Do you see?" I asked. "Now, do you understand?"

It was a ridiculous question, of course, because no one could. As a young man I'd had florid ideas about penance, submitting my coward's chest to Sol's ink gun and believing this would somehow help compensate for my crime. Showy self-indulgent displays are the opposite of atonement, of course, but it took me more than a decade to figure this out. And the tattoo did have its uses. It was evidence of the person I once was, the user who was still curled up inside me. Also, in this case baring it actually worked. The old man paid hurriedly for his copy of *No Exit* and left me in peace.

Finally, I dialed the number I'd copied down from Madeline's message. "Can I ask who's calling?" a young woman piped in a cartoonishly high voice. When I gave her my name, there was an intake of breath. No card player, she. "Would you mind holding?" she asked. "I'm gonna page Madeline right away."

I waited, holding the phone, wishing ardently for five o'clock. This was Wednesday, when the store closed early, probably in deference to church night, though Oren had never said. He'd left my check for me. Small as it was—especially after the subtraction of taxes I had never given a thought to until the age of forty—I had plans.

"Gabe!" Madeline said when she arrived on the phone. "I've been hoping you'd call. I've been thinking about you all day."

This was not what I'd been expecting. I stopped kneading my forehead and straightened, the teenager inside me stretching and waking up. There'd been that moment last night—it appeared now in my memory, indistinct but real—when Madeline had rested her hand on my leg, and I'd longed for her so fiercely that it had become all I could process or understand. Perhaps that's why, today, I had no recollection of any meetings "as per our conversation." My gin-soaked mind had been focused on trying to be covert when I stared at her breasts.

"I'm hoping we can get you in for a download," Madeline was saying. "I'm so grateful for everything you said to me yesterday. And I think we can help you reach more people, people who are hungry for your kind of wisdom. There's some real potential in this concept of ecumenical forgiveness."

"Potential?" I hunched over the counter, my body aching and wizened again. "Potential . . . as in?"

"Commercial value, Gabe. And the potential to help more people, of course. We discussed all of this last night. Remember?"

"Barely," I said, and she laughed deep in her throat.

"Oh, that's cute. You're a lightweight. Hold on, I need to shut my door."

I held the receiver and stared at the shop door, praying (literally, I'm ashamed to say) that no one else would come in.

"Okay, I'm back. Listen. I know it might have seemed like one of those drunken conversations you forget all about the next day."

"Obviously."

"But I was serious, Gabe. I thought about it all night. I even talked to a few people. I believe we have a chance to create something completely groundbreaking. Like, you know, the iPod back when Apple introduced it. *Think Different*, right? *Here's to the crazy ones.*"

My lust was dissipating. I'd been captivated by the blunt, mournful woman in front of the fire, but now everything seemed cheapened and flimsy. As if it had already happened somewhere and been translated to shorthand. Perhaps that's why Madeline was speaking in code.

"Look," I said, "I don't know . . ." I needed water again and also, not coincidentally, to urinate. The clock showed 5:01, and I was desperate to lock up so no late customer would take advantage and rush in.

"Just a meeting, Gabe, okay? That's all I'm asking. One meeting. We'll provide lunch. Or, tell you what! You come in and talk with the team, and I'll take you to lunch. Au Cheval, perhaps?"

"On horseback?"

"Excuse me?"

"You just asked if you could take me to lunch on horseback, which sounds great but a little chilly this time of year."

She chuckled again, more warmly this time. "You speak French, too?"

Too? What did she mean "too"? In addition to being a down-and-out drive-by-confession priest? But my headache was gathering force quickly—I knew from past experience that what I needed was water, food, and sleep, in that order—so I decided not to ask.

"I was in Montreal for a year, ministry internship at the Basilica. Couldn't help but pick up some French," I said, imagining for a moment the cool glory of that church, the quietly suspended golden Jesus, my sober, pious, long-haired self.

"Huh." I could hear Madeline's pen scratching on paper, and the sound carved painful lines in my brain. "Too bad it's not Spanish. More people here speak that. But we might be able to make something of the French."

I started to ask what she planned to "make" of my fifteen-year-old Canadian French but decided against it. At this point, I was willing to do whatever it took to cut this conversation short.

"So how's your Thursday?" Madeline asked, businesslike again as if she'd heard my thoughts. "Say, eleven o'clock? We'll meet with the team then have lunch around one. Do you want to check your calendar?"

"Ah, hold on," I said, putting the phone down gently and rushing to the front door. I turned the bolt and put out the ancient cardboard CLOSED sign. My head had taken up a steady beat. There were old ceramic cups under the desk, from back when Oren served midafternoon tea; I grabbed one and filled it in the bathroom with tap water. Then I stopped to check the schedule, which was the closest thing I had to a calendar of my own.

"Thursday is fine," I said when I returned. Then I gulped tinny water from the cup until I was breathless.

"Excellent," Madeline said. "We're at 220 North Wells Street. If you give me your email address, I'll send out a meeting notice."

Where is the weeping woman from yesterday? I wondered. *Or the merry, incredulous, hard-drinking one from the bar?* It was as if Madeline had superpowers, like those comic book characters that can recover from stab wounds in thirty seconds. Or else, I was just that good.

"No need for an email," I told her. "I have it down, I'll be there."

I did *not* have it down, of course. But I hardly needed a note because other than work, this meeting was my only event for the next month.

Over the years I'd counseled many couples through divorce (which inevitably became *annulment* for the sake of the Church), and in nearly every case someone would end up the loser. Men told me about the loss of family: their children off living with an ex-wife and some other man, their new apartments empty and silent at night. Women seemed to suffer most from the absence of friends, the less frequent invitations to dinner parties where everyone else would appear two-by-two, the gentle withdrawal of the social life they'd enjoyed as a couple.

All that time and I'd never for one minute put myself in their place. Yet here I was, divorced from the church and going home to my desolate middle-aged bachelor's apartment, no longer invited to the holiday meals, elegant parties, and family tables where I once was celebrated like some sort of demi-god. Being a priest had had its lonely moments, but it kept one busy.

Being an ex-priest—and I failed to consider this when I left the Church—meant infinite time to dwell on the past. It was a purgatory with no end.

I locked up now from the outside, huddled against the wind. Chicago was always fierce, but this had been a longer winter than most. And it was my first since childhood—when my mother would send me out for milk or hamburger—of actually walking to buy groceries. The sun was sinking rapidly, leaving only a thin golden glow along the western horizon. I zipped up my Carhartt jacket (durable and cheap, I'd been told) and headed east into grayness.

It was six blocks, mostly downhill, to the Jewel. My eyes were stinging and leaking by the time I finally saw it, a sanctuary with steel window grates. The automatic door whooshed open in its egalitarian way—just as it did for families and gang members and old ladies. It had never occurred to me before what a welcoming sign this was.

Inside, the Jewel was tropical. Mist sprayed from ducts trying to revive the already dead vegetables. Steam and the smell of wet coats hung in the air. I removed my scarf and placed it in a green hand basket. Then I walked slowly through the store, down every aisle, though I knew exactly what I would buy. Some nights, I stretched my shopping to an hour, but tonight, somewhere in the canned goods, the heat turned my headache sloppy and green. I hurried through the rest of the store, picking up an extra bottle of water ($1.89) for the walk home.

At the checkout counter, I unloaded the water, along with my cheese, apple, sliced turkey, canned pineapple, and package of pre-seasoned rice.

"Sack?" the cashier asked, and I nodded. She added ten cents to my total and handed me a tissue-thin bag. Our fingers met briefly, and she looked at me quickly, her eyes wary. I saw the outline of what she might say—the story of her sick baby, feverish this morning, now drugged up on Benadryl and comatose at daycare—if our circumstances had been different: if there hadn't been five people jostling in line behind me, a security guard rousting a drunkard who'd fallen asleep by the door, the overhead speaker playing a synthesized version of "Can't Fight This Feeling." I tried with one nod to convey my understanding to the woman, but, obviously, I failed.

"You need to get moving," she said as I stuffed my things inside the bag and it split up one seam. "I got other people here."

"Of course." I reached for another bag. "I just need . . ."

"You only paid for one," the clerk said.

"I know." I spoke slowly now, forcing her to look up from the beer and chips she was scanning. She watched as I reached into my pocket for a quarter and placed it on top of the twelve-pack of Old Style she'd slid my way. "It'll be fine."

"I can't give you change. I'm in the middle of another purchase." She was a woman used to fighting. A girl, actually. Tough and scared, dreadlocks coiled heavy on her head, and maybe all of nineteen.

"Don't worry," I said, holding her gaze. "Knock fifteen cents off this guy's bill." I tapped the beer with two fingers.

There was the barest glimmer of a smile, which I interpreted as success. I re-bagged my groceries and headed toward the exit, which did not open ceremoniously the way the first door had. Only entering was automatic here; in order to get out I had to back up, hurl my body at the glass, and push against the wind with all my weight.

Outside, I stopped at a trashcan with a smeared, rounded top and set my groceries there. Most of the remnants of gold sky had disappeared while I was inside, leaving only a gleaming rim against the thick gray night. The city around me was still and cold and dark, and I took a long breath. This was the winter hour I'd feared and avoided for years, holding five o'clock services even if they were attended only by me and the acolytes in their miniature white robes—anything to distract myself.

Tonight I made myself face it. I looked at the backs of passing strangers, salting my own wound, seeking out the tall, thin forms that walked hunching forward, hands in pockets, as Aidan once did. Specters outlined against the setting sun.

The sky was different in Chicago, which was one reason I'd lived here for years. There was a wideness I'd never seen before coming to the Midwest, a leaning down of the heavens as if the clouds and stars were a covering, lowered by God. But the sharpness of the air was the same as New England's, minus the tang of seawater. And occasionally, when I was tired and facing dusk, it all washed through me. The shame.

"C'mon, Gabe." I could hear Aidan's voice, high and wavering like a child's violin, anxious even at the best of times. "Please! Don't leave."

And I was back there, feeling trapped by his weakness, growing rough, snarling, mean. My breath, then and now, more than twenty years later, came fast. Leaning against a bus stop outside the Jewel, I opened and chugged my entire bottle of water despite the aching cold. This helped. Now, my head hurt only when I turned it, so I stood ramrod straight while tying my scarf and pulling on my gloves.

Then I picked up my groceries, taking care this time with the fragile bag, and began to walk home. The voice still spoke to me but whispered now, desperate. Six blocks, mostly uphill.

Mason & Zeus Advertising, LLC

Statement of Work: Forgiveness Provider
Date: February 25, 20--
Client: Gabriel McKenna
Job Number: 48011

Overview

Branding project for a sole proprietor, former clergy, who offers expert forgiveness and absolution in exchange for a flat fee that ranges from $2,000–$5,000 per sin. Business is largely word-of-mouth and relies heavily upon the character and charisma of its principal. Name, tagline, and mark should convey both dignity and accessibility with a touch of humor to reflect Mr. McKenna's personal style.

Scope

Strategist will prepare brief based on interviews with Mr. McKenna and satisfied clients, attaching comp analyses of religious and psychological approaches. Naming exploration will proceed simultaneously, focusing on "Forgive" as the primary message. Core creative and PR needs to be determined after client has reviewed initial findings and approved a name.

Goals

- Establish Mr. McKenna as the founder and originator of privatized confessing and absolution
- Build a brand that is associated with trustworthiness and relief of burden, similar to life insurance
- Triple customer base in one year and begin expanding outside the Chicago area to both coasts

Audience

Ranges in age from 21–75 but concentrates heavily in Gen X (37–53) and young Baby Boomer (54–63) sectors, especially among former Catholics. This is our primary target and will be easily expanded with digital billboards, bus covers, and interstitial ads on sites that lead to feelings of remorse (e.g., porn, swinging, Canadian pharmaceuticals). Great potential for growth in the Baby Boomer market but will require awareness campaigns to promote the concept of "guilt," which 53–68-year-old respondents to a survey reported they are "less likely" or "unlikely" to experience.

Opportunities

Research shows people in transition trend toward worry and regret. Future growth opportunities may include the recently divorced (or remarried), empty nesters, retirees, people grieving a dying or dead parent, and unemployed professionals. Client feels strongly about avoiding markets under 18 (consent issues) and over 70 (dementia). Substantial growth opportunity exists in online forgiveness, which could be offered as a low-cost alternative to face-to-face. Explore building an interface that would serve a multi-national audience on the Web.

Competition

At this time, there is no privatized forgiveness industry. Public and nonprofit competitors include the Catholic Church (Mr. McKenna's former employer), other religious organizations, and some psychotherapeutic disciplines.

Competitive Advantages

First and only concept of its kind. Requires nothing from customers except payment—no penance, church attendance, or personal growth. Caters to today's overworked parent or professional, allows for multi-tasking. May be seen as one of a suite of paid services (e.g., housecleaning, personal shopping) that busy people need.

Special Considerations

- Client dislikes/is sensitive to blasphemy and church-based humor.
- Priestly background both positive and negative; tread lightly with this.

- Cheerful, upbeat tone extremely important to ensure acceptance.
- Project top-secret due to possibility of intellectual property theft.
- Possible backlash from religious groups on both financial and spiritual fronts.
- Potential PR pitfall if business is made to look ridiculous (e.g., parody on SNL).

Team Members

Scott Hicks, Creative Director
Joy Everson, Strategist
Abel Dodd, Copywriter
Lori Inman, Public Relations Specialist
Ted Roman, Interactive Media Specialist
M. Madeline Murray, CEO & Acting Account Director

Timing

ASAP

Go team!!!!!!

From: Scott Hicks
To: Abel Dodd, Lori Inman, Joy Everson, Ted Roman
Cc: M. Madeline Murray
Subject: Priest project

Hey team—

Kickoff for the Forgiveness job isn't till next week, but I met Fr McKenna today and I had some ideas I don't want to loose. I'm seeing a white/black thing, very simple, with lots of open space and small type. Make it simple and humble and maybe a foto of McKenna off to the side. The camera's gonna like him, but for Christ's sake, we need to dress him better. (Ted, could you get on that?)

Our competition uses a lot of color, staned glass, and pics of nature. So we gotta differentiate. Joy is going to do her information thing, of course, but it's pretty obvious we're going after fucked-up people with $$. I'm thinking Kubrick. Dark but sexy, like that movie where everyone dressed up in animal heads and had orgys. Just a thought. What say you guys?

SH

From: Lori Inman
To: Scott Hicks, Abel Dodd, Joy Everson, Ted Roman
Cc: M. Madeline Murray
Subject: Re: Priest project

Love that you're thinking ahead, Scott! A couple watch-outs for this project. The comp issue is complicated. Joy is making a spread-sheet of businesses and organizations that touch the forgiveness space, and there are a lot more than we thought. So let's wait for the creative brief before we start talking concept or design.

Also, be careful of descriptors like "fucked-up." That's not going to fly with our client, and I sense he's a little reluctant as it is.

Lori

From: Ted Roman
To: Scott Hicks
Cc: M. Madeline Murray
Subject: Re: Priest project

Hi Scott—

I'm sure you didn't mean to suggest that I should be used as fashion consultant on the Forgiveness job. My role, just to review, is Interactive Media Specialist—which does NOT include reenacting episodes of What Not to Wear. I'm flattered that you like my sense of style. But sending the black man to dress some middle-aged white guy is very 18th-century. Don't make me call HR.

With regards,
Ted

P.S. Also, in case you're wondering, I won't teach him to dance. I know my people were blessed with a better sense of rhythm than yours. Deal with it.

From: M. Madeline Murray
To: Scott Hicks, Abel Dodd, Lori Inman, Joy Everson, Ted Roman
Subject: going forward

Hi Forgiveness Team—

It's been brought to my attention that there's been cross-talk about the Gabriel McKenna project. I want to do some level-setting here right off the bat.

This is a huge opportunity and an extremely important account for Mason & Zeus. We're helping to establish a first-and-only in the field of forgiveness. That means long hours, evenings, weekends, and you may be required to do things that don't technically fall under your job description. That said, let's be sensitive to everyone's contributions, and all assignments outside the scope of our SOW—fashion makeovers, for instance—should go through me.

If you are not on board with this 110% I invite you to step off the team and make way for someone who is. Your colleagues would kill for the chance, if they knew about it (please remember, this is confidential even within the walls of M&Z!!!). FYI, I'll be seeing to Father McKenna's wardrobe personally.

Oh, and let's all remember to run spell-check on emails.

Onward.
MMM

From: Joy Everson
To: Scott Hicks, Lori Inman
Cc: M. Madeline Murray
Subject: Forgiveness creative brief

Hi Scott, Lori (and Madeline)—

I have preliminary competitive findings on the environment and audiences for forgiveness services. I'll be sending out a meeting notice to the full team shortly. Please review the attached creative brief.

Yours,
Joy

Mason & Zeus Advertising, LLC

Client: Gabriel McKenna
Project: Forgiveness
Date: March 1, 20--

Key Insight:
Today's busy professionals are seeking a faster, more service-oriented route to achieve spiritual peace than traditional religion or psychotherapy.

Learnings:

Most data collected on guilt is "soft" or inferential, but several signs point to a need for more efficient forgiveness mechanisms. Many Catholic churches extend their hours for confession prior to major holidays (Easter being the big one for the "washing away of sin"). In a random survey, clergy from other Christian denominations also claim to be busier during the holidays with conferences related to absolution—often meeting someone for the first time (a non-churchgoer, or NCG) in a one-on-one to address issues of guilt, conscience, or criminality. (Note: Approximately half of all NCGs offer a contribution or "tithe" in return for the clergy's time.) I spoke to three psychologists who reported a similar uptick in patients who unburden themselves about a single wrong act—often paying out-of-pocket, so the notes on their session will not be sent to an insurer or employer—but refuse to delve into painful memories as part of the therapeutic process and/or analyze their own behavior for the purpose of changing it in the future. With this audience, repeat business is the low-hanging fruit.

Community:

Heavily weighted with former Catholics. Also parents of teenage children, repentant felons, people who are or think they are dying. Jews, Muslims, and atheists appear least likely to seek this service—until they're facing a major life event, e.g., terminal illness, death of a loved one, or loss of a job or marriage.

Conclusion:

There is a sizable gap in the market where a paid but spiritual adviser offers immediate forgiveness of guilt without any commitment on the part of the consumer.

Opportunity Landscape for Paid Forgiveness Service:

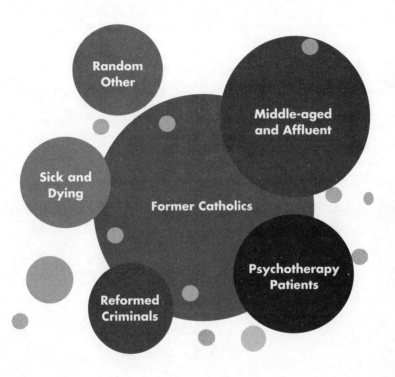

III

I WAS REACHING THE FOR THE DOOR HANDLE OF THE TAXI WHEN A MAN spoke into my ear. "Excuse me," he said, so close I could smell the sharp limey scent of his cologne. "Would you mind sharing a cab?"

Actually, I did. It had been a long day of meetings, and the French lunch had been tasty but miniature—a saucer of scrambled eggs drizzled with foie gras, and two poker chip–sized hamburgers (one for Madeline, one for me) served on an oblong plate with some snarled carrot garnish and one radish like a staring eye. I'd wondered if my brother the chef would approve.

"My parents would kill me for eating this," Madeline had said, using bread to soak up the last puddle of duck fat before closing her eyes, tipping her head back, and placing this last bite on her tongue. "All those poor little ducks with their feet nailed to planks, being force-fed till they nearly explode," she'd said after she'd finished chewing, her lips slick with grease. "Does it make you feel guilty?"

And I'd nodded, not because of the fattened ducks but because of what I'd been thinking as she swallowed. Now, three hours later, I was exhausted, ravenous, and horny, and I wanted to be alone with my thoughts.

In addition, sharing this fare would pose an ethical problem. Madeline had tucked fifty dollars into my hand before showing me out the door of Mason & Zeus, sweetly suggesting I take a cab. Pocketing half of her cash would be pathetic, if not actually wrong. I was about to say no, tell him I was a surgeon headed to the hospital on an emergency. But the man I saw when I turned was still half-boy, barely in need of a shave, and though he was well-dressed, right down to his long pointed shoes, he had an air of desperation that made me relent.

"Where do you need to go?" I asked. "I'm headed south."

"I know. I've seen you around the neighborhood, Father. That'll be fine."

"Get in," I said, stepping aside and into the slush of a sudden springtime melt. The man-boy obediently bent and folded himself into the back seat of the cab.

I briefly considered walking away once he was in the cab. It was rare for people to recognize me from my church days before I spotted them and ducked inside a florist or a travel agency to hide out until they'd passed. It wasn't that I resented or disliked my parishioners. There were, in fact, many I missed. But I could never adequately answer their questions, and this caused me frustration that bordered on muteness. My sudden departure, the abrupt absence of "calling." How could I explain to people what I did not understand myself?

I had somehow agreed, while thinking mostly about Madeline's grease-smeared lips, to think about offering my services as confessor to a clientele that she assured me was accustomed to paying for succor and could find peace no other way. It was a transparent argument, much like the rationalizations I'd used as a very young man when making money without actually doing any work. What drew me now wasn't—I was acutely aware of this—a desire to help wealthy people with their guilt, but rather a desperate need to keep myself in a relationship with this woman, with her wit and occasional honesty. But more than that, I hungered for the activity she brought into my life, the welcome newness that kept me from re-living, alone every evening, the transgressions of my own long-ago past.

Now I needed to get home, to do what Madeline and her people called my "homework." I was to write a personal statement about forgiveness that their writer could refashion into a mantra, whatever that was. I'd been assured it was important, that these words would be the cornerstone of "our" enterprise. ("Our?" I had echoed. But she'd simply nodded and gone on.) To encapsulate and deconstruct the purpose of absolution in a few paragraphs, it was a lofty task. A real challenge. And the Saturday night sermon writer in me was itching to give it a shot.

So I climbed in to the taxi and slammed the door with purpose, the set of barbells I sometimes raised and lowered while watching TV finally paying off. My posture—leaning back and against the smeared window to my side—should have indicated a wish for silence. But my cabmate was intent.

"My name's Chase," he said, proffering a long hand with a large gold watch at the wrist, glinting in the afternoon sun.

"Gabe," I responded as we shook, but the boy squinted at me as if I must be wrong.

"What are you doing downtown, Father McKenna? Church business? I hope you don't mind me asking."

"Well, actually, it was more personal," I said. *Why should I tell this young man anything?* It was none of his concern, and, besides, my errand was too difficult to explain. We had twenty minutes together in this back seat—maybe thirty, when you took traffic into account—and I searched my mind for something agnostic to say.

"You probably don't remember me," said Chase. "I was younger when we met."

"Younger than you are now?" That hardly seemed possible. He was a floppy-haired, Justin Bieberish boy.

"Yeah." He grinned, pointing up with one dexterous finger. "It's the face. Everyone thinks I'm . . . innocent." He let out a loud rather dramatic sigh. "If only they knew."

I nodded, determined not to bite at his bait. What I really wanted was a pot pie out of my own freezer and time to think about what had just happened at Mason & Zeus. I closed my eyes and willed Chase to be silent. Of course, that didn't work.

"Father?" he prompted.

"Gabe," I said, grudgingly opening my eyes. "I left the church last year."

"Oh. I'm . . . sorry?"

At which I softened, because it was as good a response as most. "Me, too, some days. But it was time."

We rode for a few moments in a companionable quiet. Dusk was melting its pink over the city and inside something had changed; we'd become partners in this ride. The cab had bad shock absorbers, and as it bumped up and down through the streets, Chase bobbed like a toy.

"Do you remember Laura Larimar?" His voice was hopeful, clear as a child's.

I startled. Yes, it was nine years ago. But how could I forget? First there was her name: Laura Larimar sounded like it should belong to a 1940s movie star, the sort of spitfire who wore pants and rode a bicycle and sparred with Clark Gable or Cary Grant. (Nights in the rectory, I watched a lot of Turner Classic TV.)

But there was also her hair, a shade of red that had never seemed real. It wasn't carroty orange or strawberry blonde. Laura Larimar was the only person I ever saw with red hair that actually *was* the color of ripe strawberries, nearly scarlet. It was thick, too, and long. There was so much of it that the makeup artist at the mortuary had to wash it in sections and lay it out on pillows overnight alongside Laura's body so it would dry.

Her family came to me on a Friday, as I was closing up. They didn't have a church. They were part of that earthbound, non-religious movement, the one espousing hemp clothing and hybrid vehicles that took hold in the wake of Whole Foods. They recycled their aluminum cans and kept an herb garden and sent money to Planned Parenthood.

That was their belief system. But when their daughter died it was all suddenly not enough.

Once, long ago, Laura's mother had been Catholic. She wanted the full treatment, with an open casket and altar boys and incense. Despite my church's ironclad policy, I agreed. After the service, her father—he had not spoken one word up to that point; I wasn't sure he could—handed me an envelope and said in a strange, high voice it was for "the priest's discretionary fund." Inside, there were ten new $100 bills.

"Yes," I cleared my throat. "I remember Laura Larimar." And in that moment I remembered the newspaper photo: a slim, frightened boy who looked, perhaps vaguely, like the little brother of this young man.

"I killed her," said Chase, as I'd known he would.

This was the point I'd been told, just a few hours before, that I'd have to learn to manage. I needed what Madeline called a "talk track" to convert people gently from free confessions to paid. It would be easy, she assured me, once I got the hang of it, once I'd developed and memorized my speech. Lawyers who were asked for free advice did this all the time; they wore it like armor at parties. It would help, she said, to have business cards and privacy forms that I gave people to sign. But here in this cab, it was just the two of us. Well, the three of us, technically, if you counted the driver. And I had a sense he was listening, though he kept his eyes straight ahead on a creeping bus.

"I'm not a priest anymore, Chase," I fumbled, caught between my revulsion at the idea of asking for payment and fury at him for cornering me in this cab.

"I know." He leaned back and scrutinized me. "So this isn't quite as lucky as I thought."

"Lucky?"

"When I saw you, I thought it was outrageous. Like a sign from God. I could finally get over all my hang-ups and stop . . . this." Chase waved his hand around the ashy-smelling inside of the cab. "Always looking for a taxi."

"You don't live South, do you?" I asked, staring again at his shiny Italian shoes.

"Nope." He grinned. "Lincoln Park."

"And why were you looking for a taxi just now?"

"I wasn't." Chase leaned forward, elbows on knees, as if we were about to make a real estate deal. "I was coming back from lunch. I work downtown."

"I see."

"Here's the thing, Father." I started to speak, but Chase held up one hand in a "stop" motion. "I know, I know. You're not a priest anymore. But you kind of are, because you can never really stop, right? And you did Laura's service. I remember it, every word. How you called her 'a barely touched soul' and talked about how God would take care of her in the kingdom of heaven. I was there the whole time. And you kind of saved me that day. Except . . ."

I waited. Now was the time I should ask him for money, for an envelope slipped my way with new hundreds inside. But how? Once I took off the collar, people stopped feeling obligated that way.

"I haven't driven a car since that day. Two days, I had my license! Two days and I was showing off in my Dad's Hummer, and I made a really stupid fast turn that killed Laura Larimar. Bam! Just like that. No going back. I got out and saw her lying there, and I could never drive again."

"Did you stop because you're afraid?" I couldn't help asking. I was genuinely curious. And of course, with my question the moment for a transaction definitely slipped away.

"No! That's what's wild." Chase leaned forward even further until our noses were practically touching. "I stopped because I'm *not* afraid. I loved that feeling, going so fast that I knew I couldn't quite pull it back. And I walked away from that accident without so much as a bruise. Humvees, man. They're built to protect the rich guy inside."

This was a conundrum. It felt like a puzzle I had to solve: If I absolved Chase of his guilt would he buy a car with his obviously sizable salary and plow into some other young girl? Because here's what most people don't understand: Forgiveness does not mean forgetting. The purpose of penance is to remind, and no one in the world understood this better than I. But I did not want to cultivate in Chase a man like myself, shaped and driven entirely by the most terrible thing he'd ever done.

"I think there's some sort of evil inside me, Father." Chase leaned over in his seat, protecting a gut pain I knew. "It's this power thing that comes out when I think I'm a big shot. Buying two-hundred-dollar ties, ordering bottle service. I don't like it in myself. But at the same time, I can't seem to stop." He pulsed forward—the pain was worse, I could tell—and shook his head.

Then he took a long breath before launching into the next logical thing. "There's this woman I've been seeing. Rachel," he said. "And it's gotten kind of weird that I don't drive. She has to pick me up for our dates, and I just thought, maybe . . ."

Abruptly, he sat back. Though the sentence hung unfinished, midair, Chase had the look of a man who had just expressed his last thought.

It was breathtaking, how perfectly God had arranged this challenge for me. Chase was my doppelganger. He'd been a couple of years younger than I at the time of his transgression; he was a little older now than I'd been when I confessed to Sol. But Chase—unlike me— had the chance of escape. He was still near the beginning. He could see a road out of his guilt and was asking for my help to get on it.

I sat and seethed for a few seconds, freshly sickened by the waste of my own young life. I wanted Chase to suffer just as I had, two full decades at least, or my sacrifices made no sense.

Look, I wanted to say to this addled, privileged boy. *You're talking right now to the grown version of yourself, a guilty man who's had sex exactly three times in the past two decades: once with a lonely widowed parishioner, once with a Canadian prostitute, and just a cou-*

ple months ago in a cringing festival of degradation with a woman who only wanted a warm place to sleep. I know what it's like to encounter a big obstacle between picking up a Rachel and driving her into bed. What's so special in your case? Talk me into this. Why should I make it easy for you?

Our own driver had apparently decided to take a side route. He lurched off Michigan Avenue and onto a block cluttered with people and posh boutiques. Chase and I were jostled together, elbows and hands bumping unintentionally. His face lit with worry. "What if we hit someone else *while* I'm telling you about Laura?" he asked. "Would that somehow be my fault, too?"

"Oh, for Christ's sake," the cabbie muttered. "Would ya rather I take Wacker all the way 'round and charge ya double?"

"Absolutely." Chase tossed his flop of hair, fancy-tie attitude showing. "That would be fine."

"Hey," I hissed, pretending it was low enough the cabdriver couldn't hear. "I have fifty dollars cash. That's it."

"The ride's on me, Father," Chase said. "It's the least I can do."

I stopped to consider this. Chase was willing to put up money in order to finish this conversation. He would pay a cabdriver a hundred dollars to keep me captive and listening—and our eavesdropping cabbie certainly had no moral problem with that. Were I stationary, sitting in an office or a coffee shop, what would be the difference if Chase's money went directly to me?

In the midst of fretting over the transaction I became calmer, and my better self won the battle with the swindler I used to be. It was wrong, I decided, to punish this boy out of a selfish sense of justice and Schadenfreude. Instead, I thought of a more priestly angle to take.

"Chase," I said, and he sat up straight like a student. "Did you take pleasure from Laura Larimar's death? Was there even the tiniest bit of satisfaction as you hit her? Did you feel a sense of achievement or power or, or . . . victory, at that moment?"

He sat considering for a full $9.60 (by the taxi's ticking meter) before he answered. "No, I can honestly say I didn't. It was horrible. The second I felt her on the car and then"—he swallowed—"under the front right tire, it was like this constant unbelief inside me. You know? I just wanted to take it back."

"You felt guilty."

Chase shook his head. "Not exactly. I mean, I knew I hadn't done it on purpose, and my mom kept telling me, 'You have nothing to feel guilty about. You didn't do anything wrong.' That's the first thing she said when she came to the police station to get me." His face took on a pinched, rabbity look that I assumed was meant to emulate his mother; I remembered her now from the church and he wasn't far off. "'Don't you start feeling guilty about this!' she kept saying." Chase switched back and forth between his own uncertain voice and a preachy, higher one. "Or she'd tell me, 'It was an accident, like an act of God.'"

I snorted. I couldn't help it. In that moment my head was filled with many thoughts—all of them unchristian. "Tell your mother you have it on good authority that your running a girl over with a Humvee was not an act of God," I said.

Chase shrank inside his woolen coat, like a man preparing to disappear in a wisp of smoke. "So you do think it was my fault?" he croaked.

It had been a long day, and I was so hungry by now that the frozen pot pie had started to sound not just essential but delicious. I put one hand to my aching gut and sent God a silent request for guidance. But it was as if I could hear Him answer. *This time, Gabe, you're on your own.*

"You killed Laura." I said it so baldly that even the cabbie drew in his breath. "But . . ." I took a breath and recalled what it was like to be this boy. I could see the dull chaos in Chase's eyes. I'd felt exactly this way: paralyzed by what I'd done to Aidan—how carelessly you could wreck a life in hours, minutes even, and never get the chance to go back!—furious with fate, afraid that my soul was ruined and the rest of my life as meaningless as a polluted river. There was a chorus of honks from outside, and I had to wait for them to die down. Then I went on.

"There was no bad intent behind your actions. No evil. None. You did something careless and human and understandable. Most of us have been that reckless at one time or another. Yes, you were the instrument that caused Laura's death. It was in some sense your fault. But it was not a fault you could control."

"I don't understand," Chase said. I half expected the cabbie to chime in, too.

"Chase." I placed my hands together and closed my eyes, as much for the dramatic effect as for the moment of contemplation. It never hurts to pull out the old clerical look. "What you did, driving as you did, was wrong and unthinking, but that is exactly what humans do. Especially sixteen-year-old boys. It caused a girl's death, which is horrifying but also . . ." Always in the end it came back to this word. "Forgivable."

"It is? My parents . . ."

"Your parents," I broke in, "thought that if you admitted to feeling remorse, you'd be held responsible and thrown in jail. Or they'd be sued for millions, and their insurance rates would go up." There, that felt good. It was exactly the sort of truth I was not allowed to say as a priest.

"So I'm supposed to feel bad?"

I nodded vigorously. "You're supposed to feel bad and wish that day had never happened for the rest of your life. But you're also supposed to learn to drive again and pick up your Rachel and, *carefully*, remembering how large the consequences can be, drive her to dinner."

"Do you forgive me, Father?" Chase asked softly.

Briefly, I was lost in memory. I had touched that girl's glorious clean hair. I had offered my arm to her mother and let her lean on me, a small woman who'd become densely heavy with grief, as we walked away from the cemetery. I'd had occasional nightmares about Laura Larimar, dreams I was not proud of that turned from funeral to orgy and featured a bizarre amount of oral sex.

"Yes," I said. And I found that I actually meant it. "I forgive you, Chase."

We rode in silence for only a few minutes before the taxi pulled up in front of my dank, smoke-hued building. To the left of the stoop, a drunken woman in rags held her HOMELESS AND DESPERATE sign. Chase peered out the window.

"You live here, Father?" he asked, his head still turned away.

"Gabe," I said, firmly this time. "Yes, I do."

When Chase finally swiveled his head there were tears on his cheeks, and he appeared suddenly mature, a boy I was ready to send back out into the world.

"What can I do, Gabe?" He was reaching into his pocket for his wallet even as he asked the question. "Please," he said placing something crisp in my hand and then closing my fingers. "I'll be careful. You, too."

I didn't look back as the cab drove away. It felt like a week had passed since I left my bed that morning, and I stood for a moment looking at the building, seeing it as Chase must have: the sheet hanging on floor three and the garbage scattered by a sub-basement unit. The shadow where the address above the door used to hang.

Climbing the stoop past the tattered, toothless woman, I stopped to look at what Chase had given me. There were three $50 bills and two twenties, probably whatever he'd had in his wallet. I paused and fought my baser instincts for a moment. Then I pulled out one of the fifties and handed it to the woman, who looked at me with suspicion.

"I'm not goin' upstairs with you," she said.

I nodded. "Be with God," I answered before I could stop myself. And then I continued climbing toward home.

Mason & Zeus Advertising, LLC

Naming Exploration: Forgiveness Provider
Client: Gabriel McKenna
Job Number: 48011

Challenge: Client needs a name that will translate easily for the general public, as well as a URL that is easy to spell and discoverable using keyword searches. Easy options (e.g., Forgiveness.com, Forgiver.com) are already owned and in use. Forgiveness.net is available—and should be purchased—but cannot stand alone due to the fact that users habitually type ".com" instead.

The following is a range of options with our top recommendation on page 2 of this document.

GabeForgives.com

Personalizes McKenna as the forgiver and offers nice layout possibilities. Would also buy GodForgives.com (surprisingly available!) and could potentially create a campaign around the two, Gabe and God, for great halo effect. Could be problematic if business were sold or incorporated.

4Giveness

Interesting play on the word that lightens the message and may make younger consumers feel more comfortable with the concept. Great ad campaign possibilities around the number "4." Primary disadvantage is that URL won't pop on word searches for "forgiveness."

YourAbsolution.com

One of our favorites because it's direct and conveys authority. Currently owned by a core strengthening exercise program ("your ab solution") but could be purchased. Concern is that 30–40% of consumers polled cannot define "absolution" and an even greater percentage would not use it to search.

Forgiveness&Freedom.com
Love the double "F" plus the ampersand. This option also speaks to the benefit for consumers of freedom from guilt. Major issue with direct competitor Emma Goldman, a television actress and "spiritual coach" who offers forgiveness services at ForgivenessandFreedom.com.

Mason & Zeus Advertising, LLC

Naming Exploration: Forgiveness Provider
Page 2

OUR RECOMMENDATION:
Forgiveness4You.com

This URL is available and offers the primary benefit of discover-ability terms related to forgiveness, absolution, and guilt. The symbol "4" gives it a slightly playful spin, lightening the weight of the word "forgiveness"; they also make clear that the benefit is to the consumer—with this service, they will receive personal forgiveness in an easy, friendly environment.

We've already purchased Forgiveness4You.com. If client is ready to move ahead, strongly advise purchasing Forgiveness 4You.net and Forgiveness4You.org, as well as Forgiveness.net and Forgiveness4You.co.uk.

From: Joy Everson
To: Jill Everson
Subject: Re: How are you?

Hi Mom—

Sorry I couldn't get back to you sooner. Work has been crazy. But I did receive the package and thank you. The pants fit great, and I love the paisley (where did you find those?). But did you have to send the cookies? I'm not in college anymore, and it's just me here most of the time—Rebecca is "in love" and I never see her unless she and her BF have a fight—so of course I ate all the cookies myself, and tomorrow I probably won't fit into the pants. Bad combination, Jill!

My job is strange. I didn't get a raise at my review, even though I got an "exceeds expectations," b/c we're supposedly in "cost-cutting mode" so investors will see that we're making money and decide to buy us. Scott says (have I mentioned Scott? he's one of the creative directors) that if we're bought everyone will get a big bonus on the day the deal goes through. That's what happened to a friend of his in New York, and he took the money and started his own shop. So Scott and I might start something together if that happens. I think you'd really like him. He's brilliant. Maybe next time you come to Chicago we can have lunch or something?

Anyway, here's the really bizarre thing that's happening at Mason & Zeus. We've got a client who used to be a priest, and he's going into business doling out forgiveness to people, like in confession, but they don't have to go to church. They just come in and pay him, like, $1,000, and he'll forgive them for whatever they did.

So I'm helping start this whole business, which seems to be something our CEO dreamed up. It's a very high-profile project, and this is probably my best chance to make director before I'm 30.

But it's all really surreal, and I'm not sure I like it. I mean, what if a murderer or a rapist comes in and pays the fee? Do they get absolution even if they're not sorry, the same as if they went to confession with Father Monahan? But then I think well that's a bad example, b/c if they're not sorry, what does it matter if the priest who's forgiving them is real or not?

And there's another part of me that's like, what about the Catholic Church? Isn't this kind of disrespectful?

But at work I'm totally on board because Madeline (that's our CEO) would replace me in a second if she didn't think I was 100% behind this concept. It's really rare for Madeline to be this involved with anything, and Scott says it's a great opportunity to get on her good side—or it would be, if she had one. Scott is so funny. And he has an adorable little three-year-old girl called Magenta; he named her because he's a designer and he wanted her to feel like a piece of art. He's such a unique person, Mom. I really think you'd like him.

I'm kind of curious for your opinion about the priest thing, since you still go to church. I keep going back and forth inside my own head b/c there's that huge sex scandal and all those abused boys, so on the one hand I think the Church isn't doing its job very well. But taking money to forgive people seems kind of awkward to me and like it might be disrespectful toward real priests.

Please don't tell me you think it's a terrible, immoral idea and I should quit, because that isn't really an option. I've got eight more months on my lease, and Rebecca can't ever find the $$$ to pay her part of the cable bill.

I hope you and Daddy have a good time on your trip to New Mexico. Happy 50th! I love you, Mom, and I'll talk to you soon!!!!!

Joy

From: Jill Everson
To: Joy Everson
Subject: Re: How are you?

Hi honey—

You ask some tough questions, and I can't really give you the answer. Our church doesn't even have confession anymore, at least not the private kind that I did when I was a kid. Now we do something called "communal confession," where Father Monahan has us think about our sins during a certain part of the service and then, after a couple minutes, he bestows a group absolution. I'm so used to it now I don't think I could go back to the old way where

I have to say things out loud. Not that I ever had much to say. That was the big problem for me when I was young. I was such a good girl I was afraid the priests were bored with my confessions! LOL

But about this Scott. He sounds very nice. How old is he? Is he divorced? I think it's very tricky to get involved with someone you work with and you should be very careful.

We'll call you from Santa Fe.

Love,

Mom

IV

I WAS WATCHING SOME LATE-NIGHT LADY-COP SHOW ON TV, MY stomach still plump and full of Stouffer's chicken pot pie, when the phone rang. It was past midnight, and when I picked it up to hear my brother's voice, I assumed my mother was dead.

It was an hour later in Boston, and Jack had called me roughly five times in the past decade. "Hey, you sleeping?" he asked gruffly. I noted that his voice, at forty, finally sounded grown-up.

"Not yet," I said. "Is it Ma?"

"Huh?" Jack sounded either slow or stoned, which I couldn't imagine. He was a whippet of a guy, sharply clever rather than smart, who worked twelve hours a day and competed in triathlons on the side. He'd had my example all his life to keep him straight. "Oh. No. Nothing like that. Ma's fine."

"Thank God," I said reflexively. Then, "Strange you should call. I was thinking about you earlier today. I was at a place called . . ." I closed my eyes and conjured up a picture of a horse. "Au Cheval, I think."

"Really? It's supposed to be great. What were you doing there?"

I clenched. How to explain commercial, transactional forgiveness in thirty seconds? To my still very Catholic brother? At 1:15 a.m.? "I had a meeting. Woman I ran into at a bookstore wanted to tell me about this project in Chicago. Helping people . . ." It was a weak answer but vaguely, mostly true. Besides, my brother wasn't interested.

"Huh," was all he said.

Then there was a long pause. This was a most unusual and unhurried post-midnight call. I reached over to turn the volume down on the TV, but left the show playing. The brunette officer reminded me somewhat of Madeline, only this woman ran and bent oddly—her blouse falling dangerously low—whenever she brandished her gun.

"How are the kids?" I asked. I'd sent my twin nieces matching Target gift cards for their recent birthday, because they'd turned eleven and I was befuddled about what they might want.

"They're good, good. Growing up too fast."

I was just about to inquire about Jack's wife, a cool Connecticut girl improbably named Inga, when he broke his own silence. "Gabe, I'm in trouble," he said, as I'd deduced he eventually would.

"What sort of trouble?" I asked, thinking immediately about women. Jack was a chef who owned a pub in the newly stylish South End specializing in what he called Colonial Irish food. His staff were buxom young ladies in small outfits that seemed torn (literally) from the eighteenth century; the rafters of his roughhewn restaurant hung with twinkling lights. We'd eaten there the night before our younger brother Sean had gotten married in a ceremony that I'd performed.

Jack let out a long sigh. Either that or my jock brother had started smoking. "The restaurant is closing. I mean . . . actually, it's closed. Nonpayment of, um, everything. Starting with my Jameson's bill. $42,000."

"For whiskey?" I didn't mean to sound so amused, but this was a figure I hadn't approached, even in my own bad old peddling days. "That's a lot of booze."

"Eh, not so much, actually." Jack took a quick, audible draw. He was definitely smoking something. "We cooked with it, too."

"So . . . I'm really sorry to hear this. It must be very hard for you and, uh, Inga." I always had to swallow before saying her name so I wouldn't laugh out loud, which had been mortifying at the christening of their two girls. I'd been a very avid *Young Frankenstein* fan back in the day.

"Yeah, right? It's goddamn heartbreaking. Sorry, Father." This was something I had never—even at the peak of my priesthood—become accustomed to. That my brothers insisted on calling me Father felt wrong in a backward, Faulknerian way. It occurred to me that Jack and I hadn't talked since I left the Church. It was possible that in his panic my brother had forgotten that part.

"Not to worry," I said. "You know I . . ."

But Jack was rambling on, "Black Irish has been my whole life for six years. Six years! A man will go to some extreme measures to save something like that, you know?"

I was yearning for bed at this point. Even the lush cleavage of the brunette police officer no longer captured my thoughts. But something deep in my brain clicked, and I reviewed what Jack had said. There was a clue embedded in it. "What extreme measures, Jackie?" I asked, picturing him at nine, scuffed and sullen, holding a hank of hair in his hand. "Wait a minute. What did you do?"

"You're one to talk," Jack hissed.

I was worn through, so his whipsaw snuck up and took me by surprise. But I breathed evenly and gathered myself. For as many years as I could remember, I'd been both the cautionary story in my family and the model of redemption that was held out. I'd fallen further than anyone, but then I'd repented and ascended to a sacred state. But Jack had never quite bought it.

He was the middle McKenna boy, sweeter and softer than we other two were by far. I was the bright, confident oldest; Sean was the spoiled baby, my mother's last, who invariably got his way. As a child Jack had been the jester, always seeking to entertain. He'd shared his candy and gum and later his cigarettes. When we'd grown up enough to see that the kid next door had problems, Jack had been the only one who stuck by him.

Sure, he'd joined in and made fun of Aidan behind his back. Back then, in our neighborhood, we'd used the word "retard" to describe so many people it wasn't sufficient for Aidan, who actually did have something missing in his head. Jack could do a dead-ringer impression of Aidan's lurching walk, of his hollow chest bent oddly over his stomach, mouth hanging open, hair in his eyes. I'm pretty sure it had been Jack who coined the phrase "Tar Boy," which was short for "retard" and was what we called Aidan among the boys on the block.

But whenever Aidan had been around, Jack had gone out of his way to pay attention. He'd listen intently while Aidan stuttered through his complicated yet empty thoughts. If someone jeered at Aidan in his presence, Jack would slip beside him like a faithful dog. He wouldn't say anything; my middle brother had no appetite for confrontation. In fact, it scared him—I'd since realized—more than haunted old houses or our father's occasional rage. Jack would simply be there next to Aidan and say soft, soothing, funny things after the bully left.

As a child, and then a teenager, Jack had never guessed that the person he should have been protecting Aidan from was me. I hadn't been the kind to be cruel right to Aidan's face, and that was how I fooled everyone. But I had been living right in his house, occupying the bedroom next door to the one Jack had to share with Sean. And all that time, it had been me pushing Tar Boy into a dark cave he could never crawl out of.

I'd done all this, and then had put on a collar and become a priest, which trumped everything. Jack had watched—infuriated, I could tell—while my mother and aunts and eventually the whole neighborhood forgave me. He'd had to show respect once I was ordained, but he'd done so grudgingly. And I had to imagine he'd been thrilled when I'd left the Church, dismantling that fairytale hero I was supposed to have become.

At least now it was clear to me that Jack hadn't forgotten any of our past. It was going to be like this, was it? Part of me was furious. The other part insisted that I'd worn that collar for fifteen years just to avoid the censure I deserved. I owed my brother patience with his disdain, and help with whatever made him pick up the phone at one in the morning.

"Let's not get riled up," I said, feeling a certain relief that we could be our real selves now, just two broken old Southie boys. "You called me, Jackie. So whaddya want?"

"Yeah, fuck, I'm sorry, Father," he said again. "It's just, I'm in a world of shit here. Inga's talking about taking the girls back to Stamford. She doesn't understand."

"Was it a girl, Jackie?" With my brother, I took on a snake charmer's tone. I don't know why, but it worked. "Did Inga catch you?"

"A . . . what? Oh, for Christ's sake, no!"

"No she didn't catch you, or no you didn't . . . ?"

"No. There was no girl. Ever." Jack sounded sullen, the way he had when Ma caught him holding a clump of Missy Halpern's hair. "I wouldn't do that, Gabe." And it was true—he wouldn't. My brother might wink and pay off some goons with a trunk full of black market beef. But he wouldn't cheat. Twisted as it may have been, Jackie had his own inviolable code.

"So . . . what?" I prodded. I was remembering now. With people from the old neighborhood—especially the ones I was related to—the best strategy was to be direct. "What did you call me for?"

Jack sighed heavily, and I imagined him on the other end putting his dark boyish face in one hand. "I owe my staff, too. About four weeks back wages. No, more like five. Plus tips. I've been holding what they made on credit cards. I thought if I used it to pay off my fish guys I could make it up later. But now we're closing, and the money's gone."

"Gone? All your money is gone?"

"Well . . ." He was scratching his face; I could hear the rasp of his thick whiskers. It was one trait Jack, Sean, and I shared. "Here's the thing."

I waited. The other trait we brothers had in common was saying "Here's the thing" before delivering an unwelcome truth.

"I have this great accountant who set up Black Irish as an LLC and an S-Corp. So technically it's a completely separate legal entity."

"Meaning?"

"Meaning I shared the profits with my partner but we have limited liability, personally, in a case like this."

"And your partner is . . . ?" I asked, though I knew exactly what Jack would say.

"Inga," I mouthed along with him.

The cop show was over, its credits rolling, the brunette gone for another night. I switched off the TV and paced for a few minutes, mostly just for something to do. "So the accountant says basically, we're covered." He was speaking slowly, starting and stopping. "The way he's got things structured, our assets are protected. We could just walk away."

"Okay, well I'm sorry about the restaurant, Jack. But it's getting late." I was about to pass my moment of tiredness. If I stayed up much longer, I'd be awake and alone most of the night. "I really need to get to . . ."

"Wait. It's not just that," he cut in. "There's also a lawsuit. A couple of the employees, including one who's got some, ah, mental problems. I hired him as a busboy. Swear, Gabe, I thought I was doing the kid a favor. He reminded me of . . . ." Jack swallowed, and I waited. This was exactly what I'd been afraid of: the topic that left me mute and defenseless. I'd have to let my brother talk about Aidan and everything that happened twenty years ago if that's what he needed. So I was deeply relieved when he went on about the boy of today. "He lives on next to nothing, this kid, rents a room some-where. The lawyer is going after me for back wages and maybe dam-ages, saying my 'wrongdoing is causing harm' because the guy can't buy his meds."

"Pay them." I was firm. This was so simple! Not like Chase and his long-dead Laura who could never be brought back. My brother knew what was right, and it was within his power to do it. "Just swal-low this. Write a check, cover the money you owe these people." I was ready to hang up.

"I know, Father, I know." Jack was tearful now, like he was back in the confessional on his knees, our mother waiting outside to quiz him about what he'd said. "That's what I said. We pay it out, start over, cut our expenses to the bone. But Inga said no. She said if I do that . . ." He paused, inhaled, exhaled. "She'll take the girls and leave."

"That's ridiculous! She's just upset, Jackie. You've been married for thirteen years. She's not going to let, what, ten, fifteen thousand dollars? come between you. That's not how marriage works." *Like I would know.*

"Yeah, you don't get how Inga works."

I acknowledged, silently and thankfully, that this was true.

"It's become this big test. I don't even think it's about the money anymore. It's about whether I love my children more than my repu-tation. Or something like that."

Poor Jack sounded crushed, and I wanted to take him out and buy him some ice cream the way I had after the incident with Missy, an evil older girl who'd kicked him in the crotch just to see what would happen. She'd heard it could render a boy unconscious, so she found a test case. She'd lured Jack in with the promise to kiss him—which he was curious about—so he'd been close enough to grab her hair when it happened. I'd told him over root beer floats that he'd done the right thing.

"What is it Inga wants?" I was gentle. There were similarities between Missy and Inga in my mind—Jack's taste in women had always mystified me—but we were talking about his wife. I willed myself to be kind. Or at least, to pretend. "Is there any way you can compromise on this?"

"I don't think so. She says it's my responsibility: I'm the one who tried to hold on and keep the restaurant open. I'm the one who was shifting money around, acting crazy. Why should our girls have to give up horseback riding camp because I'm an idiot? They're just kids. None of this is their fault. And legally we're in the clear."

I stopped to consider. Morality often had shades of gray, this was true. But generally actions were more clear-cut. Apologize, repent, repay. It was rare that I got stymied as I was offering advice. But Inga's point, self-serving though it may have been, was valid. Jack would be stealing from one faction to pay another no matter what he did.

"Well, Jackie . . ." I sat down again and spoke as if my brother were there, right across from me. "What do *you* think you should do?" The clock showed 1:23. It was unlikely that I would be sleeping tonight.

"I think I should do both, provide for my family and pay these people I owe."

I sighed. "Yes, but that's impossible, right?"

"Unless I start selling drugs." I laughed first and he joined in, as if he'd been waiting to see if I got the joke.

"Now's not the time to be a wise guy." I rubbed my own whiskery face and we made a scratching sound in stereo. "Jack?" I said after a couple minutes. "This kid, the one with mental problems, how much do you owe him?"

"Huh? Peanuts." Jack was drinking something now. I hoped it was water but doubted it was. "He was a busboy so he made minimum wage and his cut of the tips came to twenty bucks a night. Maybe forty on weekends."

"Total of what? A thousand dollars? Maybe fifteen hundred."

"Sure," Jack slurred, "about that." He was mellower now. Whatever he had in his hand was taking effect.

"Anyone else you're particularly worried about? Single mom? Any of your employees supporting a Haitian orphan or taking care of a dying parent?"

Jack snorted. "You kidding? Most of them were kids who graduated from BU and didn't want to leave town. I really think they've been stealing steaks and liquor for their parties for years—that's what kept them around." He paused, breathing like a bear. "Nope," he said after a minute. "No one I can think of who wasn't robbing me blind."

"Okay, then, what are you doing keeping me up? Pay the kid. Go to him, give him cash. You can put together a thousand dollars without Inga finding out, I know you can."

"That's your advice? Really, Father?" This time, he hit the last word with a little bit of sarcasm. "I should pay off the only likable person who's suing me, shaft the others, and lie to my wife?"

Silently, I reviewed the facts. Yes, that was my advice. "*Let us do good to everyone, and especially to those who are of the household of faith*," I recited in my best priestly voice. "You're following scripture, more or less."

"Hmm." He swallowed heavily. "You're brilliant."

"Don't forget it," I said. *And call me some time when you're not in trouble*, I wanted to say. "But, Jackie, hey!"

"Yeah?"

"You're not going to solve this by drinking. Or whatever it is you're doing."

He laughed darkly. "Yeah, true. But it's our tradition, right?"

"And, Jack," I said, intent upon following up. Jack had always been too quick to take the easy way out, never thinking about the consequences—or ignoring them. It's how we all were at heart. "Jack, listen to me. You've got a real problem in your marriage if your wife is blackmailing you. That's not how things are supposed to work."

"You think I don't fuckin' know that?" He'd tipped over into real drunkenness in the past few seconds. Nothing I said from now on would make any difference.

"Sometimes . . ." he breathed into the phone. "Sometimes I think you were actually the lucky one, Gabe." Then there was a click and my brother was gone.

To: isaac36@comcast.net
From: mmmurray@gmail.com

Dear Isaac—

I'm not writing as your friend, I'm writing as your former boss. I really need you back in Chicago, and I hope you'll consider it. I'm sure we can figure out an arrangement so you can fly back and forth to see your Texan.

Quick background: We didn't meet our numbers last year, and the venture capital who bought Mason & Zeus in '08 expecting to turn around and sell are pissed. These guys own mostly power companies and stockyards and other land-raping businesses. How they got involved with M&Z is a story for another day. (Needless to say, it involved someone sleeping with my predecessor.) But at our annual meeting last month, they said if we don't perform this year they're going to move us to . . . Are you ready for this, Isaac? Gary! As in Indiana. I am not joking. These guys know less than shit about advertising. And they honestly think that it's no big deal if we move into some moldy, old steel factory across the border where they can get a huge tax incentive. Never mind that everyone would quit.

So if they were trying to motivate me, they did. And I had what I will tell you, candidly, was probably the most brilliant idea of my life. Remember I told you about that day I walked into a bookstore and started crying? (Yes, really embarrassing.) It turns out the guy I was talking to, the clerk, is an ex-priest. And he has this effect on people—which I believe, because the minute I started talking to him it was like something came over me, this compulsion to tell the whole story about Cassidy and figure out how to make it right. So that's when I had this brainstorm. He forgave me for what I did, and he made me FEEL BETTER, and isn't that what every single person on the planet is looking for every minute of every day?

That's how we sell vodka, right? And tummy-flattening jeans. And Jamaican vacations and even insurance or mutual funds ("you'll sleep at night"). We go to massage therapists and movies and nail salons where tiny Korean women pumice our feet. Why? Because it makes us feel good. Best incentive in the world to buy something, right? So why not take what this guy has—his name is Gabe McKenna, by the way—and monetize it? I mean, people are pouring out their stories left and right; I'm a case in point. He got nothing out of the deal except the martinis I bought him afterward. And that wasn't even to pay him for absolving me. It was because I already had this idea kind of forming in the back of my mind (and also I liked him and he seemed a little sad).

But Gabe isn't quite on board yet. He doesn't understand that we have a concept for an entirely new kind of business. That's what's so incredible about this! It isn't trying to get a piece of the auto industry or fast food. It's creating something brand-new FROM THE GROUND UP and then being the person (or people) who spins it off. I see books, I see a television series, I see a franchise that goes cross-platform in every conceivable direction. Not to mention we find ex-priests or rabbis or what have you in every major market of the U.S. and set them up to do exactly what Gabe McKenna is doing here in Chicago. They listen to people's wrongs or sins or whatever you want to call them. They grant forgiveness. They collect, oh, say, $1,000 on average (I'm thinking a sliding scale). It's huge. So huge that I was absolutely sure someone else must have done it already, but our Google searches say no, it's a concept that's never been tried.

Now I can hear you saying, "Madeline, you're in advertising. That means you provide creative for existing businesses—not that you start totally new companies so you can launch their campaigns." And six months ago, or even six weeks ago, I would have agreed with you. But desperate times, Isaac . . . And I'd say being the barely qualified candidate who took over a dying agency from a jailed CEO puts me in the desperate camp.

Fact is, the economy seems to be picking up for everyone but us and growing our current accounts just isn't working. (Oh, did I tell you, we lost Northern Bath tissue? That was a blow.) So I'm going for a Hail Mary pass here (ha! Get it?) and I've already got an attorney drawing up papers that say whatever McKenna makes, we get 50%.

So why do I need you? Because, sweetheart, I've got a fuckton of PR issues brewing here. I mean, let's start with the obvious: the Catholic Church might have a problem with this whole thing. There's reputation, first, and how they react to our using the credentials of ex-priests to give it authenticity. But also, we'll be taking money right out of their hands!

Plus, there's this: I was so excited about this idea I threw a team together really fast. And I wasn't really thinking. I've got Abel on copy and Scott is designing, so the creative is nailed down. But I've got a very young, new guy on media, Ted Romans. He's local, African-American, grew up Baptist. (How do I know this? Because I have our receptionist, Candy, chatting people up over the Keurig machine, gathering highly illegal, private intel, for which I've promised her a big, fat raise.) Ted's a bit of a straight arrow, though. I'm not sure he's going to be hungry enough for this.

Then there's Joy, our strategist. She's really smart and about 25 (all the newbies are 25, it makes me feel like the maiden aunt); she wears these little zippered skirts and FM heels, great body. But I noticed the other day that she also wears a cross and—are you ready for this?—Joy is (eeewww) sleeping with Scott! Which is not only disgusting it's dangerous. (Yes, by the way, Scott is still married. That there are two women on Earth willing to get naked with him blows my mind.)

So obviously, the team could use some leadership. And then, there's this: Remember I said we did a Google search when I first came up with this idea? It was mostly around forgiveness as a business model and ex-priests. But lo and behold, look what came up? The article is attached and it's . . . well, it's a little thorny from a public image point of view. Once you read it you'll see that I really need you to come here and run some interference. You're a consultant, right? So come up here and consult. I can squeeze some money out of the budget somewhere, and I can fly you back and forth every, say, two weeks. I don't know where in Chicago I'll find a hotel that meets your extremely refined taste, but I'll do my best.

Isaac, you're the best PR guy I know, and it would mean the world to me if you'd come back. Also, I will do my very best to make you extremely filthy rich.

Yours—
MMM

***Chicago Chronicle News*—**ONLINE ARCHIVES
April 26, 20--
Losing His Religion

The flock at Assumption of the Blessed Virgin Parish on Talcott Avenue got an Easter Sunday surprise when their pastor, Father Gabriel McKenna, finished his sermon by announcing his departure from the Catholic Church.

According to many in attendance, the priest took off his stole, kissed it, and laid it on the altar. Then he told the Easter audience of approximately 350 that he still had faith but he could no longer serve the church and was leaving the priesthood, effective immediately.

McKenna, 40, was raised in Boston, the eldest son of an Irish Catholic family. He entered the priesthood in 19-- at the age of 24, and studied in Rome and Montreal before being called to St. John's on Chicago's South Side. When that church closed due to a decline in funding, McKenna assumed assistant pastor responsibilities at Assumption of the Blessed Virgin. He has been the senior pastor since 20--, when Father Thomas Kirn retired.

At a meeting of concerned parishioners last night, several people raised questions about Father McKenna's possible involvement in the ongoing sex abuse scandal rocking the Roman Catholic

Church. Lee Wybliski, police spokesperson for Chicago's 16th District, said there is no evidence McKenna is being charged with abuse and, to his knowledge, no complainants have come forward to accuse the priest.

However, records leaked to the *Chicago Chronicle* indicate Father Gabriel McKenna has a permanently sealed arrest file from 1992.

The Archdiocese of Chicago declined to comment on this story but has issued a brief statement that read in part: "We consider Gabriel McKenna to be a child of God who is struggling to find his way, as we all are. This is a deeply personal and spiritual matter, and we pray for its resolution."

Father McKenna's whereabouts are unknown at this time. The Chicago Chronicle has left messages at the rectory and on Father McKenna's personal cell phone without response. Calls to his mother's home in Boston have gone unanswered as well.

"We're certainly looking into McKenna, but so far it seems like what we've got is a guy having a midlife crisis who decided to change careers," said Wybliski. "That's not against any law."

To: mmmurray@gmail.com
From: isaac36@comcast.net

Dear M—

You know I can't turn you down when you beg. And this idea is just random enough to intrigue me. So if we can agree on a decent day rate (I'm thinking in the neighborhood of $1,200 plus expenses) I'll give you six weeks. You fly me back to Austin every two for a long weekend, Friday through Monday, BUSINESS CLASS. Last time I flew economy, I couldn't straighten my legs for a day and a half.

I'm not too worried about the article you sent. First, it's in the newspaper, and no one reads the newspaper anymore except old people and impoverished intellectuals who have some stick up their ass about saving the "fourth estate." Doesn't matter. We're not going after either group. What we want are people like you: 40-ish professionals, tons of disposable income, no time to waste on something like church (or therapy) even if you can fit in a manicure and facial once a week. When was the last time you read the *Chicago Chronicle*?

Second, I checked and this story never went anywhere. It didn't get picked up by any of the big news aggregators, there was no follow-up. Seems like what that cop said was right. This guy just decided to change careers. But I'll follow up.

I'll also check in with Ted and Joy when I get there. He might need to be replaced. But I'm hoping she and I can bond over the trauma of growing up Catholic. I'll tell her about catechism with Father Mears and how he said both masturbation and homosexuality were mortal sins. Can you imagine? I spent all my time jerking off while thinking about boys! Then I'd sit there every Wednesday night in a fiery panic. I swear, I thought God was showing me what it felt like to go to hell.

So on that cheery note, I'll sign off. Let me know if you can come up with the do-re-mi, and I'll be on a plane headed north.

Isaac

To: isaac36@comcast.net
From: mmmurray@gmail.com

Isaac—

You are a brilliant extortionist. Do you know that?

Attached is the itinerary for your flight. You leave March 8 @ 6 a.m. That's the best I could do for business class. I'll figure out a way to pay your day rate somehow. Our meeting with Red Oak Private Equity (aka The Star Chamber) is on Friday. That'll give you a few days to get up to speed.

FYI, I only get a facial once every two weeks. And I've had roughly 200 hours of therapy in the last few years, but during most of it I was so bored I thought about CRM or chocolate or made shopping lists in my head while they prattled on about the "work" we were doing together. Once I fell asleep (but it was that sleep that's so light, you can nod at the person who's talking to you so they think you're still listening), which was the most expensive nap I ever took.

The thing about Gabe is he's interesting. He listens, and he actually helps.

I'll send a car to pick you up at the airport on Tuesday. Be ready to work the full day once you get here.

MMM

P.S. I'm sorry about the priest and what he said to you. That must have been awful.

To: mmmurray@gmail.com
From: isaac36@comcast.net

Madeline—

The early flight is fine. I'm usually done with my morning run by 5:30. Sobriety has had a wondrous effect—just wait till you meet the new me. Don't worry about sending a car. I'll rent something when I get into town.

You might think about telling your personal story with Gabe when we meet with the Red Oak guys. It's very effective and it answers our, "Would you tell a friend?" question right off the bat. Something to think about.

Thanks. I'm over what Father Mears said. Mostly . . .
See you Tuesday.

Isaac

V

W E WERE AT MEN'S WEARHOUSE—MADELINE AND I—ON A
Wednesday evening. And I was standing on a little platform in front
of a tri-fold mirror while an older Indian gentleman knelt at my feet,
crisping the cuffs of my pants.

"Turn," said Madeline. "Mmm. That looks nice. But you need
a great tie, something that pops a little. Wait here."

She bounded off toward a table that displayed hundreds of col-
orful ties, and I offered my hand to the man whose nametag said Raj.
He looked at it dubiously, but I said, "Please. I know how hard kneeling is on the knees."

He smiled, a brilliant flash of white. "Thank you, sir," he said.
And I hauled him up.

"She has good taste, your wife," Raj said. He pointed discreetly
in the direction of Madeline, who was holding a tie with blues and
greens and grays that looked like river streaks in the sun.

"Oh, but she's . . ." I started to say "not my wife" then stopped,
because how would I explain who Madeline was and why she was
dressing me? Once I began, I'd have to tell Raj that other people had
been dressing me for work nearly all my adult life.

This wasn't true at St. John's, where we'd run a soup kitchen
and a van staffed with volunteers that went out in search of the home-

less and brought them to shelter on cold winter nights. We were scrappy there, the sort of congregation where a priest wore the same faded black clothes daily, four interchangeable sets, and where I would buy a jug of Tide, throwing everything into the ancient washer in the basement and setting the dial to cold.

But of course this is why the congregation disappeared. Over the two years I was there, it went from ghostly and sparse to nonexistent. The building was chilly in winter and beastly in summer: a shelter not much better than a stable, I often thought. We had no money for an organist or new hymnals. On good weeks people sang to sheets I'd photocopied and set in the pews.

"Sir?" Raj said, and I realized I'd faded into that space again, becoming like a ghost myself.

"Yes, sorry. You're right." I turned to look at myself in the mirror. Dark, whiskered cheeks and somber eyes staring back. "She does have good taste."

Madeline was walking toward us, bright lengths of silk clutched in her hands like a bouquet. I suppose I might take credit for the way she was that night: voice full of laughter, hair the same dark mane as before, her face luminous and a good decade younger than when we first met. Some New Age gurus insist that forgiveness changes people at a cellular level. And whereas I would have sworn Madeline was a woman nearing fifty when she crashed into the bookstore, I saw now that she was closer to forty, probably a few years younger than I. In a different plane of existence, she very well might have been my wife.

As if hearing my thoughts, Madeline stopped in the aisle between blazers and vests and cocked her head. She dumped the ties on a table that already held many hats then reached into the pocket of her jeans and extracted a remarkably small phone.

"Sorry," she mouthed, holding one hand up in a "what am I going to do?" gesture. Then she turned and walked in the opposite direction, hair bouncing on her shoulders in quick time.

"She could be a while," I said to Raj. And then, I don't know what came over me, but I told my first little sideways lie in exactly eleven years. "My wife"—the word felt as strange as a rubber ball in my mouth—"is the CEO of a company. She's the successful one. I'm a bookstore clerk."

Raj nodded. "This is how marriage works," he said. "Each of you does what you are meant to do. But you come like this." He brought his broad hands together and intertwined the fingers. "And your contributions mix to become one."

I was still up on the dais where men's pants get hemmed. Raj stood three or four inches below me with his hands clasped, his warm gaze beaming up.

"Are you married?" I asked. Immediately a cloud crossed the man's face.

"I was married for nineteen and a half wonderful years," he said, swaying in a way I knew was an attempt to soothe something in himself. "My wife has been gone since . . . ." He shifted his gaze to the mirror and its endless reflections. "Last June."

"I'm so sorry."

"Yes," Raj nodded again, only very slowly this time. "It was a terrible thing."

Typically, as I have said, people seek me out. They confess without prompting, even against my wishes. It is only occasionally that I meet a Raj, dignified and sequestered inside his guilt and grief. He was presenting me with a tiny gap, like a loose corner on an envelope. I could not be certain he wanted me to tear it open. For a moment, we only looked at each other through the prism of the mirror.

"How did she die?" I asked in the lowest, softest voice I own. And Raj shuddered a little, finally letting his hands separate and fall to his sides.

"It was a very windy day, more so than usual." I settled in—as much as I could while standing in pants that had been pinned for tailoring—because it was clear this man knew how to tell a story. And his lilting accent made every word sound like a jewel. "She was leaving her office building to get lunch, and a piece of the *next* building . . ." He shook his head, as if disapproving. "Not her own building, but the one to the right. It had been in some disrepair for a long time. And that day it began to break apart in the storm." *Stahrm?* "She was struck. Here." He pointed to his forehead and kept his finger there.

"She never woke up. I was called to the hospital and Divya . . . that was my wife." He glanced at me in the mirror, and I nodded. I understood that we could look at each other only in the glass. "Divya was in a bed, hooked up to many machines. There was something pumping air into her lungs. Her head was wrapped in white. I saw doctors all around her and I thought. I hoped . . ."

I had been trained at the seminary to stand on the side of God during confession, rather than on the side of man. In layman's terms, this meant I was mostly immune to the sort of empathy that hurts. But standing with Raj in the Men's Wearhouse with darkness pressing in through the windows, I fell. There was too little distance between this man and myself; I could see what he saw. The hospital with its steel and linoleum. The beautiful woman lying wrapped in white sheets.

"I went to a waiting room," Raj continued, and inside my mind I walked with him down a long bright hall. "I kept thinking, they would not be in there with my Divya unless they were going to save her. Then two of those doctors came into the room where I sat and right there they told me my wife's brain was dead. She was hooked up to those machines so they could breathe for her."

Just then a gentleman passed by us and tried the dressing room doors, shaking three in a row by their silver handles.

"Here, sir, allow me." Raj broke away from the sphere into which he and I had been locked. He took out his key and opened a little room, taking the man's purchases gently from his hands and hanging them inside. I was relieved.

By the time he'd returned to me, I was safely back inside my own mind.

"I am afraid that I am bothering you, sir. Perhaps talking too much."

"Not at all," I said, and meant it. That Raj should finish his story had become very important, for both of us. "Please."

"They told me there was no chance my wife would ever wake up. Then they said there was only truly a small chance. Two percent. But she would not be herself, ever. Because her brain waves were . . ." In the mirror Raj moved one hand, slow as a boat on gentle water, from left to right.

"Flat," I supplied.

"Yes. The woman doctor—she talked most of the time—she said it would be terrible to keep Divya alive, because if she ever woke up she would have lost her, her . . . personhood."

I nearly smiled, certain that the young doctor had not used such an elegant word.

"They needed you to make a decision." Again, we were becoming enmeshed. I saw Raj's story as clearly as if it had happened to me. "So they could use her organs."

"Yes." Raj looked up, as if he were still, all these months later, asking for help finding the answer. "I was given two hours to tell them, or they would not be able to help five other people." He enumerated what came next on his fingers. "Liver, heart, lungs, kidneys, eyes."

Madeline had finished her phone call and was walking back toward us. I beetled my eyes at her and put my hand up, discreetly. "No," I mouthed silently the way she had earlier. I was shocked at my own authority. "Not now."

Luckily, Raj was still gazing up and did not see our exchange. Madeline stared at me with rapidly blinking eyes for a moment, then looked at the small princely man who stood before me and moved quietly away.

"I could not . . ." he started then stopped. "There was no one to talk with me about this. Our children were twelve and fourteen. I have worked here"—he swept his hand in a wide circle—"for eight years, but there is no one. Divya and I, we did not often go to temple in this country. The children, they had sports on weekends. They wanted to be like Americans. The subway ride . . ."

He broke off, and I waited. But after about thirty seconds, I couldn't stand it. "What did you do?"

His reflected image went to stone. Raj was perfectly still, almost robotic, as he answered. "I left," he said. "I took the elevator down and walked out of the hospital into the very wind that had killed my wife. Because I knew that she was gone. But I could not say it. Instead I walked for so many miles, perhaps six or seven. I do not remember. It was raining and the sky got very dark.

"Finally I could walk no more, and I found a coffee shop and went inside. I looked at my watch." He demonstrated now, raising his left wrist. "Two hours had passed. Two hours and ten minutes. I had walked until it was too late, and I had stolen from all of those people, the ones who needed a new heart or eyes to see."

"Or," I said softly, "those people received organs from other donors. Or lived a decent life while blind or on dialysis due to their own diseases, which you did not cause."

Raj bowed his head, as deeply as someone ducking a ball. "I was cowardly." *Gow-ard-lee*, the word trickled from his lips like smoke. "By the time I got back to the hospital, all the doctors had dispersed. There was only Divya, in her bed with the machines, never waking up."

I saw her as he had, an empty shell of a wife.

"Five days later, she developed an infection, and I told them to remove the ventilator. It was very quick. I held her hand while she died." His left hand fluttered when he said this, as if it were remembering.

I thought this was the end of the story, but Raj drew a breath and went on. "A month later, an attorney called me and said he would give me money if I would not sue his client from the building that broke apart. I told him I did not want his money, but he said not to be this way. My children, they would have no mother now, and it would help me to care for them. So I told him fine, I will sign. I went to his office the next morning, and he gave me a check. Two million dollars." Raj sighed. "I put it in the bank."

"But you continue to work."

"This is what I do." Raj straightened, touching the tape measure looped around his neck. "How do I explain to my children that their mother's terrible accident has made our life easier? That I am a man now who can buy things because my wife is dead?"

We stood, and I scrambled for what to say. It might have been the $300 pants I was wearing—the very pants Raj had been pinning at my waist just moments before—that threw off my thinking. I, like Jesus, was probably meant to minister in tattered clothes.

"I believe," I started gruffly, having little idea of where I'd go from there. "It is how we live that makes us who we are as humans." Where was God, I wondered, and why wasn't he giving me better? Especially for this man. "Did you love Divya?"

"She was my life," Raj said softly.

"It is a perversity of our time, the decision you were asked to make." Raj opened his mouth to speak, and I held up my hand. "No. I understand there were other people at stake. But two hours? For a love like yours?" I shook my head, as if I knew anything about such a love. "Not possible." I swallowed, nervous for reasons I could not name. "That kind of love is actually more than love. It's faith. The sort of faith you can have only if you can look past the real, the concrete, and envision celestial things."

There was a small, scratching noise behind the mirror, as when a bird had gotten trapped inside the vestry. In the periphery, I caught a glimpse of Madeline's bright-colored sleeve. My face burned. The sacred trust between Raj and me had been broken.

"You, you couldn't," I stammered. Then I gathered myself. "You could not imagine a world in which Divya was dead. You had faith that she would come back to you. You could *see* it, even while she lay there in that bed, couldn't you?"

Raj looked at me with hard, tear-filled eyes, and I cringed at the cruelty of this. "You still had faith in Divya's recovery, in the life the two of you would have together. So don't you see? It would have been wrong for you to choose her death. That . . ." I paused for a beat. "That would have been something to regret. Not this. Not faith. Not doing the best you could to preserve a life and a woman and a marriage that were pure and good."

The store had gone quiet around us. It was late, the doors locked to new customers; the other sales clerks were gathered at the front, cashing out.

"Do you believe this is true?" Raj asked.

"I do," I said.

"And if, if it were your wife?" He gestured in the direction that Madeline had gone, and I imagined her bandaged and still, a small empty form on a long white raft.

"I hope . . . no, I know . . . I would hold the same faith. I would believe with all my heart that she'd return."

Madeline appeared just then, a mask of unknowing on her face. "I'm so sorry," she said to Raj. And then—it was fleeting, but I saw—Madeline touched his left hand. "I don't mean to be rude."

"Not to worry, ma'am. Your husband and I have had a chance to talk, and if we take in the waist an inch these slacks will be excellent."

"Perfect." Madeline swiveled her head slowly and looked at me with her eyebrows arched. "Let's take them. Oh, and um, sweetheart?" She held up three ties like party streamers. "Which one do you prefer?"

Madeline paid the bill while I stood by, trying to look like a doting husband rather than a ragged and libidinous ex-priest. Raj shook her hand and then mine, clasping it for a good minute and sending me warmth like the low heat from a glowing fire. I held on a few seconds longer than he did, but whether it was to comfort him or me I could not tell.

Madeline and I walked to the car without speaking. There was a scuffle as I tried to open her door while she was reaching to relieve me of my packages. We circled each other uselessly before laughing and each getting in our own sides. Then we rode in tense silence for a minute before Madeline cleared her throat and said, "I heard what you said to that . . ."

Again, the shame of exposing Raj that way gripped me, and a combination of regret and anger rose from my gut. "Please, Madeline, don't talk to me about how I should have 'converted' him into a paying customer. He was only talking because you had to take a phone call, and I don't even think I helped him that much. I liked him! I wasn't about to take his money. He probably . . ." I was about to say "makes $12 an hour," when I remembered the two million dollars in the bank and got confused. "Just lay off, okay? Not everything is about shaking people down."

There was no sound for a few minutes except the tires bumping on the road. I looked over as we passed through a bank of streetlights and rain sparkling like a meteor shower. Madeline was transformed into a Picasso of sharp angles and endless eyes. The ageless woman I'd met in the bookstore was back.

"Hey, I'm sorry." I shifted under the packages she'd bought me, $489 worth, and felt warm with shame. "I sincerely apologize. I was just so, um, affected by his story. Usually that doesn't happen, but this man. His wife . . ." I leaned back and saw again the sterile room with an unmoving woman sheathed in bandages and breathing through a machine.

"I know," Madeline finally said. Her voice was thick. "I agree with you. I heard enough to understand." She swallowed and spent a couple of seconds fussily adjusting her rearview mirror. "It wasn't like he came to you looking for something. It was almost like . . ." She glanced at me, a dark look, her face like a shadowed oracle in the night. "I felt more like he gave *you* something." Her voice was soft and low. "Does it work that way? Sometimes?"

"Maybe once in a hundred times," I said. "Or less. But yeah. Sometimes it works that way."

Madeline stopped for a light and fanned her face with one gloved hand, despite the mean, gray, late winter wind outside. "You're wrong," she said in a steely voice, "when you say you didn't help him. I can assure you that you did."

"I'm not so sure." The light turned green, and we surged forward. I stared out the window as the buildings went from tall and ornate to sagging and sad. "I felt like I was . . . off my game."

"Maybe it was the shock of our sudden elopement," Madeline said, looking straight ahead through the windshield.

It took me a couple seconds to laugh, and when I did, I felt my shoulders un-hunch. "Yeah, that came out of nowhere. Didn't it?"

"Faith." The word came out of the darkness. When I turned, I could swear there were tears gleaming in Madeline's eyes. But she never blinked. "That's what we all wish for, right? A relationship with one other person that's so close, it's like a religion." Her last four words drifted into the cold night air.

We rode the rest of the way in silence. But when Madeline pulled up in front of my apartment, where scraps of garbage hovered in the air, I felt another pull of sadness.

"Thanks for the clothes," I said as I opened my door.

"Wear the gold tie for our meeting tomorrow, okay?"

"Sure. Good night." And I thought as I gathered my bags what a relief it was to be dressed by someone else again. Wandering lost in the wind and rain, as Raj had. Making no decisions. Holding on to my faith.

March 12, 20--
Mason & Zeus Kickoff Memo
Client: Gabriel McKenna/M. Madeline Murray*
Project Name: Forgiveness4You
Job Number: 48011

Team:

M. Madeline Murray, Acting Account Director	150 hours
Scott Hicks, Creative Director	125 hours
Joy Everson, Strategist	75 hours
Abel Dodd, Copywriter	200 hours
Ted Roman, Interactive Media Specialist	75 hours
Isaac Beckwith, PR consultant**	TBD

Timing:

We're going lightning fast on this one, with phase one deliverables (see below) to be completed in two weeks (with phase two executed by April 21). Internal check-ins will occur every day at 10 a.m. for 30 minutes; this includes Saturdays and Sundays. Please accept this recurring meeting on your KompanyKalendar system and attend daily. Our goal is to be online and in market by Easter.

Deliverables:

Core creative that is consistent throughout: website, two (2) animated leaderboard banner ads, four (4) static rectangular banner ads, at least one flash concept, bus shelter ads, El-train wrap, radio spot, Facebook campaign. Isaac will work with local media to secure media coverage and interviews around the time of launch.

*This is a joint venture between Gabriel McKenna and Mason & Zeus—the first of its kind. Remember, you're working for us!
**Isaac Beckwith has joined the team and replaced Lori Inman as our PR point of contact. This is no reflection on Lori's skills or abilities. She has been re-deployed on other projects within the agency. But please be advised that our confidentiality agreement *now applies to Lori as well.* What we do as a team stays with the team.

PLEASE SEE THE ATTACHED ADDENDUM FROM ISAAC BECKWITH

To: Forgiveness Team   *Highly Confidential*

Hey Team—

It's good to be here and I'm happy to be working with each one of you. Over the next few days, I'll make the rounds and meet everyone individually. For now, let's dive in.

As some of you may be aware, there's a papal conclave scheduled for next week.

A little background: The papal conclave is a meeting of the College of Cardinals (I swear, that's what they're called) in Rome to choose a new pope. They lock themselves away in the Sistine Chapel and take secret votes until they reach a two-thirds supermajority. They can only hold one ballot on the first day. Then they can hold four on every day after that until a "final, decisive vote" is reached.

After each voting session, they signal the result by sending either black smoke through the chimney of the Sistine Chapel—indicating that they did not reach a supermajority—or white smoke, which means that a new pope has been chosen.

What are the takeaways from this?

- No one does branding like the Catholic Church.
- People are addicted to ritual and certainty.
- The more mysterious and magical the process the better.

These are things to keep in mind as we develop the look and feel of Forgiveness4You. We're not basing it on the Catholic religion, per se, but take what works. The Church has been operating successfully (and profitably) for 2,000 years.

I'll be monitoring the situation in Rome to gauge its usefulness to us. Best case, they elect a regressive pope who alienates more Catholics and broadens our potential client base. Worst case, they elect an American liberal who looks and talks like our guy. Whatever it is, I think we can leverage the results in Rome to our benefit.

Remember, you're talking to *no one* outside the F4Y war room about any of this.

Thanks~

IB

From: Joy Everson
To: Jill Everson

Dear Mom—

I'm attaching a note that came from our PR consultant, who is this gorgeous gay guy from Texas weirdly named Isaac. Basically, it says we're going to leverage the election of a pope to help market Forgiveness4You.

Did I tell you that's the name we chose? And I doubt anyone remembers this, but it was mine. We were in one of those brainstorms where everyone's supposed to "think out loud" and say whatever comes to them. Madeline had already written Forgiveness.com on the white board and then someone suggested we put a letter in, like U. So she wrote ForgiveU, which sounded like a University to me. But I didn't say so because "There are no bad ideas in brainstorms." Then I thought, what about a number? Like you use in texting. So I said, "How about Forgiveness4You, with a number 4 and a capital Y?" and she wrote that on the board.

Then we voted—which means everyone got sticky dots to put on their favorites. And after it was done, mine looked like a sunburst, with all these dots clustered around it. Scott told me later that if I was a consultant to Mason & Zeus, instead of an employee, I could bill $10,000 just for coming up with that name.

Anyway, I'm curious what you think of Isaac's note, which by the way taught me some things about papal elections that I never learned in Sunday school. I know you and Daddy are hoping for some liberal pope who's going to sanction birth control and gay marriage (and I am, too). But Scott says that would actually be bad for us because it's all the retro rules of Catholicism that make people leave the church, and then they become prime customers for us. I mean, Isaac said that in his note, but it's Scott who really explained it to me over dinner last night. We had to work late together, and he used his company AmEx to order from this really nice restaurant that even delivered a bottle of White Burgundy. It was divine.

I'm sorry I won't get home for Easter this year, but I'll be working nonstop.

Love,
Joy

P.S. Scott is technically still married, but he's going to get a divorce as soon as he figures out the financial aspects. His wife is a terrible housekeeper, and she doesn't pull her weight (i.e. make much money), and he said she's an okay mom but they don't agree on things like Magenta's bedtime. He's definitely not happy and planning to leave her as soon as possible, but he has to wait for the right time. I feel bad for him. But even though he's so unhappy at home, he's great to work with and always really funny. I know you'll love him when you meet him on your next visit!

From: Jill Everson
To: Joy Everson

Hi honey—

I'm so proud of you for coming up with the name Forgiveness 4You, which is hard to type but very clever.

However, I read Mr. Beckwith's note and must say I'm a little peeved. *No one does branding like the Catholic Church?* I assume he's talking about traditions that go back to the time of Jesus Christ. And I wouldn't say I'm exactly "addicted" to the rituals of the church. I happen to believe in them! Well, most of them. The black smoke and white smoke is a little silly, but it's probably something that started back before anyone had phones.

Your father and I struggle with many of the teachings of the Catholic Church. That's why we go to St. Ann's and volunteer on their diversity committee. We're going door to door with a petition that will be sent to this new pope, whoever he is, asking for him to lift the ban on birth control—especially in third-world countries where they have so many babies and everyone is starving to death. But we're still, in our hearts, Catholic. And we raised you that way, too.

I know I didn't say all this the last time you wrote, but I was busy getting ready for this trip (which is wonderful, by the way; we're staying in a hotel with a spa!). Later, when I was on the plane and had time to think about it, I decided charging people for confessions is simply wrong. I know *that* wasn't your idea, sweetheart, so I'm not blaming you. And we all have to do things in our jobs that we don't agree with. Just be aware.

Are you dating the married man who named his daughter after a crayon?

Love,
Mom

March 13, 20--
Transcript from the Red Oak Private Equity meeting at Mason & Zeus: Called to order, 9:09 a.m.

BOB GREEN: Good morning. Thanks to all of you for coming. Thanks to Mason & Zeus for hosting us. Great coffee. Where'd you get that?

MADELINE MURRAY: Intelligentsia.

GREEN: Beautiful. I think we owned them once. So, moving on, let's do a quick round of introductions, just so everyone knows who's who. I'm Bob Green, equity partner at Red Oak Private Equity, which we like to call ROPE.

MURRAY: M. Madeline Murray, CEO of Mason & Zeus Advertising.

JIM LYNCH: Jim Lynch, founder and equity partner of ROPE.

AMY SEE: Amy See, MBA, CPA, business analyst with ROPE.

ISAAC BECKWITH: I'm Isaac Beckwith, PR consultant to Mason & Zeus.

CANDY JOHANSSEN: Candy Johanssen, receptionist at Mason & Zeus. I'm just here to take the minutes.

KATHERINE SEATON: Kat Seaton, sitting in for my husband, Rick, equity partner with ROPE. Rick is recovering from knee surgery.

GREEN: Give Rick our best. And, last but not least?

GABRIEL MCKENNA: Uh, Gabe McKenna. I'm, um . . .

MURRAY: Gabe is our partner in a new business concept, working name—Bob, have we had everyone sign a confidentiality agreement?

GREEN: Yes, which was highly unusual. If we own something, we're generally free to . . .

BECKWITH: Sorry, that was just a precaution. Mr. McKenna isn't specifically bound to us—to you—just yet. And his new platform is so revolutionary, we felt it would be a disservice to him if we didn't offer protection for his intellectual property.

GREEN: Understood. And we're all eager to hear about this revolutionary new idea. But before we start, let's do some level setting. Okay? When we got involved with Mason & Zeus it was represented as a quick turnaround investment, eighteen months max. Margins were incredibly good, and we were going to turn around and sell to Publicis. Amy, do you want to step in here and help us understand how that all turned to shit?

SEE: It appears the margin on one account, Grain Farmers Bank, had been inflated due to a balloon payment that year. And my own forensic examination shows recordkeeping was hit-and-miss in the years prior, leaving the impression that Mason & Zeus was far more profitable than it actually turned out to be.

GREEN: Thank you, Amy. What she's saying, in a very nice way, is that fraud was committed, and the CEO who perpetrated it is gone, serving a little time on a playground they call prison. But that leaves us here, with a company we can't sell that doesn't make us enough money to warrant four of us sitting here in this room.

MURRAY: Thank you, Bob. I think that recap helped everyone here get up to speed. And I want to assure you—that's exactly why we've asked you here today. We have an idea that may spark a new revenue stream. That's where Gabe . . .

LYNCH: But does this fall under the company's charter? You can open a strip club in the office and generate money that way, but it won't make your advertising agency any more valu-able on the general market.

BECKWITH: That's the beauty of this. If we could just turn our atten-tion to Mr. McKenna and his breakthrough concept. I think you'll see that we can function as his public representatives in a way that's consistent with the mission of Mason & Zeus. But at the same time, we've entered into an arrangement that will give us a sizable stake and income stream from his activities.

GREEN: And exactly what are his activities?

MURRAY: Gabe is . . . I mean he was . . . a priest. And since leaving the priesthood he's been counseling people ad hoc. He's been forgiving their sins, ministering to their souls, sending them on healed. And he's doing all this pro bono, without representation. But we believe there's a sound business model here. People are busy. They don't have time to go to church! Oh, they might show up on Christmas Eve or Mother's

Day when the place is so packed they can barely get in the door. But regular weekly attendance? That's really old school.

SEATON: I still go to church. Every week.

MURRAY: I didn't mean . . . .

MCKENNA: Which parish do you belong to, Mrs. Seaton?

SEATON: St. Peter's.

MCKENNA: Father O'Shea. He's a favorite of mine. I used to listen to his sermons on my Sundays off and try to figure out how he made them so funny.

SEATON: Yes, he is . . .

GREEN: I'm sorry, Kat. But we need to get back on track here because I have a hard stop at 10.

SEATON: Of course.

GREEN: Go on, Madeline.

MURRAY: You know those rows of candles in a church where you can light one and say a prayer for someone, but only if you put a dollar in the box? There are no barriers: even non-Catholics are welcome to do it—as long as they pay. Well, there's our concept. This sort of transactional paradigm exists already in the religious setting. All we're doing is moving it out to the private sector. People come to Father McKenna with their guilt and pay for his absolution. It's that simple.

LYNCH: I've got two problems with this, Ms. Murray. First, we bought an advertising agency, not a small business incubator. And in my experience, the best, most stable companies stick with their core competencies. I don't see the benefit in your going off half-cocked and running this new concern on the side. Second, how is this different from the thousands of therapists out there—some of whom, no doubt, offer a religious component—who are fully covered by insurance?

BECKWITH: Madeline, if I may? Thank you. You make some excellent points, Mr. Lynch. In regards to the first, I'd ask you to consider 3M, Microsoft, Motorola, Honeywell. All of these very successful companies acted like "incubators," as you say. In some cases, their spin-offs have more visibility than the original. Who really cares about 3M tape anymore? You can buy generic, works just as well. But Imation? Well, there's a brand people know.

LYNCH: I see you came prepared, Mister . . .?

BECKWITH: Beckwith. I did. Because I believe in Madeline and Gabe, and I believe in this project. Now, to your second point, I think it's really valid. In fact, I asked the same thing myself. With everyone in the universe able to hang out a shingle that says, "I'm a personal life coach," how does this start-up get any traction? What's our differentiator? Then I came here and met Gabe McKenna, and I'm now 100 percent on board. He's our differentiator. His character, his training, his . . . I can't believe I'm going to use this word . . . aura. This is a guy who spent sixteen years in the Catholic Church, and now he carries it with him. He isn't just any old burnt-out bank teller who decided to become a social worker midlife to spice things up. This is a man of God. Not because he says he is or because we say he is. Because that's what other people sense in him. You can't spend ten minutes in a room with Father McKenna without confiding the worst thing you've ever done. I dare you to try.

GREEN: Well, ah, I think we'll keep this on a strictly business level for now. Say I stipulate to everything you've said. I agree that we've got this guy with a line to God and people will pay money to talk to him. He's still only one guy. And that's just not profitable. What's the multiplicity factor here? I don't see how this grows.

MURRAY: Think horizontal, not vertical. We aren't creating the new pyramid, where dozens or hundreds of people work under Gabe, taking confession. He's it. He's our product. I've seen him in action and I can tell you, he's good. Now, put him on digital platforms: everything from the Web to mobile to interactive TV. He's everywhere. He's forgiver to the nation. You don't have to attend church in order to receive his blessing. It's like putting that dollar in to light a candle. Anyone can do it.

SEATON: I'm not sure I like this.

MCKENNA: Mrs. Seaton, I'm not sure I like it, either.

LYNCH: Let's hear from you Mister, uh, Father McKenna. Because if you're not committed to this . . .

MCKENNA: Okay. I'm going to be completely honest with you. It's kind of an occupational hazard. *(Laughter from the group.)* When I hear forgiveness described as a business, I cringe. I want it to be an open, God-given blessing to other people. One of the reasons I left the Catholic Church was because I felt we'd failed to serve people well. To protect them. And yet . . .

GREEN: Sorry to rush you, Father, but I'm at lift-off minus six.

MCKENNA: Excuse me? Oh. I guess what I'm trying to say is that I can't keep going the way I have been. I can't, well . . . survive. People come to me. I don't know how they find me or how they know. But it's become clear that I can't just leave my old life. I no longer have the support of the church. Housing, clothes, salary, car. If I'm going to keep helping people—if that's what I was put on this earth to do—then I have to figure out some way to live. And this, maybe . . . if we could build in some sort of sliding scale for people. Or a foundation that helps the poor.

MURRAY: That would be Phase 2, of course. Our first initiative is to establish Forgiveness4You.com. *(reveals poster)*

SEATON: I like the logo.

MURRAY: Thank you, Kat. We wanted something dignified, something that matches Gabe's approach. We also needed to convey that, unlike all the workshops and counseling options out there, Forgiveness4You isn't a class. It's something real and profound that you receive from a higher source. This image, of a hand lifting a silhouetted person—could be a man or a woman—out of darkness. This shows what Gabe McKenna does. I should know. He did it for me.

(Light applause.)

MURRAY: Listen, I know this is a crazy idea. But here are the facts. Mason & Zeus needs to bring in another $2.3 million this year over last year in order to make our projections. The economy has improved, but the 20-- forecast is looking flat, particularly in business services. Meanwhile, Gabe McKenna is living hand to mouth even while he's lifting others. I've witnessed this. You go into a store with this man, and the next thing you know you're listening to someone confess that he . . .

MCKENNA: That was private.

MURRAY: You see? This is a man with principles, a man who's doing good. He's already thinking about how to make the tough choices: charge the people who can well afford to pay— probably those same people who are funding churches and basilicas all over the world—and use their support to help people who are genuinely in need. It's a win-win-win! We make money. Father McKenna makes money. The public gets this wonderful service without having to commit to some crazy religion that might not allow them to leave their abusive spouse, or marry their same-sex lover. This is that rare case where everybody wins.

SEE: It does make sense. There's no capital investment; it's all creative and intellectual. From a purely business point of view, I can't see the harm.

GREEN: It's 10:01, so I move we adjourn and discuss this at our next meeting.

LYNCH: I agree with Amy, Bob, and I don't see any reason to put this off. I move we go ahead with the Forgiveness4You project. All in favor?

SEE: Aye.

SEATON: Aye.

GREEN: Fine. Aye.

LYNCH: Excellent, it's decided then. This better work out, Madeline. That's all I can say.

Meeting adjourned, 10:02 a.m.

VI

WE HAPPENED TO BE SEATED NEXT TO EACH OTHER, KAT SEATON and I. So when the meeting adjourned and she did not stand to leave, it seemed clear she wanted me to do the same.

Bob Green hustled out first, muttering his goodbyes. One by one, the others followed. "You coming, Gabe?" asked Madeline. "I thought we might go over what the team has been doing, then get some lunch."

I felt Mrs. Seaton's eyes on me, willing me to stay. "Give me a few minutes," I told Madeline. "I'll catch up."

Madeline stood in the doorway looking at us, first me and then Kat Seaton, who sat silently, her gaze trained on the table. She lifted her water glass to drink and the diamonds on her left hand set off a brilliant shower of sparks.

"All right, page me when you're done, okay?" Madeline backed out and gently closed the door.

I turned to face Mrs. Seaton. "You wanted to speak to me?"

"Yes." She sighed. "But given what we just discussed, that whole meeting, I feel like some kind of cliché."

"Is that important to you?" I asked. "Do you feel like there's pride in being different?"

"Well . . . kind of." She turned, swiveling her chair so that her knees were pointing toward me. She had one of those tight older women's bodies. Pilates, that was my guess. Her bobbed hair was gray and her face had pretty crinkling lines, but from the neck down she could have been thirty. I wondered if that was part of Madeline's hesitation—jealousy. In a profoundly adolescent way, I hoped that it was. "I feel, Father McKenna, like there's value in thinking for oneself."

"I'd agree." I could already tell we were in a sparring match, one of those old-fashioned Oscar Wilde wars of words and wit. This lady wouldn't be a crier—not unless the tactic would help her win a point.

She looked at me, a bemused smile on her powdery face. "I had an abortion, Father."

First, in my defense, I looked over at the door to make sure it was closed. But then I said, "Mrs. Seaton, that is very possibly the greatest cliché in the Catholic Church."

"I know, I know." She nodded as if we were two scientists making a breakthrough together. "How many times have you heard this in confession?"

"Honestly, Mrs. Seaton"—I'd even slipped into a mildly Victorian style of speech—"So many, I've lost count."

"Ah, but I think my story has a slightly different . . . twist."

I settled back, hands folded in front of me; I would play my part to the end. "Tell me," I said. And she tipped her head, birdlike, to the left.

"It was 1975. Rick was finishing up at Wharton. We were engaged, and I was planning a wedding for 250 the following year. That's when I found out I was pregnant. Oh, and I was sick. Putrid! Miserable, every day. You have no idea."

"I'm sure I don't," I said.

"So. I tried to hide it from him, from my mother. I passed it off as flu for a few days. I remember . . ." Again she smiled, as if this were a happy memory. "We had to put off our appointment to taste cake. That would have been . . ." She shook her head. "Intolerable."

"That sounds very difficult."

"Oh, for heaven's sake, Father, it does not." Her tone got a little schoolmarmish, and I sat up in my chair. Kat Seaton leaned down and retrieved a small silver tube from her purse; she squirted a dollop of cream on her hand and began briskly rubbing it in. The scents of rose and patchouli rose in the air. "Lotion?" she asked, holding up the tube.

"Why not?" I held out one palm, and she deposited a tuft of the cream there before stowing it back in her purse.

"Back then, of course, I thought what was happening to me was tragic. I was terrified. Everything would be ruined, all our plans. I went to a doctor who set the due date *the same week as our wedding*. It was—well, when I look back, kind of funny." She laughed briefly, but I did not.

"When did you decide to terminate?" Despite my ambivalence, all the many years I'd spent wrestling this issue inside my own conscience, I had adopted the lingo of the other side because it seemed more humane.

"Well, I told Rick. Finally. After his thesis defense. We discussed the options, which were—remember—brand-new. The Supreme Court had passed *Roe v. Wade* just the year before. This was a new era for women. We had *choices*. You can't imagine how significant that was."

"So you chose not to have the baby."

"*We* chose not to have the baby. I was on the fence. I was embarrassed, and I wanted my beautiful wedding." She rolled her eyes, a teenage gesture in a sixty-year-old face. "But Rick made the better, more logical arguments. We weren't prepared: he was just starting a job with lots of travel, and we'd been planning to go together. Shanghai, Tokyo, Paris. There wasn't room for a baby. Not yet. Can you imagine, Father?"

She stared at me, and I remained silent, staring back.

"We decided whether to have a child based upon a week in Paris." She found a leftover dab of lotion on the back of one hand and worked it in. "It rained," she said as she rubbed, "the whole time we were there."

"Was there counseling provided back then?" I'd have been a baby at the time, I was thinking. Her phantom child and I would be around the same age. "Many women are depressed after an abortion. It sounds like you needed help."

"Not at all. I was fine. In fact, I was tremendously relieved. The procedure went off like that." She snapped her fingers. "All the horror stories I'd heard? Nothing. I went home, I rested for a day or two. It was like nothing had happened. I went on to plan my wedding, and it turned out exactly like I wanted. You should see the pictures, Father. Like Charles and Diana." She smirked. "Well, almost."

"So when . . ."

"Not until our brothers and sisters started having children, and Rick said he'd like to try. I'd been on the Pill—another new thing—even though the Church said not to. That just seemed silly." She took a drink of water, set her empty glass carefully on one of the coasters Candy had passed out. "Then my sister had a baby. Amy. Oh, she was so beautiful. I was completely in love with that little girl. But she was also like proof for me that this—pregnancy—was a real process. Do you know what I mean? I'd seen my sister sick as a dog one entire Fourth of July weekend, then growing larger and larger as winter came on and now, suddenly, there was this new person in the world. It just. Stopped me."

"Mrs. Seaton," I said, trying mightily to suppress my boredom. "There is still nothing new here. I have talked to hundreds of women who regret their abortion. And I have no doubt that God understands."

She was shaking her head. "No. No, no. Father, I have long since forgiven myself for the abortion itself. It's an option, it was for me. And I took it at one moment in my life. That, I can live with. It's what I did next."

I waited, and again she smiled. This seemed to be her defense. "So we were talking about having a baby. It was a very good time: Rick had been promoted, and we'd bought a house. All I had to do was stop taking the Pill. But I . . . didn't."

"You kept taking it?" I was more interested now. No one ever thought to confess about birth control.

"I did. And I wish I could tell you why." Her face twisted, and for a few seconds she was an ancient woman. "I would think about that first pregnancy. It had only been three years since the abortion at that point, and I wondered, why now but not then? Why this baby, not that? It was so . . ." Her hand fluttered in the air. "Random."

"What did your husband think?" I asked.

"He, ah, didn't know." Again, the smile. "He never knew, Father. He was disappointed every month."

"So you kept it up?"

"I did." She sat up straight, as if this were a point of pride. "Because I knew, I *knew* that when I got pregnant for the second time, with Rick, we would both, in our heads, think about that first time and imagine how old that child would be. Whether it was a boy or a girl. I had such a strong aversion to that. It was some form of pride, I suppose."

"Yes, it always comes back to one of the seven deadly sins, doesn't it?" I felt I was playing my part, but Kat Seaton looked at me strangely and I remembered that she had cast the deciding vote in our favor. I hunched forward, hands clasped, full priest on. "What is it that's bothering you?"

"I've lied to my husband for forty years," she said somewhat proudly, an irony that was not lost on me. "We went to a doctor once and talked about infertility. It was a brand-new specialty back then. But Rick . . ." She got a dreamy, indulgent look; it was likely she really did love the man.

"He's very Catholic, a lay deacon with our church. He wouldn't tell anyone that we actually had conceived a child once and aborted it. So the doctor did all his tests, found nothing wrong, and concluded that our chemistry just wasn't right for each other. I remember the night we got the 'results.'" She made air quotes with her fingers, a gesture I detest for no reason I can name. I stifled my irritation with a cough. "Rick was so sweet. He told me it didn't matter. Our chemistry was perfect as far as he was concerned."

"But you kept it up, even after your husband proved his love to you?"

"Yes, isn't that odd?" She peered at me. "What do you make of it?"

I was startled. Never in my tenure had anyone asked me to define their sin. This required thought. I imagined myself as a young woman in the early seventies, experiencing the equally strong pulls of the Rolling Stones and the Catholic Church. I had a tendency to idealize that period—as we all do the eras in which we're born. But to be female at a time when abortion was ten minutes legal and free love was on the news? I formed a ridiculous picture—inspired, I'm sure, by some record album cover—of a young Kat Seaton in a mini-skirt, twirling senselessly against a fiery sky.

"Whom did you tell about the abortion? Your sister, your mother?"

"No one," she said. Her tone was approving. She wanted me to find the answer, and I was getting warm. "Rick never wanted anyone to know."

"So you weren't ashamed of it, but he was?"

She sighed. "I don't want to give you the wrong impression, Father. My husband is a man of great principle. You will find, when you meet him, he's the only one on that board who gives a damn about doing the right thing. But this . . . His way of dealing with it was to erase it. Put it in the past. I believe that may have been my concern: If I'd become pregnant I might have talked about that first time. It would have hurt him."

"It takes a great deal of energy to ignore your past," I told her. *Believe me*, I intoned silently. *I should know.* "If you were protecting Rick, that's your answer. Also, and here I'm just speculating, but you were really at the beginning of something. How to be a wife and, if you chose, a mother had changed radically. There were no role models. Am I right?"

"Perhaps." She was a tough one, unwilling to give me points I hadn't earned. "But I could have sought them out. Someone. There were groups of women becoming enlightened. *Our Bodies, Ourselves.* That sort of thing." She paused. "But I do think you're right. I spoke to no one, except Rick. And he?" She held her hands up, creased palms to the sky. "He didn't want to talk."

We sat. This seemed unsatisfying to me. We'd solved the puzzle of Mrs. Seaton's, behavior but I felt no godly work had been done.

"How is your marriage now?" I asked, casting about for what we'd left unsaid.

"Wonderful. Same as it's always been." She was firm. But I took a chance, let her sit, looked at her with what I hoped was deep meaning in my eyes. "We've been lucky. We've always had enough money, more than enough. And we've traveled." More clichés. I was ready to give up. "But Rick isn't well."

"The knee surgery?" I asked. Oh, the problems of wealthy runners, I jeered in my head.

"No. That's what we told people." She knew what I thought. "He has diabetes. It's been terrible the past few years. His eyesight is failing. He had his left foot amputated. He thinks . . ." She stopped and breathed, head tipped back. "He's going to get a prosthesis and be able to pass off the limp as a side effect of knee surgery."

"He's a man who avoids the truth," I said.

"We all do," she told me sternly. "And one of the reasons he's so terrified now is," she swallowed, "there are no children to rely on, no one to inherit everything he's built. No point."

"You're right. This story is very different from what I expected."

Mrs. Seaton took less pleasure in this than I would have thought. "Do you see now?" she asked. "I can't tell him what I've done. It would damage him—us—at this point in our lives. And for what?"

"But it's hard to live with this alone."

She nodded and pressed her fingertips to the corners of her eyes, briefly smoothing out the furrowed skin.

My hips were cramping, so I stood and paced a few steps in either direction. Kat Seaton was easily twenty years older and had been in her chair longer, but she looked perfectly comfortable. Clearly, I thought, I should check out Pilates. "Mrs. Seaton?" I said from above.

"Kat, please." It seemed late to achieve that level of intimacy, but I went along.

"Kat, are you talking to me because you feel guilty, or because you're sad? I can absolve guilt. Sometimes that works. But sadness over something that's real?" I leaned against the wall, hands in pockets, a little thug-like. "There is no cure."

Finally, she placed her hands on the table and allowed her old eyes to fill. "I was afraid of that. It's why I've never confessed. But we came today, and Madeline talked all about your amazing power, how you make people . . ." A tear slid down her cheek; otherwise, she was motionless. "Whole."

"I'm very sorry." I pushed off the wall and went to sit next to her and put my hand on one of hers. "I can't make you whole, because there will always be something missing. What I can do is bear the sadness with you. We all make choices in life that cut off possibilities. We marry one person and not another. Or marry no one and devote our life to God. We have children or, in the case of both of us, we do not. And there's always something haunting us. Everyone to some degree, but people like us more than others."

She did not respond for a long time, and her hand under mine was as still as stone. Then she cleared her throat into the air and spoke in a strong voice. "I've noticed that most people get more certain as they get older. You will find this, Father. As our friends have gotten to be sixty and sixty-five years old, most insist that whatever they have done, it was the 'right way.' Everyone should hold the same political opinions or religious views. However they have lived their lives, whomever they have married, they'd do it all again. *No regrets, no regrets.*" She shook her head. "If I had a dollar for every pompous ass who's sat at my dinner table saying that."

"You know it's a coping mechanism," I said. I was way off my usual spiritual turf, but flexibility seemed to be a requirement of my new job. "What you're talking about is a type of myopia that people use so they can live with their choices. It's magical thinking. It's not real."

"Yes, well, I want that." Mrs. Seaton—no, Kat—gave me a steely, demanding look. "I was hoping you could give that to me."

"If I could do that for you," I said severely, leaning forward and matching her ire word for word. "Don't you think I'd do it for myself?"

"Yes, I suppose you would," she said, that sly smile returning as her hand finally came to life and turned over to grasp mine. "Peace be with you, Father."

"And with you," I said, grinning in return.

"I don't know that I've ever used that phrase with such an awareness of what it means," Kat said, rising neatly from her seat. She stood first on one foot and then on the other, a move I imagined she executed most often in a black leotard.

"I wish your husband great healing and faith," I said. "And I wish you the solace of knowing that you have lived as best you could."

"Thank you, Father."

I stood and picked up her coat from the back of her chair, holding it as the acolytes once held my robes so she could slip her arms into the sleeves.

"You are a very sweet man," she said turning, touching my cheek in a motherly way. "I'm not sure you'll make it in this business."

"What a nice thing to say," I told her, and meant it. "But I'm not even sure what making it means."

From: Abel Dodd
To: Forgiveness Team
Subject: possible taglines

Comrades—

Here are the taglines I've worked up for message testing on Monday. I pulled these from a much longer list that I'm happy to share if you want to see the unabridged contents of my demented mind. But I'm pretty confident these are the best options. Let me know what you think.

—A. Dodd

What would Gabe do?
Yeah, it's overused. But everyone gets it, and we could distribute those ridiculous rubber bracelets and bumper stickers with WWGD on them.

Did something? Tell someone.
Plays off the public safety message: "See something? Tell someone." Not my favorite, but it has a nice asked-and-answered rhythm that people will remember.

Absolution for Everyone
Speaks to the egalitarian nature of this service and sounds like a civil rights rally cry. Also, sounds nice said out loud.

What's the worst thing you've ever done?
This may be my top choice. It's weird, gets to the heart of the matter. And it's a twist on the typical tagline that makes assurances.

Confession: It's not just for Catholics any more.
Pushes the boundaries but you have to admit, it's funny. Will get people's attention and could make for a great campaign.

Helping You Feel Better Today
Goes immediately to the primary benefit and may appeal to the Buddhist-convert self-help crowd.

Expert Exonerations for Everyday Sins

Alliterative, a little bit sarcastic, and pretty darn accurate. People who get the irony will love it. A close second for me.

From: M. Madeline Murray
To: Abel Dodd
Cc: Isaac Beckwith
Subject: Re: possible taglines

Hi Abel—

Thanks so much for all your hard work! You've provided some excellent options here. I'm going to recommend removing the first one: "What Would Gabe Do?" I think that trope has been played out, and since our idea is completely original, we need language that's just as fresh. Everything else? Pure gold.

Just wanted to let you know, because I'm calling a check-in for this afternoon to get input from the team. We go into testing Monday morning at 9 a.m. with the goal of producing creative by late that afternoon. It's my meeting but would love it if you'd take the lead.

Thx.
MMM

From: Isaac Beckwith
To: M. Madeline Murray
Subject: Re: possible taglines

Hey sweetcheeks—

Wish you'd checked with me before calling that meeting. Whatever Scott, Joy, and the rest of the Scooby Gang have to say this afternoon, I plan to take the full list into testing. Abel's a genius. And no, I don't care how much it costs.

By the way, I saw you eyeing our client during the Red Oak meeting. What's the deal with women and priests? It's so fucking Thornbirds. Just keep your hands (and other parts) off him while he's working for us. Okay? If this thing falls apart, you can dress him up in feathers and ride him in Buckingham Fountain, for all I care.

Dinner tonight?

IB

VII

I T HAD BEEN ANOTHER VERY LONG DAY, THE BOARD MEETING AND
interlude with Kat Seaton followed by a raucous two-hour session
devoted to logos that most resembled in my mind a professional
volleyball match. I was, for once, very ready to go home to my
solitude. But at six o'clock I was still sitting in the Mount Olympus
conference room at Mason & Zeus. Madeline had broken out the
vodka and was distributing glasses.

"They're a client," she said, waving the bottle then pouring a
good three ounces over ice. "Part of your clan."

"That's Scotch, Madeline," Isaac said. "Remember, none for
me."

"Oh!" She froze, the half-extended drink rattling like a castanet.
"God, I'm sorry! I totally forgot. How could I do that? Let me get
you something else."

"It's okay." Isaac said soothingly. "Sometimes I forget myself."

He turned to me as Madeline darted out of the room. "Back
when we worked together before, I was a lush. But I went to Texas
and got sober, which is kind of like going to Texas to become a vegetarian. Which I also am." He sighed. "My man back in Austin does
love his bourbon and steak."

He laughed, and I laughed too, relaxing with my glass like we were all old friends. My desire to leave dissipated around the time I took my second sip.

Our swivel chairs were large and curved; sitting in them was like being gently rocked inside a huge hand. "I've had more to drink in the past three weeks than I had in the year before that," I said, raising my glass to look at the clear liquid. It could have been water. Or lighter fluid.

"Yup, that's advertising," Isaac said. "Occupational hazard, right? What did you say yours was? Honesty?"

"That's the virtue." I took a big slug and let it burn. "Righteousness is the sin."

Madeline returned then, her hands full of bottles and one small rectangular shape. "Okay, I have Pepsi, Mountain Dew, Perrier, and . . ."

"Whoa! Is that a juice box?"

"Cran-apple." Madeline held it up proudly. "It was in the refrigerator. I think Melanie left it the last time she brought the kids in."

"Give it here," Isaac said, and Madeline tossed the box across the table. I watched with admiration as Isaac rose without hoisting himself and swiped it out of the air.

"So, I think this week was a win," Madeline said, taking a chair and leaning way back to slip off her shoes. "The investor meeting went better than I expected. Kat Seaton was on our side. Her husband wouldn't have been nearly as supportive. His knee surgery? Gift from God."

"Ooh, bad one, Madeline. I expect so much better of you!" Isaac leaned forward and sucked on the tiny straw in his juice box. "But I'm actually glad you said it. I have to remind the team on Monday: No puns. No riffs on God. Ever. We're dead in the water if we make this thing into a joke."

"Agreed. I thought I'd have Abel start on a general lexicon: words to use, words to avoid."

"Abel?" I asked, because the vodka was working just fine and the day was becoming a pleasant swirl of noise and strange laughing heads. This was reminding me of Friday nights in my dorm at BU, before everything happened with Aidan, back when I anticipated a future filled with money and women, and believed I was in control of what happened to me.

"Abel," Madeline said, leaning back again and stretching her little body, then tucking it, legs and all, up into her chair. "The big guy."

I recalled a burly, tree trunk of a man, around six-five, 260, with a reddish Ulysses Grant beard.

"Abel's gotta be, what?" Madeline glanced at Isaac. "Forty-five? He was one of Mason & Zeus's first employees. Beautiful writer, just extraordinary. But that's all he wants to do. He's the only creative I have who isn't nagging me twenty-four hours a day for a director title."

"Yup, Abel's great," said Isaac. "Scott, now there's another story."

"Scott's a shithead, whom I am about to fire," said Madeline while Isaac leaned forward with the bottle to refill our glasses. I knew exactly what he was doing. We "recovering" addicts are always out to prove that our drug no longer has its hold on us.

"Thanks," I said, nodding at my glass but leaving it on the table. "Did I meet Scott?"

"Last week, when you first came in. Scott Hicks is our art director. Tall blond guy with those ridiculous sunglasses that he wears backward on his head." Madeline took a long draw on her second glass. For a small woman, she drank like a Marine on leave. "I can't stand him."

"So why is he involved?" Alcohol always made me braver, which I knew was its chief danger. Things usually went better for me when I was afraid.

"Several reasons. Originally I picked him because no one else was available and I knew Scott could be bought off. If I said, 'Here's a $10,000 bonus to keep your mouth shut about this project,' he'd absolutely do it. Only thing Scott cares about is Scott. So as long as I take care of him he'll do what we need. And he's a pretty good art director, even if he is a totally shitty human being."

"There is, however, a complication," Isaac said.

Madeline sighed. "Go ahead. Tell him. Because if I have to say the words, it'll destroy my appetite forever."

Isaac grinned like a jack-o'-lantern, and I found myself wishing I could learn to do that: break into happiness like a child. With a juice box.

"Turns out our strategist, Joy Everson—you know, the young woman who dresses like a hooker and isn't Candy?—she's sleeping with Scott. Or maybe just giving him blowjobs in the office. Who cares? Their 'relationship' is important to us. Why?" Isaac held up one finger and stopped, a screwed-up questioning look on his face. This was theater. And I knew a little something about that after sixteen years of raising my cup to drink the blood of Christ.

"It's important because Joy is a weak link," Madeline explained. "She's young, she's idealistic, she thinks she knows more than she does."

"I don't think she can be trusted," Isaac said. "I'm betting that when I hack into everyone's email, we're going to find out she's been breaking confidentiality up and down, left and right."

"Wait, email?" Madeline sat up, a little wobbly but alert. "We never discussed that. I'm not comfortable . . ."

"Meadow Madeline Murray!" Isaac interrupted. "What kind of a half-assed CEO are you?" His eyes were glittering, and his smile turned as sly as a snake's. I chortled and settled in to watch. This was turning into the best Friday night I'd had in years. "You *own* those email accounts! Well, Mason & Zeus does. And the law says you have access to any digital material that passes through company-owned equipment. Legally I could break into the personal accounts of every employee, if they're accessing them on their agency laptops. Which, you know, everyone is."

"Don't do that, okay? It's . . . wrong. People deserve their privacy. Even Scott and Joy." Madeline was sitting with her legs tucked up under her, like the first time we'd met. Her cheeks were fiery, her Hellenistic face tired but regal. I had a strong urge to nuzzle up and smell her that I quelled by sucking on an ice cube and reciting First Corinthians in my head.

"She hides it well, doesn't she?" It took me a second to realize Isaac was speaking to me.

"Hides what?" I asked, struggling to sit up straight in the shelter of my chair.

"Her bleeding heart. No one would guess that Meadow here is such a humanitarian soul."

"Meadow?" I asked.

"Yes." Madeline put her head in her hands. "I was conceived during Woodstock. Not *at* Woodstock, mind you. My parents lived in Skokie and they couldn't get their shit together to hitchhike to New York." She turned, head still touching the table, to glare at me. "Don't you dare tell anyone."

"I think your secret's safe with the priest," Isaac said and they both laughed, Madeline straightening and fluffing out her hair.

"But . . ." I was concentrating hard, tracing the conversation back. This day had worn through parts of me I never thought about. My ears buzzed after hours of perpetual talk. My nose was dry from the scent of dry-erase markers. It was one of those shaky highs: both pleasant and exhausting. I needed to sleep for about fourteen hours. "Why do you care if Joy and Scott are involved? What difference does it make?"

"It's always a disaster when people who work on a team together start fucking," Isaac said. "Throws the whole dynamic off every time. Weird shit happens." He stared at me pointedly, and the room grew silent.

"Well then," I picked up my glass, took a long, burning drink, then raised my eyes to meet his. "I guess I'll have to resist my desire to have sex with you."

Isaac let out a loud, braying laugh and sat back, stroking his flat stomach as if it were a pet he loved. I glanced down at my own spongy middle and pledged to start doing sit-ups in my apartment each morning. Sixteen years of wearing robes, and I'd let myself go.

"Speaking of secrets." Madeline had switched back to her official voice. "That was quite a surprise, what you said about pro bono work in today's meeting. We've never discussed that."

"Rule number one, man. Don't surprise her," Isaac said. Then he winked.

Perhaps it was that—the wink—or the vodka or the feeling that for the first time in years I was among friends, but I actually shrugged. "It's a deal breaker, Madeline," I said, having no idea where I'd picked up that phrase. "If I can't use some of our income to help people who can't afford to pay . . . I'm really not interested. I'd have thought that would be clear by now."

I looked at her and she at me. Isaac bounced back and forth between the two of us, as delighted as if we'd begun a juggling routine.

"Absolutely clear." Madeline did not blink. "And for the record, I think you're right. But I would have preferred to discuss it before we walked into that meeting." There was a moment of tense silence before Madeline said, as cheerfully as if we'd been discussing the White Sox, "Hey, is anyone else hungry? I'm starving! What do you say, guys? Take me out for something to eat?"

"As long as you're buying," Isaac said.

"This is company business. Jim Lynch is buying." Madeline unfolded herself languidly. "Give me five minutes to go brush my hair and put on lipstick. A woman likes to look her best when she's out on a Friday night with a gay man and a priest."

"Ex-priest," Isaac called, as she walked out the door, holding her shoes.

"Same thing," I muttered. "Being a priest is like being an alien. You can live among regular people and pretend. But you're never quite . . . one of them."

"Tell me about it. Remember?" He pointed to his chest. "Gay vegetarian who lives in Texas. Talk about feeling alien." We were silent for a few seconds then Isaac asked. "Why'd you leave the Church?"

"Same reason hundreds of other men did—and women, too, I suppose. I was disgusted. Disillusioned, disappointed. I woke up one day and realized I was forty years old and I'd devoted my entire adult life to this organization that lied. Allowed children to be abused. Made arbitrary rules about people's lives." I waved in his direction. "Taught that homosexuality was evil."

"Are *you* gay?"

"No. That would probably make it easier. There might be support groups, a life I could go toward."

"Did you ever touch a child?"

"God, no! But that was part of it. I never could make sense . . ."

Isaac waited without tension or judgment, and for the first time I understood how it might feel to be the person confessing, seeking answers from a stranger. Leaning forward, eager to be understood.

"It was bewildering to me that so many of the men who felt as I did about the Church, about God, also wanted to have sex with children. That felt as foreign to me as . . ." As what? There was nothing I could conjure up that I'd desire *less* than a pre-pubescent altar boy. "I don't know. It was frightening to me. Completely unforgivable. Men I'd gone to seminary with, the pastor who mentored me through ordination, people who were supposed to protect and minister. They all did this unspeakable thing. And sometimes I wondered: What made me like them?"

"So you were chaste?"

At first I pondered this question seriously, as I had for nearly twenty years. How much did my two slips as a priest count against me? I'd confessed both and received absolution. But what about masturbation? This I spoke of with no one. Was I saved the sin of pedophilia only because I regularly practiced the lesser sin of self-abuse?

Then it came to me, like a message from someone with a backbone—Madeline, for instance—that this was no one's business but mine and God's. "Is that relevant to our working relationship?" I asked in the voice I'd once used on the streets.

"You're right." Isaac ran one hand along the polished top of the table. "I apologize."

"It's all right," I said, confused because I still liked him just as much as before.

"One more question: You were arrested once. Why?"

"You've been looking into me," I said, then thought about what a strange phrase that was. *Looking into me.* It was precisely what Isaac was doing, what I did to others.

"It's my job," he said.

"That was a long time ago." The liquor helped me to not picture it. My mother in the kitchen, with fat white ducks marching along the wallpaper border. Aidan coming up the steps from the basement, his eyes wet with the swimmy pleasure I'd introduced him to. A plastic bag clutched in the cop's big hand. "I was nineteen."

"An adult." Isaac spoke slowly. "But really . . . not."

"Exactly," I said. "I was . . ."

"Ready?" Madeline was back, her hair pinned neatly to the top of her head, her eyes somehow more dramatic, drawn inside dark lines. "Let's go, gentlemen. It's nearly eight o'clock!"

Isaac rose and took his jacket from the back of his chair, and I did the same. "After you," he said, with a gesture for me to follow Madeline. And then, lower, "We'll continue this another time."

And with that, I walked out the door after a beautiful woman and into the city on a sharp, dazzling Friday night.

March 17, 20--

MARKETING METRICS

Re: message testing on taglines for Mason & Zeus, project #207

Process:

Our test group was made up of 58 people with a mean age of 42, average income level of $83,900 per household, and a mix of Catholics and non-Catholics. We issued paper questionnaires asking subjects to respond to potential taglines with a "like," "find intriguing," "don't like," or "no feeling." Afterward, we broke into four group sessions to discuss the findings and further refine feedback.

General Findings:

	Like	Find Intriguing	Don't Like	No Feeling
Did Something? Tell Someone.	8	15	22	13
Absolution For Everyone.	29	12	5	12
Confession: It's not just for Catholics any more.	14	9	31	4
Helping You Feel Better Today	13	5	12	28
What's the worst thing you've ever done?	10	34	14	0
Expert Exonerations For Everyday Sins	16	6	12	24

Recommendations:

Taglines 2 and 5 had the best testing metrics overall and clearly outperformed taglines 1, 3, 4, and 6. We recommend discarding these four and concentrating further refinement only on "Absolution for Everyone" and "What's the worst thing you've ever done?"

Tagline 2 (Absolution) offers a feel-good message and brand control, with the caveat that it contains a word that will be unfamiliar to some portion of the general public. Tagline 5 (Worst thing) is non-traditional and will, we predict, turn off up to 25% of people. But it is virtually guaranteed to be noticed and—in some cases—acted upon.

From: Isaac Beckwith
To: Forgiveness4You team
Status: High priority!

Hey y'all, as we say in Texas . . .

We've got the message testing report back on Abel's fantastic taglines, and when you put that together with my own notes and observations, it looks like we've got both our tagline and our first campaign!

Read the attached docs on your own time, but here's the skinny:

Absolution for Everyone is our tag. It's friendly and warm and people seem to like it. Not everyone understands the word "absolution," but frankly, the undereducated aren't our target audience anyway. Those are the people who still go to church . . . and probably can't pay for our services. We're going after guilty, college-educated professionals who go boating or golfing on Sundays. They'll get this, they'll love it. "Absolution" sounds smart and like something desirable. So this is where we stand tagline-wise.

"What's the worst thing you've ever done?" is our launch campaign. MMM and I are seeing ads, bus wraps, internet banners, and assorted swag (Ted, could you research the cost of coffee cups, T-shirts, etc.?) We want to see executions on this by end of day Thursday. So cancel all your evening plans and bring a pillow to the office. Not that you'll be getting any sleep.

I'll see you bright and early in the morning, which means 6 a.m. If you know of anyone on the team who isn't checking email at 11:14 p.m., please make a call. I'll expect to see you all tomorrow morning before the sun. Coffee and muffins on me.

With regards,
IB

From: Scott Hicks
To: Isaac Beckwith
Cc: M. Madeline Murray
Subject: Hey asshole!

Major decisons about messaging and concepting have always, since the beginning of time, been left up to the creative director. You just undermined my authorrity with the entire team. Good. Job!!

Scott

From: Scott Hicks
To: Isaac Beckwith
Cc: M. Madeline Murray
Subject: About last night's email

Hey Isaac—

I probably shouldnt of sent you that note I did last night. I was mad and kind of wasted and the baby was up crying til like 2. Anyways, I'm sorry for calling you an a-hole but I still think I should have ben in on the creative decisons. Is this something we can talk abt today?

Scott

From: Isaac Beckwith
To: Scott Hicks
Cc: M. Madeline Murray

Hey Scott—

Don't worry about the email. Tempers tend to get out of hand when we're working this fast. It happens.

But you should know that because of the unusual nature of this project—and our client—we're going to have to make some decisions without involving the creative team. I'm sorry, that's just the way it is. If that's something you can't deal with, please talk to Madeline about it. I'm sure she has a solution in mind.

Thx.
IB

From: M. Madeline Murray
To: Isaac Beckwith
Subject: Scott

Nicely done. I sent Scott's "Hey asshole" message to HR. We're building a file. If he sends you anything further without cc'ing me, please forward. I'm not going to fire him yet, because I think he can crank out something really fantastic on the Worst Thing campaign.

I may be a little late to your 6 a.m. work session. That's a ridiculous time for a meeting, you freaking sadist. I'll see you at 8, when civilized people start work.

xo,
Madeline

From: Isaac Beckwith
To: M. Madeline Murray

MMM—

You're missing all the fun! We've been here for an hour and a half and other than looking like a week-old corpse, Scott's been a prince. (His hangover is so epic I can almost feel it. You know how I never talk about how grateful I am to be sober because I hate all that bullshit? Well, today, I'm almost grateful.) He's working on three directions for the Worst Thing campaign.

Meanwhile, fucking Abel! Love that guy. He wrote a manifesto already—I think he walked in with it at six o'clock. I don't know when the guy sleeps, but I don't care. Also, he ate six muffins. SIX. But Jesus, if he keeps working like this, I'm thinking of just handing him my credit card for lunch (which I suspect he may take around 11). See what you think of this:

We believe.

In you, no matter who you are, where you live, which religion you were raised in, or what you've done.

We believe.

That forgiveness will help you live a better life. Loving more, earning more, giving more. Becoming more, every day.

We believe.

Everyone deserves absolution. Without prejudice. Without judgment. Without the artificial rules of a faceless church.

We believe.

In raising you up with empathy and understanding. Purging your guilt. Bringing you to peace with your past.

We believe.

Less burdened, you will go on to live a happier, healthier, more productive life.

We believe.

In you.

    IB

From: M. Madeline Murray
To: Isaac Beckwith

I'm loving the manifesto, except for the "artificial rules of a faceless church." Somewhere inside Abel there's a Marxist dictator plotting to overthrow Chicago. Can you schedule a three o'clock for the three of us to brainstorm on this later?

I'm going to stop by Gabe's and pick him up on my way to the office.

MMM

From: Isaac Beckwith
To: M. Madeline Murray
Subject: KEEP OUR PRIEST PURE!! eom

VIII

I N ORDER TO EXPLAIN WHAT HAPPENED WHEN MADELINE SHOWED up Monday morning, I need to go back to Friday night.

Madeline, Isaac, and I had walked into four restaurants downtown only to find they were packed with patrons who glared as three more tried to approach the maître d'. Waits of more than an hour, we were told everywhere.

"Fuck this economic recovery," Isaac said as we left the last one. "When the recession was on, you could always get a table." Madeline bumped him with a sisterly shoulder and told him to be quiet, but I could see from the deep sway in her step how badly she needed food. I offered her my arm and she took it, leaning her full sprite's weight against me. I felt as if I could lift her in my palm.

We ended up at a small Thai place with a linoleum floor, heat pouring out of the registers overhead. It met our criteria: tofu for Isaac and immediacy for Madeline. I had no criteria. I was, I thought as we sat, one of those people who kindly stays out of restaurants to the benefit of those crowding the foyers and showing newcomers their hostile, hungry eyes.

But the nine-page laminated menu overwhelmed me. Sections titled Red Curry, Green Curry, Sticky Rice, and Noodle Dishes were followed by numbered items going up to 252. The descriptions were sparse and elusive. There seemed to be scallions in everything. I had stood at the altars of cathedrals in Rome and Paris and Montreal— praying to the same God in Italian, Latin, and French—but I could not decipher *rama* or *tom yum*. Plus I was exhausted, the day's meetings still squabbling in my head.

"Not a big fan of Thai, Father?" Isaac's voice was surprisingly gentle.

"I have no idea." I drank the entire contents of my tiny water glass. "We didn't have a lot of Asian food in my neighborhood growing up. And this isn't the sort of restaurant where priests go in groups." I kept studying the menu, like it was cypher I could decode.

"Don't worry about it. I'll hook you up." How many times and in how many dark places had I heard those words? I glanced up quickly, half expecting to see some kid from Southie, hunched in an oversized coat and holding out his goods. But it was still Isaac, a grownup wearing a peacock-blue silk shirt.

When a man came to take our order, speaking in something remotely like English that lulled me with its secret sounds, Isaac ordered for me—a dish that when it appeared just ten minutes later was steaming, full of chicken and carrots with dark chili-flecked gravy. We ate in grateful silence, and it was one of the top five meals of my life.

Sated, finally, we stood. There was a brief exchange at the front counter during which I held back like a child. I had yet to obtain a credit card.

It had begun snowing—that light March variety—while we were inside the steamy little café. We walked, warmed by the food we'd just consumed, and our silence continued. Madeline was steadier now. She and I preceded Isaac who stayed a step behind, like a father duck protecting his young.

It was during that walk—seven long blocks—that I understood fully the life I had left at twenty-one. It wasn't just the dingy warehouses, dark, puddled underpasses and cars idling in parking lots.

These I relinquished willingly. But I failed to forecast the changes, the other lives that might have followed. Certainly I'd considered the fact that I was giving up marriage and children. But I had never before realized I was also sacrificing cheap ethnic meals and quiet walks with friends through spring's winter. The occasional, thrilling touch of a woman's hand on my arm as we navigated slick streets. This loss struck me with force.

When we arrived at Mason & Zeus, Madeline led us through a door to the right of the building and into a small garage where only two cars sat side-by-side.

"It's ridiculous that you're driving separately." Madeline's voice startled me, but she broke into regular conversation as if the past half hour of vestal silence hadn't occurred. "Now we're going to get in our individual cars and burn a metric ton of fossil fuel just so we can end up in the same place."

"Your bleeding heart is showing again," Isaac told her. "Anyway, it's hardly a metric ton. And this way we can live like adults, rather than me relying on you for rides. Besides, I've always wanted to drive one of these." He waved in the direction of the sportier car. "I got an amazing rate."

"Do *not* bill that to the job," Madeline warned, grinning. "I'm serious, Beckwith. You have squeezed your last drop of blood out of this stone."

"Father?" Isaac turned to me. I'd thought the first time he called me that it might be irony, but I now I saw it was simply his childhood training. "Can I take you home?"

I paused. The "live like an adult" comment played through my head, and I wanted to refuse. But the prospect of taking the El sounded thunderous and cold.

"I know where he lives," Madeline said. "And you probably have a mileage limit on your ridiculous rental. I'll do it."

Something was transmitted, a glance or a gesture that I almost missed. I was too busy ruing twenty years of cloistered living without Thai food, fast cars, or women in my bed. In addition, I didn't like being passed between them like a teenage babysitter who needed to be transported. Yet, I went obediently to Madeline's car and climbed into the passenger seat.

Gloom crept up on me as we rode. I was facing an empty weekend—not unlike most of mine, but a cavernous contrast to this loud, long day. We arrived at my building before I was ready, and when I looked out, its windows leered in the quickening snow.

"Gabe," Madeline said, then abruptly stopped. I released my seatbelt, but she remained strapped in. "Good night." She leaned toward me and put one gloved hand on my neck, a spot no one had touched in about a decade. I came forward, intending to the best of my recollection to kiss her cheek, but I met her lips instead and stayed there, tasting briefly the evening's worth of iced vodka, red curry, and dark Oolong tea.

Then I felt her tongue, small and slightly rough, lapping at my lower lip. Startled, I jerked away from her and smacked my back flat against the passenger door. "I didn't mean to kiss you!" I said, before I'd had a chance to think.

Madeline glanced down, her head bowed for a moment as if in prayer. But when she raised it, her gaze was scornful and amused. "We've had too much to drink, both of us. I probably shouldn't even be driving. Go." She put her hand on the stick shift and said it again. "Go. I need to get home to bed."

I seriously considered putting my hand on hers, unbuckling both our seatbelts and drawing her close. I wanted to. My ache for a woman went deep into my bones, and so far in my life, Madeline was the one I knew best. But she looked, sitting there bundled and flinty behind the vast windshield, like a woman who might burst into flames.

"Good night, Madeline." Gathering every bit of courage I possessed, I reached out with one bare hand to touch her cheek, and she allowed this, though she continued to stare straight ahead.

"Good night," she said to her own reflection. "Get some sleep, Gabe. Good work today."

This confused me, as I had not performed much of a function. It was a mostly passive role I fulfilled at board meetings and "creative brainstorms." But then I remembered this was exactly what she and Isaac had said to each of their colleagues—Scott and Joy and of course Abel, whom I liked immensely—as they left the room. In fact I believed I'd heard Isaac and Madeline say it to each other, like passing unction.

"You, too," was my ridiculous response.

With that, I opened the door and stepped out onto the damp, chilly street.

The next morning, sky and air blended in a shroud of gray. I walked to Starbucks for coffee, my one planned outing of the day. And within that shop I watched couples with fat babies in strollers, happy despite the weather pressing in from outside. A woman raised her left hand, causing that unmistakable spark of gold and diamonds to catch the light. I might have married them, this very couple. How many times had I stood by while some stranger worked a ring onto the finger of a woman I had made his wife?

Also in the coffee shop that morning was an older man with reading glasses on a chain. He worked a laptop diligently while the woman across from him at the table sipped from her cup and knitted and smiled at him whenever he looked up.

I lingered, reluctant to leave the circle of this place. And I watched as a woman came in, younger than I by at least a dozen years. She was furtive and pale, dressed in a new but ill-fitting coat and a jaunty triangular hat, her long wheat-colored hair spilling out underneath and down nearly to her waist. I watched as she ordered, counting out four worn dollar bills for the cashier.

She took her coffee to a corner where she wedged herself into the least comfortable cranny behind a table—it was the only seat open but I knew instantly that she also desired it. Nooks and angles suited her. She was accustomed to being cramped and out of the way.

I watched from the safety of my book. She blew on her coffee and looked around with a strange lack of curiosity. There was something very out of place about her. Or rather, I thought, it was out of time. She seemed to be traveling without electronics: no laptop or tablet or smartphone. Around us, there were only people talking to their companions or madly pushing buttons—in many cases, both. Even the knitting woman had pulled out a device that she pecked at with an intensity that caused folds to form on her brow.

With neither companions nor gadget, the girl was like a visitor from some deep country. Not unlike me. I felt an irrational kinship with her that grew in my imagination as I watched.

We did not speak, though I sensed she knew I was observing her. Halfway through her giant cup of coffee—I was looking so intently, I could measure her progress—she stood, hat in one hand, walked to the trash can and dropped the cup in. Then she turned and left as if something had made her angry. She took no more than three steps before disappearing into the fog.

What impelled me to return the following day was not the girl, but fear. This was not my pattern. Typically, I would visit Starbucks on Saturday and work at Brooks Books on Sunday, drinking watery Folger's from the ancient Mr. Coffee in the backroom. But as if he were in collusion with Madeline to make me receptive to any random moneymaking scheme, Oren had announced earlier in the week that we would no longer be open on Sundays; business was very slow, bringing in less than the $95 or so it took to pay me for the day. He'd apologized in his gallant way for the short notice, and I told him it was fine, though I knew Sunday would arrive like a monster's gaping maw.

It had been one of the chief benefits of the job, aside from surrounding me with books—that I would be safely tucked inside, serving a purpose, when the church bells began to ring. When this Sunday morning arrived, even warmer—almost muggy—but with a pelting rain, I rose, showered, and dressed, found my umbrella, and headed out.

I was nearing the intersection where the Starbucks sat, just over the threshold of where our neighborhood started to "improve," when someone fell in step with me. It was the woman from the morning before, her boat hat gone, a slick green raincoat covering her from her head to her knees. "Do you mind?" she asked ducking under my umbrella with me and peeling the hood from her hair.

"Of course," I said, moving over as much as was possible under the shelter of a small umbrella from the drugstore discount rack.

"I saw you yesterday," she said. "You kept staring at me, and I thought maybe I knew you from somewhere. I almost went over to talk to you then, but I decided that was insane. Some random guy in a coffee shop. You could have been a serial rapist for all I knew."

"Could still be," I said.

She nodded gravely. Up close, her face was lightly freckled and free of makeup. With her long shining hair, she looked like those women in documentaries about the sixties: wholesome yet untamed. In the distance, the ringing of the bells began.

"I should be there," she said, pointing in the direction of the sound.

"Church?" I asked, and she nodded. How many people, I wondered, thought exactly the same thing when they heard those bells?

We came to the door of Starbucks and I pushed it open over her head. Inside, the noise was crushing: people laughing and milk being frothed. We stood in line together, and to anyone who had been watching it would have looked as if we were together, another happy couple out for their morning coffee. It felt good, false as it was.

Despite the rain and the echo of the bells, I played at being lighter, less serious—the ordinary man I might have become, if not for Aidan. Out for coffee with my girl on a lazy Sunday—that's what I imagined the world saw.

"What do you want?" I asked when it was our turn and she ordered her coffee, exactly the same as yesterday, a fact that I tucked away. We went to a table together and sat. "I'm Gabriel," I said, and she answered, "Jem."

What was I intending? Certainly nothing sexual. She was too young for me, first, and a sort of eccentric that bordered on vulnerable. So I wasn't trying to charm Jem—only pretending, just for an hour, to have a normal life. But I do recall that she tucked in close at my side, the way a woman does with her husband or brother, and this made me feel protective. The wet rain suit still hung around her shoulders, and for the second day in a row I watched her remove the lid of her coffee and blow.

"It's a baptism," she said finally. "I was going to be the godmother. But last night, my friend disowned me and kicked me out of her house. I think she called her sister instead."

I trust I did not give away the dull pain that started in my chest and traveled down, all the way to my legs. But in that moment, my sense of belonging ebbed away. Jem was just like the others; she only wanted to use me to confess. If I waited she would launch into her tale of guilt. And, sure enough, by the count of three she did.

She was raised in Pennsylvania, or Ohio—she mentioned both; I gleaned the difference was small. There was a friendship during high school with a girl much prettier and more successful than Jem herself. I pictured what this would mean at seventeen in a rugged steel mining town: a girl with Egyptian eye makeup and tight white T-shirts who belonged to the dance line that sometimes precedes football games. In their senior year, the other girl—name of Stacy, not surprisingly— became involved with an unlikely boy.

"He was more my type, you know?" Jem asked, stirring her un-drunk coffee with a wooden stick, though she'd added nothing to it. "He was nerdy and skinny, obsessed with dolphins and whales."

The boy wanted to be a marine biologist and had been accepted to a university in Oregon where the study of ocean life was, in Jem's words, "an actual thing." But it made no sense: Stacy and Jared, which was the boy's name. Jem would quiz Stacy when they were alone together, and her friend could never pinpoint precisely what she liked about him. She had no great love for sea animals and would be entirely unsuited to Oregon.

"Stacy was the kind of person who assumed that a woman who wore hiking boots *must* be a lesbian," Jem explained.

Graduation was looming. Jem had dated a couple of boys from their high school, but they all paled next to Jared, whose bedroom (which she had visited once with Stacy) was painted a dark blue color and papered with images of shining orcas and narwhals the size of small ships. Being there made Jem feel genuinely happy, for the first time in her memory. It was like living under the surface of the water. She ached to lie on Jared's extra-long twin bed.

Her recitation was unhurried and so vivid I could picture every scene. Jem still sat in her green coat. My coffee was mostly gone.

"Stacy didn't deserve him. She didn't love him." Jem held me with her frank green eyes.

"But you did." It was the first time I'd spoken since we sat down.

She shrugged. "I don't know. The truth is, he never for one minute noticed me. Even though it would have made perfect sense! I was one of those girls who got A's in science and liked listening to Collective Soul in the dark. But Stacy . . ." She shook her head. "She got drunk one night and said some things about him when he wasn't around. About how, um, weird he was. Like she was dating him as an experiment. Just to prove she could."

"So . . ." She paused. For a very long time.

"So?" I asked. "At this point, all you've given me is the plot to a bad Molly Ringwald film."

"Try *Gaslight*." She gulped down three hits of cold coffee so her cup was more or less at the half-full point she'd left it the day before. "Hey," she said, rising. "It's not raining any more. You want to walk?"

This is how we ended up leaving together, Jem and I, walking in the direction that came naturally to me, which was south and east toward the building where I lived. After a block or so she took my arm, tucking her hand in the crook of my elbow, and I let her. My umbrella swung from my other hand.

"What's your story?" she asked, startling me, making me remember with a jolt my last encounter with Madeline. That kiss. Were women always so difficult to predict?

"Wait. You were in the middle of telling me about gaslighting someone."

"Yeah, that can wait." Jem hugged my arm to her like we were old friends, and I let her. "I can't tell my life story to a total stranger. This is a two-way street, buster. You have to give to get."

"All right, what do you want to know?"

"Where did you grow up?" she asked.

"Boston."

"How old are you?"

I considered subtracting a few years but didn't. "Forty-two."

"What do you do for a living?"

I slowed, and she tugged at me a little before adjusting. "Well, that's kind of a hard question to answer . . ."

"Does that mean you're unemployed?"

"Not exactly." We'd come to a dilapidated park, one of the few in my area. The only bench was occupied by a sleeping man covered in a tarp, so I led her to the slide where I took off my coat and spread it on the wide chute children sailed down. I sat, leaving her room, and Jem plopped down at my side like the little sister I'd never had.

"I used to be a priest," I said.

"For real?" She was looking up at me, her face dancing with delight.

"It was very real," I said. "These days, I work in a bookstore, which is a little less real. And I'm kind of doing this other crazy business thing that's completely, well . . . I don't know yet."

"Wow." She thought for a moment. Then she said, "I'm an interventional radiologist."

This struck me as completely unbelievable, but given that I'd just told her I was an ex-priest turned entrepreneur, I didn't feel I had much room to judge. "Where?" I asked.

"Cleveland Clinic," she said. "I'm older than I look."

"Why did you become a doctor?" I still couldn't tell if she was making up all of this. Maybe she was trying for some reason to gaslight *me*.

"Like I said, I was good at biology, chemistry, all that stuff. I got a full ride to Oberlin, ended up in pre-med. You know. OSU Med School was the next logical step. But when I got there, and we started doing patient rotations, it was pretty clear I don't, ah, do well with people."

I tapped her leg, which would have seemed forward had it not been touching mine. "Yes, you're very standoffish," I told her. I was relieved when she laughed.

"Sick people. People who need comforting. I'm not great at that. But I'm very good with instruments, very careful and precise. I love figuring out which specific treatments to use for a particular disease. So I went into a field where I could help people without having to hold their hands." She gazed into the distance then said softly, "Most of my patients have cancer." And I believed her. "Is that why you became a priest, to help people?"

"No," I said before even considering her question. "I became a priest because I was a drug addict, and when I got into trouble, it seemed like the only way out other than prison."

"Mmm. I can see that." She sat very still, her head against my shoulder. The wet sand gave off a fresh, nearly edible smell. We were silent, looking out at the sodden park.

"And then . . . I turned out to be good at the comforting people part."

"I could tell that, too," she said, nodding her head against my shoulder, edging even closer. "I could tell that yesterday when I didn't even talk to you."

"So." I was beginning to worry about what this arrangement on the slide might mean to Jem. She was lovely but girlish, and whatever attraction I might feel was accompanied by a strong aversion—my own personal ban on priests and young people, plus the shame I still felt over Laura Larimar. "What about Stacy?" I asked, desperate to distract her—and myself.

"Well, we'd watched *Gaslight* in Film Appreciation, junior year. And I just decided, one day, to do that. It was kind of like, she was experimenting with Jared so I experimented with her."

"And how did you accomplish this?"

I cocked my head and looked down, just in time to see a ghost of a smile cross Jem's face. "So first, I stole things from her. It was easy; we were together all the time. I took her keys, her school ID— which we needed for graduation—makeup, underwear, one shoe of a pair. This went on for, like, two weeks."

"And?"

"She was pretty . . . unsettled. Also, she got into a lot of trouble, you know, with her mom. And the school. But it didn't really affect her relationship with Jared. He kept being really nice to her, and she let him. So I . . ." She swallowed. "I mean, I was already in. I'd started. So I just went for it."

"Meaning?"

"We were in the same AP English class, Jared and I. So I suggested that we study together, and I started leaving the things I'd taken from Stacy's house, one by one. I'd excuse myself to go to the bathroom and stick her favorite bra into his sock drawer. Or put her ID under his desk. Then I started doing slightly sick—well, sick-*er*—things: like I'd leave an old piece of sandwich under his bed with something of hers. An earring or a book she'd been reading. It was lucky I was smart. I basically had no time to study I was so busy stealing stuff from Stacy and planting it."

"And no one suspected it was you? I mean, it seems obvious. Doesn't it?"

"You had to know me at the time." She blushed, her freckles reddening first. "I was that weird kid in high school. So quiet, most people didn't even notice me. I was always good. Always. It's what I was known for. When you really think about it . . ." She paused as if she were doing just that. "It's like I was madder because they *didn't* suspect me. That only made me try harder to drive them both crazy. And it took a while, but it worked.

"Stacy had lost so many school library books, she was on probation. Those, I just threw away so she couldn't get them back from Jared and return them. But at the same time, he was thinking there was something really wrong with her. Because he kept running across random things in his room." Jem paused. My hard-on had passed, which relieved me greatly.

"They probably would have broken up all on their own," she went on. "But in April or so, Stacy lost it and accused him of messing with her; then she spent about two weeks just 'resting' at home. She was seeing a therapist who had her on Prozac, which I told myself she probably needed anyway. I brought her schoolwork to her every night. Her mother used to give me pie and tell me what a good friend I was."

"Stacy's the one whose baby was baptized this morning?" I said.

"Yes." Jem gazed, puzzled, at her knees. "I get that I'm not a 'conventional' person. I live alone, except for my guinea pig, Lou. I'm a good doctor, I think. But being Stacy's friend has always been the most normal thing about me, so when she asked if I'd come here and be the godmother to her baby, I just booked a ticket. Then, when I saw her new house and her husband, who actually kind of resembles Jared—so maybe she really *did* like him—I remembered that whole bizarre spring of our senior year. And I had to tell her. I mean, she had to know that if I was going to become the 'spiritual adviser' to her child."

"I agree."

"Yes," she said. "I suppose you would."

"So she threw you out . . ."

"I could not *believe* how furious she was. I started telling her, and she just flipped out. I don't know what I expected but it's been, what, sixteen years?"

"It's a really pivotal time for people, the end of high school. The end of anything, really," I said. "She probably felt embarrassed. Cheated out of something."

Jem leaned against me, slipping one arm behind my back. "She had a right."

I patted her hair in what I hoped was a fatherly way. "So, you're homeless?" I asked.

"'Til Tuesday afternoon," she said into my chest. "That's when my plane leaves."

"I'd be happy to help you find a hotel," I told her.

Beside me, Jem was quiet. When she spoke, her voice was small, hopeful. "I know I can afford it. But I just . . ." She swallowed. "I don't want to go back to the Holiday Inn tonight. It makes the fact that I'm alone so, I don't know, *clear*. Like it's punishment for what I did."

This was a feeling I knew—exactly this. And the equation

seemed so simple: We could, each of us, be with someone tonight rather than alone. I paused and ran through scenarios in my head. If Jem came on to me, would I have the will to say no? The grace to do so in a way that did not wound her? Or would I end up giving in to the flesh and closing my eyes, imagining Madeline in place of this lost and lonesome girl?

"My apartment is close," I said finally. "It's not nearly as nice as the Holiday Inn. But we can go there and watch TV if you'd like."

"Thanks," she said softly. "I'll try to stay out of your way."

I laughed. "Yeah, wait till you see how small my place is. Come on." I stood and offered her my hand, though she needed less help rising than I. "I'm hungry."

But I was, in reality, thinking about many things other than food. I was thinking of Madeline in the car on Friday night, her proud, tight face as she drove away. Of Chase handing me cash and saying, "Father, it's the least I can do." Of Isaac and the Red Oak investment team agreeing I deserved some sort of compensation for hearing the troubles of others every day. Of my empty apartment: its sad table and square, sagging bed.

I righted Jem and stood up behind her. As we passed the bench, I stuck a few dollars underneath the homeless man's tarp and wordlessly Jem did the same. Then we started to walk, and silently, because there was no one to listen, I gave myself and my sins up to God.

• • •

I was not expecting Madeline at my door on Monday morning.

By this time, Jem and I had been living as a pair for some eighteen hours, which is long enough to feel like half a life. We'd left that park, gone to my apartment in the deep quiet of Sunday afternoon. Once inside, I'd made tea—redundant, as we'd just had coffee. And Jem had found enough in my refrigerator to put together grilled cheese sandwiches with ketchup, which she'd informed me was "her thing."

"These are everyone's thing," I'd said, taking a bite of the perfectly browned bread, amazed that the items needed to make something so good had existed here all the time, right under my nose.

After cleaning up, we'd watched the evening news on my tiny television. There was a soft, sagging futon where we'd sat side by side.

The whole day had felt like dusk, with its gray, rain-filled skies. So it had been easy to move into bed early, and there we'd lain still dressed, talking with our bodies touching gently at the ankle or shoulder, simply a reminder that the other was there. Without my saying anything, we hadn't gone further. Jem had burrowed close a few times, as she had on the slide, but she'd never slid in a suggestive way or climbed on top of me—for which I was grateful. I am animal enough that I might have succumbed.

None of it made any sense: why I invited Jem to my apartment or that she came. I had never had an encounter anything like it before. It made me think of stories I'd heard about men who paid women only to hold them and sleep next to them. But in this case, we both seemed to need someone. I could sense her quaint oddness, and it matched mine in the way of a puzzle piece that locks snugly. It wasn't just guilt holding Jem back; it was she, herself. Her bewilderment with the world.

We'd talked until nearly midnight, about Jem's life in Cleveland and mine in Chicago, about the Catholic Church and the reasons I left. It had been the first time I'd told anyone about my rage and confusion. The Church had disappointed me so cruelly, I wondered if this was why I'd gone along with Madeline's plan. Was I simply vengeful? Jem had listened carefully and posed excellent questions: *What would I do if not this? Was it possible to help people this way? Why not be compensated for hearing confessions, as she was for treating disease?* Then she'd outlined the terms I should ask for, turning from homeless waif to shrewd negotiator. Commission, stock, trademark. It was my name, she'd said, and I should protect it at all costs.

"Never let them own you," she'd said, her voice sleepy and slow. "Because life changes. And you never know what you're going to want to do next."

Jem had repaid her debt to me two or three times over, until I could no longer say that I'd heard her confession without stipulating that she'd done the same for me. My gratitude was profound; I'd actually understood in that moment how this business might work. I had been about to make my real confession—about Aidan—when Jem had leaned back, her skin ashen from fatigue, and asked if I would mind if she slept.

I had given her an old T-shirt, and she'd taken it into the bathroom along with the small case we'd retrieved from her hotel. When she'd emerged five minutes later, covered to her knees in my clothing, her face had been scrubbed and her eyes had been heavy. In my bed we'd drifted off, curled up like puppies, and I'd felt contented, grounded, certainly less alone. But I'd never even kissed Jem except once, like a benediction, on the top of the head.

Of course, there was no way to tell that to Madeline, who appeared at my door without warning to suggest I dress immediately, go to the bookstore, and quit my job. The time had come to start selling my services, she said. Our website would go "live" at the end of the week—whatever that meant. I was just about to ask her when Jem wandered out from my bedroom in a faded XL Maroon 5 T-shirt I'd picked out of the rummage pile at St. John's.

Madeline was still straddling the doorway, no doubt due to our awkward misunderstanding a few nights before. But when she saw Jem she pulled her right foot back as if she'd just dipped it in scalding water.

"Oh!" she cried. Sometimes, I said to myself, life really does sound like a film. Not *Gaslight* but something slightly more modern, starring Meg Ryan and Tom Hanks.

"Madeline, this is Jem," I said. Because it seemed to me this is what Tom would do. "She got, well, stuck here in Chicago, and I offered her a place to . . ."

"Hey, whatever gets you through the night," Madeline said, each word bright and hard, like something radioactive. "Gabe, you're just amazingly progressive for a priest."

Jem was grinning, sweeping one green-painted toe around her body like a dancer. I stood between the two women, my face burning, feeling irrationally fearful. Some evolutionary impulse, no doubt. "Madeline, it's really not. I don't just do. I mean, it wasn't like that at . . ."

"I'm going to go now," Madeline interrupted. She was rooting around in her vast over-the-shoulder bag. "I apologize for barging in. But Gabe, it's very important that we see you in the office this morning. This is not the time to get sloppy. We're just days away from launch."

"It sounds like you're going somewhere in a spaceship." Jem had come to stand next to me, bare feet nudging my slippered ones. I'd told her all about Forgiveness4You and the ad agency, but I hadn't mentioned the complexities of my relationship with Madeline herself. Chaste though we were, it would have seemed indelicate to talk about another woman as we lay side by side. So I couldn't blame Jem for appearing half-undressed and rumpled from my bed, standing next to me like she owned me and extending her hand. "Very nice to meet you." She used her grown-up doctor tone; I could hear it. "Gabe's told me a lot about you," she said.

Madeline shook Jem's hand awkwardly then drew another step back and returned to her purse. "Here!" She handed me an engraved business card with a logo that depicted a trowel and a lightning bolt.

Jem, still hovering by my arm, put her finger to the image and laughed softly. "Ah, I get it!" she said. "Mason . . . and Zeus."

Madeline ignored her. "Just get in a cab and give it to the driver. Tell him we'll pay the fare." And with that she turned, pulling the door closed with a thwack.

From: Abel Dodd
To: Forgiveness4You team
Subject: copy deliverables

People—

Here's the copy for a magazine launch ad, banner ads, and two radio spots. I did some research into motivators based on Joy's audience profile, and I'm using the themes of "regret" and "guilt" alternately. Both provoked anxiety and interest among our test groups—which is a positive response, as long as it's followed quickly with assurances that we can fix what ails them.

Let me know if you have any feedback. I know we're moving quickly, but let's avoid on-the-fly edits, okay? I never want to repeat the verb-tense debacle of 2010.

—A. Dodd

ATTACHMENTS:
Magazine ad (print buy: *People, Redbook, Esquire, AARP*)
(headline)
What's the Worst Thing You've Ever Done?
(subhead)
We can help you admit it, work through it, put it behind you, and move on.
(copy)
Regret. It can weigh heavy, causing emotional problems, family tensions, even physical illness. But now, no matter what your religious affiliation, there's a way to rid yourself of regret and go on. Visit Forgiveness4You.com to find out how you can attain true peace of mind today.

Banner ad (to run on USBank, AARP, various legal sites)

(headline)

What's the Worst Thing You've Ever Done?

(subhead)

We can help you admit it, work through it, put it behind you, and move on.

(call to action)

Forgiveness4You. Start improving your life today.

Banner ad (to run on Weight Watchers site)

(headline)

Guilt eating you so you can't stop eating?

(subhead)

We can help put a stop to the cycle by freeing you from the weight of regret.

(call to action)

Forgiveness4You. Start improving your life today.

Banner ad (to run on Runner's World and Nike sites)

(headline)

Guilt slowing you down?

(subhead)

We'll help get you back on track by lifting away the weight of regret.

(call to action)

Forgiveness4You. Start improving your life today.

Flash banner ad (to run on Christian, gambling, and porn sites)

(animated headline against chaotic, graffiti-filled background)

What's the . . .

      Worst Thing . . .

          YOU . . .

            Have Ever Done?

(light breaks, screen glows)

We can help you admit it, get forgiveness, and move on.

(build)

Our spiritual leader understands. No matter what your religion—or your sin—he will move you closer to your God. Stop suffering with guilt. Forgiveness is available to you.

(call to action)

Forgiveness4You. Start improving your life today.

Forgiveness4You	3/12/--
Radio spot #1	1:30 AD

"THE END OF SLEEPLESS NIGHTS"

SFX: BUSY CAFÉ, PEOPLE TALKING, DISHES CLINKING

WOMAN 1: Sorry I'm late. My head's so foggy. I haven't been sleeping.

WOMAN 2: Sit down! You look really tired. Anything wrong?

SFX: SCUFFLE OF CHAIR MOVING

WOMAN 1: It's, oh it's a long story. Nothing I can really talk about. But there's this thing from my first marriage that's been weighing on me. I lie awake every night just . . . regretting.

WOMAN 2: I understand. I went through something really similar. Family problem. And I didn't know where to turn. Then I found Forgiveness4You.

SFX: MUSIC UP

ANNCR: You don't have to live with sleepless nights and guilt. Forgiveness4You is a spiritual service, but it's not affiliated with any religion. We're here to listen and help you move on, freeing you from the burden of regret. This is absolution for everyone.

WOMAN 2:   Forgiveness4You really helped me.

WOMAN 1:   Is it like counseling? Or confession?

WOMAN 2:   Forgiveness4You takes the best parts of both of those but leaves the psychobabble and religious punishments behind. I've never felt so free.

ANNCR: You deserve a clean slate, a life free of guilt. And you can achieve that today, thanks to Forgiveness4You.

WAITER: Can I get you something, miss?

WOMAN 1: I'd like a cappuccino. *(Voice noticeably lighter)* Thanks. And from you, my friend, I'd like the number for Forgiveness4You.

woman 2: That's easy. Just dial 1-8-6-6-4-G-I-V-E-4-U. Or you can go to their website Forgiveness, 4 like the number, capital Y-o-u.

WOMAN 1: Perfect. I'm going to call right after I finish my coffee. Soon, too much caffeine will be the only thing keeping me awake.

SFX: WOMEN LAUGH SOFTLY.

ANNCR: Forgiveness4You. Absolution for everyone. Our URL is Forgiveness, number 4, Y-o-u, all one word. Or dial 1-8-6-6-4-G-I-V-E-4-U. And sleep better tonight.

Forgiveness4You	3/12/--
Radio spot #2	1:45AD

"SHOULD I TELL HER?"

SFX: FOOTBALL GAME ON TV, MEN'S VOICES CHEERING AND BOOING

MAN 1: Hey, commercial break. You got a minute? I need to ask you something.

MAN 2: Sure, brother. Let's go outside and have a smoke.

SFX: MOVEMENT; DOOR CLOSING; FLARE OF MATCHES BEING LIT

MAN 1: I'm thinking of telling Abby about . . . you know . . .

MAN 2: You mean about the girl? What, are you insane? Why would you do that? It's only going to make your wife miserable. And she'll hate you. And then you'll get a divorce, and you'll be living in my basement. Jeez, no! C'mon, get ahold of yourself.

MAN 1:   I know. I thought about all that. It's over and there's no way I'd ever do such an idiotic thing again. But the guilt, man. It's just eating away at me.

MAN 2:   So tell someone else. Tell me. Okay, you did that. Tell a priest.

MAN 1:   That would be great . . . if we were raised Catholic, you moron!

MAN 2:   Yeah, too bad the rest of us don't have a place to go and confess.

SFX: MUSIC UP

ANNCR: Now there's a place for non-Catholics who want the experience of confession and absolution. Forgiveness4You is a spiritual service, but it's not affiliated with any religion. We're here to listen and help you move on, freeing you from the burden of regret.

MAN 2:   So, did you tell her?

MAN 1:   I was about to. I was headed home to sit her down and spill my guts. Then I saw this sign that said Forgiveness4You, and I pulled out my phone on the spot and got on their website.

MAN 2:   And . . . ?

MAN 1:   It was exactly what I needed. I talked to a guy who helped me deal with the guilt. So I don't have to destroy Abby with it.

MAN 2:   That's great. I think Forgiveness4You probably saved your marriage. And it saved me having my idiot brother in my basement.

SFX: BROTHERS GUFFAW.

ANNCR: You deserve a clean slate, a life free of guilt. And you can achieve that today, thanks to Forgiveness4You.

MAN 1:   If you told me last month I was going to sign up to "talk about my feelings" (jeering tone), I'd have said you were crazy. But it's easy at Forgiveness4You.

MAN 2:   You're going to have to give me their contact info. 'Cause you know, godlike as I am, I may make a mistake someday . . .

MAN 1:   Yeah, yeah. Just dial 1-8-6-6-4-G-I-V-E-4-U. Or you can go to their website Forgiveness, 4 like the number, capital Y-o-u.

MAN 2:   I'll keep it in mind. You want to get a beer?

MAN 1:   Okay, but just one. I have a date with my wife tonight.

ANNCR: Forgiveness4You. Absolution for everyone. Our URL is Forgiveness, number 4, Y-o-u, all one word. Or just dial 1-8-6-6-4-G-I-V-E-4-U.

IX

WHEN I LEFT JEM ON MONDAY MORNING I KISSED HER ONCE more on the top of her head—still the only place I had ever kissed her—to bless her on her journey. "Call me when you're back in Cleveland," I said, feeling guilty that I would not be accompanying her to the airport.

Jem nodded and slipped her arms around my neck. "Thanks for putting me up." She smelled toasty and warm, like sleep, and I held on for one blissful moment. "It was really . . . nice."

I walked several blocks to hail a cab—none would stop in my end of the neighborhood—and read the Mason & Zeus address off the card Madeline had given me. My driver grunted. He had a large wooden cross hanging from his rearview mirror and a statue of Mother Mary, in plastic, next to his clicking meter. Soft Christian rock on the radio. I sprawled in the seat, wishing I could ask him to drive around the city until the sun set. Here in this halfway place, maybe I could figure out my life.

An announcer came on the radio to describe the scene in St. Peter's Square where hundreds of thousands of people were waiting in a rainstorm to see the smoke that would foretell the next pope. I had not seen Rome in more than a decade, but I could picture it as clearly as I could my childhood home. A few men I'd known at seminary had gone on to become bishops, including one of the worst and most calculating—a priest I'd suspected of being deviant long before the sex abuse news began to break. For years I'd been checking the newspapers, surprised every time that his name wasn't among the accused.

I thought about how it would feel to don a dark robe and collar and walk among that crowd. People become dazed in Vatican City. They would reach out to touch me: the lame and poor of Italy and the businessmen from Seattle alike. Being a cleric in Italy was something like being a child TV star; you had celebrity but not the wisdom to use it. Moments of grandeur were followed by long hours of lonely self-doubt. The young priest within me ached to be there at the foot of the Sistine Chapel, filled with hope. The older, jaded man I'd become was glad to be here, in a taxi, watching the Blessed Virgin bob with the bumps in the road. Hope was too often followed by despair.

We pulled up in front of Mason & Zeus before I was ready.

"Keep the meter running," I told my taciturn but faithful cabbie. "I need to call up."

Madeline didn't answer on my first or second attempts, and I could feel the driver getting agitated, preparing to call the police and report nonpayment of fare. "I know she's there," I said, sweating as I dialed again. This time, listening to her message, I heard her prompt me to push "0" and page her. I did just that, waiting for another tense period, until finally Madeline's ragged voice came on the phone.

"I'm downstairs," I said. Then, because she seemed not to remember our deal. "In the cab?"

"Any way you can pay him and we'll expense it out for you, Gabe? I am getting slammed up here."

I glanced at the meter, which read $41 . . . click, now $42.25. My wallet held roughly $23, plus maybe a dollar's worth of change in my pants. "Sorry, Madeline," I told her. "I'm stuck."

"Okay, tell the guy I'll be right down. Why I didn't just leave my American Express with you, I don't . . ." Her voice faded and she hung up. And I thought how glad I was that her face-off with Jem had not ended with Madeline's pulling a credit card out of her purse.

She arrived at my window, her haunted, older-looking face peering through the glass at me. She was like two different women: the Madeline overwhelmed or filled with guilt, who appeared tattered and fragile, versus the laughing, drinking, kissing version of Madeline with her soft skin and endless, grateful eyes. "Here," said Madeline version one, wearing a trench coat and pushing her credit card through the crack my backseat window allowed. "It's my card," she said, flashing her driver's license. Then to me: "Pay him, tip him, come upstairs."

It flashed through my mind that I should tell the cabbie to take off. We'd have a good hour before Madeline, this strung-out version of her, realized I'd left and called her bank to put a stop on the card. By that time I could be somewhere else, with new shoes and fine food. Perhaps with a ticket to Rome. Only what good would that do me? The hotels were no doubt filled to capacity; now that I was defrocked, none of my old friends from the Vatican would have me on their couch.

I could fly toward my mother in Boston, but I had destroyed her faith twice—first, when I'd destroyed a life, then when I'd quit the priesthood—and could offer no way to fix it. There was Jem, now headed back to her life in Cleveland. What would she say if I showed up at her door with presents for Lou the guinea pig and no plans to leave?

"Here." The taxi man shoved a scrap of paper at me and indicated I should sign the bottom.

"Thanks. Have a nice day." I looked around the backseat, but there was nothing for me to gather.

"Yup," said the man. His eyes said, *Get out*.

Upstairs, Candy squealed when she saw me and came out from

behind the desk to kiss my cheek. "The team's been waiting for you, Father Gabe," she said, walking ahead of me backward—so she could face me as she talked—teetering on transparent shoes, her gold-painted toes sticking out. "They have some amazing work to show you!"

"Where are we going?" I asked as Candy led me toward the elevator.

"We have a war room on eight," she said, as if that phrase explained everything.

We took the elevator to a large warehouse-y space with many tables and cloth bulletin boards for walls. The tables held candy, soda cans, pizza boxes, at least fifteen dirty coffee cups, a mostly-empty bottle of Scotch, and what looked like the remnants of a kindergarten: paper-cuttings lay strewn about with brightly-colored pens, scissors, and glue. The walls were a collage. Under a card that read "Inspiration," there were photos of the ongoing papal conclave, cardinals bowing in their red hats; illustrations from the Bible; ads for weight loss products and Alcoholics Anonymous; and Oprah Winfrey—probably the only television star I knew because she was from Chicago, and besides, who on this earth does not recognize Oprah?

Walking to the right, clockwise, the cards read "Print," "Web," "Bench & Bus," "Radio," "Mobile," "Word-of-Mouth," "Rewards," and "PR." Under each was something that might have been ripped from a catalog: images of extended hands, women talking at a table, men drinking beer, a large old-fashioned telephone, crowds of people looking up, a couple kissing in a park, people holding small children, an elderly woman beaming from her wheelchair, again Oprah—and me. There I was, wearing vestments, hands up, in prayer before the crucifix. Under this image, the words "Absolution for Everyone." I flinched then moved in for a closer look. Where had they gotten this photograph? It was completely unfamiliar. I barely even recognized myself.

"Hello, Father," Isaac was slumped behind one of the tables looking hairy and unclean. "Welcome to our cluster fuck. T-minus-three and counting."

"Madeline told me you needed . . ."

"Hey, excuse me," Scott said, jostling past with something he pinned to the board. It was one sentence spelled out in Gothic letters on a license plate: "What's the worst thing you've ever done?" I stared at it.

"Yeah." Isaac rose, stretching. He had wide armpit stains that gave off a skunky smell. "We need to start thinking logistics. Like where you're operating, day one. And how we respond to media requests. You okay doing interviews? I'm thinking *Good Day Chicago* is going to eat this up."

"You'd go on with him, right?"

I turned to see Madeline at the door, wearing jeans and a tight Chicago Cubs T-shirt, tossing a shiny black smartphone from hand to hand.

"Um, here's your card." I handed her the piece of plastic, and she stuck it in a back pocket, her shirt—I couldn't help but notice—straining over her breasts. "Thanks for the cab ride."

"You're welcome, Gabe. I'm glad you're here. We have a lot to do." I checked for signs of the morning, for hints about the kiss. But she was impassive. "First things first. Tell me you've quit your job."

"No, in fact I'm due there . . ." I checked my watch. "In two and a half hours."

"I think you need to tell them—"

"Wait a minute." Isaac was rocking on his feet. His thinking stance; I already understood this. "Let's explore this for a minute. We've got a humble priest working at a *bookstore*, which is as wholesome as you get. It's local, that kind of sweet little corner shop deal." He looked at me. "You're not selling porn or running numbers out of the back or anything like that, are you?"

I thought about the raunchy books all the ladies came in to buy. It was too difficult to explain. "No," I said simply.

"I say he keeps the job, reduced hours. We can use it." Isaac was addressing Madeline, not me. "I'll go in this afternoon and talk to the manager or the owner . . . ?"

"Owner," I supplied. "Oren Brooks."

"Perfect. I'll talk to Mr. Brooks and convince him that this is the greatest thing that could ever happen to his little bookstore. He's going to have a local celebrity working there. It'll bring in droves of people. He'll bend over backward to make scheduling work."

"And what about when people start going into the bookstore, asking Gabe for a freebie?" Madeline asked. I decided she was pointedly not looking at me, and it became my mission to get her attention. Just like that, I was back in junior high.

"What about when they pretend they're looking for *Anna Karenina*?" Madeline went on, making me crave her attention more, the more aloof she was. "But really they just want to tell Gabe how they skipped their kid's birthday party to go to Vegas and now they feel bad?"

Isaac shrugged. "We'll just give him an elevator speech. 'I can't speak to you right now. I should be working. I'm committed to my employer during these hours.'" He shifted back to me. "That'll work for you, won't it, Father? You wouldn't take time away from your actual job to forgive random people."

"Ah, but he did for me." Madeline's voice was triumphant, and there was a moment of tension where I struggled to figure out what this meant in the context of the conversation—and Friday night.

"Totally different." Isaac waved one hand. "He was doing that out of the goodness of his heart, which means he puts morality first every time. Helping you over working for Oren Brooks? Sure. But when he's being *paid*, when it's all become commerce, that'll be different. Am I telling the truth here, Father? Help me out. I say that once forgiving people is your business, you'll put it behind everything else."

I stared at him for a second then nodded. I couldn't have parsed it so clearly, yet Isaac had nailed exactly how I would behave.

Madeline laughed, and the brazen, beautiful version of her that I'd been longing to see reappeared. I was momentarily pleased then disappointed, because some artifact of my twelve-year-old self wanted her to be inconsolable that she'd found me with Jem.

"You are not making me feel better, Beckwith!" Madeline cried. Was it possible, I wondered, that she was trying a little *too* hard to appear carefree? "Your argument is that once we get this business going, our only service provider won't care about it."

"Precisely." Isaac leaned against the wall and scratched himself. "That's one of the most appealing things about Father Gabe."

"Well, if I'm going to get to work, I'm going to have to catch the train in . . ."

"Don't be silly. I'll make sure you get to work," Madeline said. "We've actually got something we'd like you to do today. Sort of a dry run."

"It was her idea," Isaac said, poking his thumb toward Madeline. "We gave a 50 percent friends-and-family discount to everyone in the building and told them to sign up ASAP, so you're not booked with outside clients. Do you know how many takers we got?"

"Uh, three?" I said. I always guess three. Habit, I suppose.

"Nineteen!" Isaac stretched again. I was getting used to his odor. Oddly, at this point, I almost liked it. "Including four from our own agency. We're billing you at $100 per hour online, $150 by phone, and $180 in person. So these are people willing to pony up $90 bucks apiece, no questions asked."

"But I haven't . . ." I cleared my throat and reminded myself of what Jem and I had talked about. "I don't remember signing a contract. So far it's been just talk—and you two buying me clothes and meals and cab rides, which I appreciate. But what happens when I start working? I don't even know what the terms are?"

Jem had coached me as we lay in bed on Sunday night. "I don't know if they have contracts for priests" she said. "Maybe you had some ritual involving holy water. But out here in the real world, they have to promise you some percentage. I'd fight for 60 and settle for 50."

Now Isaac looked at Madeline, and she looked at him, and I thought she might burst out laughing again. "You're right, Father." Isaac bowed his head. "We've been moving so fast, we've let go of some of the important stuff. Tell you what: We have a meeting set up for you in twenty minutes. Some woman from downstairs, reception-ist at an architecture firm. I think her name is Sandy. If you're willing to talk to her, I'll have Mason & Zeus's lawyer draw up the contract at the same time. Should be fairly simple."

"What terms, exactly?"

This time I heard it. Madeline chortled behind me, and I felt her fleeting touch on my sleeve. It disturbed me slightly that one woman's advice was winning me attention from another, but I told myself this was one more tradition among lay people that I'd have to learn.

"We own the idea, the design, the tagline and the franchise rights. If this becomes a movie or a TV show, we own that, too. We might use you and pay you a performance fee; we might not . . . We can hire or fire you—and anyone else—at will. We use your image and reputation to sell the idea." Isaac rattled these off so rapidly, even I could tell several conversations had been had.

"You take away 50 percent, clear, from the sessions you do per-sonally," he continued. "When the time comes that we hire other peo-ple—I'm already assembling a team of spiritual counselors from other faiths—your commission drops to 15 percent on those. You don't get an ownership stake at first because the entire start-up investment was made by Madeline and her people. But we can revisit that after a year, maybe offer you 5 percent."

I stood stock-still. The only thing Jem and I had discussed was my percentage, and Isaac had met the number she threw out as she reclined with her hair spread like sunrays on the only pillow I owned.

"Do you have an attorney that you want to look at it before you sign?" Madeline asked. "It might not be a bad idea, Gabe. For you to have representation of your own."

"No," I said. Once, my congregation had been full of lawyers who fed me steak and relied on me to forgive—without a set hourly charge—their misdeeds. But to call one of them at this point would be excruciating. "Draw it up just as you said," I told Isaac. "I'll sign."

"All right, let me show you your workspace." Madeline took my arm lightly, the way she had Friday night. "*You,*" she said to Isaac. "Go take a shower. You stink."

We walked out of the room like a couple strolling through a park. And it was in this moment that I reconciled myself to the fact that I would never understand women, ever, at all. I would have predicted that Madeline's showing up to see Jem that morning had destroyed something fundamental. Possibility, trust, both . . . But here she was, acting easy and treating me like an old friend.

Then there was Jem herself. She was peculiar in ways that created a distance between us. Yet it was she who had asked the only question that mattered, the one I'd been trying to answer for myself. "Why are you doing this?" she'd asked yesterday, on that long rainy afternoon. "It doesn't seem like you: taking confessions for pay. Though, personally, I don't think there's anything wrong with that." She'd placed a palm on my chest. "I'm just curious. Why?"

I'd paused. It was partly her hand over my heart. The place no one had touched since I'd bared it for Sol and his ink gun, years before. But also, I'd been scrambling for an answer that made sense.

"I'm good at one thing," I'd told her, placing my hand over hers. "I was a good priest. Maybe someday I would have been a great one. But I couldn't . . ." I'd stopped, and she'd raised her head to give me a questioning look. "Being a priest meant being silent about things I could not abide. I had a pastor who was . . . I don't think he was *molesting* kids. Teenagers, actually. It wasn't so clear-cut, you know? It wasn't ten-year-old altar boys. He had more, well, I suppose, acceptable tastes. Sixteen-, seventeen-year-old girls. He spent a lot of time with them, and I think he only . . . well, I'm not sure what he did. None of them ever complained."

Jem had lain back, but I had felt her still listening.

"Then there was the money. I wanted to stay at St. John's. That's where I was needed, serving the poor. But the politics were crazy. We were collecting millions of dollars in the congregations like St. Hedwig and Holy Name. But all that money had to be used for maintenance. For rebuilding. For the archdiocese. I couldn't get $5,000 to run a van and pick up the homeless in January. Don't even get me started on the last pope. He looked the other way when children were being abused. His politics were very fourteenth-century. I just couldn't serve . . ."

"You're not answering my question." Jem's interruption had been abrupt enough to sound mature and for just that moment, I hadn't felt like a dirty old man. "Why this? Why start up with some shysters who want to charge people for confessing?"

"Because." We'd stayed there for a long time staring at the ceiling. Finally, I'd given the only answer I'd been able to come up with. "I don't know what else to do."

From: joytoyourworld@hotmail.com
To: Scott143@gmail.com
Subject: Abel's spots

Scott—

I almost forgot and used our work email accounts for this message! That would have been awful. Cuz I'm pretty sure Madeline is spying on every single thing we write.

So I've been reading Abel's radio spots, and I really don't like the one about the married guy who had an affair, but I'm wondering if I should say something. The other one's okay. Actually it's pretty good, except I can't in a million years imagine sitting down at a table with another woman and listening to her problems, then giving her some toll-free number to call. Maybe it's a generational thing.

But the second one makes a joke of adultery and the Church, and I'm not feeling good about that. I think I'll talk to Isaac. I mean, I am a Catholic, and I think we should take sin more seriously. Plus my mom and dad are hanging on every bit of news, waiting for the new pope to be announced. So what do you think?

By the way, I have a surprise for you tonight. <3 <3 <3

    xoxo,
    Joy

From: Scott143@gmail.com
To: joytoyourworld@hotmail.com
Subject: RE: Abel's spots

Christ, Joy, do I have to be the one to remind you that YOU are having an affair with a married guy???? WTF? Why do you always want to cause trouble?

155

Abel's a little wierd, but his spots are great. Plus, Madeline thinks he's a genius and the priest guy seems to like him, so please, just let this go. Also, I forgot to tell you I fucked up and shot off my mouth to King Isaac so I have to lay low for a while and that means YOU DO TWO!!! Okay?

Tonight may be tough for me. I have Magenta and anyways I'm kind of tired. Can the surprise wait til Friday?

S

Jabber IM session—March 12, 20--

@IBeck: What do u think of Abel's work?

@MMM: First spot sounds canned to me. I wd never sit down at a table with a friend and dump like that . . .

@MMM: The other one is brilliant. Love the pay-off.

@IBeck: Concur. I'll talk to AD. What's up w Gabe?

@MMM: Coming later. Had some things to do.

@IBeck: Some things, or someone?

@MMM: u r disgusting.

@IBeck: Kidding!

@IBeck: You OK?

@MMM: Tired. This idea has to work. Jim Lynch is up my ass in a bad way.

@IBeck: Getting close to new pope and I'm worried. Cd be a decent guy this time.
@MMM: What're the odds?

@IBeck: We shd have a backup plan if pp like him. Fewer Catholics defecting . . . .

@MMM: That's where cheating guy comes in. Church will never okay adultery. Great space for us to play in.

@IBeck: Agreed. That 2nd spot is brilliant. Going to talk to Abel now.

@MMM: Bring good chocolate. Always helps.

From: Isaac Beckwith
To: Forgiveness Team
Subject: Launch date

Hey Team—

I know you're all wiped out, and I want you to know how much we appreciate your hard work. The campaign is starting to come together, and everything looks great. Kudos to Scott and Abel for being creative around the clock!

Heads up, sources say they're probably going to announce a new pope tomorrow and he won't be a Nazi, like the last one. So if this guy is someone people feel good about, we're going to have to tread a little lighter around the Catholic issue. The PR team is standing ready to take people's temperature as soon as the announcement is made.

Our plan is to launch this sucker on Friday, if there are no surprises. So it's going to continue to be a long week. Please apologize to your families from me personally, and let me know if you need anything (toothbrush, Vitamin Water, Adderall—just kidding!) to keep working. This is all going to be worth it in the end.

Cheers!
IB

X

MY WORKSPACE ON THE EIGHTH FLOOR WAS A SMALL MEETING room next to the lavatories that shuddered every time someone flushed. I had a laminated wood table and three adjustable office chairs that I positioned so two of them faced each other. This reminded me of my years of Pre-Cana counseling, and I wondered if Madeline and Isaac had considered a couples rate for my forgiveness services: spouses who had, for instance, conspired to cheat a relative out of an inheritance. I started to say something, then remembered that I didn't have a stake and shut my mouth.

"I know it's not ideal," Madeline said, adjusting the shade of the floor lamp that sat in a corner. "We're looking at spaces a couple blocks away, in a building that has a lot of law offices and psychologists. But for now . . ."

"I'll need to leave by one o'clock," I said, more gruffly than I intended.

"No problem. We'll cancel the appointment after this, and I'll make sure there's someone here to drive you. Oh, and I'd like you to take this."

Madeline handed me the black phone she'd been juggling, which I'd assumed was hers.

"It's a smartphone," she said. "We need to be able to get in touch with you."

"I have one," I said, pulling out my battered flip phone.

"I know. But this one's got all our numbers and email addresses programmed in. There's a calendar function, which is how you'll know when we've got you scheduled to see someone. We'll send you text alerts. You text, right?"

I shook my head, and Madeline sighed. But there was some tiny part of her, I sensed, that was pleased.

"Don't worry," she said, though I hadn't been. "One of us will show you later. It's easy. Six-year-olds can do it, literally. But right now . . ." She grasped the phone I was holding and turned it so she could see the time. "Oh! We have to hurry. I'll be right back. Please don't leave."

She disappeared for a moment while I wondered about that strange last request. She came back with a file folder that held several forms. I could see they were hastily drawn up and copied, providing me the most basic information. Sandra Nelson, age 51, married, resident of Winnetka. Even this felt like too much. My first "client" had become a two-dimensional cutout of a person before even walking into the room.

"Okay, I'm going to leave so you can do your magic." Madeline was simultaneously checking her watch and backing out of the room.

"Wait." I shut the folder and put it on the table, resolving never to look at another of those forms again. "I want to explain about Jem."

"It's none of my business, Gabe. You just . . ."

"No." I know how to project my voice, and this one syllable made her stop. "It's important to me. She was here in Chicago, in my neighborhood, there was some mix-up with the place she was staying. All I did was give her a . . ."

"Gabe." This time it was Madeline who halted me, but by uttering my name so softly that I had to strain forward to hear what she would say next. "It's really. Not. My business. There's nothing for you to explain. You're an adult and so was your friend. End of story." She sighed. "I shouldn't have showed up unannounced at your front door, and that won't happen again. But beyond that, I like you. I think you should live your life."

I yearned for the weeping Madeline I'd first met. This one, with her constantly changing looks and mood that ranged from steely to kittenish, only confused me. But I nodded as if we'd come to some resolution, and that's when a portly woman with a platinum bob spoke up from the door. "I'm Sandy Nelson," she said. "Am I too early?"

"Not at all!" Madeline stuck her hand out, and the two women shook. "You're right on time. And we're delighted that you're Gabe's very first client. Congratulations!"

This made me it sound as if I'd been won in a grocery store raffle, but I shook Sandy's hand as well and gestured for her to sit. She cleared her throat as Madeline closed the door.

"I'm here to talk about my friend, Carol," Sandy began abruptly. "I've known her since sixth grade. She has MS."

"I'm sorry to hear that," I said. Like the sacrament of confession, this forum felt bloodless to me: people presenting only their sins without any context that I could use. I realized with a start that one of the things I liked about the random bookstore or taxicab encounter was their feeling of intimacy. This arrangement pushed me backward. Now, if I wasn't careful, I'd start muttering about Hail Marys. I resolved to engage with this brusque woman and made eye contact, but this only prompted her to blink rapidly, as if I'd turned on a bright interrogation light.

"We were very close for, um, I suppose thirty years." Sandy was clutching her purse in her lap, as if she were sitting on a bus.

"Tell me," I said, leaning back in my chair. This actually prompted her to relax and put her purse on the floor, which I counted as a small victory.

"Carol stood up for me at my wedding. She's godmother to my oldest, and I'm godmother to hers. We were in the same book club together. Once, oh about ten years ago, Carol and her husband and Ron and I went on a cruise. To Alaska. It was spectacular. Have you ever been?"

"No. I haven't." Alaska did sound spectacular right now. I wondered if there was a market for me up there. Probably not. I read once that it was a state that already had too many men—not unlike the priesthood. "So you and Carol are very good friends."

"Yes." She pursed her lips. "We were."

"I see."

"Carol was diagnosed with multiple sclerosis in '04. It was a shock! But Ron and I were right there for her. Every step of the way. I remember even the night they found out, we went over to the house and talked and talked . . ."

"That sounds very supportive," I said. But I was beginning to worry. Something basic was missing; I felt nothing from this woman. Sandy could have been an actress sent by Isaac to test me. In fact, from what little I knew about him, this was something he might very well do.

"It was little things at first." If she was acting, "Sandy" was pretty good. She played the frumpy woman with great skill, and her voice had that infuriating mosquito's buzz of constant complaint. "Carol's vision got blurry. She said her hands felt funny. Tingly, kind of. And she was tired. But we hung in and prayed a lot, thinking things would get better."

"Better? I must admit, I don't know much about multiple sclerosis but isn't it . . . progressive? I mean, doesn't it just get worse?"

"Exactly!" Sandy looked pleased for the first time since entering the room. "And in Carol's case, it got worse so fast. Two years later, she was using a walker and even then, she'd get off balance and fall, so if you were out to lunch with her you had to be constantly worried about how she was sitting on her chair. You had to get up and leave your food and go to the ladies room with her.

"Then . . ." Sandy shifted her eyes so she was focused on the blank wall. Her face reddened. "The ladies room became a non-issue, because she lost all her bladder control. And the other one, too. You know . . ." she dropped her voice to a whisper. "Bowel."

"That's awful. Very sad."

"It was. Awful for Carol and, frankly, awful for whoever was with her and had to deal with it. I have changed more than my share of adult diapers, let me tell you."

"You sound like a good friend."

"You think so?" Sandy looked at me hopefully then shook her head. "Anyway, not anymore."

We sat in uncomfortable silence until I remembered this was a timed session. Minutes were slipping away. "Did Carol die?" I asked, mustering as much care as I could.

"No, no. So far as I know she's still alive."

Sandy seemed grateful I'd prompted her, so I kept going. "Did something happen between the two of you?"

"Nothing, really." She took a breath, as if preparing for a high dive. "Nothing except her MS. And I just got to the point where I just couldn't . . . take it . . . anymore."

"What do you mean?"

"You have to understand, I had kids at home. Well, my daughter. She was still in high school. My son had gone off to college. But there was my husband, too, and he's a handful. We've been married for a long time, and we both work in the city, so by the time we get home it's late and I have to make dinner, clean up, all that."

"What . . . ?" I was about to ask what this had to do with Carol, but Sandy just kept going.

"My parents are in Arizona, and my mother had a stroke last year. It turned out to be something small, thank God. It didn't even cause damage, because Dad called 911 right away and they gave her that drug. You know? The one that stops strokes." She looked at me, and I shook my head. "Never mind. Anyway, I flew out there to help my parents, and once I was away from Chicago, I realized how *heavy* this thing with Carol had become."

There was a knock on the door, and a girlish voice I didn't recognize said, "Five minutes, Father."

"I'm sorry," I said to Sandy. "It seems we need to hurry."

"Well, that's it," she said, picking up her purse from the floor. "When I got back from Phoenix, I just never contacted Carol again. She called a few times, and I let the machine pick up, and I, um, never called her back. It needed to be done. The whole situation was just too much. But sometimes . . . I feel guilty. I have trouble sleeping. And I need you to help me put it, you know, in the past."

Usually, I knew exactly what to say. With Madeline and Raj and even Chase, who were harder on themselves than any judgment they might seek, my part had been obvious. I hadn't even had to think. Now I sat for thirty precious seconds reconstructing Sandy's story in my head, looking for my role here and concluding, finally, that I had none.

"You say Carol is still alive?" I asked. "She lives here in Chicago?"

"Yes." Sandy sounded wary. "But I've heard through the grapevine that she's gotten very bad. She's in a wheelchair now. Mostly confined to home."

"I think you should go see her," I blurted. Three minutes and counting. "You're asking for forgiveness from the wrong person. The source of your guilt is, well, ongoing. She's sick and probably very scared. You can go to her and spend an afternoon, give her your friendship, admit your mistakes." I paused and took a breath. How to wrap this up?

"I think that will make you feel a lot better," I said.

Sandy appraised me with cool, unblinking eyes. "Yes, well, I'm afraid I'm not comfortable doing that," she said. "It would be too awkward. We haven't spoken in, oh, ten months, and I think I'm just going to leave well enough alone."

She waited, pointedly, like a customer who had not yet been handed her dry cleaning. I swallowed and wished I'd brought a bottle of water into this little room. "I'm sorry," I told her for the second time. "But I can't offer you anything. I understand your dilemma is difficult, but it's not . . ." The temperature in the room, or in my head, had risen at least five degrees. "Look, you still have a chance to make this right, and I sincerely encourage you to do so. But I cannot absolve you of a sin you have the power to change."

"A *sin*?" This syllable cut the air between us like a blade. "I would hardly call it a sin! I'm not even Catholic."

I closed my eyes, briefly, wondering where my timekeeper had gone and why she wasn't pounding on the door insisting we stop. At precisely that moment, a vibration started in my front pocket where I'd stowed the phone Madeline gave me. The sensation it produced in my groin further threw me off my game.

"Perhaps that was a poor choice of words." I said, rubbing my forehead and promising myself glasses of water—whole pitchers full— once I was out of this room. "But I just . . ." The knock finally came, more timid this time than before, but I nearly dropped to my knees in thanks. "I'm afraid I cannot give you what you want. Please see who- ever you paid for this, uh, meeting and tell them I said you should get a full refund."

"Fine." Sandy rose, clutching her purse to her body, shaky on her low heels. I reached a hand out to steady her, but she moved quickly away and to the side. "I think this is a very poor way to run a business," she said. I ached when I heard the thick tears in her voice.

"Yes. Yes, it is." I wanted more than anything to stay in my chair staring at the carpet's green nap. But she was a woman, standing and poised to leave the room. So I rose and held out my hand. I was surprised when she took it.

"I wish you all the best, Mrs. Nelson," I said. Then the high voice came again from the other side of the door.

"Hey, Father Gabe? I'm sorry to keep bugging you. But you're, like, going to be late for work?"

At which point, Sandy pulled her hand from mine, opened the door, and fled.

From: joytoyourworld@hotmail.com
To: Scott143@gmail.com
Re: Father Gabe

Scott—

I just had the best idea! At least, I think it's a great idea, but I'd love your expert opinion. Here's the story:

While I was eating lunch with Candy, Madeline came up and asked if I would use her car to drive Father Gabe to some bookstore where he works down south. I'm afraid even to drive that way, but of course I said yes. She was in a big rush and really rattled—which is unusual for Madeline. I think she has a crush on Father Gabe. She doesn't stand a chance with him: She's way too old, and there are hordes of younger, more attractive women that think he's hot (Candy said she'd do him in a minute). Not me, of course. You don't have to worry   But Madeline's smart, and I think she senses that I'm not going to compete with her. So anyway, she told me to go up to Floor 8 and knock on this random door at exactly 12:45 on the dot, then give him five minutes to finish what he was doing and knock again.

So I did that. I knocked. And I gave him the five-minute warning, but he didn't come out. So finally I knocked again, and then this lady came, I swear, running out of the room like he'd done something terrible to her. I looked inside, and there was Father Gabe, all sweaty and holding on to the table like he was going to have a heart attack. He asked me for some water and I got him some, and after he drank it I felt better because he didn't look so much like he was going to keel over.

So we went down to the garage and got in the car (and I start driving toward this place that is honest to God in gangland), and I asked him about the woman—if she was okay. He said he hoped so, but it had been a "difficult" meeting. He was really stressed so I tried to distract him. I told him about my parents and their church

167

and how they're waiting to hear about the new pope, how we all hope it'll be someone who lets people use birth control and says women can be priests. And he actually smiled when I said that! So we started talking for real, and he said he's hoping this pope will go back to supporting "service," though I wasn't sure what he meant by that. But I acted like I did, and he told me about his old church where they used to feed homeless people and how he could make a Thanksgiving dinner for 500 people.

He was inspiring, Scott. There are all sorts of things we don't know about Father Gabe, such as the fact that he used to go out and save homeless people in the middle of winter. He's like some hero who comes out in secret or at night. And you wouldn't believe how he gets when he's talking about stuff like this. He's actually kind of cute! (Not as cute as you, of course ;)) But he has a really nice smile, and I started picturing him in his robes. With a great haircut and some funky glasses, I think he'd have a ton of social media appeal. There's something very Clark Kent about him.

So here's my idea: We should set up a Facebook fan page for Father Gabe and build a whole campaign around making him look like a superhero. It can be subtle: just the way he stands and maybe even a phone booth in the background. It's a little bit funny but it's also a little bit true, you know? Like his superpower is coming in to take away people's guilt and suffering and cure their lives.

Ted already has a Facebook page and a "like" badge started for the business, and that's great. But I think this should be like the fan page for Justin Bieber or Michelle Obama. We could run little video clips of Father Gabe standing like Superman while saying quotable things and I bet anything they'd go wild on YouTube.

So what do you think? Isn't that a great idea? And what are we doing on Friday? I can totally get rid of my roommate if you want to come to my place.

xoxoxoxoxoxo

Joy

From: Scott Hicks
To: Ted Roman
Bcc: M. Madeline Murray, Isaac Beckwith
Subject: Facebook

Hi Ted—

I had this idea last nite as I was going to sleep. What if we made a Facebook fan page for Fr Gabe and made him look a little bit like a superhero? It can be subtle: just the way he stands and maybe even a phone booth in the background. It's a little bit funny but it's also a little bit true, you know? Like his superpower is coming in to take away people's guilt and suffering and cure their lives.

He's not a bad-looking guy when Madeline gets him cleeaned up and we could dress him up in those preist robes and make some YouTubes of him blessing people and stuff. I think making him like som rock star online mght be the way to go.

Sorry if I'm stepping on your toes. I just thougt it was a good idea that I shd really share.

Scott

From: Ted Roman
To: Scott Hicks
Subject: Re: Facebook

I have to admit, that's a pretty brilliant idea, and I like to think I would have come up with it myself eventually. We'll need to get Father Gabe in here soon for a photo shoot. I'll need budget for that (would you maybe put in a good word with Madeline?). Plus, it would be really funny if we add a mash-up; nothing too outrageous, maybe Gregorian chant with DMX's "Lord Give Me a Sign". I'm going to get on this right away.

Thanks, Scott. I'm sorry I jumped all over you about the What Not to Wear thing. Glad we were able to start fresh.

Ted

Jabber IM session—March 18, 20--

@MMM: Hey, did you see the email Scott sent Ted? It's a really great idea! Surprised that idiot thought of it.

@IBeck: Yeah. But he's a slimy motherfucker. You see he bcc'd us? And I'm pretty sure he stole it. There was a section in the middle that wasn't misspelled. Cut and paste job.

@MMM: Let's pretend we never got the email and give Ted credit. Drive him crazy.

@IBeck: Sounds like fun. But we've got other things to worry about.

@MMM: Whaaaaattttt?

@IBeck: I got a vm from Sandy Nelson this a.m. She was angry. Something strange happened w/Fr. Gabe yesterday.

@MMM: Bad?

@IBeck: Apparently. He refused to forgive her. Offered her a refund instead.

@MMM: Why?

@IBeck: No clue.

@MMM: U going to refund Sandy the $$?

@IBeck: If she tells me what happened.

@MMM: Hmmmm. Not good PR for 1st time.

@MMM: I'll talk 2 Gabe. Maybe we set some ground rules?

@IBeck: Like?
@MMM: Customer's always right? No, that won't work. What if he gets a murder confession? Or a pedophile???

@IBeck: Now you're just making up bad shit. Relax.

@MMM: K. I guess that can wait. But I'm putting our other beta clients on hold, til we work this out.

@IBeck: Sounds good. You on board with the superhero motif?

@MMM: Love it. Set it up. But remember, ALL TED'S IDEA.

@IBeck: U R an evil woman.

@MMM: I know . . .

From: joytoyourworld@hotmail.com
To: Scott143@gmail.com
Re: MY idea

I could not believe it when I got the memo from Ted this morning saying he was going to make a FB fan page for Father Gabe where he comes off like a superhero. I honestly believed that we had both come up with this great idea at exactly the same time because THAT'S HOW STUPID I AM.

But I went to talk to him, to see if I could help and maybe give him some of my other ideas from yesterday. And when I told him I thought of this, too, he looked at me like "oh you poor thing," and he asked if I'd told anyone. I almost said no, because you've got me trained to protect your farce of a marriage. But I said yes, that I mentioned the idea to you. And then he showed me your email. Scott, you are such a fucking asshole (literally) and I can't believe I let you do that to me the other week. For the record, I hated every second of it and spent the whole time praying for you to be done.

I told Ted there's no way you'll let him take all the credit. For sure, you let Madeline and her gay boyfriend know about this somehow. Forget about your surprise on Friday. I never want to see you again. And be prepared for all your work on Forgiveness4You to tank. It's a shame that other people have to suffer, too. But I've never been comfortable with this whole campaign, and I think it might be time to do the right thing.

By the way, I was looking through your phone log the other night. I have your wife's cell number, and if you breathe a word to anyone at Mason & Zeus about me not being on board with F4Y, I'll call and tell her everything.

J

From: joytoyourworld@hotmail.com
To: Jill Everson
Subject: You were right!!!!!!!!

Mommy—

It's me. I'm writing to you on a Hotmail account I set up for private stuff and this definitely qualifies.

Scott, that guy I was sort of seeing, turned out to be a jerk just like you said he would . . . Okay, you didn't actually say it, but I could tell you were thinking it and you were right. He's still married and even if his wife is a shrew and a total shopaholic (which I'm not sure I believe any more) it was wrong of me to get involved with him and I know that now. It's over and I promise I won't make that mistake ever again.

And Forgiveness4You, which I not only named but thought of a huge, great idea to market, is about to launch. But I'm streaming the pope election on CNN, and it's really getting to me! I see why you and Daddy have stuck with the church even if some of the priests turned out to be molesters. Because there's something really beautiful and historic, and I'm thinking now that maybe we shouldn't be turning confession into a business. Because it's really only for true believers, right? And it's not about money. I don't care what Madeline and Isaac say.

I'm sure I'll say this over and over throughout my lifetime, but you were right about everything and I'm so glad I have a mom like you.

Love,
Joy

From: Jill Everson
To: joytoyourworld@hotmail.com
Subject: Re: You were right!!!!!!!!

Hi Sweetheart—

I only have a minute because I volunteer today at the Somali refugee center.

I'm glad you're done with the married man. Those things always end badly for the woman—believe me, I know. Someday we'll talk.

As for the priest project, I think you should do what you know in your heart is right. But remember, we all have to make compromises to survive. For instance, your dad hated representing Monsanto in that big class-action suit a couple years ago, but he did it because it was his job and we had a daughter (you!) in an expensive college. So sometimes you have to weigh a lot of factors . . .

Must run. I'm in charge of opening up the food pantry, and there was a bit of a panic last time our ladies showed up and the doors were closed.

Love,
Mom

XI

I AWOKE TUESDAY MORNING TO THE SOUND OF A BIRD TRAPPED IN my apartment, an insistent chirping that had me up looking on window ledges and under the bed. There were only so many places it could hide.

I could see the bird nowhere, yet the chirps went on, stopping for a moment during which I—still on hands and knees in white underwear—listened intently. Then it started up again. I was crawling over my pants, which were lying where I'd discarded them on the floor, when I felt a vibration along with each twirp. I stuck my hand into the pocket and pulled out the phone Madeline had given me yesterday, now suddenly alive with motion and sound and lights.

I tried pushing "buttons," but the screen was smooth and flat and nothing happened. Eventually the phone went dead in my hand. Then it started up for a third time, and when I poked at the picture of a telephone receiver, Isaac's voice came through the device, tinny but real.

"Hey Father, sorry to wake you," he called from the little black box. I put it tentatively to my ear. "I was hoping we could get some breakfast before work. I'm in your neighborhood. Okay if I pull up?"

I looked at the clock. It was 6:30 a.m., an hour that I avoided because I used to spend it in prayer. Waking at dawn but without my ritual, I felt furtive and unprepared. "Yes," I said slowly. "But I really need to shower. Can you make it 7?"

"Sure," Isaac drawled. "I'll just wait here." And that's when I knew he was already in his car downstairs.

I hurried, dressing in the "business casual" outfit Raj had sold us. I once read in a magazine at a barbershop that men should dress to feel powerful. At the time, I hadn't understood it. But now I had a sense I'd need my olive green shirt and bold purple tie.

"Looking good, Father!" Isaac said as I opened the passenger door of what looked like Batman's car and folded myself in. "You must have read my mind. One of the things I want to talk about is a photo shoot we've got planned for 10 a.m. So don't spill any anything on that Versace, okay?"

Thus, I sat in a booth at the Daybreak Diner swathed in napkins, drinking my coffee with an anteater's extended lips. The room clattered and buzzed around me, that low happy noise that makes even a place you've never been feel homey. "Listen," Isaac said. "I want to understand what happened yesterday, with Sandy."

"Here ya go, gentlemen." A woman wearing a nametag that said "Dora" and hair in a beehive straight out of 1965 slid our plates onto the table. "Egg white omelet and dry toast," she said to Isaac, "and the Farm Hand special for you," she cooed, turning toward me. "You're my favorite. I like a man who eats ham in the morning." Then she winked one spidery eyelash and walked away.

"I'm not sure I can talk about it," I said, fork suspended above my plate. I was starving but stopped by this question. "Isn't what people confess to me confidential?"

Isaac was already eating; he shook his head and swallowed. "We wrote the language of the contract very carefully. It's got all the standard outs that priests get: You have the right to go to the police if some guy tells you he's got a sex slave locked in his basement. But we also put in a clause about being able to discuss the content of your sessions 'as a whole' for business purposes."

"As a whole?" I pierced one perfect egg, and it oozed steaming yolk.

"Yeah. You've had one session so far. With Sandy. She *is* the whole. Go ahead and eat, Father."

I piled a bite of egg and ham on toast and bit into it, closing my eyes and giving up silent thanks to God. When I opened my eyes again, Isaac was pushing his plate away. "Uh, I've gotta get going in about ten, fifteen minutes, and we have a couple things to discuss. So, about Sandy?"

"I felt I couldn't offer her anything, under the circumstances. She'd abandoned a very ill friend who needed her—who *still* needs her—and she wanted me to forgive her, both from what she'd done in the past and, as I understood it, what she plans to do in the future."

"But isn't that the way it works? A guy comes in to confess every week, says I slept with my secretary, the priest blesses him and gives him ten Hail Marys with the understanding that he's just going to go out and do it all over again? Isn't that what Indulgences are for, perpetual forgiveness?"

I laughed involuntarily. "Your Catholicism shows up in random ways," I told Isaac. "Like the way you have everyone at the agency calling me Father Gabe."

"It's a disease that leaves something inside you," Isaac said. "Like chicken pox and shingles. I'll never quite be cured."

"Why did you leave the church?" My stomach was straining, but I was still hungry for something. I soaked up the last of my egg yolk with toast.

"The real answer is probably long and complicated and has something to do with my inability to be faithful. But the short answer is: because the Catholic Church teaches that who I am is perverse and a 'violation of divine law.'"

"You could have gone to confession every week or month, or however often you chose, admitted that you sinned and received absolution. Many gay men do."

"How does that make sense?" Isaac asked. "I'm still a gay man, and I intend to have sex with men. With *one* man, at this point—if I ever get to see him again. But receiving absolution every week like I'm punching a ticket? That sounds . . ."

"Pointless?" I was finally sated so I pushed my plate to touch Isaac's and tore off the napkins that draped me. "What the Catholic Church teaches about homosexuality is wrong, on so many levels. But it's also really shrewd. People buy it. Gay men and lesbians who've never done a thing to hurt anyone, at least not where sex is concerned, spend a lifetime feeling guilty. And Church doctrine locks them into this ridiculous merry-go-round of so-called sin and absolution—like a lifetime membership."

"Excellent retention tactic." Isaac waved at Dora and made a scribbling motion in the air.

"Then again, maybe not," I said. "It didn't work on you."

"I'm smarter than most," he said, grinning like a boy.

"So am I," I said. "I have nothing to offer someone who comes to me and says 'I've hurt someone and I'm going to continue to hurt her, though it's in my power to change things, and I want to be forgiven.' Would the Catholic Church offer Sandy weekly redemption? Probably. But I can't hand out my blessing like some . . . some . . . paid flower delivery."

"So what you're saying . . . Thank you," he said to Dora when she dropped the bill in a puddle of water that had sweated off his glass.

"You come back soon, sweetheart," she said to me, grazing my hand with her red-painted nails before she left.

"So what you're saying," Isaac began again as we left the café and climbed into his Batmobile, "is that we're running a for-profit business with higher moral standards than the Catholic Church?"

"I wouldn't say higher, necessarily." The spires of Michigan Avenue loomed and glittered in the bright morning sun. "Just different."

• • •

By the time we arrived downtown, Isaac had spoken at length about a photo shoot, "social media entry points," and some campaign to make me a forgiveness hero, which sounded silly in the way so many wildly popular television shows do if someone tries to explain them to you.

He dropped me off at a salon a block past Mason & Zeus with instructions to go inside and submit to whatever Henry deemed best. "You're irresistible, Father," Isaac said. "Did you see that waitress? She wanted to rip your clothes off right there in the booth, despite your $9 haircut. Imagine what a really good style will do."

I couldn't imagine, or I was afraid to. I'm not quite sure which. The shop was still technically closed, so it was just the two of us. Henry—a man-and-a-half size person with long, graying golden locks of hair—draped me with something soft and began by massaging my neck with oil, which was startling at first. I might have objected, but it felt too good.

He talked in a shouting voice during the entire shampooing portion of the procedure. I could have sworn he said, "I was on a Bugis Schooner." But the truth is, I wasn't really listening. With my eyes closed, I could pretend it was Madeline holding my neck and rubbing fragrant soap gently on my head.

"Indonesia!" Henry boomed, as he toweled me. "No one here understands. It's not like any place else on earth. Seventeen thousand islands! No way anyone could see them all. That gives me hope!" He propelled me back to the chair and gave a little shove on my back that meant I should sit. This was a little like ballroom dancing, with its gentle leading cues.

Henry had taken my glasses so his reflection in the mirror above my head was downright lion-like in its fuzzy unreality. I could imagine him in the jungles of Bali or Borneo (though I had no idea whether either place actually had lions), crouching as he did now to examine my right temple. "What do you think, Father? Highlights or just a cut?"

"Just a cut," I said, inferring that "highlights" was the more involved process.

"All righty then." Henry moved around me as if I were prey. "I think I can work with this. Have you ever been overseas, Father?"

"Paris," I said. "And, well, Rome, of course."

"Not a big fan of France." The scissors made a soothing, snippety sound. Full of food as I was, I could have drifted to sleep in Henry's chair. "Now, Rome, on the other hand. Loved it. But it was mostly the food. Fagiole! You ever had fagiole, Father?"

I searched my memory for such a thing, but by the time I'd come up with the bean dish Mother Aemilia would serve on Sunday evenings, Henry had moved on. "Prague. Christ, I had more amazing women in Prague than anywhere else on this earth, literally." He spun the chair to the left, my own little teacup ride. "You know where I never got, though, Father? South America. Would you believe it? Right down south, and it's the only continent other than Antarctica that I never set foot on. Peru. There's my goal. I mean, how hard can it be? It's even the same time zone! Nothing to get used to. Except my Spanish is pretty rusty. But still."

He paused and it roused me, the way the sudden absence of an engine sound will. "What took you to so many places?" I asked. "Was it a job?"

Henry snorted. "Hardly. More the opposite. I kept leaving jobs, because I'd get this feeling and the only thing that would make it stop was *moving*. Somewhere, anywhere. Except it had to be new."

"What feeling?" I asked. I'd known people like this: priests who asked for assignments in remote locations, addicts who surfed from city to city always looking for something they never found.

"Loneliness." Henry had stopped cutting, and he stood stock straight behind me, his blurred reflection looming in the mirror. "I can't explain it. But when I was in one place for too long—and I'm talking *months*, not years—I'd get this feeling like I was going to die. The only thing that helped was to pick up and go to a place I'd never been. Where I didn't know a soul. I know it sounds backward, but that's the way it's always been for me."

He bent again and went back to the business of my hair, but he was slower, more deliberate now. "That's how I ended up doing this," Henry said, smoothing a section on my crown. "When I was younger, I worked construction and utility and docks. All hard labor. But a body can only do that for so long, and I knew this girl who taught at Aveda. We worked out a deal. You know."

"So now you stay in one place," I said. Henry circled the chair and crouched directly in front of me, pulling strands down on either side of my forehead. "What changed?"

"My parents died." He sighed heavily, and his breath smelled like cinnamon gum.

"I'm sorry."

"So was I. But not for the right reason. All those years, they were the people bringing me back. I'd work until I had enough cash for a one-way ticket and maybe two, three, four weeks of fun. Then, when the money was gone, I'd call my mom and dad and tell them how I was broke and stuck in Jakarta or Port-Au-Prince or Istanbul, wherever I was. And they'd wire me the cash to get home."

He sighed again, from behind me, and I could feel the air on my neck in places that used to be covered. "When they died—my mom first, then my dad about six months later—there was nothing left. In fact, less than that. They'd taken a second mortgage on the house. It took me four years to pay it off."

"The bank probably would have forgiven that," I said. I'll admit, this was a test.

He shook his head, and his ringlets swung; that hair had to have something to do with Henry's getting this job. He looked like the man on the cover of the pornographic romance novels I sold—or rather, the way his much-older uncle might look.

"It was my debt," he said. "Mine to pay. The sad thing is, I didn't get that 'til after they were gone." Then he turned on a hair dryer and our conversation disappeared in its roar.

When he was done, Henry holstered the hair dryer and handed me my glasses. "Have a look." My reflection gazed back at me from underneath a neat businessman's cut with an exotic fringe in front. "See? You look just like that guy on *Mad Men*," Henry said, and I nodded, though I had only a vague idea what he meant.

He removed my cape, holding it carefully to cradle the fallen hair. "You know, your parents . . ." I said, but Henry backed away and held up one hand. He had to let go of one side of the fabric in order to do this and dark wisps fluttered to the ground as he spoke.

"I know what you do, Father. Isaac told me. And I'm not asking for your forgiveness. I know what I did, and I know I'd probably do it again. It's how God made me, but that still don't make it right."

I could find no hole in Henry's logic, yet it didn't make sense. But he was determined now. "Bill's all paid, and I got a nice tip," he told me, offering me his huge hand as I dismounted. "You can just go."

Walking the block to Mason & Zeus, I turned my face toward the pale sun. If I were about to go back into that room where I met Sandy, I'd need the memory of light.

"Father Gabe?" Candy squealed when she saw me. "I didn't think you could get even cuter. But I was wrong!" She rose from her desk in an outfit so tight and intricately laced I wondered if she'd have to be cut out of it at night.

But instead of taking me to the eighth floor, Candy led me to the conference room where we'd met with the investors the week before. The large table had been shoved to one side and all but one chair removed from the room. There were lights on stands and large translucent discs like enormous Frisbees. Two of the younger people— including the girl, Joy, who'd recently driven me to work—sat on the edge of the table, waiting.

"Ready for your photo session?" Joy came forward with her hand out, but I didn't know where to look. Her breasts were high and mostly exposed, a thin gold necklace with a cross disappearing between them. I was afraid if I moved I might touch one. When I didn't shake her hand she stretched up instead to kiss my cheek. "Don't worry. You're going to be great. Have you met Ted?"

A young black man with my exact haircut came forward. He wore a shirt striped like Joseph's coat of many colors and a small diamond stud in each ear. I wondered what these dazzling people would have thought of the younger me, trading in his Levi's and Freddie Mercury glasses for a novitiate's robe. "Good morning, Father. Ted Roman. I'm in charge of interactive media."

"Nice to meet you, Ted," I said, shaking his hand. "I have no idea what that is."

He grinned and clasped my hand with both of his. Ted was slender and boyish, but his grip was sure. "Facebook, Twitter, Tumblr, Instagram, Snapchat. Basically everything that happens on a device."

I shook my head.

"It doesn't matter, Father Gabe," Joy said, darting in front of Ted to take my arm. I sensed a tug-of-war with myself as the rope; if this was the case, I was hoping he'd win. "We'll talk you through this."

But "talk" turned out to be not what this was. I was placed in a chair where Joy hovered over me with a container of makeup in her hand. "There's really nothing to do here," she said, wiping me here and there with a little puff. "The five o'clock shadow really works for you. Maybe just a little . . ."—she leaned straight over, and the cross popped out of her shirt to dangle in front of me—"right here around the eyes."

By the time she'd pronounced me done, there were three more men in the room. I reached for my glasses, but Joy put her hand out and said, "No, try these," handing me a pair of frames with no corrective lenses. "Perfect!" she cheered somewhat too effusively, as I wobbled to stand. It would be a day of wandering blind as my blurred vision made the shifting glare of the lights even more intense.

Across the room stood a grizzled wolf of a man, two cameras hanging on thick straps around his neck. The other two men—black-clad Ted-aged creatures from what I could tell—milled around with more enormous lighted shells. I was placed in the midst of these and blinked madly in the glare. The wolf came forward. "Try to stay still, Father," he growled. "Just relax. You'll get used to the lights."

My body was contorted into positions that seemed outlandish: one hand to my chin; head forward and arms behind me as if I were skiing; legs spread apart while my arms were crossed. "That's great, just great, love. Sorry . . . Father," the wolf said. He was lying at my feet, camera pointed up. "There! Hold that. Don't. Move!!" His shutter clicked as fast as machine-gun fire. I grimaced and sweated in the lights.

"I think we need something a little more natural." I heard Madeline's voice and turned toward it, but her body, her face, were veiled by light. "Here . . ."

There was a shuffling as she came toward me, first just luminous movement and then, gradually, the form of Madeline emerging from the glow. When she got right under my nose, I saw she was in a pale blue dress that wrapped around her body in different, confounding ways. Why was every woman in this place wearing clothes that seemed like puzzles I wanted to solve?

"Gabe, why don't you try this?" Madeline pushed me gently to sit on the edge of the table. Then her hands were on my tie, loosening the knot.

I looked down and my lips brushed her hair. It was accidental, and no one seemed to notice—not even Madeline—but it was as if an animal in my body had woken up. It was more than just the hard ache rising against the front of my pants. That, I was used to. But this? There was urgency everywhere in me, my chest and legs and neck, pulsing with the desire to touch her. I crossed my arms, clenching my hands inside soggy armpits.

"No, no. Let's take these out." Madeline began prying at my biceps, which only made me tighten my grip. "Gabe! This isn't funny."

By this point, I was wild. The wolf and his assistants were watching me. Ted was pressing a bottle of water on me, asking if I needed to rest for a few minutes. Madeline stood close enough to lick, and I felt certain that if I let myself lose vigilance, I would turn and lift her off the ground, drive her against a wall, and rip through the maze of her dress.

I don't know what would have happened next if I hadn't been saved by Joy, who must have left the room unnoticed at some earlier point. Now, blessedly, she burst back in. "There's white smoke! They've elected a new pope. Isaac says we should all go to the war room to watch. This will definitely affect our strategy going forward."

"Christ," said the cameraman. "Fine, but you're paying me for the time."

Madeline backed away a few inches, and my heart rate improved. "Shall we?" she asked. And I looked into her dark eyes, not at all sure what she meant. Everyone else was filing out. My relief at no longer being on display was too immense to contain. I loosened my arms and sat back on the table, reaching for the water Ted had left there and drinking half the bottle at once.

I closed my eyes and recalled the smells of Vatican City. Seawater and the dust of old stone. The metal-and-earth scent of a thurible packed with incense. I could still feel the weight of the chain in my hands. I did not know if I was actually longing to be there, in St. Peter's Square, or if I only wished to long for it. Whichever it was, yearning unfolded in me, and I felt the hope that I had during two previous papal elections: that this would be the man who could show me the lighted way.

Years ago I had applied for a papal audience, believing I could finally unburden my soul. That was during the reign of Pope John Paul II. I showed up at the appointed time and had been waiting for three hours when handlers—Italians who looked and dressed oddly like Tommy Lee Jones in *Men in Black*—told me that the Holy Father had been called to Church business, and that I should come back some other day. The next available slot was nineteen months hence.

Madeline came and sat next to me, hoisting herself primly up onto the tabletop—which made my heart pick up again. "This is ridiculously hard on you, isn't it?"

I considered her question carefully. To say yes struck me as unmanly, certainly unpriestlike. We were trained to remain as oblivious as possible to earthly things. Nothing mattered but one's relationship to the Church and to God. I'd spent years "praying away" both lust and fear.

But to say no would be a lie.

"I have to ask. Why are you doing this, Gabe?" Madeline inched closer. "I know I started it, so that may seem like a strange question. But I've been watching for the past few days and this just isn't . . . you."

I sat heavily. It was clear that Madeline was providing me with an escape. This time there was no need for tearful, confusing speeches. I could leave all this—the photography sessions and frantic cab rides, Isaac's early-morning chirping from my phone—and I could go back to . . . what? I would continue to be haunted by memories of Aidan and hear the guilty stories of nearly everyone I met. But I would do so without these people who fed me Thai food and got me drunk and cut my hair like some madman on TV.

"You're right, this isn't me," I said to Madeline. And in the single bravest act I've ever committed, I took her hand. "But. Nothing is."

She clasped my fingers in her tiny, steely grasp. Then Madeline drew closer, her breasts grazing my side from inside that wonderfully perplexing dress. She tilted her face up, and this time I kissed her, just the way I had imagined a hundred times since that night in her car. Her lips were chapped, parted. She smelled of coffee and a peachy hair gel—or perhaps that was me.

"Gabe." Madeline stood to slip her arms around my still-damp chest. Then she leaned against me, her body tight between my legs, and I lost consciousness everywhere else. The room and its scatter of lighting equipment were gone. I was kissing Madeline slowly and it was wet, and I was feeling her swivel against the thing I had become. Hard, hot, huge to bursting. My mind was erased, filled with nothing but the need to be inside her. In the combined history of my mostly disappointing sexual encounters, I had never experienced this.

"Father Gabe, they've elected a . . . Oh!" I focused as well as I was able on the doorway beyond the soft, dark hair in my hands. A blur that seemed to be Joy stood there, hand clapped to her mouth. Inside my arms, I felt Madeline curl in defeat for the briefest second then turn with determination to face Joy.

"We're going to need a few minutes here," she said. "Could you get the door? And please, sweetheart." She paused to draw a breath. "Keep your mouth *shut.*"

I was frozen, waiting to see what would happen next. Humans have free will; it's one of the first things young priests grapple with.

You can never assume where choice is concerned. But Joy backed away, still watching us, dragging the doorknob in one hand. When finally the door clicked shut Madeline—now facing out—slumped back against me and lay her head on my chest. "Oh, we are in a world of shit," she said, rocking gently from side to side. "That girl is telling someone right now. I guarantee."

I adjusted myself discreetly then reached up to stroke Madeline's hair. I'd deflated to a degree that was, in one sense, more comfortable. But I could tell what had happened before was imminent. My body was lying in wait. Should Madeline turn to face me or put her hand on my thigh I risked pushing her up against the door and lifting her skirt. Just thinking about it, my breathing became ragged. I calculated her weight and whether I could lift her sufficiently to enter her while standing. I decided I could.

"Gabe?" she said, and I heard something lonely in the word. "What are we going to do?"

"We're going to fix ourselves up and go out there," I said, pulling her in closer until the friction made me nearly lose the thread of what I was thinking. "We're going to find out who has been elected to lead the Church. Then what happens is up to you. But I'm hoping we'll go somewhere together and find a bed." My mouth was so near her ear I had lowered my voice to a whisper, which made me braver. "Or, it doesn't have to be a bed. A couch. A car seat. A park bench. Anywhere but here."

Madeline laughed, and I was elated. There was a flicker of my old self, counseling the new; this predicament was of the earth, utterly human, hardly dire.

"What a story that would make," she said. "Ex-priest and local executive arrested for public indecency. I don't know if that would kill our business or help it! You could get a bad boy reputation: the Anthony Bourdain of forgiveness."

I tightened my arms around her and placed my chin on her

shoulder. I felt more at peace, more certain of my place, than I had since my early days in the priesthood. But I knew this was a fiction. As soon as we stepped out of this room, the pressures and constraints of the outer world would come upon us. I reminded myself that God was with us, He had made us this way. It was our duty to find grace in freedom.

"You're right," Madeline said, as if she could hear what I was thinking. "We need to go out there."

She pulled away to check herself, running her hands over hips, breasts, and hair to make sure everything was smoothed down and contained. Once she was satisfied, Madeline shook her body slowly from her pointed high heels all the way up to her shoulders, rolling them back as if marching into battle. I imagined her doing exactly that move naked under me, and before I could think of something else, something somber or gruesome, every drop of blood in my body surged toward my loins. "Ready?" she asked.

"You go," I said faintly. "I need . . . a little time."

Madeline was wearing her CEO face now. "But you were the one who said . . ." Her voice was strained, her mouth set and verging on grim. "All right, fine. I think it's important that you make an appearance though. Go on about the day. We're launching in forty-eight hours, you know."

"I know." I looked down at my lap, which I realized ten seconds too late looked weak. Like avoidance or betrayal. When I was really only doing the thing I remembered so clearly—so painfully—from adolescence: looking to see if the tent in my pants was obvious. Waiting sweatily for it to collapse.

As a young Catholic boy, I had taken the warning against masturbation to heart. But in my late teens, I'd run like a freight train over all the lessons of my youth, jerking off two, sometimes three times a day between hazy hours of getting high. It was brilliantly effective. A couple quick strokes in a men's room could relieve me. And there were half a dozen times I'd reverted to this out of necessity as a priest: before a baptism or a dinner party when I could not crouch or stay seated. I assumed that God in all his wisdom would understand.

Madeline, however, did not seem to. And shame over my lack of control, my arrested, still-adolescent approach to sex, made it impossible for me to explain.

"All right." She walked away, and the distance grew between us. "I guess I'll see you later," she said softly as she opened the door. And then she was gone.

Reuters
Breaking story . . .
March 18, 20--

Pope Vincent to Lead the Catholic Church

White smoke poured from the Sistine Chapel today when Chilean Cardinal Alejandro Antonioni was named the new pope.

The first South American pontiff in history, he has taken the name Pope Vincent in honor of St. Vincent de Paul, the seventeenth-century priest who dedicated his life to serving the poor.

Pope Vincent looked timid, hesitating a moment on the balcony of St. Peter's Basilica before stepping out to greet the huge crowds gathered in the square below.

"I ask a favor of you . . . pray for me," he said, explaining that the 114 other cardinal-electors "went almost to the end of the world" to find a new leader.

A Jesuit, Pope Vincent has spent his life as a priest focusing on service to the poor and marginalized. He is known for favoring simple vestments, driving his own seven-year-old car, and refusing the luxuries afforded bishops in the Catholic Church.

"What the church needs most today is the ability to heal wounds and to warm the hearts of the faithful," the new pope said, before blessing the cheering crowd.

From: Isaac Beckwith
To: Forgiveness Team
Re: Pope Vincent

Okay, people, I hope you're studying up. This is what we've been waiting for, and let me say, in case you haven't figured it out already, Pope Vincent is throwing a monkey wrench (what does that phrase even mean? Abel???) into the marketing plan for F4Y.

Remember, we're basing audience response among former Catholics—our primary market at launch, according to Joy's Opportunity Landscape—on people feeling distanced and disillusioned by the Church. But this new pope may change the game. I wish I could tell you I saw this coming. But never in my wildest dreams did I think the conclave would elect a guy like this.

First, he's a Jesuit. Literally that means he's part of the Society of Jesus, a band of priests that wears rags and lives in poverty, serving the poor and the sick. These are the saints who wash the feet of the homeless. They consider themselves "soldiers" in the battle to make this world a better, more godly place. These guys rescued hordes of Jews during the Holocaust! Bottom line: Jesuits rock. Great historical PR.

Second, people love him already. Think Obama, November 5, 2008. Pope Vincent is the great white hope, so to speak. Right now, Catholics are a little high on his goodness. They're relieved to be done with the old, cranky bad pope and feeling better about who they are.

What does all this mean? A) We may have to change tactics. For instance, we might have to remove all references to the Church. B) We're going to reassess how to talk about Father Gabe. We might want to drop the priest connection altogether. Or we might go ahead and tie him to the Church but do it carefully, with reverence. I've got a couple focus groups working 24/7 to tell us which. C) We're going to delay launch by three days. I think it's ill-advised to go out there the same week as this papal election. So let's start fresh next Monday. By that time, we'll have more information and a revised creative brief.

Any questions, please see me or Madeline personally. I cannot stress this strongly enough: YOUR DISCRETION IS CRITICAL. Don't talk about F4Y to anyone—and by anyone, I mean your wives or husbands or brothers or sisters or one-night stands. If you need to talk to someone, call me. Midnight, 4 a.m., I don't care. Just keep it between us.

Also, if you have any weekend plans, cancel them. We'll be revising straight through, Friday to Sunday. No excuses. Let's get this sucker launched!

IB

From: joytoyourworld@hotmail.com
To: Jill Everson
Subject: I'm going to get fired!!!!!!

Mommy—

Before you get upset, I want you to know you should be proud of me. I did the right thing and called some people about what Madeline and Isaac are doing with Father Gabe. It's lucky Daddy is a lawyer because I violated my non-disclosure agreement and I probably could get sued, but it was worth it and I know you're going to think so, too.

I'll be honest. I've been drinking tonight. Cosmos, because I was feeling very Carrie and Samantha and remembering how we went to the first Sex and the City movie together back when I was in junior high. I was with the whole Forgiveness team tonight. We worked till like 9:30 then went to McGill's for a "planning session," which was really just a big drunkfest. Scott was there, too, but we totally avoided each other.

I don't think I really explained everything that happened, so I'll start at the beginning. A few days ago, Madeline asked me to drive Fr Gabe to the bookstore where he works. (I know that sounds strange, but he does.) So we got in Madeline's car and he was really tense because he'd just had a forgiveness session with some older woman who got v. angry and stormed out.

As we were driving, Father Gabe loosened up with me and started telling me things about his childhood and how he felt about the pope. It was nice and I started to really like him. That's when I had this brainstorm about making him into a "forgiveness hero," making that his brand. It's the kind of creativity a strategist doesn't usually get to contribute, so I was really proud. But I stupidly told Scott, who STOLE my idea! That was the day I broke up with him and maybe you're thinking I got what I deserved because what we were doing was dishonest. Well, don't think I haven't thought of that! I do feel guilty for sleeping with a married man. But you have to remember, Scott lied to me when he told me how unhappy he was and made it sound like he was definitely leaving his wife.

Anyway, this morning I saw the older lady in the elevator and asked her what happened w Fr Gabe. At first she told me it was none of my business and I said fine, I was only trying to help; then she said she was sorry, but it still made her upset. She paid for a forgiveness, but then she got into the room and Fr Gabe refused! He said he wouldn't forgive her at all and he wouldn't give her a good reason so she thinks the whole thing is a rip-off b/c she's been trying to get ahold of Isaac to get her money back and he hasn't returned her calls.

Part of me was on the side of admiring Father Gabe. I mean, this woman must have done something really terrible if he wouldn't forgive her. I really believed this was about his integrity. But then, after we had a photo shoot (where he looked really hot thanks to the haircut and glasses I suggested), I found him making out with Madeline!! Seriously, they were going at it right on the table in the conference room. And this is while the new pope was being announced! I mean, there was white smoke coming out of the chimney, and I thought, "Oh, Father Gabe shouldn't be missing this," so I went to find him and that's when I saw them. It was so gross. Madeline is practically your age. No offense.

Then, after all that, Madeline came into the room where we were all watching TV. It was right at the moment when Pope Vincent was coming out to talk and bless people. But she made us turn it off so we could work another 29-hour day. Later, I saw her talking to Isaac (he's the PR guru from Texas), and next thing you know we're getting this memo that says the pope is all bad news for us because he's a Jesuit and Catholics might like him enough to stick with the Church instead of confessing to Fr Gabe.

Well, I'd just gotten to a boiling point where the hypocrisy was making me furious. So I told Candy that I had a really bad period and I needed to go home and change my clothes, maybe take a nap, so could she cover for me? And she did. She watched my email and sent vague answers that said things like, "On a research call right now. Can I get back to you in 30 minutes?" Then I took my iPhone (thanks for still paying the bill for that, by the way) and went to a coffee shop a few streets over and called every newspaper and TV network I could think of.

The first two were like, "Yeah? So what's the big deal? There's a priest starting a business in Chicago. Doesn't sound like news." So I got an iced mocha, and I tried to figure out how Isaac would talk to people about this. So the next call I made, I kind of spun the whole story about how it was the very same week that the new pope was elected and Mason & Zeus was going out with this very anti-Catholic start-up and did that seem like just a coincidence?

I lucked out this time because the woman I was talking to said her station wasn't really interested but I should call the religion reporter at the Chronicle. She even gave me his direct number. So I called and talked to this guy who sounded like he was about 100 years old, but he said, "Oh, yeah, Gabe McKenna . . ." and it turns out this guy covered it when Father Gabe left the priesthood. And here's the amazing part: He also remembered that there was some cover-up, like a police record on Father Gabe. And I said that makes sense, because there's something wrong with him and I think he's a total manipulator.

Finally this old dude said he was going to find the business reporter, the guy who covers stuff like advertising, and maybe they could work this from two angles and come up with a story, because it sounded interesting. But they absolutely had to have someone who was willing to speak on the record. Without it they'd look stupid, like they were just harassing a Chicago-based business, plus an ex-priest who never hurt anyone. And I said fine, I'm done with Mason & Zeus anyway. They're all liars and cheats.

I'd been gone like two hours, so I had to call Candy and say the cramps got so bad I had to make a hot water bottle and take six Advil, but I'm finally on my way back. And she was sympathetic, but she said Madeline was looking for me and I should hurry. I'd been planning to go somewhere and buy a different pair of pants so Candy wouldn't think I was just using her, but at that point I decided it wasn't worth it, I should just go back and see what happened.

So it was after five o'clock and I knew I'd be in big trouble. I went into the office and found Candy right away to thank her and promise I'll take her to lunch next week—which I'm probably not going to do because I doubt I'll still be working there. But she was very sweet and said I should go find Madeline and tell her the truth (which was actually a lie) because like five people had noticed I was gone. And SCOTT, that jerk-face, was making a big deal about how everyone else was staying late but there seemed to be different rules for me.

But when I went to Madeline's office she was actually nice to me, which was kind of confusing b/c it could have been real or she could have just been worried I'd tell everyone at the office about her kissing Father Gabe. She said she appreciated my hard work and told me how valuable I was to the team and I was starting to regret talking to the reporter, but at the same time I could feel my phone vibrating over and over and I knew he was trying to call me back.

By this time it was about six o'clock. We had dinner where they served bad, soggy pizza and talked about strategy for about an hour. We were going to go out with a whole alternate ad campaign that doesn't use words like "absolution" (because it's too religious)—this was Scott's idea. But I said I think it's a mistake because you want your advertising to be consistent, and we can't have one billboard saying one thing and another one saying something else. I mean, does Nike say "Just Do It!" in New York but something else entirely different in DC? No.

Then the most amazing thing happened: Madeline said I was right and she told Scott to stick with the campaign we have, just tweak the language a little. Also, it turns out they're interviewing like three guys to back up Father Gabe and one of them is an ex-priest but two of them are like ministers or rabbis, I'm not sure. Afterward, Isaac came up to me and said, "Good work," and I decided right then that I wasn't going to call the Chronicle back for sure.

Only you're probably wondering why I still think I'm going to get fired? Because after we got to the bar, finally, after working till nearly nine, and I had a little more to drink than I should have, I went into the ladies room and checked my messages. And you're not going to believe this. The reporter had left two voice mails and a text telling me that he was going to put the story about Forgiveness4You in Thursday's paper, along with information about Father Gabe BEING A COCAINE DEALER. I swear, that's exactly what he said.

And maybe it was the Cosmos, but it all just totally added up in my head: the business, the scene with Madeline, the way I can't get a read on Father Gabe. Now this drug thing. So I texted back yes, they could go ahead with my quotes and use my name, and then I went back out to the bar and had one more drink—because I didn't want to look suspicious—before I left. (Of course, I took a cab.)

So I just wanted to warn you and Daddy before the story hits.

And I need to confess a few things. My new apartment overlooks the lake, it costs $3,200 a month, and Rebecca moved out last November, which I never told you b/c I knew you'd be mad. Also I got a little behind on my credit cards. All to say, if I get fired I'm either going to need to come home for a while or $12,000 to tide me over. Maybe both. But you'll get every penny back. I think I'm pretty good at my job, and if it weren't for all the craziness going on around me, I might have been promoted to associate director next year.

I'm going to bed now. And I'll probably be hung over in the morning, so if you want to call me please don't do it till after noon.

xoxoxoxoxo

Joy

XII

URING THE YEARS I WAS IN THE MONASTERY—AND AFTERWARD,
as a novice—I also attended Narcotics Anonymous every Tuesday and
Thursday night. But I hadn't been to a meeting for a long time. I left
NA around age thirty, when the group's version of a higher power
began competing for authority with God the Father, insisting that my
sobriety was more important than anything—including my faith in
Him. Defecting was a dangerous decision. I'd been clean in the in-
terim. But I wasn't, as they say, "working the steps."

And though I'd never been to McGill's before, it was strikingly
familiar. Nostalgic even: the tattooed bartender who doubled as a
bouncer, the jittery fellow hanging out by the men's room. Seventies
country-rock on the now-digital jukebox, swivel stools with scarred
vinyl, and everywhere the wet doggy smell of beer and sweat. Social
media was a complete mystery to me, but here was a culture I knew.

I sat at the end of our long table—now mostly empty as people
were up milling and dancing—gripping a sticky mug full of some kind
of ale. This was one of the only ways bars had changed since my
youth: everyone, it seemed, was now brewing their own craft beer.
No more weak, flat, urinous Schlitz; even dive bars like this one had
huge stainless steel vats and served home brew with names like Genius
and Barking Frog. I had opted for the former.

The noise was crushing and I sank into it, exhausted, relieved. There were ten months—literally forgotten now—when I lived only at night in places like this, alighting at dawn to sleep at my mother's house through the daylight hours. A vampire. That was my other calling, and I imagined myself now if things had gone differently, the man I might have become.

At forty-two, my other self might be a customer of the jittery man—or, more likely, his boss. That Gabe would go out into the fray, catch Joy and laugh off the scene she'd walked in on earlier. He would sit next to Madeline, one arm flung casually behind her shoulders. He would offer to take her home at the end of this endless evening, decipher her dress, and mount her in the back of a cab.

Just as I was picturing his/my hand disappearing into the warmth under her skirt, the television over the bar shifted to an image of the new pope, grinning and waving, his round elfin face wearing my grandfather's jutting chin. This man would understand my conflict, I was fairly certain. His face was without costume, full of wonder. Finally, just after I'd departed the Church, one of the good guys came in.

Bleary, I imagined picking up a phone to tell the pope about what I did to Aidan, about what I wanted to do to Madeline, about my fleetingly impure and confusing thoughts regarding Jem. Even better, I could buy a plane ticket to Rome! I still knew people there. One of them might help me get an audience, and it would go differently this time. Forget what the man in the back of the bar was selling. What Pope Vincent had was a different kind of drug—less immediate but more powerful when it worked.

"Mind if I join you, Father?" Scott shouted. It was the only way to communicate in this place.

I nodded, and he sat in the chair to my left. We had hardly spoken prior to this moment, and I looked at Scott as if for the first time. He was boyish and blond and big-muscled, like an actor in a television show about surfers. If I were to close my eyes, I'd picture him with a shark's tooth around his neck.

Instead, I tilted my head and scanned the crowd, picking out my Mason & Zeus colleagues. Ted, small and dapper with his thin, striped tie. Isaac, leaning his tall, hard body against the bar. Candy and Joy moving like shiny little stars among the cloddish beer-swilling patrons. They looked ready to be cast in a movie about young professionals in the big city. I flashed drunkenly on the scene where I had stood, newly shorn and wearing someone else's glasses in my Superman pose.

"I slept with her, you know. Joy?" I turned to Scott who was looking down at his left hand, the gold circle on his ring finger dull. "I cheated on my wife."

I nodded, secretly admiring his oxen approach. "Yes, I know."

"You do? Man!" Scott rolled his lazy eyes up to the ceiling, and I could see what he was thinking as clearly as if it were printed across his forehead: *Even the priest heard about me and Joy? That's it. I'm dead.*

"I didn't mean to. Really. I never . . ." He paused and gulped from his glass. "Okay, there was one other time, but that was years ago when Dana was pregnant. Never since then. 'Til . . ." He tipped his head in Joy's direction. "Her."

He stopped, looking darkly miserable. But I couldn't decipher if it was related to infidelity as a concept, or to Joy herself.

"She's, like . . . witchy," he shouted in my ear, then looked around as if he'd been caught at something. "Is that a word?"

"Sure." I clapped him mildly on the arm. A guy gesture. "Very Shakespearean."

"Yeah," he said. "Like that. I mean, I wasn't planning on doing anything. Sure, I'd noticed her in those short little skirts and the FM heels." I let this one pass, assuming I'd find out later what radio had to do with women's shoes. "But I was being good, keeping it in my pants. Sorry, Father. Then one night I was working late. The baby had been up like nine nights in a row, and I was toast. Couldn't get anything done during the day. So I stayed by myself after work on a, um, Tuesday, I think. And I'm at the copy machine, printing out a deck when Joy comes up next to me. Like *this* close." He held his hands maybe three inches apart.

He paused to breathe. "I didn't like her. I mean, I didn't even know her. But it was really late, and she was, Jesus . . . really hot. So we stole a bottle of Chardonnay from the executive conference room, and the next thing I know we're going at it on the media table." He shook his head. "I was just a guy thinking with his dick, you know what I mean?"

I froze. Because, in fact, I knew exactly what he meant. My scan of the room had pointedly excluded Madeline, because one look at her might set my own to aching and commandeering my thoughts again.

"It's the most fucked-up thing, Father. When I got to know her, I really didn't like her. She's kind of spoiled and whiny. Always looking for an angle. Seriously, I think she might be a . . . what do you call it . . . psychopath? Psycho-something. But that didn't stop me. It just made the whole thing this sick, sexy game. She'd be talking at me in that, Christ, nagging voice of hers, and I'd get so angry, I'd cover her mouth with my hand. But then we'd both get turned on, and it would morph into this crazy bondage thing.

"When she was really getting to me, I mean *grating* on every brain cell . . ." he gazed into the distance with his lazy California eyes as if he were composing something profound. "Then, I'd fuck her in the ass."

I sat for a few seconds, trying to come up with an appropriate reply. Finally, I defaulted to the old standby. "Do you love your wife?" I asked.

"I don't know." His voice was ragged, and when I glanced at his face, there were tears in Scott's eyes. "Things have sucked between us since before our daughter was born. We probably shouldn't have had her. Magenta." He grimaced. "That was Dana's idea. I wanted to name her Grace."

"You had the baby to save the marriage?" I asked and took a long swallow of beer. I was warming to Scott by the moment, making a note to tell Madeline—if I could ever face her again—that she should give him another chance. But if he was going to stay on this prosaic route: shaky marriage, baby, infidelity, etc., I might as well drink. This old story I could counsel with half a brain.

"Yeah, I guess. Stupid," he said, then grinned at me exactly the way Aidan used to, with only the right side of his mouth upturned. I gripped the table, holding on because very abruptly it was like I was both here with Scott and more than twenty years in the past.

The last time I was in a bar like this, I'd had an expertly-made fake ID in my wallet, and Aidan was with me. He'd just washed out of an auto repair program, and his father had called, pleading with me to talk to him. He had to learn to stand on his own two feet, Aidan's father pleaded. Yes, his son had problems but other "slow kids" eventually made a life. Underneath it all I heard the man's real wild cry: He felt bound by his son, anchored by him. The man was terrified.

I agreed to do what he asked, but when I called, Aidan didn't want to talk. All he wanted was to watch the lights over a tiny dance floor while "Rhythm Nation" thumped through the speakers. His head swung just out of time with the music, and he wore a dumb, dazed expression on his face that had only deepened with the drugs.

He wanted coke. My coke. It was finals week at BU, and I had five, six hours of studying to do every night if I wanted to pass Physics II. The gram in my pocket was essential to getting me through the next several days. But at a certain point during that evening, somehow both long ago and now, I pressed the small manila envelope into his hand and stood, draining my beer, willing to give anything to be done straining to hear his high, nasal voice. Those kindergarten words he used.

"Dana wanted to get pregnant." Scott's flat voice brought me back fully, and I was grateful to leave Aidan in the past. "She thought a baby would help our marriage. And I didn't really want to, but I went along to shut her up." He rubbed his cheeks and his late-night whiskers made a pleasant scratching sound.

"But Magenta," he went on. "She is the best thing that ever happened to me. I would die for her. You want to know what happened? Right after she was born I was carrying her down the stairs and I tripped, but instead of putting my hands out . . ." He demonstrated, palms flat like he was saving himself from a fall. "I just tightened my arms around her and took the entire staircase on my back. I had bruises for like six weeks. And my neck hurt like a mother." He shook his head. "But that didn't matter. My daughter was okay."

"So what are you going to do?" I asked.

Scott's face clouded. "I don't know. I was hoping you'd have, uh . . . advice."

"Stop having sex with a woman you don't like who is not your wife," I said.

Scott laughed, a surprisingly jolly sound. "Yeah, right? You're a genius, Father."

I raised my sticky, empty glass. "Like the beer."

"What about Dana? he pressed, moving even closer. I could smell his meaty sweat. "Do I stay just because we have this kid?"

"You're getting out of my area here. I used to be in the business of telling people to stay together. But these days, I just help them deal with what they've already done."

"I get that." Scott stared at his feet. "I'm not asking you to forgive me because what I did was pretty shitty. I mean, I wouldn't forgive me." But he gave me the look of the hopeful.

"What you did was pretty biological, Scott. I can't speak for your wife but on a broader world level, infidelity is part instinct: it's as old as time and probably forgivable. Just quit it, okay? Try to figure out what's best for your family."

"Deal," Scott said and raised his hand with two fingers up, for the number of beers we needed. "This one's on me."

"She's leaving," I said rather abruptly.

"Who?" His questioning face was childlike. Even I could see why women were taken in by his dumb surfer's charm.

"Joy." I pointed to the door. "She just slipped out, and it looked like she didn't want anyone to know." I didn't tell him that I'd been watching because I was terrified Madeline would leave with everything unresolved between us, and the next time I saw her she'd act like nothing happened and we'd never get back to where we were.

"Yeah, Father, you gotta watch out for Joy."

"You mean in general or me personally?"

"Uh, both, I guess. Thanks." He handed our barmaid a twenty and waited while she counted back four one-dollar bills. Eight dollars a beer? So many things had changed over the past eighteen years. "So, Joy grew up Catholic, and she's been having these, like, random moments of guilt about what we're doing to the Church. Or at least, that's what she says." He took a long draw and blotted his mouth with the back of his hand. "I think she just likes fucking shit up."

He leaned closer. "You know what else I did?"

I shook my head, wondering what—after he'd already admitted to sodomizing a woman not his wife—would qualify for this more covert unburdening.

"Joy sent me a note with a suggestion for the campaign that wasn't half bad; it's the one that got you into this whole photo shoot today. So anyway, I told Ted and Madeline and Isaac, and I acted like it was me, my idea. I've never stolen like that before, ever, in my whole career. I don't know why I did it now; it was stupid and I'll probably get caught. But she makes me . . ." he gripped his beer so tightly his fingers went white and waxy. "God, I just wanted to *do* something, show her she can't go around manipulating people to get whatever she wants. Give it back for once."

We sat for a few moments in silence, listening to the whisky-laced voice of Willie Nelson sing about Spanish angels.

"Okay," Scott said, rising as if something had prodded him out of his chair. "It's almost eleven. I should probably get home. Thanks for the talk, Father." He held out his hand and I shook it.

But Scott walked only a few feet away from the table before doubling back. "Listen, I gotta be honest. I'm gonna smoke a joint before I take off and I was just wondering if you want to . . ." He trailed off, looking at my no-doubt startled expression. "No, I guess not. That was stupid. Sorry, Father. No harm, no foul. Right?"

"No, no." I was, inexplicably, nodding. "That's not it." I stood swiftly; my body had made this decision long ahead of my brain. "Let's go."

I filed through moving bodies, my eyes on Scott's broad back. And I could feel that thing happen: anticipation cracking open like a sunrise, filling me with its golden light. We pushed through the door and out into the cold wet night.

"I'm over here." Scott pointed to a black SUV that hulked over the other cars, taking up one and a half spaces in the lot. When I climbed into the passenger side, I had to place one foot on the sideboard and use the other to spring me off the ground.

"You sure we're going to be okay out here?" I asked as I closed the door.

"Absolutely." Scott was digging in a compartment between the huge, padded front seats. "Cops have so many murders to worry about this year. Two numbnuts smokin' a doobie downtown just ain't worth their time."

"Where'd you grow up?" I asked.

"Why? Is my redneck showing?"

"Kind of."

"Tulsa, Oklahoma." He pulled out a tightly-rolled joint and a Zippo, leaning to one side—he must have had long hair when he started smoking; old drug habits rarely die—as he lit up.

"South Boston," I said, taking the joint from him. "It's the reddest-neck part of New England. Trust me."

Then I concentrated. First, I sniffed the thin gray smoke coming from the tip. It was good, Hawaiian or perhaps Colombian. Green and piney with a little bit of spice.

"Hey, Father?" Scott was already round-eyed, melting into the seat. "You've done this before, right? I'm not, like . . ." He paused, puzzled, searching for the word. "Corrupting you?"

"Yeah, I've done this before." I raised the joint to my lips and drew steadily, then swallowed the hit and sat perfectly still.

"Yup, I guess you have." Scott reached, and we passed as I exhaled.

I waited, thinking that it had been twenty-one years—exactly half my life—since the last time I had smoked pot. Then that thought trailed off into softness, and I lay back against the seat, which felt more plush and comfortable than any bed. In my mind, it detached from the car and flattened so I could sleep. Scott could go where he liked. I would stay here in this cocoon.

"You want one more before I take off?" Scott said from far away.

I reached, eyes closed, and took another long hit. "Thanks."

"Hey, sorry, Father. I really have to get going."

I was tempted to ignore him. What, after all, could he do? Scott had a critically drug-addled priest in his front seat, drugs in his car, and a psychopathic (probably sociopathic, I corrected silently) mistress ready to call his wife. He was not a man in charge of much.

But I roused myself and fumbled to open the door, turning to look at the cement ground from my perch. It was a long way down. "Thanks," I said, as I started the treacherous slide: one foot on the running board, my hands gripping the seatbelt and using it like I was rappelling. "I'll see you at the . . ." I bumped onto solid ground. "Office."

"Ten-four, Father," Scott said and waved. Then he turned a key, started the engine with a rocket ship whoosh, and drove away.

That's when I realized I was stranded. Buses ran infrequently at this time of night, and walking my Southside block was not advisable—particularly if you were an out-of-shape middle-aged ex-priest stoned out of your mind. For all I knew, everyone from Mason & Zeus had left the bar while I was in the car with Scott. But all these thoughts came to me very, very slowly, and I did not judge but simply acknowledged them with interest. There was no reason to worry because everything felt like it was happening according to some wise master plan. I might have been standing there two minutes or twenty when I heard a voice.

"Gabe? What are you doing out here?" Madeline appeared in front of me, her face lit by a streetlamp, and I blinked with righteous fortune. "Are you all right?" she asked.

Without thinking—because I did not need to; the world was as predestined as a dream—I walked to Madeline and drew her to me, lifting her. She was so light in my arms I imagined the lupine photographer had cast some spell, giving me superhuman powers as I struck his ridiculous poses.

"Gabe, why do you smell like . . . ?

I didn't let her finish but kissed her hard, hungrily, the way I'd wanted to earlier. Now I was brave. This, I reminded myself utterly without shame, was why I used to enjoy smoking pot.

Time stretched on. I heard a group of people leaving the bar, laughing, but it sounded as if they were separate from us—on some other plane. Madeline and I remained joined, mouths and tongues, hot darting whispers, her heart against mine. She put her hand to my hard cock and my legs buckled slightly but held. It was miraculous to me how long I had been lifting her. I felt immensely powerful. Also, suddenly, painfully thirsty. I needed water to continue this, gallons of it. I wanted it nearly as much as I wanted her.

"Where's your car?" I asked hoarsely and turned us both in the direction she pointed. "Now. Let's go." We walked together briskly. I was calculating as quickly as my stagnant brain would allow. "How far is your place?" I asked, and it came out almost angry. I was about to apologize, but Madeline moved in closer and leapt a little to glance a kiss off the edge of my jaw.

"I'm right downtown. About a mile and a half from here."

It sounded like a forty-day journey through the desert to me. But I calmed myself by thinking about her sink, the water gushing out of it. Or maybe she would have a refrigerator stocked with many green bottles of cold, bubbly exotic water, as so many of my Assumption parishioners did.

We rode through Chicago's streets, alternately dark and illuminated with showers of light. But unlike last time when I'd been lulled by the drive, I leaned forward, urging Madeline with all my powers to go faster. I could think about only two things: slaking my thirst, then ramming into Madeline with the pent-up force of twenty years.

We bumped down a ramp into an underground garage, and Madeline drove slowly through the aisles—too slowly—until she came to the spot marked 2213. I was rabid but working to appear calm, unsticking my tongue from the roof of my mouth. "We're here," she said, presaging a talking moment that I knew I had to deflect.

I opened my door and jumped out. "Let's go," I called, resisting an urge to knock wildly on the top of her car.

She came silently then and we walked, my arm wrapped around her so that I could have closed my eyes and simply been led.

We took an elevator that rose grandly, with barely a lurch. Her apartment was 2213. When I made the connection with her parking space I felt proud, then vaguely aware that the high was wearing off.

Once inside, I scanned for a sink, a tub, a fountain, anything with water. It was hard to make words in my sticky mouth but I said as casually as I could, "Do you think I could get a drink?"

Madeline looked startled. "I may have some gin. But there's nothing to mix it with."

I shook my head and swallowed. Entirely dry. "No, water," I said.

"Oh!" She laughed but it was hollow. "Sure."

I followed her through a living room I barely saw; there were large dark chairs hulking in a manly way. Then we were, blessedly, in the kitchen, a black and gray stone place with wrought-iron stools. She opened the refrigerator and took out a pitcher of cold water. I was riveted, following her hand like a hunter. She took out a glass, poured, handed it to me.

When I drank, finally, the relief was greater even than I could have imagined, washing my mouth, my throat, then everything below. I felt saved. I set the empty glass down and Madeline refilled it. That's when I noticed she was on one side of the shiny countertop and I was on the other. Somehow we would have to come back together. And it was clear now that the drug that had emboldened me was wearing off.

"Thank you," I said to Madeline, placing my hand on the one she rested on the tile. It took every ounce of my courage to do this, but she did not pull away. "I was very thirsty."

"Gabe? Where did you go when you left the bar? I thought maybe you'd called a cab and gone home."

"I was talking to Scott."

"Scott Hicks? Our Scott?" A look of disgust crossed Madeline's face, and she wavered ever so briefly between being the woman I desired and the one I did not.

"Yes," I said and got up to circle the counter. "He needed to talk in private. We went out to his car." I gave mental thanks to Scott, who I knew would forgive me for using him this way. "He's a better man than you think, Madeline." I put my hands on her shoulders, testing. "You should give him a chance." I moved in closer, and she put her arms around me, resting her head on my chest. "Let him work."

"Okay," Madeline whispered into my shirt. We swayed for a moment, locked together. Then she asked, "Gabe, what are we doing here?" And her haunted voice filled me with longing again. But it was different this time.

My mind was clear and quiet. I was no longer high. Madeline felt like a small, warm spirit against me; I stroked her hair and she made contented sounds. "I am here to understand you," I whispered. "To worship you."

The noise she made then sounded almost like anguish, but she took my hands and pulled me to the threshold between kitchen and living room. The front door was to my left. A shadowed corridor ran toward the recesses of her apartment to my right.

"Will you come with me?" she asked.

"Yes," I said. "But I need to tell you something first." I held her chin and tipped her face up toward mine. "I did not have sex of any kind with Jem. I could never move from one woman to another like that. You are the first in . . ." She put her fingers to my lips and gently pressed them closed.

"Let's go to bed," she said.

But it was I who led her back through the darkness and laid her gently on the vast, king-size expanse. It was like an altar where she began untying and unlocking the mysteries of her dress. Moonlight spilled through the window, and I backed away from the bed, breathless with awe. Then Madeline watched from the glow as I removed my own clothes, dropping them to the floor piece by piece. I walked toward her, and she stretched one hand toward my pounding heart.

"Oh, Gabe," she said, tracing the tattoo on my chest with her fingers. I could feel her make the sign of the cross then touch three times, anointing each drop of blood.

"Should I go?" I asked, confused suddenly by the intersection of Madeline and Aidan, worried that the past would rise up and swallow this moment, as it had so much of my intervening life.

But Madeline shook her head and drew her to me murmuring, "No, no, no, come." When our bodies met, the mark of my guilt touched her soft skin, and I sank into her, wild with desire and relief.

From: Jill Everson
To: joytoyourworld@hotmail.com
Subject: RE: I'm going to get fired!!!!!!

Hi honey—

Your father and I went out late with the Larsens last night. So I was still up brushing my teeth when your message pinged in on my phone. I read it. Your dad read it. Then we stayed up most of the night talking. So on very little sleep, here's what I have to say.

Kitten, I think I've done a disservice to you all these years, letting you destroy or walk away from anything that bored or irritated or just plain didn't suit you. Remember that field trip to the Como Park Conservatory when you were 12? You asked to go to the restroom and called me from the cell phone you weren't supposed to have (that we allowed you to have, I know; but that was for emergencies). You begged me to pick you up and said you didn't feel well, but the minute you got in the car you were laughing and telling me about how "lame" the whole thing was and hinting that you were hungry. Next thing I knew I was taking you to Pazzaluna for lunch, and we were ordering those silly pink drinks and personal pizzas . . . I knew that was the wrong thing to do, but I did it anyway, because you were such fun.

Oh, you were. So bright and cute and sure of yourself. I didn't want to break your spirit. But also, it was selfish. Your dad and I agreed to have only one child, and I always felt like I'd won the lottery. I got this great kid who never even went through an awkward period, and I just wanted to enjoy every minute. As you got older, that meant doing the things you liked to do. I never told you this, but your dad and I fought over those all-day shopping trips you and I took to the Mall of America, He'd ask me: "Why are we buying $200 shoes for a 15-year-old?" And I'd make excuses and insist that good leather shoes would last for 10 years. Eventually, I'd just shut him up with sex because—let's face it—that never fails to stop a conversation with a man. And somehow, even though we never discussed it, I think I taught you to use sex that way, too.

Since you've been living on your own, your dad and I have had a lot of time alone together. I'll admit, I didn't like it much at first. When you went away to college I felt like my life was over. But the last few years have been eye-opening, and one of the things we've discovered is that we're more than just your parents. There, I said it. (You have no idea what a huge step I've made! My therapist and I have been working on that single sentence for a long time.) And we've entered a whole new phase of our life. Your dad is working a little less. We eat when we're hungry. We started taking couples yoga. And we're planning to travel more! Next month, for instance, we're going to Hawaii. And in the fall: Reykjavik! It's the new destination city. All our friends have been.

Joy, I love you, but it's time for you to live your own life. (My therapist and I have been working on that one even longer . . .) You'll have to figure out your credit cards and rent situation. But really, honey? $3,200 a month??? Our mortgage is two-thirds of that, and we have five bedrooms.

As for your problems at work, that's what has your father most upset. He thinks you may be guilty of libel or in violation of some contract you signed at the agency. It was almost 4 a.m. by the time we talked about this, and I'm a little fuzzy on the details. But anyway, here's what we're offering: If you get sued, your father will represent you free of charge. We want you to learn to stand on your own two feet, but not from federal prison. Sometimes, honey, you jump into things without thinking them through.

Now the final thing I have to say is woman to woman. It has nothing to do with your father, or even my therapist. I don't know what your problem is with this woman Madeline, but from what I read she didn't do anything wrong. She was kissing an ex-priest, right? Neither of them is married (which, I'm sorry to be blunt, is more than we can say for your recent relationship). And you were angry because . . . why?

Well, I have an idea. You have never liked it when another girl was getting noticed. I was always a little anxious when I sent you out the door to prom or Spring Fling, because I knew chances were good you'd come home slamming doors and crying. We never talked specifically about the reason, and I'd tell myself it was because those nights were so emotionally weighted, which was unfair to teenagers. But I knew the real reason. And I wish I'd said it then: "Get over yourself, Joy. You can't always be the center of attention." Maybe if I had, you wouldn't be in this situation today. Forgive me, kitten. I wasn't tough enough for so many years. But I promise to make it up to you now.

I am giving you the gift of my total support and my faith that you will figure this whole thing out. Remember that your dad is available to help you with any legal problems that arise (as long as you can avoid May 5–21, because we'll be in Maui!). Now it's not even noon, and I'm so tired I think I'm going to take a Klonopin and try to get a nap in. Call tonight if you want to talk.

Love,
Mom

XIII

For THAT MOMENT BEFORE WAKING, I THOUGHT I WAS BACK IN MY
mother's house in Boston. The phone was ringing and I could see it—
a beige pushbutton that fit together like a clam trailing a thick, coiled
cord—but I could not reach it. It rang again, a shrill sound, and I
woke abruptly in Madeline's bedroom. Through the window came
the muddy, glowing lights of dawn.

I raised myself. She was gone, the side of the bed where she'd
been as blank-looking as if I'd imagined last night. But then Madeline
darted into the room, wearing a short red robe. She looked as if she'd
been awake for some time: Her hair was gathered loosely on top of
her head; her cheeks were scrubbed clean and flushed. She was carrying a huge cup.

With a quick nod to acknowledge me watching from my spot,
she snatched her phone up from the bedside table, pressed something
and said—in the voice of midafternoon—"Hello, this is Madeline
Murray." I lay back down and stole a glance at my own naked body
before pulling the covers to my chest.

"Yes," she said, lowering to sit on the edge, her back to me. "Go
ahead." I debated touching her gently. Was this right? What was cus-
tomary after a night like ours? Were there special rules for when a
woman was on the phone?

"I'm going to need a couple hours." She was the terse CEO Madeline. I drew my hand back. "Give me 'til noon, and I'll get back to you with my response."

She set the phone down and turned to place her back against the massive mahogany headboard. Everything in Madeline's apartment was oversized, as if built for Vikings, and this gave her the appearance of being even smaller than she was.

"Can you make my phone sound like that?" I regretted the question the minute it was out. What a stupidly unsexy thing to say.

"Like what?" she took a drink from her enormous cup, and the smell of coffee wafted over.

"That old-fashioned ring." I moved closer, and Madeline handed me her coffee, motioning that I should drink from it. I had put my mouth on every inch of her body last night. Yet, raising her cup to my lips felt like the most intimate thing I had ever done. "Isaac set my phone so it sounds like a cricket. Or a bird. I'm not sure . . ."

"Gabe?" Madeline was staring out the window, into the glowing dawn. "That was a reporter from the *Chronicle*. Someone leaked the story about our business. Probably Joy. I should have . . ." She stopped and rubbed her face, which looked younger and far more beautiful without makeup. I made a mental note to tell her that someday.

"They're going to publish something on it tomorrow, and at this point, there's nothing we can do. But he asked if I knew about your, ah, past." She shifted and her robe fell open a crucial inch, the breasts I'd touched and licked just hours before nearly visible. My penis stiffened, and I was seized with two urges, simultaneously. To remove Madeline's robe and splay her against the colossal headboard, pressing my cheek against hers as I re-entered the temple of her body. Also, to urinate. Before anything else happened, there was no question, I had to pee.

"Madeline, I'm sorry, do you mind if I . . . ?" Like a bashful third grader, I gestured toward the open bathroom door.

She nodded. "Go ahead."

I rose from the bed aware that Madeline would see my naked-ness, including my large and perpendicular erection. This seemed both unclerical and just plain awkward given our professional relationship. But there was no other option, so I moved like someone walking a diving board: apprehensive but determined. Once inside the bathroom I stood, one palm flat against the wall, and winced as the river inside me tried to push its way down a swollen path. The pain actually helped, causing me to wilt. A trickle began, and I aimed at the water. Finally, I sighed and let loose.

After this was done, I washed my hands slowly and rooted through Madeline's cabinetry until I came up with a small bottle of mouthwash. I took a swig that stung the insides of my cheeks, so I checked the label to be sure I hadn't accidentally used perfume or glass cleaner. But it clearly said "mouth rinse" and "prevents gum dis-ease." I spit and made a cup of my hands to catch cold water then drank from them. When I straightened, my scruffy face appeared in the mirror, droplets trailing from the corners of my mouth like blood.

I turned so my back faced the mirror and craned my neck to see what the view looked like to Madeline as I left her in bed. Not bad. I hadn't begun to sag, the way my father had at my age. Saturdays, when we'd played basketball at the Y, I'd watch with enchanted hor-ror as he stripped in the locker room and leaned to pick up his shorts, his testicles in their wrinkled purple sacs hanging halfway to his knees. They'd been stretched, perhaps by years of use: the production of five pregnancies—resulting in two miscarriages and the births of me and my two brothers—as well as twenty-five years of hunching under other people's sinks in his ill-fitting plumber's pants.

Three years out of seminary I'd officiated at my father's funeral, which had appeared to comfort my mother as profoundly as if Jesus Christ had descended to deliver the eulogy himself. The casket had been open. At fifty-nine, my father had had the grizzle and jowls of an eighty-year-old man. Yet, when we'd stood side by side looking down, my mother had smoothed his waxy cheek and remarked what a handsome man he still was.

"You look just like him, Gabriel," she'd said. "It's wasted on you, I suppose. But you're the one of you boys who takes most after his side."

I turned now to face the mirror and saw what she meant. My father's gray eyes, the color of ocean surf in a storm, assessed me unblinkingly. I had his broad chest matted with silver and black, and underneath it the belly that rounded like it held a small animal. His had been raccoon-sized, whereas mine looked like it contained only a possum. I turned to the left and sucked it in. A chipmunk, if I tried.

When I went back to the bedroom Madeline was exactly where I'd left her, but there was a second cup of coffee steaming on my side of the bed.

"Thanks," I said, picking it up to take a sip, brazenly naked for a few seconds before slipping back beneath the sheets.

"Gabe?" Madeline asked, as if uncertain who I was. "That reporter who called? He said something about you . . ." She laughed and shook her head. "Were you stoned last night? I know that's a crazy question, but I thought I smelled . . ."

She looked at me with wide, disbelieving eyes, and I thought that maybe I loved her. Right in that moment. "Pot," I said. "Yes. Scott and I smoked a joint in his truck."

"Wow. Okay. Well, I'm not complaining. The effect was, uh, magnificent. I guess." She laughed, and I blushed, which made her laugh even harder. Coffee sloshed crazily in her cup, and I saw the wisdom in her velvety black sheets.

"I didn't plan to do it," I said when she'd quieted. "I hadn't in a very long time. But then Scott asked and I thought . . . Well, I don't know what I thought."

"Gabe?" She was abruptly serious now. "This may sound insane. But were you ever arrested for selling drugs?"

I sighed deeply, letting out a breath I'd been holding for two decades. "Yes," I said and sat very still, frightened but also exhilarated. There was a gentle rush in my head and my veins. But everything felt orderly and right, even preordained. It was as if I'd been waiting all those years for this moment—and for Madeline—to speak the truth.

We had only a few minutes, so I couldn't tell her everything. But I described my life back then, when I was arrogant and reckless, as honestly as I could. Madeline only listened. And when I was done, she put her hand on mine and told me, gently, that we needed to hurry. She showered and dressed while I finished my coffee, then left discreetly so I could scratch and put on yesterday's clothes and use the bathroom alone.

Heading out of her room, I heard voices and assumed she had turned on a television. It would have been believable that Madeline checked the stock reports first thing. It wasn't until I rounded the doorway into the kitchen that I saw Isaac. He was wearing what looked like a wrestling singlet and black shorts that clung to his groin like Saran Wrap, drinking from a bottle of something iridescent blue.

"Father," he said very slowly. I stopped, my heart racing like a teenager who's been caught. I had completely forgotten he was staying with Madeline, if I ever really knew.

"More coffee, Gabe?" Madeline asked, holding up the half-full carafe. The woman was good, not a crack in her cool.

"Uh, sure. But I left my cup back in the . . ." I glanced in the direction of the bedroom and felt my entire face, including my ears, flush hot and red.

Isaac guffawed. "Christ. You two are soooo *Dawson's Creek*. I feel like we've all been waiting for you to stop tiptoeing around and just do the fucking deed. What do you say? Now that you've made your holy two-headed beast, can we just get on with business?"

I glanced at Madeline, who looked like she was about to cry. Or laugh. This seemed like a test. Rolling my shoulders the way I used to before a big score that might be a narc's trap, I straightened and faced Isaac.

"What we do behind closed doors is *no one's* business," I told him. "Not Joy's. And not yours."

We squared off against each other for a few seconds. "Yeah, well." Isaac put down his blue bottle and held out his hand. I took it and he clenched mine, knuckles up, the way street kids do. "No offense intended, Father. You know I'm on your side. Hell, maybe I'm a little jealous because I haven't had sex in . . ." he paused and gazed up at the ceiling, calculating, "twenty-two days. Anyway, it sounds like we have a situation?"

"We're going to need to address it by lunch," Madeline said. That's what I told the guy at the *Chronicle*."

"Go get him fixed up," Isaac said, dropping my hand and starting toward the hall. "I'm going to shower and think about how to deal with this." He turned. "We'll talk, Father? I'm going to need to know all about your arrest."

I nodded.

"Okay, I'll see you kids in the office," Isaac called, raising an arm to expose one hairy armpit and wave as he loped in the direction of what I assume was his room.

Madeline drove me to my apartment and waited in the tiny living room, sitting on my shabby plaid Goodwill couch while I showered and hunted for clean clothes.

When I came out in fresh jeans and a hippie-style linen shirt I'd bought along with the couch, she was on the phone. "Check the years 1989, '90, and '91," she was saying. "Cross search with 'McKenna,' 'Boston,' and 'narcotics.' Print out anything you find. Thanks, Abel."

I was barefoot, and Madeline eyed me as she slipped her phone back into her purse. Her hair was gathered on top of her head, large, studded sunglasses propped on top of the mass. I remembered the day she'd come into the bookstore and put on those same sunglasses, as if preparing for a burst of light. It had been only three weeks. Maybe all this was that flash unfolding, the one she'd sensed.

"You going to wear sandals with that outfit?" she asked with a squint.

"I wasn't planning on it," I said.

"Do it." She rose and twitched her skirt, as if sloughing off the bad upholstery. "And don't shave. You'll look like Jesus, sort of. That can't hurt."

I found a pair of rubber flip-flops that I'd purchased at CVS for some long-ago trip to the beach with the after-school kids from St. John's. "These?" I asked, holding them up. "It's a little cold out."

"Give them to me." Madeline stowed my dime-store shoes in her enormous bag. "You can wear boots and change at the office. But hurry. We're running out of time."

We had driven this stretch from my apartment to Mason & Zeus, the two of us, half a dozen times. Never before had this meant that Madeline spent a portion of the previous night kneeling between my legs, delivering the first slow, wet, dreamlike blowjob of my more than four decades on earth. I wondered if her employees would sense something different, if they would be able to see that I had been re-born into my body at the hands of their boss.

"We need to keep this all-business today, Gabe," she said, as if reading my thoughts. And I nodded. "But whatever shit storm comes down here today . . ." she paused to park in the space painted with M. M. MURRAY. "I had a really good time with you last night. And that's, ah, separate."

I took her hand, and after a quick glance around, she let me. "Do you know you're the only one who calls me Gabe?"

"No." She laughed nervously, and I realized this whole scene had an eerie serial killer set-up. The abandoned parking garage, an unshaven man with a secret.

"Everyone else calls me Father. Even Isaac. And if they swear around me, they apologize."

"Yes, well, at this point I've done so much more than swear." She was getting anxious, glancing at the elevator bank. "Gabe, we really need to . . ."

"I know," I said. "I just wanted to say thank you . . ." Did this sound pathetic? Self-serving? Because that was not my intent. I wanted only to exalt this woman who had taken me in. "You are amazing, Madeline."

She stared at me for a moment then leaned in and kissed my cheek. "Now let's go," she said, prodding me in the side. "Isaac is waiting for us."

But when we got off the elevator, Madeline spied Isaac and rushed off, closing them in her office alone. Candy was not at her post; instead there was a card alerting visitors to an electronic bell I'd never noticed. So I wandered back through the labyrinth of Mason & Zeus.

There were only a couple of real offices with doors. Madeline had one, as did the controller, a tall thin man named Wilson who wore a narrow dark tie and seemed as if he'd time warped from 1962. Everyone else sat in open areas festooned with posters and strings of Christmas lights and cartoon figurines. They had individual enclosures and there was an elaborate color-coding system: The group where Ted sat had red chairs and between the desks were stretchy dividers that doubled as bulletin boards. Ted waved as I walked by and asked, "Can I help you find something, Father?"

"Coffee?" I said, though what I really wanted was food.

"Sure thing." Ted stood and led me rather than simply pointing, the way grocery store clerks are trained to do. "I'm sorry, Father Gabe. Someone should have given you a tour so you could make yourself at home here. Do you have time to do that right now?"

"If I'm not pulling you away from what you're working on."

"Yeah, right now, *you* are what I'm working on."

Ted bestowed that warm white grin that made me feel both protective and taken care of. That's when I saw that someday he would be like me, hearing strangers' confessions and sadness and fears. I could imagine him out in the city with his friends, riding the El, feeling the tug of other people's doubt. He was young enough that he probably hadn't realized: Not everyone heard the whispers of passersby and felt their pain. It would be years before strangers would come to him for counsel. But once it happened, he would become a doctor or a therapist or a preacher. This office was a brief stopping place for him. Ted would go on to do better things.

I decided all this as I trailed him through a hallway lined with bright posters. "Sit-in against hemorrhoids!" proclaimed an ad for medicinal cream that featured a picture of at least twenty-five middle-aged people in hippie garb sitting cross-legged on the floor of a flag-draped political office. "Gold Health Raises You Above the Rest" appeared above a diagram of a patient in a hospital gown being levitated by a man in a business suit above a maze. Then simply "RUN" above a photo of enormous neon shoes in mid-stride, their ghostly, absent wearer racing along a misty road.

"Some of our work," Ted said, waving at the wall. "That hemorrhoid campaign won a Bronze Effie. We had a YouTube video and a song. Customers could post their 'sit-in' status on Facebook. And they were doing it. It's crazy what you can get people to talk about online!"

"Where was it taken?"

"The mayor's office. No fooling. One of his aides got us in over a long weekend, but the deal was we had to let him be in it. The aide,

I mean." Ted tapped a wild-eyed man with a long beard and a suede vest. "That's him."

"He looks like the Unabomber," I joked.

"Who?" Ted asked.

"Uh, 1994, '95?" I tried to place myself when Kaczynski was in the news.

"So I was, like, six," Ted said. And we both laughed. "Also, I think we were out of the country that year. My dad ran his company's division in Milan for a while."

"*Parli Italiano*?" I calculated that I was in Rome at the same time, about three hours from young Ted.

"*Sì*," he said. "But I've forgotten most of it. Not much use for a black dude who speaks Italian in Chicago."

"Ordering in restaurants? You could really impress your dates."

"Yeah, well, if I had dates my wife would kill me."

"Your . . . ?" It was as if the six-year-old from Milan had spoken of marriage. I looked down and saw the shiny new ring on Ted's left hand.

"Four months," he said and lit the hall with his smile. "And I still just like saying it, you know? Wife."

"No, I actually don't know," I said. "But I can imagine."

Ted laughed and it had the mellow sound of an old singer. "I suppose that's true, Father. But someday? Maybe?"

We moved on, and Ted pointed out the account team, purple; public relations, orange; and creative—a deep jewel of a color that wasn't green or yellow or blue but a combination of all three. Everywhere I looked, someone was examining a printout or a screen related to Forgiveness4You. My own image was on at least half of these: posters and flyers and what looked like a bus ad on a young bandana-wearing boy's enormous computer screen.

"This is everyone who makes stuff: writers, designers, infographics guys, and animators," Ted said. And then, as if he heard what I was thinking, "Right now, about two-thirds of the agency is working on you."

I stood watching dozens of people click and mark my face, baffled that such a thing could be true. Slowly I realized how many salaries and lives were now tied up with mine—how many people would be hurt when the buried part of my past came out. I began to sweat imagining this throng of earnest young people stilled, all their hard work undone by an awkward and regretful middle-aged cleric still coming down off the high of last night. Just then I caught the familiar outline of a surfer dude and felt a calming rush of comradely goodwill. I waved at Scott, who was standing at a mammoth copier. He waved back in the awkward way of a junior high friend you'd made on a field trip who wasn't sure he wanted to acknowledge you in school.

"Okay, so here's the café," Ted said as we entered a sunlit room.

When I was a child, *Willy Wonka & the Chocolate Factory* ran on the local Boston channel at least one Saturday every month. It was my favorite movie, and I wished for a place where I could live and play and eat candy all day long. Mason & Zeus seemed to be answering my long-ago childhood prayer.

I turned with wonder, from the row of dispensers that poured out every sweet, brightly-colored, marshmallow-studded cereal of my youth—Lucky Charms, Froot Loops, Trix, Cap'n Crunch—to the bins of Lay's Potato Chips, Nacho Cheese Doritos, Little Debbie snack cakes, and the cooler stocked with chilled Snickers bars, cans of soda, seltzer, iced coffee, and beer.

"There's yogurt and cheese and OJ in the refrigerator," said Ted, oblivious to my Charlie Bucket moment, pointing to a bank of silver appliances. "Coffee's over there. We have tea in the cupboard, if you'd prefer. Uh, I think that's it."

Abel sat alone among the tables, reading the *Wall Street Journal* and eating from a large bowl of something.

I turned to release Ted. "I know you have to get . . ."

But he was quiet, staring down. He had the look, which surprised me. Because this man was not a drive-by confessor.

"Do you still pray?" he asked and then blushed, which I felt rather than saw on his dark skin. "I mean . . . I'm sorry. That was a bizarre question."

"No." I put my hand on his. "No, it wasn't. And yes. I still pray. All the time."

"Could you pray for my brother? He's my twin. Tyler." Ted looked shy and young, hands stuck in the pockets of his designer jeans. For the first time, he seemed uncertain about what to say. After a long pause, he started rattling off facts. "We grew up with a lot. Our parents are rock solid, married twenty-nine years. We had a nice house with six bedrooms and a pool. We went on great vacations."

"I'm not seeing the problem yet," I said, thinking of my parents' apartment with its creaky, slanted floors and closet-sized rooms.

"That's because you're not black. You go out into this world as a black man who grew up easy, it's like you're already a traitor. Some places, I mean. Not everywhere. But Tyler was ashamed. After high school, he started hanging out with 'hood kids.'" Ted blinked. "That was his name for them, not mine. But it's like he's on this crusade to . . . I don't know . . . prove his street worthiness or something. He's been arrested a couple times. He's into drugs. Heroin, I think."

"Oh, God," I said.

"I don't want you to think he's some junkie." Ted recoiled stiffly. "I mean, he's just really messed up."

"It could happen to any of us," I said, crouching a little to meet his eyes straight on. "Sincerely, Ted. As a priest and as a man, I understand exactly what you're saying." I was never one to take the medallions they pass out like Boy Scout badges in my NA meetings.

But now, I wished I had one so I could pull it out and place it in Ted's hand. "I will be praying for your brother, every day."

"Thank you, Father Gabe."

And I couldn't help saying, because I felt it was true at some level, "You're welcome, my son."

After Ted left me, I picked up a bowl and poured a stream of Cap'n Crunch that *tap-tap-tapped* exactly the way it would have in Willy Wonka's world. Then I went to the refrigerator and peered inside, but there was only yogurt, beer, and cheese.

"The milk is right behind you," Abel called from his table.

I went back to the bank of cereal dispensers and looked: nothing.

"To your left. Raise the lever," Abel intoned from afar. I lifted the silver handle on what looked like a keg, and milk squirted out all over the countertop. "Now put your bowl underneath next time," Abel said drily. I was the only one who laughed.

I cleaned up the mess with a paper towel and let milk into my bowl until the cereal was coated but not mushy—a precise calibration I'd learned by the age of five. Then I got some coffee from the urn behind me and weaved my way through the empty tables.

"Mind if I join you?" I asked, approaching Abel.

"Please," he said, leaning back, his legs extended for what seemed like seven feet in front of his chair. The clock on the wall said 10:32, and everywhere else in the expanse of colored pods people had been rushing around brandishing papers and electronic devices, but Abel was composed and seemed to have nowhere else to be.

"I can't believe how much food they provide," I said, lifting my spoon and breathing in the scent. It was the peanut butter kind; I marveled at my luck.

"Synthetic trash," Abel said precisely as I inserted the first spoon into my mouth. "I wouldn't call it food. I bring my own from home: Granola. Real cream. Some fresh strawberries." He waved at his empty bowl. "That's been breakfast every day for the past twelve years. Of course, the fruit varies with what's in season. Peaches in summer. Blueberries in August. Winter's hard. Sometimes I have to resort to raisins or dried apricots."

"Bananas?" I offered. "They're always in season." Now that Abel had pointed it out, this cereal was awful. It had a gritty perfumed taste and sharp corners that cut the inside of my mouth.

"I don't like bananas," Abel said gravely. "They have a texture I just can't place. There's no word for it."

I thought about this for a few seconds and had to agree with this, too.

We sat for a bit in a silence that I would have filled by eating, but I could not face another bite of the industrially sweet cereal. At least last night's ganja had been just as good as I recalled—better when you factored in the sex that followed. Not all of my adolescent memories were being dashed.

"Tell me about yourself, Abel," I said after taking a few furtive sips of coffee I did not want. It was a little late to be getting to know people here; everything we'd started together might soon come to an abrupt end. But I was jacked up on sex and caffeine, plus I was curious. Abel was the first human being I'd encountered since entering the priesthood whom I needed to prompt to talk.

"Well," he drawled, "I've worked here since 2001. I have a dog named Killer; he's a Chihuahua, naturally." He dropped off, and I thought he might be done but it turned out he was only thinking. Then another fact bubbled out: "I've lived with my girlfriend, Eve, for twenty-four years."

Abel and Eve? I wondered if this could be true. No one ever pranked a priest, so I was out of practice spotting sarcasm and tall tales. "Twenty-four years? You must have been, what, eighteen?"

"Something like that." Abel stretched back even farther. His body now formed a plane at a forty-five-degree angle to the floor. "We met in high school, and there's been no real reason to change things since." He stroked his long beard, the fingers of one hand disappearing into the tangled fur. "We're not married," he volunteered, "for exactly that reason."

This took me a moment to parse, and while I was at it, Abel followed with, "I don't believe in God." Most people are challenging when they say this to someone like me, but Abel was singularly matter-of-fact. It was as if this statement and the information about Killer the Chihuahua were on par.

"Now you," he said. And I could hear in his voice the molasses of some near southern state—Kentucky, perhaps.

"Now me what?"

"I showed you mine." He might have smirked but it was impossible to tell under the beard. "Now you show me yours."

"Okay." Just two spoons of Cap'n Crunch plus the caffeine and sugar in my coffee had set my middle-aged heart to racing. I decided as long as it was happening I should just relax and enjoy it. Lean in. I took another sip. "I live in a decrepit apartment on the south side, partly because it reminds me of my first congregation here in Chicago, but mostly because it's all I can afford."

I paused to think. This was hard. Every piece of the biography Abel had given me was as clear and hard as diamond. I could from the few sentences he'd uttered construct an entire person: devoted to one woman since high school; owner of an ironically-named dog; loyal employee of a dozen years; nonbeliever in marriage and in God. I owed him a similarly terse but evocative sketch of my life.

"I'm Catholic, always have been, and though I don't hold with the Church I still talk to God every day."

I cut my gaze to check with him. Abel was unmoved but still listening.

"I'm a recovering drug addict with nineteen years of sobriety." *What about last night?* asked a voice inside my head. *Does that episode in Scott's truck set me back to zero?*

"My drug of choice was cocaine," I said, explaining both to Abel and myself.

Finally Abel reacted, his eyes behind thick glasses bugging forward, his body ratcheting up a touch. "No shit?" He shook his large head. Then he settled back down. Surprise had a very short half-life for this man. "You're okay, Father," he said in his standard twangy monotone.

"I like your writing," I said, because it was true. Something in Abel brought that out. "You're very funny without being mean. That's a gift."

"Thanks." He seemed, if anything, to be sinking further into repose. "I've been working on a screenplay." He chuckled, a low rumble like the shifting of tectonic plates. "That's my embarrassing confession. It's the most banal thing about me: What copywriter *isn't* working on a screenplay?"

"Well." I scratched my cheek, and it made a sandpapery noise. "I'm feeling a bit hackneyed myself."

"I don't know." Abel's gaze was like a lizard's. "Ex-addict ex-priest. It's pretty interesting. Maybe I'll write a screenplay about you."

"You're welcome to the material."

"But I wouldn't put in any of this bullshit about forgiveness for hire. That's just stupid."

"Yes." I filled with relief—someone had finally said it—and sat up a little straighter. I was the emperor, and Abel the incredibly large little boy who named my naked state. "Yes, it is."

"There is a luxury in self-reproach," Abel intoned like the preacher I never was. "When we blame ourselves, we feel that no one else has the right to blame us." He paused then added, "Oscar Wilde."

"Gabe!" Madeline appeared at my side as if she'd teleported into the room. "I've been looking everywhere for you. Isaac has drafted a media release, and I'd like you to take a look at it." She turned. "Abel,

I'm so glad you're here. Why don't you join us? You can give us your expert opinion."

"Certainly." Abel rose, unfolding slowly until he was like a mighty tree over Madeline's head.

Rise up and shine, for your light has come, I thought.

"Isaiah 60," answered Abel.

I stopped, crouched, on my way to standing. "Did I just say that out loud?"

Madeline took my arm and hauled me the rest of the way. She was—as I'd discovered during the thigh-clenching woman-on-top portion of the night before—much stronger than she looked. "You all right, Gabe?" she asked.

"How did you know that?" I asked Abel. "I thought you didn't believe in God."

"Just because I'm an atheist doesn't mean I don't read," he said. "Sheesh!" Then he caught my eyes and nodded deeply—a small but unexpectedly benevolent gesture. My nerves calmed for a moment and, grateful for his kindness, I bowed my head in return.

March 19, 20--

FORMER PRIEST AND MASON & ZEUS JOIN TO OFFER WORLD'S FIRST NONDENOMINATIONAL FORGIVENESS SERVICE

Media Release

Chicago, IL

For thousands of years forgiveness has been a discriminatory practice, available only to those who tithe or pledge loyalty to a particular church. Mason & Zeus saw a gap—in the marketplace and in our culture—where forgiveness could be provided to the everyman. We have developed a service to meet this need and we're calling it Forgiveness4You.

Together with Gabriel McKenna, a priest in good standing for sixteen years who served at Assumption of the Blessed Virgin until his resignation over philosophical differences in 2011, we have created a model for absolution that relieves people of mental burdens regardless of their age, race, religion, or sexual orientation.

As spiritual leader, Gabe McKenna brings a rich breadth of experience. He has studied in Rome and at the famed Notre-Dame Basilica of Montreal. A leader in our own community, McKenna once ran the community service program at St. John's, serving indigent and low-income individuals and families citywide. He brings personal understanding to this project, as well.

More than twenty years ago, McKenna was arrested for possession of a controlled substance in his hometown of Boston. His case was suspended, and he was placed in a diversion program for young offenders that led him eventually to the priesthood. He knows what it is to stumble and right the course of one's life. He is a living example of the power of forgiveness and wants to share that gift with the world.

Forgiveness4You is a unique service that meets an urgent need in our marketplace. Like a hospital, Fair Trade food organization, or private adoption firm, our agency will work on a paid model designed to provide the most good to the greatest number of people.

Tomorrow, an article will appear in the Chicago Chronicle announcing the creation of Forgiveness4You and disclosing Gabriel McKenna's arrest record. We welcome your questions about both and suspect this is only the beginning of the media's attention to a genuinely breakthrough business concept whose time has come.

Please contact Isaac Beckwith directly for more information at 512-345-8921.

Chicago Chronicle—ONLINE EDITION
March 14, 20--, 11:56 p.m.

Ex-Con. Ex-Priest. Entrepreneur?

While the faithful everywhere followed news of a new pope this week, Chicago had its own Catholic drama unfolding—only ours is less world-worthy and more news of the weird.

According to a source inside the ad agency Mason & Zeus, the company is about to launch a satellite business that offers forgiveness for a fee. And the person they've selected to lead this venture is former priest Gabriel McKenna, who came to our attention last year when he announced from his pulpit on Easter morning that he was resigning from Assumption of the Blessed Virgin due to differences with the Catholic Church.

McKenna served the Church for sixteen years, including a stint as pastor at St. John's on the South side, where he managed a $1.2 million budget for the homeless shelter there. But it's since come to light that McKenna has an arrest record from 19--, filed in Halifax County, Massachusetts, that was processed through drug court and subsequently expunged.

Reporters from the Chronicle have spoken to a source at the South Bay House of Corrections who confirmed that the former Father McKenna was detained in that facility for two weeks, pending trial on a felony charge, then placed in a diversion program for youthful offenders.

"I don't recall the particular case," said Sgt. Tom Bradie. "But any time we get any kid through diversion and he turns his life around, I think that's great."

Neighbors tell a different story, however. "You couldn't trust him," said Eve Daniels, who lived next door to the McKennas. "Gabe was a real smart boy, but he was trouble. He used to sell drugs to twelve-year-olds! Makes you wonder what he was doing all those years as a priest."

After entering the priesthood at age twenty-four, McKenna held posts in Rome and Montreal before being called to Chicago as lead pastor of the mission church St. John's. That congregation was shuttered for lack of funds in 20--, the year the archdiocese of Chicago removed eleven priests from clerical work due to the ongoing sex abuse of minors. Subsequently, McKenna was placed at Assumption of the Blessed Virgin, where he served until his abrupt resignation in 20--.

Since that time, the former priest has been working as a clerk at Brooks Books in Bronzeville. Oren Brooks, owner of the store, claims to know nothing about the forgiveness business. "Gabe McKenna has always been a good employee," said Brooks. "He's very knowledgeable about literature and the customers love him."

How McKenna became involved with the ad agency Mason & Zeus remains a mystery, but one of the agency's own tells the Chronicle that the former priest is participating in a campaign designed to "smear the Catholic Church."

"As a Catholic, I'm just not comfortable with the way we're marketing this service," says Joy Everson, brand strategist with Mason & Zeus. "I believe only Jesus Christ can offer real forgiveness and what we're doing is making a mockery of my religion."

Everson admits that she played a part in developing the new absolution business, even coming up with the name: Forgiveness 4 You. But after seeing marketing materials that made light of infidelity she had a change of heart, voicing her concerns to the agency's creative director and withdrawing from the team.

Isaac Beckwith, spokesperson for Mason & Zeus, says Everson is free to hold her own beliefs and claims she will not be penalized. "Of course, I wish she'd come to us first," said Beckwith. "As to her concerns, I'm incredibly proud of what we're doing with Gabe McKenna. Forgiveness4You is the first of its kind: a secular service that will ease people's guilt without prejudice."

A fee-based, for-profit business, Forgiveness4You will operate under state and federal human rights laws that prevent bias based upon race, sex, age, religion, disability, national origin, or sexual preference.

XIV

IT WAS ISAAC WHO SHOWED UP AT MY DOOR ON THURSDAY MORNING with two coffees in a cardboard container and a folded copy of the *Chicago Chronicle* shoved under his arm.

"It could have been worse, Father," he said as I flung open the door in hopes of finding Madeline. Ever the addict, I'd been doing little since my breakfast with Abel but crave more of her; sex was all I could think about. I'd bounded from bed to the door with my flannel robe loose around me. When I saw it was Isaac I tied it tight.

"What time is it?" I asked, my voice hoarse with disappointment.

"Six-thirty." Isaac walked into my hovel, arranging the cups on either side of the overturned crate I used as a coffee table. "I picked this up on the way over," he said, opening the newspaper and refolding it neatly to reveal a specific page. "I read it online last night. Well, this morning actually, around two. Then I spent the next hour raging at myself for not vetting you better. Jesus, Madeline should fire me."

"When do you sleep?" I asked.

Isaac smiled, but it was more of a scowl, and I saw the hollowed-out look of his eyes. "Not much these days, Father. You?"

"I'm sleeping better than I have in twenty years," I answered truthfully.

"Well, that's good." Isaac sat in a springless chair and sank nearly to the floor. "One of us should be conscious today."

He drank his coffee steadily while I hunkered on the couch and read the story. *Miss Daniels!* I chortled when I remembered my mother's tiny, cranky next-door neighbor, always—even in the middle of the day—wearing a nightgown and shawl. *She was still alive?*

"What's funny?" Isaac had revived a little.

"Just remembering," I said. "Eve Daniels is still a hothead."

"So you *didn't* sell drugs to twelve-year-olds?"

"Not directly," I said, putting the paper aside and picking up my coffee. It was good; Isaac had put in my two sugars. "I wasn't hanging out at middle schools, pushing heroin on sixth graders. But that's splitting hairs, isn't it? If you sell drugs, they're out there. Kids have access. Whether you can trace the exact supply chain or not." I was, for the first time in twenty-four hours, not plotting my next move with Madeline. "I wouldn't disagree with what she said."

Isaac sighed loudly. "You're making my job impossible, you know."

"I know." I stretched out to lie on the couch, arranging my bathrobe carefully, and gazed at a smoky-looking stain on the ceiling. "What will this do to the agency? To Madeline?"

"Good question." I craned my head to look at Isaac, and he stared back with tired, saggy eyes. "That's exactly what I was asking myself all night. In the beginning, I thought I was coming back here to save the agency. I know . . . delusions of grandeur and all that. But also, I wanted to help Meadow make the biggest career move of her life. God knows, I owed her. She'd yanked me through one long, incredibly dire drunken year. Cleaned me up, paid my bills, kicked my ass 'til I finally hit the wall and went to treatment." He stiffened, sitting up a little and squinting fiercely. "She's a far better person than she lets on. Do *not* make me remind you of that fact." Isaac leaned back again, closing his eyes and murmuring, "I don't exactly relish the idea of beating the shit out of a priest."

"Ex-priest," I said.

He sighed. "Still."

"So you said that was the beginning. What about now? Why are you still here? What are we doing?"

"Which question do you want me to answer?"

I stopped to think. "Do you believe what you said in the paper, that we're providing a 'non-discriminatory' forgiveness service to people?"

Isaac's head popped up. "Of course not! Jesus. Don't you know that's the one question you never ask? Do I believe one brand of toothpaste is better than the others? Or that the psychotropic drugs we're pushing on people will really improve their lives? That the candy-flavored vodka we market mostly to sixteen-year-olds makes their parties sparkle and twirl like the ones we show online?" He had broken out in a light sheen of sweat, which probably had more to do with fatigue than with anything I'd said. "But I don't sit around thinking about these things, because if I did, I wouldn't be able to sell anything. I just, you know, take a leap."

"I see. So really, that's your job." I was still lying with my head perched on the arm, which was beginning to make my neck sore. But I didn't move because I'd learned over the years that gravitas requires a certain outward peace. "You believe ardently no matter what your doubts, and in doing so, you encourage others to believe as well."

Isaac bellowed, a huge laugh, and his eyes were gleaming. He looked, dare I say, healed. "You bastard!" he choked. "The only thing that makes this shit-show worthwhile, today, is that you're such a smart and weirdly fucked-up kind of priest."

"Thank you," I said, gathering my robe in the most dignified way I could muster and rising from the couch. "I'm going to get dressed now. If you don't mind waiting, we can go into the office together."

Isaac slumped back in his seat. "Take your time, Father."

Instinctively as I passed him, I reached out to place my hand briefly on Isaac's forehead. He bowed his head, and I felt the blessing pass from my fingers into his skin.

When we got downstairs, Isaac pressed the keys for his hot little sports car into my hand. "I'm so fucking tired," he said. "You can drive, right?"

"Of course!" I said, trying to remember the last time I'd done so. Perhaps eight years before.

St. John's had owned a creaky old van that I drove most nights in winter, looking for homeless people in the killing cold. You'd think they might have come toward us, me and whatever volunteer was working at the time. But instead, the people we sought ran; they separated and dove into drainage ditches or corners to hide. Wearing layers of thermal clothing and carrying thermoses of hot cider—partly because the people we served needed both warmth and calories, partly just to keep our hands warm—my angels and I would dive after these frightened souls and argue, citing windchill and death statistics and eventually leading them back to our van.

But that had been an ancient Chevy with a "three-on-the-tree" transmission. This was a low-slung little thing, flat-nosed like a snake, with a stick that showed six gears—double the number I was used to and excessive, it seemed to me. I slid into the driver's seat and its leather cupped my body. The clutch was stiff, manly. And the engine, when I turned the key, growled like an animal that meant business.

"Go north 'til you're out of the hood," Isaac advised, then closed his eyes and began (real or not, I couldn't tell) to snore.

If I lurched and ground the gears a few times, there was no one but me to notice. And within a few miles, I was smoother. I'd decided to ignore the upper gears, just work with the ones I understood. At a stoplight, I pushed a button and successfully turned the radio on. Country music filled the car, twanging in a way that made me irritable as I lurched toward the next red light. It was a blessedly long one, allowing time for me to find a station playing George Michael and settle back.

As I pulled forward, there was a chuckle from the passenger seat. "Not a fan of Kenny Chesney?" Isaac asked, his eyes still closed.

But I heard this as if on a time delay; Isaac was back asleep by the time I thought to answer. So I thought about the scene this music conjured up: Aidan's mother's basement, with its tile floor and mishmash of old furniture, "Faith" playing on the stereo, the sweet smell of cheap pot mixed with the scorch of incense.

Aidan had been after me all week to come over, as if we were still in grade school making a date to play with the little Army men that filled the one gallon ice cream bucket on the shelf. He looked like a six-foot-two-inch ten-year-old, his body gangly and childlike for eighteen, all hollow, rubbery muscle. As soon as I got there, I pulled out a stub of an old joint and said I was going to teach him something. I took the first hit and passed it to him, but he reached for it all wrong, palm up as if I were going to drop it into his hand.

"Like this." I remembered it as clearly as if I'd been right there, watching myself at seventeen—half a year younger than Aidan but far more schooled in the ways of men. (Or so I'd believed.) I'd flipped his hand over roughly, making a pincer of the forefinger and thumb. "Now," I'd said, pressing the burning roach in between, "inhale the smoke, then take another little breath and hold it."

Aidan had had trouble with this direction. He'd been confused by the word "inhale," and even after I'd explained, it was like I'd asked him to rub his stomach and pat his head. He hadn't been able to get the order right; twice, he'd sucked the joint into his mouth and had had to remove it with his fingers. I'd given up on sharing it with him and had spent the next thirty minutes coaching him until he'd been left with nothing but a charred bit of paper. We'd actually laughed a few times; I'd felt like I was doing something unselfish and that my mother—if we took the pot out of the equation—would have been proud. Aidan's eyes had been glassier than usual, full of lostness and wonder. I had told him he could eat the last little shred of the joint and he had done it.

It was in the midst of this memory that I saw the bar where Scott and I had smoked in his truck—a quarter century of my life collapsing into bookend stoner events—and realized I'd gone too far. I made a U-turn, grinding the gears, and Isaac woke again with a hideous face.

"If this were my car," he said, "I'd kill you."

"We're almost there," I said, slowly coming back to the day, to Isaac and my still-adolescent middle-aged self.

"Park in the garage." Isaac flipped the visor down to look at his grizzled face in the mirror. "Fuck, I'm kind of scary today. Eh. Maybe that'll help when I talk to Joy."

"What are you going to say?" Every word of this conversation helped me put more distance between this moment and Aidan's mother, still living in that same house with the beat-up futon in the basement and the huge stereo from 1975. "Isn't it settled? You told the *Chronicle* she had a right to her opinion."

"Yeah, that was total bullshit. She has a right to her opinion as long as she keeps it to herself, but she's legally bound by her contract never to disclose Mason & Zeus business. That's airtight. She's in violation, and we're not only within our rights to fire her, we could sue her for breach."

"So why did you tell the reporter her job was safe?" I turned carefully into the garage, and Isaac handed me a card to flash in front of the ticket machine. The car was so low, I had to strain up and out the window, waving the card until it took and the mechanical arm slowly rose.

"PR, man," Isaac said. We entered the darkness, and I drove blindly until my eyes could adjust. "I wasn't going to hash out our employee policies in the media. And since we're talking about *forgiveness* here, I couldn't afford to come off as vindictive either. But that doesn't mean we can't deal with Joy in our own way, in our own time."

"What about the reporter?" I parked and cut the engine, filling the car with stuffy silence.

"Are you kidding?" Isaac seemed to have revived completely. Even the bags under his eyes were fading. "He doesn't care. You're the story. You and your 'checkered past.' Joy could walk down Michigan Avenue naked and never see her name in the paper again."

We exited from our respective doors, Isaac easily while I had to clamber, with one hand on the headrest hoisting me out. "She's young," I said as we walked toward the elevators. "You could give her another chance."

Isaac pushed the button and stood, hands in his back pockets, tipping forward onto his toes. "And what would that teach her, Father? I'll tell you what. The same thing she's been learning all her life: that she can do whatever the fuck she wants without ever suffering the consequences." He kept looking up but his voice got softer. "I think, actually, I'm the one doing her a favor. Maybe she'll learn from this and do the right thing next time."

But all this turned out to be moot when we exited into the lobby of Mason & Zeus and found Madeline waiting for us, hair pulled up on her head much the way she'd worn it in bed (was this purposeful, I wondered?), a big bronze necklace like a shield around her neck.

"Joy is 'on vacation,'" she said, making little hooks with her fingers in the air. "I found a message on my office phone—you know, the one I never answer?"

"She's running scared," said Isaac. "Have to admit, I'm relieved. One less thing to deal with today."

"Don't get used to it." Madeline was all business this morning, which helped calm me. All that corporate attitude masked her appeal. "She only has two and a half days of PTO saved."

The three of us walked back to the Mount Olympus conference room, the one where I'd had my photo shoot and where we'd sat before our Thai dinner just a week before. I remembered the warmth of that night and it came to me all at once that none of this would have happened if I weren't lonely. Simple as that. The things that go on in mankind's world—decisions that affect whole populations of people, accidents, bombings, scientific discoveries—often result from one person's desires. To be loved, to be important, to escape.

"So what's our plan?" Isaac asked as we sat around the table in exactly the configuration we'd been in that much simpler night.

"You tell me." Madeline gave him a wide-eyed stare. "Why do you think I brought you all the way up from Texas, Million Dollar Man?"

"Okay, is there any reason to change our agenda for today? Any reason you can see that we shouldn't just go ahead, prepare to open for business on Monday?"

"Gabe?" It was the first thing she had said to me since we walked in: my name.

I looked at her, and she wasn't angry, only curious. In fact, there might have been a flicker of new interest in her eyes.

"Is there anything else we should know?" she prodded, the CEO talking. "Any more, um, history that could come out?"

I pictured the funeral. Not Laura Larimar's but the one that I'd caused when I was a little older than Chase. The church had been dotted with cops in full uniform, not because of me but because our neighborhood was full of the guys who patrolled Newton and Wellesley but couldn't afford to live there. After the service, one of them had put his meaty hand on the back of my neck and pulled me outside.

"Yes." I said to Madeline, still feeling Officer Pilot's palm, sweaty but sheltering. His touch transmitted knowledge; it confirmed what I'd done. Two decades later, my stomach still went liquid at the memory. "There are a few things you should know."

"Hey, Father Gabe?" Candy poked her head through the door. "You've got a phone call. Should I just send it on in here?"

I looked around for a phone but didn't see one. "Right there," Isaac said, pointing to a black thing in the middle of the table that was shaped like a turtle with a speaker on its back.

I couldn't think of a soul that would know I was here, other than the thousands of strangers who'd read about me in the paper. "Did you get a name?" I asked Candy.

She looked at a piece of paper in her hand. "Jemmalyn Smythe," she said, pronouncing the last name with a drawn-out sound.

I shook my head. "I don't know any . . ."

"Jem," Madeline said softly. She got up, brushing something I couldn't see from the front of her skirt. "C'mon," she said to Isaac. "We can continue this later. Let's give Gabe some privacy so he can talk."

Isaac sat looking up at her, though, even standing, she only barely cleared his head. "But I want to know what Gabe was about to . . ."

"Really. I think we need to go." She had moved to the door, face flushed. "Now."

Isaac stood slowly and gave me the same look Officer Pilot had so many years before: a mixture of pity and accusation. "Fine. You've got another pre-launch discount session today at 11. The widow of one of our old maintenance guys. Do me a favor and forgive this one, whatever she's done, okay?"

I paused, bracing myself for his response to the truth. "I can't make any promises."

Isaac sighed loudly and shambled after Madeline, who was using her entire body to prop open the heavy door. "Yeah, this job would be so much easier if I were still getting drunk."

Once they were gone, I stared at the black turtle. Was I supposed to push a button? They were all marked with mysterious arrows and arcs. But as I was about to press the only red one, Jem's voice popped out, raspier than I remembered, from the speaker box. "Gabe? It's me. Are you all right?"

"I'm fine!" It felt comfortingly familiar, speaking aloud to a disembodied voice. "How are you?"

"Good. But . . . I read the newspaper article this morning, and I just thought . . ."

"Wait. The story got picked up in Cleveland?"

"Nooo." She sounded wary. "I know this might be hard to believe, given my history. But I'm not stalking you!"

"Excuse me?"

She sighed, and I wondered how I was managing to exasperate everyone I talked to today. "So, I set a couple of Google alerts after I left Chicago. Just to keep up, you know, on this business idea of yours."

"It wasn't my idea," I said, more defensively than I'd intended.

"I know." Jem was unflappable. She took a breath, and when her voice came out of the box next it was the one I recalled from my apartment, talking to me through the dark. "That's why I called. It seemed like you were just going along with all this. And now, all of a sudden, people are talking about you being a drug dealer."

"But I was." I leaned back in my chair, released by her stark language. That's when I noticed the mural of Zeus, with his wild hair and thunderous beard, looking down on me from the ceiling. "I was a . . . drug dealer. When I was younger. It's true."

"Oh, Gabe, we were all something," Jem said. "That's not important now."

"I sold cocaine to high school students," I said, savoring every word. "And I loved it. Not just the money—when I was nineteen, I'd carry around a wad of hundred-dollar bills like it was pocket change—but the power. People needed me; they waited for me. It was great. It was so much more important than being a priest. So much more . . . straightforward."

"So why did you stop?"

I thought back. The answer I wanted to give—the one I'd been telling myself for twenty-three years—wasn't accurate. Alone in that conference room with only Jem's voice, the truth bubbled out of me. "Because I got arrested."

"So the system worked, right? You did something wrong, you got caught, you changed."

"No!" The word echoed off the walls of the large empty room, and there was silence from the turtle. "I'm sorry," I said to the table. "I didn't mean to shout at you."

"It's okay." She sounded very far away. "Listen, Gabe, I'm really worried about you. But I have a guy coming in. Stage Four lung cancer, I'm his last hope. Can we talk later? Will you call me?"

"Sure." I breathed slowly and reminded myself this was not Jem's fault. She had no way of knowing these were the questions I'd been avoiding for a lifetime. "Do I have your number?"

"I thought so. Didn't we program it into your phone?"

"You're right. My old phone. I switched . . ." I looked at the shiny new one Madeline had given me; the only people who used it were from the agency. Scott had called the night before, asking in a whisper if I wanted to split a quarter ounce.

"Oh. That's why you haven't returned my calls." I could hear distraction in Jem's voice; a dying patient was about to walk through her door.

"Go heal the sick," I said gently.

She snorted. "I'm afraid there's almost no chance with this one."

"I have faith that whatever you do will improve this man's life."

"Maybe." She was silent for a second. "Maybe letting him die in peace would improve his life."

I blinked at the turtle. Her responses were never quite what I expected. "Thank you for calling, Jem. It helped. I'll talk to you very soon."

There was a click, and her presence vanished from the room. "There is a luxury in self-reproach," I told myself, speaking aloud but softly. "When we blame ourselves, we feel that no one else has the right to blame us."

I bowed my head, tenting my hands so that the fingers pointed to my forehead in a purposeful priestly pose. I had been punishing myself and trying to avoid public blame for two decades, first out of fear and then—or so I told myself—from a twisted sense of duty to the Church. But now the floodgates were open and regret rushed into me with the force of a storm. Soberly, I told myself I deserved whatever came next.

• • •

Forty minutes passed before Isaac came to retrieve me. I noted this by using the phone from my pocket, which reflected my face in its dark surface. Sagging jowls, wild eyebrows. It was as if going back and talking about Aidan had broken some magic spell. I was aging like the junkie I'd been intended to be.

"Whoa," said Isaac when he pushed through the door. "You all right, Father?"

Our time apart had had the opposite effect on Isaac, who appeared rested and unhurried. I imagined that he'd eaten some soy-rich power bar and gone for a run. This was the unwholesome man whom the Church shunned, while I was its ambassador? I chuckled quietly, with derision. A little madly, judging from Isaac's eyes.

"What's going on?" he asked, sitting in the chair next to me.

"Gabe?" He turned and put a hand on my shoulder. "I'm getting a little worried. It looks like you're coming unglued."

"I'm not sure I was *glued* to begin with," I said. "Maybe taped. Or just propped, you know. The way you do when you're a child and you break something; you fit the pieces back together like its whole and just leave it for someone else to find." I stopped. Isaac's hand was still on the small of my back, rubbing small circles the way my mother once had. "You called me Gabe," I said. What Isaac was doing was making me sleepy.

"Yeah, well, thinking of you as a priest will make it harder for me to kill you if you're cheating on Madeline with this doctor. Christ, you get a lot of action."

Despite everything, I grinned. "The appeal of the forbidden. Some guys go into seminary just for this purpose. Nerds and virgins? They put on clerical robes and women just go nuts." I shifted, like a cat nuzzling. "That's why the dropout rate is 50 percent. Around junior year, the students who just wanted to get laid finally leave."

Isaac pulled away from me and leaned back in his chair. "But you didn't leave."

"I was looking for something else."

"What?"

After all this time, all these meetings and conversations where the word was tossed around, I still couldn't say it. I could not admit aloud that my entire career with the Church had been so self-serving and small. Penance. Atonement. The search for absolution.

"I killed someone." I hadn't meant to say these words, but they came out loud and confident, unlike anything else I'd said all day. Isaac's sudden jolt was satisfying. I sat up strong in my chair.

"I don't mean I shot him or even that I set out to hurt him. But I caused his death. Recklessly." I took a deep ragged breath. It hurt. "Worse, perhaps. I caused him pain, terror—him and his family— for a long time before he died. Months. And I knew it was happening.

Only I blamed him for it. He was weak, ignorant. This is what I told myself. The truth . . ." I knew saying this would damage both of us, Isaac and me. Things would never be the same. But I was hurtling toward something, and I couldn't stop. "The truth is that he *was* weak and ignorant. Probably learning disabled. Maybe even mildly retarded. He had issues; he didn't understand cause and effect. He was tortured as a kid: lonely, unpopular, friendless—except for me. And I . . . I?"

The picture in my head shifted to Aidan huddled in his windbreaker on a corner in Jamaica Plain. I'd pulled up to sort out the cash he'd collected. Aidan had struggled with math; he wouldn't have known if I'd cheated him. Usually, I hadn't. But sometimes I'd take all the money and pay him in hash. I'd even roll the joints, because he'd been too uncoordinated. Eventually, I'd bought him a small wooden pipe and had presented it like a gift.

A sharp knock on the door brought me out of my reverie. Isaac stood but didn't move to open it. His cheeks were red and raw, as if he'd been struck.

"Who is it?" he asked.

"Um, it's me? Candace?"

Candace. Had I met a Candace? I concentrated. Then the answer popped into my head. *Candy!* It was like solving a particularly challenging crossword clue.

"There's a woman here who says she's Father Gabe's eleven o'clock. Her name is Georgia Wright?"

"Shit!" Isaac's whispered, checking his watch. "It's 11:05 already. Should I tell her we have to reschedule?"

I looked at the door. Candy was still waiting on the other side; I could feel her crouching close. I let my head fall back and saw Zeus thrusting his scepter toward me.

I closed my eyes. "No, I'll do it." I stood, eyes still shut, and took two steps forward, reaching out to touch Isaac's arm. He flinched but let my fingers stay connected. His body was so different from mine: tight sinew and hard muscle, strong as Zeus yet a mortal man's.

"Whose soever sins ye remit, they are remitted unto them," I murmured.

"What the hell does that mean?" Isaac's eyes were wild, and it occurred to me that he might think I was making a pass at him. There's a reason people refer to making love as "transcendent," calling out for God as they climax, the way I had done with Madeline. The line between spirituality and sex is very fine.

"It means I am leaving my sins in your safekeeping, and you will help bear them," I said, removing my hand so there would be no confusion. "That's what we do when we hear others' confessions. We pick up their burdens." I breathed and nodded at him in thanks. "You have taken mine."

When I opened the door, I half-expected Candy to tumble into the room, ear turned conspicuously toward us, in the manner of an old screwball comedy. But instead, she was waiting to the side, scrolling through the messages in her phone.

"Oh, good, Father." She was vague, no longer riveted by my presence. This was interesting. Had the effect worn off for Candy now that she knew about my past or had something changed when I confessed to Isaac, reducing my godly aura? I brushed closer to her and set my face in a perplexed expression. She smiled and took my arm, tucking it in next to her spectacular breasts. And I'll admit I was relieved that I had not lost all of my charm.

"We're going to Floor 8," Candy said the way everyone here did, like it was a distant planet.

She chattered as we rode the elevator. It had been a busy morning. Madeline had to be reminded twice about the earnings report that was due. This woman, Georgia, was unusual. Hard to place, Candy told me; I'd see what she meant.

Ted was waiting outside my workspace with a tall woman in a

long striped skirt who turned as we approached. I mean no disrespect when I say that Georgia Wright had a purely animal look, as if she had only recently transmogrified from being a leopard or some other large cat.

"Gabriel McKenna," I said, extending my hand to meet hers in a strong, sure grip.

"Nice to meet you," she said in a very low voice.

It is not my habit to categorize people by race. Yet I found myself searching Georgia Wright for clues because she looked unlike anyone I'd ever met. She was tall and quite old, her face deeply lined in shades of gold: skin, lips, and eyes. Her hair, in contrast, was pure white and pulled back in a braided style.

"I'll be back in forty-five minutes, Ms. Wright." Ted turned toward me with a questioning look. "Father?" he asked. *How could you?* his eyes were saying. *You have lied to me about who you are. Why should I trust you?*

As Georgia Wright slid into the room with feline grace, I took Ted's arm exactly the way I had Isaac's moments before. "I'm praying for your brother, Ted. I understand his pain and I will carry it for him. He is my brother, too."

Ted hesitated then nodded and bowed toward me, hugging me with stiff arms before walking briskly away.

When I entered the room where I heard people's lives, Georgia Wright was settling silently into a chair. I sat across from her, breathing in the unexpected scent of ginger and nutmeg. Or perhaps it was cinnamon. Whatever it was, it seemed to be coming from her breath.

"You are young," she said, flashing three gold teeth.

"Not really," I said, hunching forward, hands clasped between my knees. "In contrast, maybe."

She laughed wickedly. "Ooh, I do like you."

I liked her too, everything about her, from her wrinkled amber eyes to her smell. Aidan remained in my mind, but the thought of him became almost bearable now that I was sitting here, in the presence of someone who felt so right in the world.

"I can't imagine what you're doing here," I said. All my filters seemed to be gone. "You don't seem like the kind of person who needs to confess."

"We all need to confess," she echoed. "*Confess your sins one to another and pray one for another, so that ye may be healed.*"

"James 5:16," I said, and she nodded like a teacher. "That passage is about the cleansing effect and healing that comes from confessing to a righteous man."

"That would be you," said Georgia Wright, and she pressed her lips together in a considering expression.

"I'm not so sure of that," I said. "Being righteous is a much higher bar than being a priest."

"Well, of course it is." She raised the spectacles she wore around her neck on a chain, placing them on her nose but only so she could look over them at me. "Being righteous is as high as a man can go. You don't get that in any *school*." She spat the last word.

"I suppose you're right." I leaned back and summoned the courage to meet her eyes. "What brings you to me today, Ms. Wright?"

"I'm dying." She laughed, a rumbling croak. "I mean, not specifically, but I'm eighty-six. So I figure it's time to sort through all the evil, the mistakes."

"All right." I was uncertain what to ask.

"My first husband, he was a drinker," she said. "He said it was the war that did it to him, but I always doubted that." She checked my face. "World War II."

"I assumed."

"He was ten years older than me and quite good looking. But by the time our second was born, I already hated him." She sighed. "Him, our house, our marriage. But not those babies. So I moved out, and I took them."

"That sounds wise."

"You think so? Because I don't. Especially not back then. I did what I wanted, but it was terrible for my kids. Better I should've stayed and been unhappy for a while. Let them grow up with their dad. He wasn't a mean drunk, just a stupid one." Georgia Wright rolled her eyes on the word "stupid." "It was mostly my pride, you know. I couldn't stand to be associated with a man like that."

"Many of us make bad choices in young adulthood," I said, then repeated the phrase to myself. It sounded stilted and weird.

"Uh-huh. Only my bad choices didn't just affect me. I had a son, a daughter."

"And what happened to them?"

"My daughter is fine. She lives in California. She's an accountant." Georgia Wright looked at me a little bug-eyed. "And a grandmother, would you believe?"

"And your son?"

"He died almost forty years ago. Drowned. He was twenty-four."

"I'm so sorry," I said.

She waved a large hand. "By that time, I had a whole new family, with my second husband. Three more girls. He went wild, that boy. And he got lost. I let him get lost. Biggest regret of my life."

We were quiet for a moment. "There were women, you know."

I looked up, puzzled.

"Between my husbands, I was with some women." She sat very still, watching me. This was the first confession that seemed to discomfit Georgia Wright.

"There's nothing wrong with that," I said.

She shifted in her chair. "Maybe." There was a long pause.

"Ms. Wright?"

"Yes?"

"What can I do for you? I'm hearing you talk about things you didn't cause, or that didn't matter—at least not where God and your conscience are concerned. My job is to forgive people their sins but I need something . . . I've got nothing to absolve here. It seems like you've just lived life the best way you could."

I saw those gold teeth flash. Then Georgia Wright leaned forward and gathered my hands in both of hers. "Isn't that what all people do?" she asked. "We just knock around in this world, one careless thing to another? And we never know until later how it's all going to come out. Well, I'm here to tell you: I'm an old lady. And nothing happens the way you plan. I wake up now and think: This? This is what I've done? Phptt." Again she showed me the clamped, disapproving lips.

"It is *nothing*," she whispered. "And it's over."

I sat with her hands grasping mine, and you might think this was uncomfortable, but it wasn't in the least. "Georgia Wright?" I asked, using her full name because that's how I'd been thinking of her all along.

"Yes?" she said for a second time.

"You are forgiven for all errors and sins and hidden faults. Your life is lifted by the sanctity of God and of our savior Jesus Christ." I stopped, confused. I had not uttered that name in two years.

"Thank you," she said, starting to draw her large hands away from mine.

I caught them, reversing the grip so I now held her. "You are loved," I said.

I don't know what I expected: solemnity, or perhaps tears. But instead Georgia Wright winked at me broadly, her face breaking out in a crocodile grin.

"You too, Father," she said, swaying our joined hands and rocking a little. "I think you may be a righteous man after all."

"Some days," I said, then repeated it to myself silently. *Some days, I am.*

URGENT MEMO

Subject: All-staff meeting of the Forgiveness team

Time: 6 p.m. CST—dinner will be provided

Location: Executive conference room

Required: M. Madeline Murray, CEO

                    Isaac Beckwith, PR consultant

                    Ted Romans, Interactive Media Specialist

                    Scott Hicks, Art Director

                    Abel Dodd, copywriter

                    Rabbi Nathan Kahn, spiritual forgiveness counselor (Jewish)

                    Yoshii Adrami, spiritual forgiveness counselor (Buddhist-Hindu)

                    Roberta Fox, lay forgiveness counselor (atheist, non-religious)

                    Father Gabriel McKenna, Forgiveness founder

                    Jim Lynch, founder of Red Oak Private Equity (ROPE)

                    Bob Green, VP and equity partner at ROPE

                    Amy See, business analyst for ROPE

                    Rick Seaton, equity partner at ROPE

Due to this morning's newspaper story about Forgiveness4You and Father Gabe McKenna, we're convening a special session of the entire Forgiveness team to discuss issues of timing, staffing, and process going forward. THIS IS A MANDATORY MEETING!!! We expect your utmost confidentiality and look forward to seeing you there.

XV

SAYING GOODBYE TO GEORGIA WRIGHT WAS HARD. BUT THE THIRD time Ted knocked on the door she winked and said, "I think they're beginning to suspect us of something." Then before I could stop her she called, "Come in!"

That's how he found us hunched together, my hands clasped in hers. "It's, uh, 12:15," he said, averting his eyes as if we were also naked. "I'm supposed to take you downstairs."

"All right," she told him, all the while looking at me. "I'll be needing a taxi."

"Yes, I called a cab. He's waiting."

"Well then . . ." she stood regally, dragging me up with her. "I'd better be going."

"God goes with you," I said.

"And with you, Father." Her golden eyes narrowed, and I had one more image of Georgia Wright prowling on large leopard paws. "He walks alongside you, too, Father. Remember that."

After she left, I felt motherless. I had not told Georgia Wright about Aidan, though the impulse had been great to lay my head on her hands and confess everything. It wouldn't have been professional, but I'm not confident that's what stopped me. She was a woman who had lost a child. Aidan's mother and Laura Larimar's, Georgia Wright and the Blessed Virgin. They made up a vast sorority of women that cowed me with their suffering. Nothing could compare. I had no right to complain.

It was 12:30 by the time I could locate Isaac to tell him I was due at work in half an hour.

"But you're *at* work," he said, craning up from the table where he'd been going over layouts with Scott.

"No, the bookstore. My shift starts at one. Every Thursday, one to close."

Isaac blinked repeatedly, as if he were trying to swallow this information with his eyes.

"Dude, you're still working there?" Scott asked. *Dude*. Getting high with him had been a grave mistake in so many ways.

"Isaac thought it would be a good idea," I said stiffly. "Wholesome, I believe he said."

"Christ, I did, didn't I?" Isaac rubbed one hand over his forehead. "Okay, fine. But we're supposed to have a meeting at six. Can you maybe get off a little early?"

"I close the shop. Alone." There was a clock on the wall, and I glanced up. Twenty-five minutes to one, and there was no way I could make it to Brooks by bus. "I hate to ask, Isaac. But could I use your car?"

"Aw, Father, please don't ask me that. According to the rental contract I'm the only one who can drive it. I know, I shouldn't have asked you to this morning. But, Christ, you ground the shit out of those gears."

"Here." Scott rummaged in the pocket of his baggy cargo pants and pulled out a set of keys that he pushed into my hand. "Truck's downstairs, Level B. I'm gonna be here all night so you may as well take it."

"Are you sure?" I asked.

Scott shrugged. "It's an automatic. Gas tank is full. Go for it."

Finding Scott's SUV wasn't difficult. It dwarfed every other vehicle on Level B. I swung up into the driver's seat and inserted the key, then spent five precious minutes moving the seat, steering wheel and mirrors so I could see over the car's ludicrous hood. I'll admit, I prayed out loud as I started it and the radio blared on. "God, please watch over me," I said under the heart-thumping bass. "Don't let me kill anyone with this beast of a car."

I inched it backward, one foot on the accelerator the other on the brake. There was so much power in this engine, I was terrified of pressing down too hard and plowing backward into another car—or worse, through the garage wall. When I reached the gate, it seemed impossible that I should be able to drive this enormous thing—far larger than my little church van—through the opening. Sweating, barely breathing, I eased my way between two metal posts and out onto the milling street.

There were people walking across the intersection a hundred feet in front of me. This made me nervous. I stayed back, watching. When the light turned green, I hesitated long enough that drivers started honking. I cruised through on yellow, leaving the others stranded. In my mind, I reversed the route Isaac and I had taken that morning. At the next light I checked the digital clock on Scott's dashboard; it said 3:42 a.m. That was no help.

The crowds thinned as I reached the edge of the city, and once I crossed 35th, it was like I'd entered a different world—broken-down and unpopulated. But ten blocks farther south, there were people congregating—not the people one usually saw in this area but men in suits and women dressed like librarians. There were maybe thirty of them, and they were all walking in the direction I was driving, which made me nervous, because every once in a while someone would step off the curb into the street. I slowed nearly to their pace, and we proceeded like a parade to the front door of Brooks Books.

It had never occurred to me that I'd have to worry about where to park Scott's truck. Oren had a small parking lot that I'd never used, which typically had fewer than six cars in its ten spots. Today, however, there were cars and minivans and motorcycles parked randomly—at least thirty packed into the tiny space. The street was lined with cars, as well. And in front of the bookstore, there was a table set up with two people sitting behind it, handing out coffee and flyers. Protesters, many with children, stood in front of the shop holding signs on sticks. As I passed, I read the banner that hung above them all: CATHOLICS UNITED TO PRESERVE THE CHURCH.

This explained all the people walking. They'd parked a half-mile back in a neighborhood most of them had probably never seen before. I kept driving seven blocks until I found a spot large enough for the SUV. I ran back toward the bookstore, slowing as I approached the crowd. Chances were good one of my former parishioners was there and would recognize me. I made a sharp left and headed to the back entrance, jumping onto the loading platform where the UPS man dropped cases of books. But when I tried the door, it was locked.

I removed my confusing phone from my pocket and, after a few failed attempts, managed to dial the bookstore number. It took nine rings for Oren to answer. "I'm in back," I said. "Can you let me in?"

"Sure thing," Oren said, as if this were a perfectly reasonable request. "I'll be right there."

Inside, the shop was eerily quiet, despite all the activity out front. "Hello," I said, shaking Oren's hand. Something about this occasion felt formal to me. "I assume all this is my fault?"

"Seems to be," Oren said cheerfully. We walked toward the chairs where Madeline and I had once sat. There was a new display on a table next to them: Maritime Literature with *Moby-Dick*—Oren's all-time favorite—in the center. Around the Melville, Oren had arranged *Treasure Island*, *The Old Man and the Sea*, and *Heart of Darkness*. I'd worked at Brooks long enough to know this table would never be touched by a customer.

"They started off in front of that advertising company of yours, that's what one of them told me," Oren said as we sat. "But security chased them off. So I guess they thought they'd come here instead. Started showing up about ten."

"I'm really sorry, Oren. I was hoping the publicity would be good for business."

"Well, you never know." Oren leaned back and tented his hands. "Things change. Could be tomorrow all the people who want forgiving will come in and buy books."

We sat for a few moments listening to the buzz and clamor of the people outside. Someone named Barbara had arrived, to the delight of the assembled crowd. Calls of "Barb!" echoed in a chain.

"So it's an odd thing you're doing, Gabe," said Oren. "Forgiving people for money. How does that work?"

"I'm not sure it does," I said. "So far, all it's yielded is . . ." I pointed toward the front window where we could see a bald man shaking someone's hand. "This."

"People don't really buy books anymore," Oren went on. "But they'll pay for someone to take away their guilt?"

"Yes, that pretty much sums it up." I thought for a minute. "Read anything good lately?" I asked.

"Ah, just you wait!" Oren's old, hooded eyes glittered for a second. "It comes out in summer. I just finished the galley, and I'd give it to you, but Ruby is reading it right now. Story about a young widow who time travels back and meets the people who caused her husband's death. But better than that sounds."

"Does Ruby like it?" Ruby Brooks—Oren's wife—could identify a great story within twenty-five pages. For the year of my employment I'd been reading directly behind her.

"Ruby loves it. You will, too. Tell you what. I'll send you a copy when it comes out."

I shifted in my chair. "That sounds like a message, Oren."

"You don't need this job anymore, Gabe. Want some coffee?"

"No, thanks," I said.

While Oren got up and ambled into the back room with his cup, I looked outside. The people in front were five or six thick. They were socializing, mostly. Two women had set up lawn chairs on the sidewalk. At one point, they tried to flag down a teenager who was walking past, but he just crossed to the other side of the street.

"They're waiting for the news guys," Oren said from behind me. "One of 'em told me earlier. As soon as they get some coverage they'll go home."

"I'm not sure that's going to happen," I said. "I don't think I'm very big news."

"Oh, they'll make sure it does." Oren seated himself carefully, holding the cup out from his large body. "If this goes on another hour or two, they'll pull out something more dramatic. Set up a confessional out front or release fifty doves or something." He winked at me. "I might have even recommended it myself."

"You're coaching your own protesters?" I laughed.

"Well, if a thing's going to be done, you know. May as well be done right."

"So are you firing me, Oren?"

This was the first time he'd looked uncomfortable all morning, his broad brown face wrinkled up with concern. "No, no, Gabe. If you insist on staying, I'll make a place for you. I always have."

"Is that what it's been?" I asked. "You making a place?"

"It's the reality of running a bookstore these days. You're not doing it because it's good business. You're doing it because you want to. And if you hire someone, well . . ." Oren shrugged. "That's really more of the same. It doesn't take many people to sell books no one's buying."

"So why did you hire me?"

"I like you, Gabe. You're interesting; I appreciate your opinions. When you came in to apply, Ruby and I hadn't been on a vacation in three years. So I thought, 'Here's a sign.'"

"From God?"

Oren looked at me over his cup, eyes lit from deep inside. "Sure," he said. "Why not?"

"But you really don't need me?"

"I think," he said slowly, "it's also that you really don't need *me* anymore. You don't need this. You have plenty to keep you busy."

"That's true." I sat for a minute then got up and poured a cup of the Folger's that Oren had made, half-decaf and extra-weak. "Mind if I sit for a while before I leave?" I asked when I came back.

Oren looked up and nodded. "It would be my privilege, Father," he said, though he had only ever called me Gabe.

• • •

It was midafternoon when I left the bookstore through the back door. I walked around the building to peek out front and grew more brazen when a white-haired woman waved me over. "Are you here to join us?" she asked.

"I'm just . . . here to see. I'm Catholic. Or, I used to be."

"Plenty of people leave the church for a while," she said taking my arm. Hers was plump and powdery. It was the year's first spring-like day, and she and a couple other people had shed their coats, even though the temperature was a brisk fifty degrees. "But if you were baptized, you're always a Catholic. It's like a tattoo. You can cover it up or have one of those surgeries to erase it, but it's always going to be there. Under your skin."

Instinctively, the fingers of my right hand—the one that wasn't clamped under her elbow—went to my chest. She smiled and tightened her grip further. It was like she knew.

"People," she announced in a loud voice as we approached the group, "this is . . . ?" She turned to me with a questioning look.

"Aidan," I said.

"Welcome, Aidan," said a man in a lawn chair who looked to be about eighty. I scanned the crowd, which had thinned considerably over the course of the afternoon. There was no one I recognized, and apparently there was no one who recognized me.

"We're just waiting for the news people," said the white-haired woman. I turned to look at her and realized she wasn't nearly as old as I'd assumed. Her girth and her hair color combined to give the wrong impression. It was clear, looking at her tough skin and hardened jaw muscles, that she'd lived through some very difficult times. But she was only about a dozen years older than I.

"Why?" I asked, just as I glimpsed Oren standing at the front window, watching the goings-on with amusement on his face.

"Why what?" asked the seated man.

"Why do you want the news to cover this?"

"Why do *we* want the news to cover this?" corrected my companion. She must have been a schoolteacher at one time. Or at least Sunday school.

"Yes. Why is that good for us?" I appeased.

"People need to know," volunteered the man from the chair. "This is serious business, confession. It's not like soda pop you can sell to any old person on the street."

"So are you, are *we* saying that only Catholics deserve to be forgiven?" I knew I was stepping out of character, whatever that character was. But it felt important that I stand up for something I believed in. And I had very little to lose, even if they figured out who I was. More people were gathering up their things, and it appeared that soon only the three of us would be left.

"Of course I'm not sayin' that," said the man, trying twice—unsuccessfully—to rise from his chair. I pulled free from the woman's grasp and put my hands under his elbow.

"Ready?" I said. "One, two, THREE!" I hauled the man up and helped set him on his unsteady feet.

"Thank you, son," he said. Upright, even bent a little, he was as tall as I was, with beetled, long-haired eyebrows and a hawkish nose. "Everyone deserves to be forgiven in their way, by their people. The Jews have their rabbis and the Baptists have their preachers and the Arabs, the what-do-you-call?"

"Muslims?" I asked.

"Yes! They have this system, I believe, where they kneel on the floor facing east."

"But if everyone deserves absolution, why not . . . ?"

"Because." The man's voice boomed. "This one is ours. It means you believe with us, it means you're one of us. We don't take other people's holidays or go into their churches and light up all their candles. We stick with what's ours."

The woman had been looking at me oddly ever since I separated from her arm. "It's diluting our faith," she said, speaking as if this were something she'd heard or rehearsed. "It's using something that Catholics hold sacred and making it . . ." She waved one hand on the air dismissively. "Nothing. It's taking it away. From us."

There was a sudden shift around us. Voices, louder than before. People were on the sidewalk streaming back. "We saw them!" a woman called to where we were standing. "The news truck. Channel 7. They're coming!"

About twenty people who had been in the process of leaving rushed to re-open their chairs and set their coolers down and shrug off their coats. At the corner, a News 7 van nosed its way toward Brooks.

"You're him, aren't you?" I thought I'd imagined someone saying this until I turned to see the white-haired woman, arms crossed, glaring at me. "You're that, that fallen priest."

"I'm . . ." The van was parking, slowly. They seemed to be in no hurry to unload their camera equipment and interview the united Catholics. "Yes," I said to the woman. "And I should be going now."

I didn't quite run. But I walked so swiftly I began to sweat in the cool, dimming afternoon. When I got to Scott's truck, I swung myself up into the driver's seat, locked the doors, and started the engine with its mighty roar. When I saw the sign for the expressway, I took it. No experienced driver would have made this mistake.

I had often heard it said that there is no "rush hour" in Chicago, only two small stretches around noon and midnight when the traffic is not so bad. When I checked Scott's clock, it now said 7:22, which I took to mean it was somewhere near four. The line of cars I entered was still. I gazed out from my perch above all the others and the scene was apocalyptic. Metal roofs glinted as far as the horizon. With the windows rolled up, everything was silent. There were no birds. Nothing moved.

I turned on the radio and found a traffic report, relaxing as the announcer's voice joined me in the cavernous cab. There had been a crash at the intersection with Interstate 55 involving a semi and at least nine cars. Traffic was backed up for twelve miles to the south, she chirped. *If you're on the expressway, you're not going anywhere soon!*

And true to her word—which she repeated many times over the next hour—we were there for an hour by the clock. I could practically watch the gas gauge needle tick back; Scott's behemoth of a truck rumbled and exhaled a full quarter tank. Finally, I turned the truck off and sat in the dusky light shivering. When my feet and fingers grew dead with cold, I'd turn the truck back on for a few minutes, run the heat on high, and switch it back off to save gas.

As the sky darkened, a few cars maneuvered and turned, driving on the median and up over the shoulder to turn around and head the wrong way up an exit. Twice, the radio woman warned us not to do this, saying it was dangerous. I considered it, but I was afraid I'd damage Scott's truck, and besides, I could barely fit into a wide-open lane of traffic. There would be no edging into small spaces. But each time a car escaped, I advanced a few feet.

Well after a new announcer told us the crash had been cleared, my line of cars finally started moving. I'd been waiting dumbly, hungry and not quite sleeping, so it took me a few moments to get my bearings and figure out where I was going. I turned right on the Eisenhower and there was another, lesser traffic jam. By the time I arrived at the agency, I'd been on the road for longer than it would have taken to fly to New York.

The elevator took me up from the garage level, where I'd parked Scott's truck in the same place I'd found it, only with an eighth of the gas. Candy was not at her desk, so I wandered through the abandoned offices. The conference room we usually occupied, the one with Zeus looking down at the assembled, was dark and empty. I kept going and heard a voice coming from a room in the back of the building, near the café. When I leaned on the door, it swung in to reveal a huge room paneled with windows that offered a sparkling view of the city and a long banquette lined with chafing dishes. A dozen people sat around a table the size of half a tennis court, eating noodles with plastic forks.

"Gabe! Where have you been?" Madeline asked, and it was unclear to me whether she was speaking as CEO or the woman who had begged me to fuck her faster.

"There was a crash on the Expressway." I looked at the clock on the wall. It was nearly 6:30. "Sorry to be late."

"We were just getting started," said a man in a gray undertaker's suit. I remembered him from the meeting a few weeks ago. "Why don't you have a seat?"

"I'm sure Father McKenna is hungry." Isaac's voice was challenging. "He's been working all day."

"Yes, well, your agenda said half an hour for dinner, and I for one don't want to be here all night." The man turned to me. Jim Lynch, I recalled. Even his face was gray. "If you wouldn't mind helping yourself while we start the discussion, Father? Then we can stay on task."

I walked behind Scott on my way to the buffet, and he turned in his swivel chair, jostling me with his knee in the way of a ten-year-old showing allegiance to his best friend. Something animal and warm bloomed inside me, and I reached out to grasp his shoulder as I passed.

"Let's start with the financial prospects for this forgiving business," said Lynch. "What's the state of the state?"

I lifted the lid on the first of seven chafing dishes and saw that someone—Madeline?—had ordered Thai food, maybe from the very same restaurant where the three of us had eaten the night I kissed her awkwardly in her car. I still didn't know the names of the various noodles, rice medleys, and meat stews. But I heaped my plate with a bit of everything and took a can of ginger ale from the ice bucket at the end of the line.

"The prospects are extraordinary."

I turned just as Madeline began to speak, and she was looking directly at me, her face winsome and sad. She was in the wrong costume for this meeting, I ached to tell her. *Go put on your armor. Be the CEO.*

Since this morning's newspaper article appeared, we've had . . ." she looked down to consult a set of notes, "114 calls and 346 people contact us online—all requesting an appointment, or at least more information about how to get a forgiveness session. Preliminary data shows we're converting 58 percent of all inquiries into a commitment, either in person or by Skype. And word is traveling fast." She took a quick breath and drank some water before going on. "Currently, we have Forgiveness4You clients registered in twenty-three states, plus one call from Belize."

"We're already seeing the need for a bilingual forgiver," Isaac added. "Five of our requests so far are from people who would prefer to speak Spanish. We expect that number to grow, especially when we go out with translated ads in the Southwest."

The only open chair was between Ted and a man I'd never seen before. I took it and spread a napkin on my lap, then began devouring my food as discreetly as I could. Those hours on the highway in Scott's cold truck had left me empty and wanting. This meal wasn't nearly as good as the one I'd had in the restaurant with the cracked linoleum floor; after spending time over little gas burners, the noodles and rice had taken on an identically sticky texture and taste. But I didn't care. It felt like I was feeding a fire inside.

"Are you telling me," asked the stranger to my right, "that this response is based entirely on one newspaper article? No marketing, no outreach of any kind on our part?"

"That's exactly what we're telling you," Isaac said. "We're not scheduled to run our initial campaign until Monday."

"So perhaps this young lady did you people a favor?" The man moved his hand under the table, and I saw he was gripping a cane that had four little feet with rubber stoppers on the ends. I thought of Kat Seaton and her description of her kind, now disabled husband. This must be Rich. Then I lifted my gaze to see, on his other side, a ghostly white female face with wide frightened eyes.

I hadn't recognized her when I came through the door. But now I sat just feet from Joy, who had traded in her shiny lip-glossed style for the look of a woman in mourning, or shock. I tipped my head in recognition and smiled, even though there was a good chance I had something in my teeth. She cringed and bowed her head.

"No, no. There is absolutely no chance Joy's disclosure helped us." Isaac was tight, working to control his temper. "What today shows is how much potential there is for this project. But frankly, we anticipated that going in. That's why everyone here . . ." he pointed in the direction of Abel, Scott, Ted, even me, "has been working so damn hard. It would have been far better for us to control the message and launch this concept right."

Joy gasped a little and looked as if she might be sick. I noticed there was only a can of diet soda in front of her. No gummy noodles, which was probably good.

"As it stands, we've got a lot of interest. But we've also got some publicity challenges right off the bat."

Madeline cleared her throat. "Along with the 114 calls for forgiveness service, we received 72 from people who were complaining or angry. Two bomb threats, which we called in to the police." She alone looked completely unmoved by any of this. It was as if she were reading from her grocery list. "We also logged 569 protest emails. But most of those were just copies of a petition that someone generated in, um . . ." she re-checked her notes, "Barrington, Rhode Island."

"What's their objection?" I asked, surprising even myself. But I was curious.

"All over the map," Isaac said. "Some of them think we're doing the work of the devil, drawing people away from a spiritual life. Others say we're preying on people's misfortune." He turned to the gray-suited man and the one with the cane. "Same could be said of divorce lawyers or funeral parlors—anyone who makes money when other people are in pain."

"And the others?" I prodded, still scooping up heaping bites of curry and remembering the taste of Madeline's mouth.

"Most of them call for us to fire you, Gabe." Isaac did not blink or avert his eyes, for which I was grateful. I put my fork down and folded my hands on the table.

"For what reason?"

"Well, we've got Catholics who say you're blaspheming the faith and a wacko contingent that has you lumped in with priests who molest children. We discounted all of those." He was quiet for a moment then went on. "But about half the mail is from anti-drug groups saying your history makes you an inappropriate choice to lead a business that's more or less in the field of mental health." He held up his hand. "Not because you used drugs. There are thousands of therapists with a history of addiction, including every single chemical dependency counselor I know. Their problem is that you hid it. The Catholic Church helped you hide it. They feel like this is just one more church cover-up."

I thought about this for a moment. Every pair of eyes in the room was trained on me, but this was not uncomfortable in the least. It was like being in the pulpit, chalice held high above my head, people in the pews following my every move.

"They're wrong about that," I said, finally pushing my plate away. "I'm not saying they're wrong about my inappropriateness as a leader, or having me removed. That's a different discussion and one that I think we should have. But they're wrong about it being a cover-up. The priesthood was my penance. Also, probably . . ." I looked from Scott to Madeline. "My salvation."

There was a rustling, but no one spoke. It was a familiar sort of quiet.

"I think Father McKenna has helped locate one of the problems with this model," said a man a little older than I with a thick beard and Santa Claus-ish spectacles. "If we as clergy are presented as super human, we will all fail to live up to that image."

"It happens with athletes all the time," said Isaac. "Tiger Woods, Lance Armstrong."

"Yes, but they are hired to be strong, attractive, powerful. For us the stakes are even higher. We . . ."—he held his arms out to encompass me, the curly-haired woman by his side, and a bald man wearing flowing white clothes—"are hired to be *good*. Faithful. Almost godlike. Who among us can deliver on that? Not I."

Isaac groaned. "We're going to have to trash the whole super-hero campaign. That photographer cost me . . ."

Madeline cut him off. "So we know the problem. Let's figure out the solution. We've got hundreds of customers lining up already. People seem to be responding favorably to the name, most of our creative concepts will work, we're all ready to go on Monday. Let's figure this out."

"But we still have the problem of Father McKenna." Lynch rose and pointed at me. "Right now, the attention is focused on him."

"So I'll resign." I said it so quietly, even I barely heard myself. But everyone quit moving and again, there was that hush.

"Are you sure you want to do that?" asked Isaac, but he sounded hopeful. I glanced at Madeline. She looked like she might weep.

"I'm sure. It sounds like the only insurmountable issue right now is my history—which I probably should have told you about. It just seemed . . ." I was stopped by a memory of Aidan, his hand out, face screwed-up and pleading; then my own hand reaching into my pocket and handing him the bag. "So long ago."

"But will that take care of it?" Lynch's voice was grating, like a rusty gate. "Even if we make an announcement. Won't people always associate this thing with Father McKenna?"

"No way." Isaac looked more relieved than I'd seen him in days. He was practically melting into his chair. "That's the public's form of forgiveness. They forget quickly, every time."

"I'd love to take your word for that," said the man with the cane. "But do you have data? Some kind of proof?"

"Remember that very famous Chicago comedian who was arrested a few years ago and charged with child abuse?" Isaac asked.

There was a long silence, raised eyebrows, pensive looks. "That sounds vaguely familiar," said Lynch. "Remind me of the name."

"Exactly!" Isaac leaned back and crossed his hands over his

stomach. "I won't tell you the name because that's the point. You see this guy on television every week. You don't remember. People forget. They forgive without even knowing they're doing it."

• • •

The four from Red Oak filed out first, including the man next to me, who needed my hand to get out of his chair and balance with his cane.

"Sorry it had to come to this, Father," said Rich Seaton, to which I shrugged.

"It may all be for the best," I said with absolutely no conviction; when I left this building I would have no job, no car, no income, and no purpose. He nodded and stumped out behind the others, who did not even give me a glance.

But the bearded man circled the table and shook my hand. "Good to meet you," he said, showering me with all that goodness he'd claimed he was too fallible to have. "Nathan Kahn."

"Rabbi?" I asked, and he looked at me with merry eyes.

"A rabbi, a priest, and a yogi walk into a bar . . ." Next to him, the bald man sputtered out a laugh.

"Anything I can do for you two, let me know."

"Three, actually." He tipped his head in the direction of the curly-haired woman. "Roberta Fox is our secular humanist. Brings in the non-believers."

"Do you mind if I ask you a personal question?" I sat on the table, woozy from the day, the drive, and all the starchy food.

"Sure," said the rabbi.

"Why are you doing this?"

"Twin daughters headed to college in the fall. One at North-western, her sister at Yale. We're very proud, also very broke."

"And you?" I asked the bald man.

"My practice used to be spiritual," he said in an unexpectedly deep voice. "But these days it's mostly Highland Park housewives and retired attorneys. Buddhism has become a very popular hobby. Doing this feels more authentic than selling rock fountains and gongs."

"How about you, Bobby?" Rabbi Kahn said, as the curly-haired woman approached us. She was younger than I'd originally thought. With some makeup and a more revealing outfit, she could fit right in at Mason & Zeus. "Why are you doing this? Father McKenna wants to know."

"Mostly for my dissertation," she said. "I'm writing about guilt as a motivator for moral behavior, trying to tease apart how much is due to an individual ethical system and how much comes from societal pressures, both good and bad."

"Excellent," I said. "This should be perfect."

"Like a gift from God," she said with a wicked grin. "Plus I'll make a little pocket change. My stipend doesn't quite cover the bills." She tilted her head, and the entire, wondrous mass of her hair moved with it. "And you? Why did you start this? Why are you leaving? Like Isaac said, the whole drug thing will blow over by next week."

"Ah, you ask good questions." I peered at the girl, who reminded me vaguely of Jem. "Unlike all of you, I never had a good reason for doing this. I sort of stumbled into the enterprise with a unique set of skills. But no . . . purpose. Or calling? I'm sorry, that's a vague answer. But it's the truth. I never really belonged here in the first place, so now it's time for me to go."

"Not before we have lunch, I hope?" Rabbi Kahn pulled a wallet from his pocket and rooted inside it until he found a card. "Call me next week, okay? I think it would help all of us to hear what you have to say."

"Let me know where you're going, and I'll take care of the check." I turned to find Isaac standing right behind me. "In fact," he said, "if you want to make it a regular thing, we'll just start an account wherever you choose."

"That's very kind of you," said the rabbi. Then he shook my hand with both of his, and it felt like saying goodbye to a cousin I'd never known I had. "I have to run. It's Friday tomorrow so I've got a fifteen-hour day ahead of me. But I'll talk to you soon?"

"I'll call on Monday," I said, putting his card into my own battered wallet.

"Could I talk to you for a few minutes?" Isaac asked.

"Sure," I said, though I suddenly felt worn and dull, as if I had been awake for days. I shook hands with Roberta and the monk and moved aside with Isaac to a small empty spot near the congealing food.

"I want you to know, I really appreciate what you're doing," Isaac said. "And we're going to re-write the contract so you get 3 percent, founder's cut. Meadow and I already discussed it, and she's calling the lawyer in the morning. Also we'd like you to be a director, once we get our shit together to form a board. You can be the conscience of the organization. There will be a small salary, of course."

I eyed him. "Is this guilt talking?"

"Maybe partly." He swayed, a little zombie-like. "Christ, I'm exhausted. And it's making me all emotional. But the truth is we need you. And I don't want you to disappear on us. I've grown attached."

"All right." I couldn't tell how much I was being offered. Three percent could be just enough to help me replace my wallet—or prop up the bookstore, fund the shelter where St. John's used to be, and buy a car. I had no idea.

As if he heard my question, Isaac said in a low voice, "If this thing grows as fast as we think it will, we'll start up in Seattle, Providence, Western Connecticut, and Austin by the end of the year. I'll work out of the Texas office."

"You're staying on?"

He nodded. "That's the plan."

"And Madeline?"

We both looked in her direction. She was talking with Roberta Fox, and both were smiling. They looked like they could become friends.

"She's um," Isaac said warily. "Acting kinda strange. This whole forgiveness thing was her idea, and it's huge. I mean, she could end up on the cover of *Forbes*. But right now, she's totally lukewarm on the business. Says maybe she shouldn't have started it. She's not sure it's 'good for the world.' It's so odd. The other day, I heard Meadow talking to her mother on the phone."

"I doubt they were all bad, her parents," I said. "Sometimes we have to leave the tradition we grew up in to see its true value. Take back the pieces that make sense to us."

"You sound like a shrink," Isaac said. "New career path?"

I'd had it. My day had started before dawn. I'd driven (twice) for the first time in years. I'd been fired, essentially, by a man I would deeply miss and tried to pass myself off with a group of agitators, then sat in traffic cold, bored, and lonely for several hours. I hadn't been able to touch or really talk to Madeline following our intoxicating night. My feet hurt, and I had a touch of indigestion. Sighing more heavily than I meant to, I backed up against the wall. "I think I *need* a shrink," I said.

"Oh, don't look now. But I think Joy wants to talk to you!" Isaac spoke in a jubilant whisper. "I guess her dad was on the phone with Lynch this morning, talking about free speech *and* freedom of religion. It's a constitutional two-fer! I got a call mid-day saying we can't fire her yet, and she needed to be at this meeting."

"You going to keep her on?" I asked, watching Joy approach. The girl looked five pounds thinner than the last time I'd seen her.

"Thinking about it," Isaac said. "She's wicked smart. And we could probably get her back on better terms. Less salary, longer hours." He snorted. "If that's possible."

Joy seemed wrapped in rags compared to her former self. She

wore a plain dark dress and bowed her head as she neared me, the way old women did at early morning mass. "Could I speak to you alone, Father?" she asked.

Isaac drifted a discreet distance from us. But not, I suspected, so far that he couldn't hear.

"I want you to know I'm . . ." Joy began, then looked at the floor between her feet. "I'm sorry," she whispered. "I really don't know why I did all that. But it wasn't right."

"You were angry," I said, watching Scott talking to Abel out of the corner of one eye. "And none of us was behaving very well, myself included."

"Still." Joy said. "I didn't mean to make you leave."

I stood contemplating my options. I could have given her absolution; that would have been easy, but also a little cliché. So I went instead with what I was really thinking.

"I hope you'll stay on with Mason & Zeus, even if the terms are harsh," I said and saw her wince. "I genuinely think it would be good for you to work through this. And some of your criticisms of Forgiveness4You—more appropriately expressed—could be helpful."

"My mother said the same thing." Joy looked off into the distance for a moment. "I made this mess, and I need to stay and fix it. Stop being so defensive, look at things from a bigger point of view, grow up and be a better person." She shrugged, and maybe it was only weariness, but I saw a glimmer of something oddly admirable: Joy was able to forgive herself.

"Hey, Father?" Isaac bobbed up next to me, and Joy averted her eyes. "I hate to interrupt you, but we need to draft a new media release tonight, and I'd like to pass it by you. Get your blessing, as it were."

"As it were," I echoed his arcane construction. Then I turned back to Joy and put one hand to her cheek. She waited, head bowed, no doubt expecting wisdom and grace.

"Just stop messing with people's lives," I said, surprising even myself. "I truly believe you can learn from this. But if you have any true feeling for the Catholic Church, you must quit using it like a weapon to get what you want."

She nodded, tears dribbling from her eyes.

"I've seen enough of that for a lifetime," I said more gently. Then I gave up—delirious with fatigue—and hugged her. "Go." I said. "Be good."

March 21, 20--

FORGIVENESS4YOU EXPANDS BEFORE OPENING ITS DOORS

Media Release

Chicago, IL

Just two days ago we announced plans to launch Forgiveness4You, a first-of-its-kind forgiveness service that helps people resolve guilt and regret. Despite the fact that we are not yet officially in business, customer demand for our services has been overwhelming. So we're revising our business plan and expanding before even opening our doors.

We're happy to announce the addition of three forgiveness practitioners. Nathan Kahn is the assistant rabbi and director of adult education at Temple Mazel in Skokie. Yoshii Adrami studied Buddhism in Nepal and at the Institute for World Religions in Berkeley, California. Roberta Fox, a fellow in the philosophy department at the University of Chicago, is a leading expert in moral non-belief.

We are proud to welcome them and believe their services will make forgiveness available to an even greater number of people.

Due to commitments elsewhere, our founder, Father Gabriel McKenna, has stepped down as acting director of Forgiveness4You. He will remain on the board. We are engaged in a search for a priest or other Christian pastor at this time. We thank Father McKenna for his extraordinary work and for the inspiration that brought us this far.

Forgiveness4You will hold a grand opening in mid-April. By that time, we expect to have dedicated space with more than a dozen on-site consultation rooms and supplementary service options, including a massage therapist trained to help clients cleanse and relax after catharsis.

As always, we thank you for your interest and welcome any questions about this fast-growing enterprise.

Please contact Isaac Beckwith directly for more information at 512-345-8921.

XVI

"WHAT COMMITMENTS ELSEWHERE?" I ASKED ISAAC FOR THE third time. We were back in the smaller conference room where I felt the comforting presence of Zeus overhead. "I have no job, no parish, and no plans. My family is doing fine, except I left the church and broke my mother's heart. Exactly what do I tell people when they ask what I'm doing?"

"They won't. Don't worry. Everyone knows why you're leaving."

"Then why not be honest? Or say nothing?"

"Because," Isaac sighed, "in PR, this is the way it's done. I didn't make the rules, man. I'm just really good at using them to my own advantage."

"When do you have to file the release, Isaac?" We both turned. Madeline had crept up to the door so quietly neither of us had noticed her. She was leaning against the frame in a simple black garment. She'd taken off her amulet. Her feet were bare.

"If we want to get into the Sunday news stream, by midnight tonight."

"Fine." Madeline rolled against the doorway and peered up at the clock. "That gives us two and a half hours. Let me talk to Gabe, and we'll get back to you by 11:55."

"No, don't worry about it." I stood. "Go ahead and do what you think is best."

Isaac tilted back in his chair until he was nearly reclining and closed his eyes. "Just so you know," he said to no one in particular, "I'm going to stay with a friend tonight. So you'll have the apartment to yourself."

"What friend?" asked Madeline. "I thought we were your only friends in Chicago."

"Funny," he said, righting himself so he could glare at Madeline. "If you must know, Abel's girlfriend is at a mandolin festival in North Carolina this week. So I'm staying at their place, in her practice room."

"You didn't tell him . . . ?"

"I didn't tell him anything. He offered, completely out of the blue, as he was leaving tonight. Abel just seems to know shit. I have no idea how."

Isaac gathered himself and his papers and edged wearily toward the door where Madeline leaned. I felt like we were saying goodbye after a long voyage together. He had showed up at my apartment, already exhausted, at dawn. Somewhere in the middle of the day I'd told him about Aidan. Not everything, but more than I'd ever disclosed to anyone else.

"Hey." I caught Isaac's arm, startling him. "Thank you."

He yawned, wide, like a bear. "No problem, man. I'm sure Abel's couch is fine."

"No, I don't mean that. I mean. Just thank you."

He reached toward me, exposing a large, round armpit stain. I went to him and though I had to reach up to do it, I gathered him in my arms and tipped his head down to kiss it. Isaac gripped me hard for a moment then pushed me away and waved at Madeline. "See you tomorrow," he said and disappeared.

We were quiet for a long time, both of us listening to him walk down the hall, waiting for the elevator to come, open, and close.

"Gabe?" Madeline finally said. "What do you want to do?"

"I want . . ." I stopped to consider the many things I wanted: Madeline herself. A design for my life. Proof of faith. Absolution. God. "I want to go home with you." She took my hand in her own, which was cold. I turned it between mine, rubbing gently to warm it. "I'd like to have a drink," I continued. "And if you don't mind, I want to tell you the truth."

• • •

It had begun to rain. We were silent on the way to Madeline's apartment, traffic darting around us, buildings melting overhead. She drove slower this time, deliberately centering her car in its underground parking place. She turned off the car, and the engine quieted. Neither of us got out.

"The *truth* sounds a little ominous," she said softly. "Is this something I'm going to hate? You have a wife somewhere, this priest thing was all a cover. You're really gay, I was just an experiment. It's really Isaac you prefer?"

"No, nothing like that."

"What, then?"

I'd imagined doing this upstairs in her apartment with a big glass of whisky in my hand. But now this spot seemed like the most appropriate place in the world. It was dark and quiet, and the two of us were contained in the little vessel of her car.

"I was one of those kids . . ." I started, picturing myself at eight, twelve, fifteen, based on photos my mother kept in silver frames on her mantle. "I was happy, smart, lots of friends, everything came easy."

"That surprises me," she said. "I thought you'd be one of those tortured boys."

"No, that came later. First year of high school, I was cocky. And I got away with everything: breaking curfew, cheating on tests. My parents were tired and perpetually broke. My teachers had forty students in a class. No one had time to worry about a kid who was basically doing okay." I shifted to look at her. "I didn't mean that to sound pathetic."

Madeline shook her head. "Don't worry about it. Someday I'll tell you about the trauma of having a mother who breastfed my little brother until he was five."

I laughed, despite myself. "I look forward to that." There was a pause, a few seconds of lightness. But I had to go on. "Anyway, sophomore year in high school, I had this friend who was a senior. He always had money. Great clothes. He drove a red Jaguar with a sound system wired through the trunk. It was . . . everything I wanted. So just before he graduated—Peter, that was his name—he showed me how he did it."

"Drugs?"

"Cocaine. Peter didn't bother with the small stuff. Pot, psychedelics. Most of us had been getting high since we were about twelve. But cocaine was what successful people did. Movie stars, bankers. We were guys from Southie. It wasn't hard to sell coke as a kind of . . . aspirational drug."

"Nice branding reference," Madeline said. "I can tell you've been paying attention."

"Thank you." I reclined my seat, realized I was positioned like a patient at a therapist's office, and ratcheted it back up. "So when Peter graduated, I took over his business. It was like magic. I'd pick up a pound of coke in Dorchester. Take it back to my room and weigh out single-ounce bags. Peter's customers came to me. I was clearing $3,000 a week. At sixteen."

"Were you using?"

I sighed. "Not at first. I wasn't stupid. I knew my money came from feeding other people's habits. But then someone new came to me, a kid who'd transferred in, and he'd seen some movie where the guys buying heroin made the dealer do some to prove he wasn't a narc. He cut some, handed me a $20 bill, said, 'Snort it.' So I did."

"And you liked it?" Madeline sounded distant, like she was talking to a stranger. I suppose in some ways, she was.

"I loved it. Coke made me feel powerful, like I could do *anything*. No doubts. No weakness."

"Sounds terrifying," she said.

I nodded. "It was. Only I was too young, too full of hubris, to understand." I stopped to gather a breath. "But really, this story is about my neighbor Aidan." Saying his name felt like touching a bruise. "He was . . . slow. A little older than me, but he ended up in my grade in school. He had . . ." I stopped and swallowed, and Madeline reached out to touch my leg, but I drew it aside. "No! Don't comfort me. I don't deserve that."

"All right." She withdrew to her side of the car, and I felt a familiar loneliness. As if she were already gone.

"Aidan had something wrong with him. He was skinny and his chest sort of caved in. He walked like his legs were attached wrong." I pictured him, shambling along the hall at school. "My mother made me play with him when I was little, so we knew each other. He thought of me as his friend. He was always hanging around, so one day he was there when I sold a gram to one of the baseball players. Mean kid. I remember he looked at Aidan and said, 'You better not tell anyone, Lurch.' And that's when I thought: *Aidan's safe. He's got no one to tell.*"

For the second time that day, I was shivering in a stopped car. But I resisted the thought of going upstairs and getting into Madeline's large, warm bed. Instead, I wrapped my arms around myself.

"He started carrying for me. Aidan. Taking care of really low-level sales. Sometimes I paid him in cash and sometimes in drugs. I taught him how to do it. All of it." I stared out the windshield at the cement wall of the garage. "I bought him a roach clip once, because he wanted one like mine. He was easy. A little pot, a few lines, he'd be happy. He just wanted to hang around with me."

"What happened to him?" Madeline's voice was tight, resigned.

"He got hooked. Imagine you're a kid like Aidan. No friends, not very good in school. And this drug comes along that makes you feel great about yourself. Who wouldn't . . . ?"

Madeline sat up and grabbed my hand roughly, but this time I let her.

"So, eventually, I got caught. It was the beginning of senior year. I was very lucky: I was two weeks shy of eighteen. So instead of going to prison, I was put in this diversion program for young offenders. I had to go to classes and get drug tested—stay clean for six months."

"Did you?"

"Sure." I could still remember lying on my bed, counting down the weeks until I could be done stopping by the police station Mondays and Thursdays to urinate in a cup. "I had plans. I was going to go to BU, full ride. Six months? I just put my head down and got through it. But Aidan . . ."

"Did he quit with you?" Madeline asked hopefully.

"Uh, no. He was on me every day, showing up at the house, looking for drugs. I was furious! My parents were already devastated and ashamed. This was a close neighborhood; everyone knew. To my mind, Aidan was just making things worse for them. It wasn't *my* responsibility, of course. So I took him and introduced him to the guy who'd taken over. Really mean kid we called Nob." The boy's sneer surfaced in my memory. "I told Nob that Aidan would do anything. Just give him a little coke, and he's yours for life."

"Did he ever get caught?"

"Aidan? Don't know. It's possible the cops caught him a couple times and just gave him a lecture and sent him home. Everyone knew the deal with Aidan. He wasn't masterminding anything. I doubt they would have put him in jail."

"Did you stay clean?"

"Are you kidding?" I'd always thought of Madeline as the worldly one of the two of us. But about this, she knew nothing. "My friends and I had a party the night I was done with diversion. I got wasted, high, low, everything. I was destroyed for about a week. But I did quit dealing. That much I understood: I could take all the drugs I wanted, but if I ever got caught selling again, I'd do hard time."

"And I'm assuming Nob wasn't about to give up his business."

I was impressed. She might know nothing about drugs, but Madeline understood commerce.

"That helped, too," I said. "I graduated, started college. I was a Physics major. Had wild dreams about grad school at MIT."

"You weren't . . . religious?" Madeline asked, as if the question were impertinent.

"I was Catholic, just like every other kid who grew on up my street. I didn't question it. I'd study, smoke a joint, go to church. That's just how things were. So, finals week, freshman year." I realized I was clamped onto Madeline's hand like a vise and made myself loosen my grip.

"Gabe?" she said. "Do you want to go upstairs now? You can tell me the rest of it up there."

"No." Madeline was freezing, and I hated doing this to her, but moving felt like a cop-out. "There's not that much more." I waited, and she didn't say anything, so I went on. "Aidan was an addict, but he wasn't. It's so hard to explain. He didn't have the cognitive ability to understand what was happening, so he acted more like an animal who was hungry. Starving. All the time."

Madeline shivered, from the cold or what I'd said, or both.

"He was like that when he came to find me. I was studying for a big exam, but he didn't understand that. He just kept asking me to give him coke. He didn't have any money; everyone else had turned him away. Finally, I just pulled out the bag and kind of threw it at him. I told him to take it and leave me alone." We sat for a moment. I was staring down at our clasped hands. "His mother found him the next morning."

Madeline shifted but said nothing.

"She found him," I whispered. "That's one thing I cannot . . . tolerate. His *mother* opened his bedroom door to tell him the coffee was on or his eggs were ready, and she found him dead on the floor."

I looked at Madeline. There were tears on her face, but she wasn't making a sound. "But you know what bothers me even more?" I wondered why I wasn't more upset. I'd never told anyone this—I'd been holding it in for twenty-two years—but now I was reciting it like a sermon I'd written. "He didn't have anyone to do it *with*. He didn't have a party to go to. Even holding a gram of good coke, he didn't have a friend he could call. Aidan was completely alone. So he just." I breathed. "Snorted it all himself."

"And it killed him?"

I nodded. "Probably. The autopsy showed he'd been drinking, too. And there was something wrong with his heart. Marfan's Syndrome. That's why his chest had that strange concave shape." My voice broke on the last syllable.

"Oh, Gabe," Madeline murmured. "What did you do?"

"Skipped my Physics final." I squinted, remembering those days, that week. My parents grim and gray-faced, glancing at me as if I were a dangerous animal. They must have heard things, but they never asked me. Our conversations were limited to what we were having for dinner and whether my black suit was clean.

"After Aidan's funeral this local cop, James Pilot, took me by the back of the neck." I reached back and pulled on my own collar to demonstrate. "He was huge, Pilot. He took me around the side of the church and told me they knew the coke Aidan used was mine. He said with my first bust, I was looking at three to five years minimum."

I could still hear his low workingman's voice in my ear. *Tree to five yee-ahs.*

"Only . . ." I could still see the prison cell that should have been mine. In my dreams, I'd been living there for two decades. "I didn't sell the coke to Aidan. I gave it to him. That made it harder to prosecute. The district attorney wanted to charge me with manslaughter, and there were maybe four or five months where it looked like that would happen."

I had lived with my parents during that entire time, watching my mother age a decade in less than half a year. No matter how delicately I entered a room she would startle every time. It was as if she'd never seen me before. Her house had been invaded by the monster I'd become.

"It was the Marfan's that saved me." I winced at the word *saved*. Because it had not. "His heart was weak and that muddied things, made the case against me too convoluted. It was the week of Thanksgiving by the time we found out. I'd been working at a tire store, preparing myself to go to prison. Then, one day, it was done. Over. I was actually . . ." I searched for the word. "Bereft."

"You wanted to be punished?" Madeline hadn't spoken for so long, her precise Midwestern voice sounded foreign, as if she'd landed in the middle of South Boston circa 1991.

"Yes, I wanted to be punished." The cold had seeped into my feet, and they felt blocky, useless. "Don't give me too much credit. I was relieved that I wasn't going to prison. But I couldn't just go back to college and live like I hadn't . . ."

I half expected Madeline to say the words: *Like you hadn't killed someone.* But she didn't. She was quiet, so I went on.

"A couple weeks before Christmas, I went out and got the tattoo. I drove to Rhode Island, because I wanted a place where the ink guy wouldn't know who I was. Still, how many twenty-year-olds ask to have a cross dripping blood tattooed on their chest? They could tell something was off. When I left, I heard them lock the door."

I could see myself walking down a dark, cold street in Providence, my chest aching with a thousand tiny needle stings, head down, hands stuffed in my pockets. "It was literally the last plan I had, getting that tattoo. Once I'd done that, I was out of ideas. My life was a total blank."

"What happened?"

"My mom eventually called her priest, because that's what women like her do. Father Murphy. He was kind of an old drunk but a nice one. He listened, and he asked if I really wanted to atone for the things I'd done. There was a priest shortage." I shrugged. "He offered me a way out."

"So you chose a different kind of punishment?" Madeline asked.

"Maybe. But not exactly. Once I got to Holy Cross and started taking classes, it was okay. I started going to NA meetings. I was surrounded by a completely different kind of people. Everything I'd done before. The drugs. Aidan. All of that began to fade. And it was a relief. But also . . ." I turned to Madeline and looked at her. "It made sense to me. I was good at being a priest. Every time I helped someone it felt like a very tiny bit of what I'd done was being erased."

"So why did you quit the priesthood? Was it done? Had you gotten to the point where you no longer felt guilty so you resigned?" She sounded angry, as if it had been she—rather than the Church—I'd walked out on.

"Not even close," I said, my hand creeping to the spot on my chest where I could still feel the sting. "What I did to Aidan isn't gone. It hasn't left me. But I realized one day that what I was doing wasn't honorable. There were men all around me hurting children, boys, and they were doing it with Rome's tacit permission. Everyone knew. No one was doing anything. How was staying in such a system going to reverse my sin?"

"Reverse?" Madeline gathered herself and seemed to grow somehow, large enough she could reach over and pull me to her. Her grip was powerful, and I let her lay my head near her throat. My arms slipped around her. Tears ran down my throat. "Gabe, you can never reverse what you did. None of us can. That's not how it works."

"How does it work?" Now that I'd spoken the truth I felt like I was drowning in it. "Because I need to do something. I cannot live with what I did."

"Jesus, Gabe . . . I'm sorry." I could feel her breathing, and I tried to breathe with her. "Listen to me. What do you think we've been doing all this time, packaging up forgiveness? This is exactly why. To help people live with the things they've done that they can't change. That's what this whole business is based on: people feeling exactly like you do. And with *one* exception, you understood. You forgave them. You forgave me for running out on Cassidy. You forgave that man who sold you clothes for not donating his wife's organs. You forgave . . ."

"There's a difference." The words came out of me threateningly, like a growl. But Madeline just held me tighter. "Your stepdaughter isn't dead. She ended up with a new family. She's fine. Raj doesn't know what happened to the people who were supposed to get his wife's organs. But he did what he did because he loved her. There was value in that. I just used someone, for no reason other than my own personal gain. I treated a vulnerable person like he was less than human. I took his life, and I wasted it!" My voice was rising, and the windows had a fine layer of steam. "I did something evil. Not just wrong, not just human. But *evil*, Madeline. There is no forgiveness for that."

"You're wrong," she said simply. "What you're saying makes no sense. Cassie could have died because of me. She could have walked out in the street and been hit by a car because her dad was frustrated and overwhelmed and she had no one else watching over her. She could have gotten depressed and swallowed all the pills in the house. The fact that she's happier today has nothing to do with me. I abandoned her." Madeline was cradling my head against her chest and rocking back and forth, creating the lulling sensation of being on a boat. "And we know that Raj left that hospital without donating his wife's organs because he loved her so much. But how do you think the people whose teenager was waiting for a kidney would feel? They wouldn't care. To them, he's a monster who took away their son or daughter's best chance."

"Madeline . . ." The gentle rocking felt so good, I almost believed her. "You're trying to use logic in a situation where it doesn't apply."

"No," she said, and now she was stroking my hair. "Actually *you* are trying to use logic. You've constructed this equation where because Aidan died you are evil." She stopped moving but placed one hand inside my open collar, her cold skin against my heart. "I don't know much about your religion, your God. But I can't imagine you're that powerful. You didn't set out to kill him. You weren't the only person involved. You were cruel and selfish, but we all are at that age. Your stupid acts combined with the Marfan's and his addiction." Her voice dropped low. "With luck."

"The Bible does not recognize luck," I said into her neck. "Read Job."

"No. It's all about God's will, right? So according to you Catholics it was God who gave Aidan Marfan's and allowed Peter to introduce you to cocaine."

I straightened, lit with frustration. "That is completely wrong," I told her. "God gave humans free will. *The righteousness of the righteous shall be upon himself, and the wickedness of the wicked shall be upon himself.*"

"No fair," Madeline practically shouted. "I'm positive there's some verse to support my point somewhere in the Bible, but I just don't know it. Come on. Give me something."

I sat, torn between my sense of fairness and my desire to win this debate—even if it meant proving my own irredeemable sin. Madeline met my silence with a steely stare. Finally, I sighed and recited, "The race is not swift, nor the battle strong, nor bread to the wise, nor riches to the intelligent, nor favor to those with knowledge, but time and chance happen to them all."

"Ha!" Madeline was practically dancing in her seat. "Time and chance, exactly what I was saying."

I looked at her for a moment, her cheeks flushed with triumph despite the damp cold. Then, without thinking, I leaned forward and kissed her, and she let me. In fact, she pulled me in, turning her head so that we fit together, her hands under my coat and everywhere on me the way I'd imagined when we'd first met.

After a couple of minutes, I broke away. "You're still . . ." I started, embarrassed by what I had to ask.

"Still what?" she prompted.

"You're still willing to . . ." I swallowed, "touch me. Even knowing what I did."

She smiled sadly. "Yes, Gabe. We're both kind of broken people. That's been clear for a long time, at least to me. But I think that's part of what works. We're both trying to be better. And we *make* each other better." She paused and thought. "This is the first time in my life I've been able to say that. About a priest! That is so . . . ironic."

Then we were quiet for a time, just holding hands. Enclosed in that car in that garage in Chicago, it felt like we were the only two people on a tucked-away planet. Finally, in a rusty voice, Madeline spoke. "Do you want to go upstairs with me?"

I groaned, my head back against the seat. "Madeline, I want that more than I want anything in this world." Everything in my body was telling me to shut up, take this woman upstairs, and fuck her hard. "But I need to be fair to you." I took a long breath and measured what I was about to confess, the clear fact that had come to me in the middle of the afternoon on the highway in Scott's truck. "Whatever happens tonight, I'm going to leave."

My words echoed, and Madeline bowed her head.

"I know that," she whispered, as if imparting divine knowledge. "I understand that this is our last night." When she finally looked at me, her eyes were shining. "Please, come upstairs," she said.

And I did.

Pope Breaks Through Vatican Security, Kisses Disabled Girl

Only Renata Fay knows what Pope Vincent whispered in her ear, and when anyone asks her, she simply smiles and shakes her head.

Vincent "bestowed an extraordinary Good Friday blessing" on Renata's Michigan family when he broke through his own security to embrace the eight-year-old, who has cerebral palsy, in St. Peter's Square. The photo of Vincent hugging and kissing Renata has captivated the world, appearing in the New York Observer, the Wall Street Times, and on every major nightly news show.

"I was awestruck and moved to tears," says Renata's mother, Michelle Fay.

The family knew they were unlikely to find seats when they arrived only an hour and fifteen minutes before the Easter morning mass began. But as the Fays waited to enter the square, space near the front of the crowd miraculously opened up.

As the Popemobile passed, several ushers stepped into its path and stopped the procession directly in front of Renata. Gently pushing security guards aside, Pope Vincent stepped out of the vehicle to sweep Renata into his arms and hug and kiss her before waving to the crowd and getting back in.

"It was like he was pulled to my daughter," said Fay. "He sensed her goodness, and he only wanted to make a connection. We are truly blessed."

XVII

I WOKE BEFORE DAWN TO THE SOUND OF LOU SCRATCHING AND ROOT-
ing in his bed of cedar chips.

When I stood above the aquarium where he lived, the guinea pig
looked up at me with glittering catlike eyes. I petted him with one finger and poured a little of his dried food into a dish, moving quietly
because Jem would not need to get up for a couple more hours. Interventional radiologists, I'd discovered, worked a regular nine-to-five
shift.

I walked through the condo without turning on any lights. It
had been less than a month, but everything was familiar to me. The
beige couch. The IKEA desk stacked with books. Jem's mountain bike
that she rode everywhere and stored in the living room at night. The
décor here was easy and artless, like the city where we lived.

Cleveland would be tabula rasa, Jem said when we'd first talked
about my moving in, and I remember feeling a tug of fondness for
these two words of Latin. It was a perfect place to start over, she'd
told me. A city with no spotlight on it. It wasn't like Chicago; no one
ever talked about Cleveland. The Catholic community was scattered
and quiet. I could take some time, unnoticed, and decide what I
wanted to do.

It was late May now, and suddenly the earth had turned warm

and wet. I wore a pair of plaid boxers and a white crewneck T-shirt from the package that Jem and I had bought at Kmart when I first arrived. My feet were bare on the linoleum as I moved around the kitchen, measuring out coffee and putting water on to boil. Standing, waiting, with a mild breeze coming through the windows, I pictured Madeline. Her small, bare yet regal body and solemn eyes. My thoughts were fierce and hot, filling my head as I recalled each detail of our last night together.

This was my morning ritual. It was the only time I allowed myself to indulge in memories. But during the time it took for my coffee to be ready, I let myself go there and sometimes even whispered aloud as if Madeline could hear.

I'd devised this habit to avoid the dissonance I felt about bringing her into my new life. She didn't belong here. I had vowed to leave her in the past. But the pre-dawn hours were mine alone, and I knew from experience that a craving denied would only rear back up. So I gave myself this pardon each morning to close my eyes and let myself imagine her mouth on my face, my body, the marks on my chest.

When the teakettle whistled, it woke me like a hypnotist's snap of the fingers and I put the memory away. With the first sip of coffee I came back to my real life, the one I'd chosen. I took my cup and walked back through the living room, where Jem's bike stood against the window, outlined in a faint gold light.

On the desk were the papers of incorporation I'd been going over last night. Jack's signature was on the top sheet, and there was a small yellow tab marking the place where I was to write mine. I'd read everything last night, suspicious of all the passive legal language, then had called my brother one last time to confirm that he meant what he said.

"I swear to God, Father," Jack had said. "I've already talked to the Catholic Charities out here. There's a social worker in Quincy who has some kids coming out of their . . . I don't know what you call it. But it's a school they go to after high school, when there's nothing else for them to do."

"And Inga's going along with this? She's not going to decide you should take the money and send your girls to Disney World?"

"Jesus, Gabe!" Jack had said. "Do you really think my *teenage* daughters would be caught dead at a theme park? If they got their hands on your money, the three of them would go to Paris. But, no. She's not a partner this time. It's just you and me."

"And you really think people are going to want to eat in a restaurant where they're served by kids with Down Syndrome and schizophrenia?" I'd braced for my brother's pious bullshit.

"Not a chance." Jack had said, and I'd relaxed. "I did talk to a couple people about making it public. There are a few places, one in Denver and one in, uh, Wisconsin, I think. They do a lot of PR around hiring disabled workers, and it gets them stories in the local newspapers. Which is worth what, exactly? It's not like anyone even reads the paper these days."

I'd grinned, thinking of Isaac. My brother might resist the comparison—so would Isaac, actually—but they were, I'd realized, quaintly alike.

"The truth," Jack had continued, "is that Pope Vincent can go around kissing as many little handicapped girls as he wants. Most people still aren't going to want *that* around when they're out for a nice dinner. Guilt ruins pleasure, you know?"

"Yes," I'd said. "I've heard."

"This isn't about hiding people." Jack had paused, and I'd heard the tiny whoosh of a lighter. He'd taken a quick breath in then exhaled slowly, like someone doing yoga. While smoking. "This is about giving jobs to people who need them while running a business. Hey, what do you think of Chapel?"

"As an activity?"

"A name," he'd said. "The name of our place. I thought it

would, you know, give you some credit. Keep things in your camp."

I'd thought of the site we'd chosen: a small stone building on the water in South Boston, near our old neighborhood but in an area that had been discovered by artists and hoteliers and gay couples starting families.

"I like it." Jack and I were careful to remain stoic with each other. After years of estrangement, our new partnership was fragile. But I'd slipped up with what I said next. "You're doing a good thing, Jackie. I think a place like this might have helped Aidan."

I'd broken our pact by mentioning Aidan, and as soon as I'd said the words, my face had gotten hot. I was again that nineteen-year-old skulking around his mother's kitchen, afraid to go out into the neighborhood and face the people who knew what he'd done.

"Nah." I had almost forgotten Jack was still on the line, my transformation had been so complete. "Let's be realistic, Father. We aren't going to have the resources to deal with a kid like that."

"What do you mean? I thought that's what we were talking about, giving jobs to young people with, uh, problems."

"We are. And I'm committed to that. Mild retardation, autism, maybe, what are they calling it now? . . . transgender? But c'mon, I can't deal with junkies. We'd be in business like two days. I hope you're not expecting . . ."

"But don't you think, if Aidan had had an opportunity to do something like this before . . ." I'd swallowed. "Before he got messed up with drugs? He might have been all right."

There'd been a moment where I'd waited, and when my brother's voice had come back it was gentle, as if we'd changed places, he now the older brother and I the younger, he the confessor and I the repentant.

"Gabe," Jack had said. "Aidan was never going to be all right. His father was a drunk who smacked him around. His mom thought he was punishment from God. Aidan was sneaking booze from the time he was fourteen. Poor bastard was hard-wired that way. In addition to being a little deformed and messed up in the head, he was an addict to his core. Who knows why? But there's nothing anyone could have done."

"I'm not sure I understand."

The night before, holding the phone to my ear, I'd stood staring out the living room window and listening to Jack's breathing, as familiar to me as my own. Jem's townhome was perched on a bluff and below us the Cuyahoga rushed northward, toward Lake Erie. I'd watched as a light flickered above the writhing water.

"You were a fuckin' asshole back then, Father. I for one couldn't stand you. But you didn't kill the kid. Life did that." The river beneath me had moved like a serpent's tail, and the weight I had carried for twenty years had fallen away, leaving only sadness. I was washed clean.

• • •

Still holding my coffee, I went to the small guest bathroom and quickly showered. Afterward I wiped the steam from the mirror and saw my face appear—ghostly and mottled at first, then real and more confident. I watched the transformation as I shaved.

Every day, I looked a little more like myself. Since coming to Cleveland, I'd lost both the gauntness in my cheeks and the soft paunch in my midriff. I'd all but quit drinking since leaving Chicago, except for a glass of wine on Sundays. Jem had loaned me her old bicycle—far less valuable than her new one, so it stayed outside chained to the side of the garage—and I rode it everywhere I went.

The summer would be hot, she warned me. I would probably need a car by July, or I'd be showing up for work rank and covered with sweat. I had no money to buy a car now, because I'd turned over my founder's fee to Jack so he could start building the restaurant. But the Forgiveness4You board was scheduled to meet in June, and Isaac had emailed to tell me to expect a check for 3 percent of the profits to date.

"This thing is a fucking goldmine," he wrote. "We're already up and running in Austin. Seattle goes online in August and Portland in September. Stamford, Connecticut, sometime after that. We're scouting Minneapolis, Denver, and Asheville, North Carolina, right now. We're staying away from Cleveland for the moment, at your request. But we are engaged in global awareness campaigns. Internet, satellite TV. We've added an entire digital team to create a mobile app. Even if we don't move in next door to you, this isn't going to stay contained. Not if I have anything to say about it."

I responded saying I understood, but in the very small world I'd set up in Cleveland, I doubted anyone would notice. I smiled at that, even as I typed, imagining that Isaac would see this as a challenge. We'd settled into a regular email correspondence that sustained me through the first very lonely weeks. Next to Madeline he was the person I missed most.

This was, I knew in my heart, most of the reason I had agreed to return and serve on the board. There was the possibility of dinner with Isaac and perhaps Madeline, though I had not spoken to her since our last night together. And popping up on her email seemed crass, too informal for a relationship like ours.

A few days after Easter I had written her a letter by hand, with pen and paper. It had felt like a brave and gallant thing to do, but once I'd dropped it in a mailbox—wondering if anyone even checked them anymore—I'd begun to worry that it might seem distant or contrived, an act designed to maximize the space between us. At least a dozen times I'd picked up the phone to call her, but I'd seized up when trying to think about what to say. How to explain.

· · ·

Madeline had taken over the Forgiveness4You Foundation and managed all the pro bono work. "We're giving away 28 percent of our services!" Isaac had complained in his latest message. "Meadow's gone off the deep end. She's freakin' Mother Teresa!" But he had to know this would make me yearn for her even more and question my decision to leave. Isaac could be exacting and a little cruel that way.

It was 6:30 a.m. by the time I was shaved, dressed in black, and helmeted. I let myself out the front door and walked around the little car Jem hardly ever used. "Take it whenever you like," she'd said when I arrived. "I'll leave the key."

But this had not felt right. Jem had offered me a home and a new start. She stayed up with me talking, helping me patch together my new life. But I could never be anything more for her; my heart, my allegiance, lay elsewhere. She never spoke of her disappointment, and when I'd asked her once, she'd shrugged it off.

"It takes two people with similar levels of passion to make romance work," she'd said in her scientific way. "Friendship is more forgiving. You can put that together with anyone you love."

There was affection between us. Each of us, I think, was starved for someone to touch. Often, while we were making dinner in the evening, jockeying in her small kitchen, our bodies would brush. When we watched the news at night, she might rest her head on my shoulder, lightly, and once, when she seemed particularly lonely, I stroked her hair. But our boundaries were clear. After the news was over and we'd cleaned up our glasses and plates, we said good night and each went into our own separate rooms.

Bicycling through the cool, clear morning, the sun rising at my back, I watched Lake Erie harden and brighten and shine. Traffic was picking up on Memorial Shoreway with a rush of semi-trucks and early morning commuters. I turned left and coasted down a long, narrow street. It was in the diocese building around one of these corners that I had discovered I was still, technically, a priest.

I'd come to Cleveland intending to apply for a chaplaincy at the hospital where Jem worked. I'd been nervous about the background check, afraid that my old arrest—now unearthed—would show up and disqualify me. Instead, what had come back was proof that I was a fully-ordained priest consecrated by the Catholic Church. I'd gone to the diocese with my story.

I'd walked away from my congregation! I'd told the nun who officiated over their front office. Surely that was reason enough for the Church to be done with me. She was Margaret Thatcher in a wimple and a slate gray dress, austere, even a little regal. She'd simply shaken her head and said no.

"Many of our young men question their calling at some point," she'd said. "We can't have all of them running off. So we give them time to reconsider."

I'd asked how much time, and she'd said ten to twelve years, or until they married. "Usually, that's what triggers a transition," she'd said. "But my sense is the Vatican is becoming more lenient there, too." The nun had given me an exasperated look and I had been able to tell that she did not completely approve. "We have a few former Anglican priests who came into the Catholic Church due to a need in the community. If they're married already, we look the other way. I wouldn't be surprised if it works that way for men like you someday."

At first, I was furious. I felt trapped, like a cult member who thinks he's escaped, but realizes he's only been living on the outer edges of the compound, trying to rebuild a life while his captors keep their hold. The chaplaincy went to a recent divinity school graduate who had less to "sort out." I began the process of laicization, but it was foggy and unclear.

I would be immediately defrocked if I joined the military, Nun Thatcher had told me. Then she'd appraised me with unblinking eyes that matched the gray of her dress. "But you're looking a little long in the tooth for the armed services. I doubt they'll have you. Marriage is your best bet."

We'd become almost friends by this time, and I'd found out her name but I never used it. She was always Thatcher to me. I had happened to be in her office Monday morning after Easter to deliver one of the documents she'd said might or might not convince the Church to let me go. The newspaper had lain between us on her desk, its front page nearly filled with a photo of Pope Vincent undefended and cradling the little girl, Renata, in his arms.

"He's a good one, isn't he?" she'd said, when she'd caught me looking down.

I'd nodded. I had watched him sweep her up over and over on CNN the night before. And I'd felt something stirring, though I'd been trying to ignore it. Wily Nun Thatcher had seen it at once. She'd reached across the desk and patted my hand with her long claw. "He will change the canon. Mark my words." The next week, when Vincent had responded to a question about gay clergy and uttered five words that changed the Catholic Church forever—"Who am I to judge?"—I had thought of the tough old woman and sighed. In the fight for my soul, we'd both known who was winning. And it wasn't me.

Thoughts of Nun Thatcher stayed with me as I approached the little scorched-looking building where I worked. The parking lot was surrounded by a rusted fence and empty but for the old station wagon someone had abandoned there last week. It sat with its hood gaping open a foot or so. There was green glass and the remnants of a bottle near the passenger door, so I stopped to see if perhaps someone had crawled inside to sleep. But whoever had used the car was gone. I made a mental note to call the impound lot, then locked my bike and went in through the back door.

The entryway was musty, a place for spiders and mice. I hung my messenger bag, which contained my lunch and a book that Oren had sent me on Ruby's recommendation. Then I hurried into the small makeshift vestry and opened a cupboard door. Ours was a poor church, so I washed and folded my own vestments, but I kept them here so they wouldn't get wrinkled on my bicycle ride.

When she'd told me about this congregation the nun had been brutal, making it sound even worse than it was. I'd been imagining crack pipes in the pews and bars on the windows. Walking in to find the church simply dim, filthy, and barren, I'd felt a little gypped. After nearly four weeks, I'd learned how shallow my first response had been. The people of this tiny place were poor and tired and mostly angry with God. But they were still looking for Him. This, I understood.

I had no acolytes during the week, so I shrugged myself into a plain white cassock, lifted a stole from the cupboard, kissed it, and placed it around my neck. Then I entered the sacristy and looked out onto my congregation. There were three souls, which was standard for a Thursday morning. Once I'd arrived to an empty nave and had, after considering the matter for a couple of minutes, performed an entire service by myself.

The point, I'd realized that day, was my own communion with God, my service to Him, whether or not I had "customers" with their own expectations and needs. It had been during that low mass, as I'd read the scripture portions I'd chosen aloud, that I had secured my own commitment. Here I faced my God squarely, with no demands or delusions. I had made my full confession, done penance in His name, and He had received me back.

"I am a priest," I'd written to Madeline on that night in mid-April, telling both her and myself. "Not out of guilt or because it's an escape. But because this is who I am."

This morning there were people facing me, asking me to lead them out of darkness. And in doing so, again and again, I would lead myself. I dipped my fingers in the holy water on the altar and crossed myself. In the pews, an old man wept quietly. A teenager glared at me over her tightly crossed arms. Lenora, my Thursday morning regular, folded her hands and bowed her head.

I lifted my arms to hold my tiny congregation. "May the peace of the Lord be with you always," I said. Together the three small voices rose up, "And also with you."

The morning smelled of wildflowers and incense. And low inside my head I heard my brother's words from the night before. For the first time, I pictured Madeline from the altar and her clothes gleamed like lightning. In my chest, under the old tattoo, I had the sensation of something breaking open. The golden light of sunrise. Faith as Raj described it, vast and clear. It had begun.